"The law of the novelist: to give a personal impression of life."
— *Henry James*

For Vin Carafiello
In Solidarity
Manny Fried

This publication is made possible in part by the Arts Council of Buffalo and Erie County Regrant Program with public funds from the New York State Council on the Arts.

WORKS OF EMANUEL FRIED

PREVIOUSLY PUBLISHED
Meshugah and Other Stories, fiction
Elegy for Stanley Gorski, play
Drop Hammer, play
The Dodo Bird, play

PLAYS PRODUCED
Brothers For A' That — Rochester, Pittsburgh
(Semi-finalist in Denver Center Theatre Play Contest and Beverly Hills Theatre Guild — Julie Harris Award Play Contest. Honorable Mention in Perkins Play Contest sponsored by International Society of Dramatists)

The Dodo Bird — New York, Toronto, Chicago, Pittsburgh, Cleveland, Buffalo, Los Angeles, etc.

Drop Hammer — Los Angeles, Kansas City, Buffalo

The Second Beginning — New York, Pittsburgh, Kansas City, Buffalo (Midwest Playwrights Program Selection, New York Writers Theatre Selection)

Elegy for Stanley Gorski — Buffalo

A Piece of Cake — Pittsburgh

David and Son — Buffalo

The Peddler — New York, University of Arkansas (Fayetteville)

Triangle — State University College at Buffalo

Brother Gorski — New York

The Judge — Pittsburgh, Buffalo

Rose — New York, Detroit, Buffalo

Mark of Success — Catawba College (Salisbury, N.C.)
(New American Playwrights Contest Winner)

PLAY: STAGED READING
Cocoon — Boston, Kansas City, Buffalo
(Playwrights Platform Selection in Boston)

NOT YET COMMERCIALLY AVAILABLE
(Circulating in manuscript form)

The Un-American, novel

Lasting Out, novel

People Are Not Sheep, novella

Old Haunts, collection of short stories

Union Leader Stories, collection of labor short stories that appeared weekly in Buffalo Union Leader

Pardon Me, Your Class is Showing, collection of essays

SCREENPLAYS FOR FEATURE FILMS
The Dodo Bird
(Optioned twice by Canadian film companies, but film never made; seed money provided by Canadian Film Development Corporation)

Lasting Out

BIG BEN HOOD

A Novel
by
Emanuel Fried

Textile Bridge Press
Labor Arts Books

FIRST EDITION
PUBLISHED, DECEMBER, 1987

Published by Textile Bridge Press
(A Division of Moody Street Irregulars, Inc.)
in association with Labor Arts Books

TBP ISBN: 0-938838-20-2
LAB ISBN: 0-9603888-5-0
Library of Congress catalogue card number: 87-50361

Copies may be ordered from:

Labor Arts Books
1064 Amherst Street
Buffalo, N.Y. 14216

Printed in the United States of America
by union printers

50

This one is for the people I worked with when I worked in the factories myself and when I was a union organizer — my friends and my enemies inside the labor movement and on the other side of the bargaining table — who so deeply enriched my life when I came to them from my early career as an actor.

ABOUT THE AUTHOR . . .

Emanuel Fried conducts the Western New York Playwrights Workshop and is chairman of the Labor Arts Committee of the Greater Buffalo AFL-CIO Central Labor Council. Professor Emeritus in English following retirement from the full-time faculty at New York State University College at Buffalo, he still teaches one writing course there. He has been a factory worker, a union organizer, a drama and film critic, a reporter, a candidate for Congress, an insurance broker, and with the stage name Edward Mann, an actor on Broadway who studied with Lee Strasburg, Benno Schneider, Elia Kazan, Harold Clurman, Morris Carnovsky, Bobby Lewis, Clifford Odets and others. He acted in New York in over a dozen plays, including the lead in **The Young Go First** directed by Kazan, a supporting role with John Garfield in **Having A Wonderful Time** directed by Marc Connolly and a smaller role in the short-lived production of **Dance Night** directed by Lee Strasburg, and he danced under the direction of Martha Graham in **Panic,** the verse play by Archibald MacLeish. Currently, he is in much demand by theatre companies in Western New York, accepting roles occasionally to keep the feel of performing on the stage — a sense of the dramatic scene — which he believes serves him well in writing both fiction and drama. Back in the Thirties in New York he was a member of the Theatre of Action and acted with the Theatre Union. More recently, he used his play **The Dodo Bird** to bring together the people who formed The New York Labor Theatre.

Born in Brooklyn, one of nine children, Fried's parents brought him to Buffalo while he was a young child. He wrote his first play while he was in high school, about the prostitutes he met while working nights as a bellhop at a hotel — his discovery that they were human beings just like other people. When he graduated from high school he worked for several years in the Dupont Cellophane and Rayon factory before going off to the University of Iowa for one year and then on to New York City to become an actor. In 1939 he returned to Buffalo to direct the Buffalo Contemporary Theatre. The theatre company came apart in 1941 as its members went into the armed services during World War II. Fried went to work in the Curtiss Airplane factory where he became co-chairman of the union organizing drive of the United Auto Workers. Fired from Curtiss because of union activity, he was hired by the United Electrical, Radio and Machine Workers of America (UE) and headed up organizing drives at heavy industry factories during the period when that union swelled its ranks to represent 30,000 workers in Western New York.

Fried took time out from union activity to serve almost three years in the infantry, ending up a first lieutenant, returning from Korea in 1946 to again head up the union's staff in Western New York, where he negotiated contracts and guided union members in many strike situations. In 1956, District 3 of his union voted to go into the Machinists Union to get out from under the heavy barrage of redbaiting being thrown at their members.

He had been summoned before the House Committee on Un-American Activities in 1954 because of his union activities and told Committee members that it was none of their business what he believed or with whom he associated, and challenged them to indict him so he could make a court test of the Committee's right to exist under our U.S. Constitution; they did *not* indict him. He was called again before the Committee in 1964 —because of what he was writing, the FBI told his new employer, Canada Life Assurance Company. Fried again refused to answer any questions, telling the Committee it was none of their business what he believed or with whom he associated.

However, in 1956 the Machinists Union executive board, by a one vote majority, surrendered to McCarthyism and fired Fried from the organizing staff. Blacklisted, with the FBI intervening to get him fired by every American employer who hired him, Fried finally hooked up with the Canadian insurance company, whose top officers rebuffed the FBI. While selling insurance, he continued writing both plays and novels and completed his college education — getting his BA in 1971, his MA in 1972 and his Ph.D. in 1974. As the result of getting several plays produced during his 16 years on the blacklist, Fried finally got hired in 1972 to teach Creative Writing at State University College at Buffalo.

Through it all, from the time he wrote that first play at the age of 15, he has been stubbornly writing, writing, writing — getting his experience down on paper, for future generations — if not the present generation — to know what it was really like to be on the inside of that turmoil in which he lived and survived.

AUTHOR'S NOTE

Some readers may try to match real people they know with the characters in this novel. While this novel is based on reality, both the circumstances and the characters are composites altered much further by invention — and some are completely made up — and any resemblance of the resulting characters in this novel to actual persons, living or dead, is purely coincidental.

BIG BEN HOOD

Chapter 1

Every night the past week and all day Saturday and Sunday the weekend before Big Ben had worked on his old Buick. And now this Saturday he tested it out on the highway, driving about two hundred miles west to Cleveland in a little over three hours.

He took in a football game, the local Western Reserve team playing some other college outfit, and he didn't care who won. It was just something to do on the weekend before heading back to his little room above the tavern back in Niagara.

"Thirty-one, just old enough to keep the hell out of the draft," Big Ben told the girl he picked up at a bar after the game.

But he also quickly told her that his kid brother Tommy was already over there in Vietnam getting his ass shot off and one in the family is enough.

She had been out of circulation for a while, she told him after he bought her a drink.

"An auto accident, a couple ribs cracked, a bone fractured in my thigh, and I just got out today after ten weeks in the hospital. So jumpy, I'm ready to scream."

They talked only a few minutes, each quickly trying to read the other's thoughts and intentions.

She liked his appearance, a well-built man about six feet tall, broad shoulders, brown hair, a nice face with an easy smile showing big teeth, an awkward boldness mixed with some fleeting touches of modesty and shyness, and his clothes were all right, nothing fancy, his dark suit not sharply pressed, a white shirt fitting him loosely around the neck, and a tie that was knotted loosely and not pulled up tight under the tabs of his shirt collar.

There was an easygoing quality there that went well with the challenging look in his eyes. Dark brown, they seemed to be warm and they seemed to be telling her he wanted to take her to bed quick and he was confident but not boasting about what he could do there.

At the same time, Big Ben, looking her over, thought she was a little flatchested and somewhat bony, but that was after ten weeks in the hospital and the eager look he saw on that pale

13

face which responded to every word he said told him there was a
strong urge there and he did not have to waste time here with
unnecessary talk.

He invited her back to his hotel room. She said she had to
catch a bus. He asked when it was leaving and she agreed there
was plenty of time. They went to his room and everything went
fine. He was considerate and gentle and careful at this sort of
thing, concerned for his partner.

She lit a cigarette.

"Thank you. A ton lifted."

When they left the bar they had introduced themselves,
giving real names, but paying little attention since they'd never
see each other again. But now while they rested in bed, both
smoking, they seemed to feel a need to get to know more about
one another.

"Sara Hankinson, and I was working in the main office of a
supermarket chain here. But now I'm going home for a while to
rest up. I got a boyfriend there and he wants to get married. I
don't know."

He told her his name was R. Benjamin Hood and people back
home where he worked called him Big Ben because there was
another Ben working with them in the machine shop, a little
guy. She was too polite to ask what the R. in his name stood for,
so he told her.

"Robin, my first name is Robin. Robin Hood, named after my
grandfather, a wild, drunken, agitating bastard of a coal miner,
a digger with a pick and dynamite, deep mining, back there in
the hills of Pennsylvania. And he tried to live up to his name.
He was one of those guys who went up into the hills with his
hunting rifle and took potshots at the Pinkertons,
strikebreakers, when the coal companies tried to bring them in
on rafts down the river. Stupid bastard, he burned himself to
death, smoking in bed in his furnished room. He moved in there
after his wife, my grandmother, died and he insisted he wanted
to live alone. An independent old bastard. That's something I got
to watch out for in this furnished room where I live, smoking in
bed."

She smiled. "Robin's a nice name."

"I don't like being called Robin. Anybody calls me that at
work, he better duck. I let fly with a hammer or a hunk of steel."

They were sitting up in bed, both naked, her shoulder

touching his. Her breasts were small, but he thought they were just right for her. She had a nice body. He guessed she was a little younger than himself.

"Are you married?" she asked.

"I'm still having too good a time to get married. But I got a family I support. Not my father, not my mother, not my brother, not my sister."

"Did you get careless and get some girl pregnant?" she guessed.

"No."

"Divorced?"

"No."

"Annulled, separated?"

"No."

"I give up."

"Back when we still lived in Clearfield down in Pennsylvania I was a wild guy with a motorcycle. A dumb kid. I took the neighbor for a ride and I tried to whip him off. He lost hold onto me and he got killed. I killed him. He had a wife and three kids and she got money from the insurance compnay. She said she didn't want none from me. I keep sending her a money order every week. Twenty bucks."

There was still plenty of time before she had to catch the bus and he was enjoying himself, using whatever she said to open up about himself, telling her things he didn't talk about with the people back in the shop.

She had graduated from high school and she would have liked to go to college. But with eight younger brothers and sisters at home she had to go to work. Her father drove a truck for the farm cooperative down home.

She drew the covers up around her waist. "A journalist, a reporter, that was my dream. If I could get the education for it. And if I knew somebody with a newspaper who would give me a job."

Big Ben unconsciously patted his soft bare belly in quick response to this information and told her he had done some writing himself.

"A mystery novel. I started it, but never finished."

"I wrote some poetry."

"So did I. None of it any good."

"I'd like to write short stories. I wrote one to sell to True

Confessions. I read through a pile of old copies of the magazine to get the idea on what they wanted. Then there was something happened with a boy I knew back home when we were still in high school. After the dance at school, the two of us in the car. We fooled around, both scared, and we never did go all the way. But in the story I made her pregnant and desperate because she couldn't afford an abortion and her father kicked her out of the house. I don't even remember exactly how I ended it. It's home somewhere up in the attic."

"Dig it out and finish it and send it off."

"What I'd really like to do is write a play about some of my experiences. I started one. Wrote only a few pages."

"I used to act in plays in high school."

"So did I."

"I liked it."

"I did too."

"That's great."

"Yeah."

Big Ben got out of bed and went to the writing desk, still stark naked. "Give me your address, just in case I ever pass through there."

"Sara Hankinson — 373 Genesee Street — Johnsonville — southern Illinois — corn and hog country."

She gave it to him slowly, but too impatient to wait until he finished writing it down, she went on. "I saw a play in Chicago, a musical, *Hello Dolly*. Did you see it?"

"No, but my sister works in New York and every so often I grab a plane and fly down to visit her. She knows some people in show business and she promised next time she'd get me some tickets to see a Broadway play."

He went to the bathroom and got a towel and wrapped it around him. He never expected to see this girl again. So it was easy to speak freely and honestly.

"A speech teacher in high school talked me into joining the dramatics society. Some weird guys belonged. But I played football and I played baseball and basketball. So that kept anybody from ribbing me about acting. The same teacher started me on poetry. She gave me a book of poems for a present. For no reason. You'll like this, Robin. And I did. I like poetry. Not that I'd let on to any of those dumbheads I work with in the machine shop. Those poems she gave me, I read them over and over until

I knew a lot of them by heart. One I'll never forget. She asked me to pick out my favorite poem and read it to the class. *The Man With The Hoe* by Edwin Markham. The lines are gone. But the idea is still there in my head.

"That serf in Europe who seems so dumb. The heads of government better start worrying. Because some day that dumb bastard is going to start rebelling. And when he does, watch out. All hell is going to break loose. Last week down in Mike's Bar. Right across from the plant where I work. I live up over the bar. It's where the guys from the shop hang out. There was a guy there. I didn't know him. But I seen him around in the plating room over in the shop and somebody said he's got a son got all shot up in Vietnam, a basket case. He was drunk and he was sounding off at the president, Nixon. Drop the damn A-bomb or get the hell out. Then he said something what reminded me of that man with the hoe, that dumb serf in Europe. He said the way this country's heading now there's going to be a bloody revolution. People getting their kids killed and if you're not a college student you got to keep your mouth shut or you're out of a job. But pile it on and pile it on and then watch it blow. Blood, there's going to be blood. Blood, lots of blood. He was drunk all right, but he was saying what he was really thinking down deep in his gut. He reminded me right away. Edwin Markham, *The Man With The Hoe.*"

Their earnest conversation changed their relationship. Big Ben slipped on his drawers and pulled on his undershirt. She put on her underclothes and slipped into her dress. Big Ben went on dressing while the words poured out.

He asked if her boyfriend did any fishing or hunting and then went on about himself.

"I like to fish and hunt, and once I tried to write a story about that. You're supposed to write about what you know. And I know something about hunting. A bow and arrow is what I use. More sporting. Give the deer a chance. When I was a kid my uncle give me my first bow. There's a spot about a hundred miles south of where I live now. It's down near the Pennsylvania border. Our game laws, we're allowed one buck per hunter. I got this place staked out in the woods where I can see for over a hundred yards through the trees. See that buck coming up the trail. The wind there is good most of the time. From him to me. It never fails, every year, the first day. Take careful aim. First shot, one arrow, that's it, usually. But I might sit there from before dawn almost all day before I get that clear shot. All day I stay there and I don't move a muscle. At the base of a big tree. A forked trunk and I aim right through the fork. Like a big slingshot with me and my bow and arrow in the bottom of the fork."

He looked into the mirror above the dresser while he knotted his tie. But he didn't stop talking. He ran on, enjoying the chance to tell somebody.

"I tried to write a short story about that. Get into it how I felt. Excitement and satisfaction and a lot more I couldn't describe. How I felt when I looked at the buck lying there dead and had the crazy thought that he was a father and had a wife and children. — When I catch fish I always pull the hook out and toss them back in. I try not to rip them up getting the hook out. Fishing, I fish only for the hell of it. Hunting deer, the same. Only for the hell of it. I'd rather just hit a buck with an arrow and then pull it out and set him loose. But then they say there'd be too many deer if we didn't kill off so many a year. Like people. You don't want to say it, but if we didn't have a war like that going somewhere all the time where the hell would we put them all? — So if you're going to kill any deer you try to bring them down with one shot. One arrow. If that don't do it you got a mess. They take off and you have to chase. If they're bleeding a lot they leave a trail. But they can outrun you. And they are smart, they head for a stream and break the trail by swimming in the water. Maybe not go up on shore until they've gone downstream another hundred yards. Then maybe even double back. Don't cross. Come back and go around behind you. But if you lose them like that they still may die. And then it's a waste. — I get a buck I bring home the carcass and I give it to the Salvation Army or something. When I was living at home down in Pennsylvania I'd bring back a buck and my old man would skin it and cut it up and divide it among the neighbors. Last year — the deer season — our shop was out on strike. And a bunch of us went down and brought back three bucks. I got all three, but I give the others credit for two. The women running the strike kitchen soaked the meat in brine all night and we had venison stew there for a while. A seventeen week strike. Over new rates set by time study. People in the shop still talk about that venison stew.

Anytime it looks like trouble in the shop. Ben, get out your bow and arrow and go get us a deer. *Venison stew!*"

She was fully dressed now. She got a word in edgewise. "My daddy took me along when he went fishing."

"My old man took me from almost as soon as I started to walk."

"My daddy taught me how to bowl too."

"I learned by myself. With other kids."

"The bow and arrow. You're a real Robin Hood. Rob the rich and give to the poor."

She opened her purse and took out her powder case and lipstick. She looked into the small mirror inside the top of the case. Her silence while she intently painted her lips gave him a free field.

"I wrote an Archery Bulletin for a while. For our Sportmen's Club. One long mimeographed sheet. Every two weeks. With my name up on top as editor. Once for the hell of it I wrote it all in rhyme. Like poetry. I was trying something. Trying to get at what it is that makes a man go so strong for archery or bowling or whatever it is. Like a real nut. Every minute of spare time. Like some guys do. And then that don't satisfy you. You need something more. Whatever it is you do, whatever it is you got, you always need something more. Some people try to fill that in with religion. With some it works. With some it don't. With me it don't. I'm not against God. I'm not against the Church. It just don't do it for me. I was raised Protestant. I got aunts and uncles and cousins who are screaming Baptists. But that ain't for me. I still got that big hole in there in me. In my head or my heart or somewhere. And I don't know what it is will ever fill it, will ever satisfy it."

"Catholic." She closed the compact case. "I'm Catholic. But I never ask what's your religion. I think there's a God. Don't you?"

He shrugged. "I don't know, and I don't worry about it. And I won't argue about it."

She put her lipstick away. "Neither will I."

He put his feet up on the chair, one at a time, untying and retying his shoe laces. "Man's restless. Builds things. Makes things. Writes. Paints. Makes statues. Men in the shop, they fool around with their cars. Bowl. Fish. Hunt. Join the archery club. Get married, have kids. They're all searching. And they

don't even know what for. And you never find it. It's a good
thing you don't. Because that's how we get progress. Searching
to find something that we never find."

She smiled, letting him know how much she enjoyed their
conversation. "This is what I miss with my boyfriend. He's got
everything else. We're good with sex. But you need to get
intellectual with somebody once in a while. Or you feel awful
dumb. And he doesn't talk about anything. Nothing like what
we're talking about now. He just ain't there. Not for that. Other
than that I can't complain. Maybe when we get married I can
teach him to talk like this. I'll try."

"What kind of work does he do?"

"Garage mechanic. His own place now. Works seven days a
week."

"Maybe he's all worn out. Too tired. You get too tired, who
the hell wants to make loose conversation?"

She looked at him, thanking him for the touch of kindness
toward her boyfriend. "No chance you ever getting down to
Johnsonville."

"Some weekend I'll hop into the car and sneak over."

"Write first. Or phone"

She gave him her phone number and asked for his. The
number he gave her was for the pay phone in the tavern.
Anyone who answers will get me down from upstairs in my
room.

He went down to the street with her. His car was in the
parking lot across from the hotel. He drove her to the bus
station. She picked up her suitcase from the checkroom. They
shook hands. Goodbye. It was nice. I enjoyed talking to you.
See you again some day. I hope so. She walked away.

It was dark already. He had intended to stay overnight and
drive home in the morning. But it might be a good idea to
check out of the hotel and drive back right away. The barroom
downstairs back home was open until three in the morning.
Some second shift men working Saturday overtime would be
there, drinking and playing cards after getting out of work.

He drove around, looking for a place to eat. Then he noticed
he was beginning to see only colored people on the sidewalks
and in the automobiles. He locked both car doors and at the
first corner he made a right turn into a wide avenue. The fronts
of most of the stores still standing on both sides of the street

were boarded up. In between them were open areas piled with
the ruins of burned-out buildings. Fronts of some frame
buildings were scorched dark by fire, their windows broken.
Looks like somebody dropped an A-bomb here. He made a right
turn at the next signal, hurrying to escape out of the disaster
area. He didn't want to be the stupid white sonofabitch from
out-of-town who by mistake wandered into the wrong
neighborhood and got himself mugged, beaten up or robbed by
some mean black dudes who were still getting even because
last year a stupid white bastard used a high powered rifle to
drill a hole in that Martin Luther King and splattered him all
over the second floor balcony of a motel down in Memphis,
Tennessee.

Feeling safe again back in a white neighborhood, he drove
slowly in and out of some side streets until he found what he
was looking for. A dingy corner tavern with a sign in the
window. Home cooked meals.

Chili con carne was the Saturday night special. He ate a big
bowl of the stuff at the bar, washing it down with two bottles
of beer.

The TV set was back of the bar and there was a brief flurry
of tempers at one point when the news broadcast showed the
North Vietnamese delegation returning from Hanoi to
participate in the stalled Paris peace talks. Someone made a
wisecrack about President Nixon's secret plan to end the war
("so secret it don't exist") and that prompted a sharp exchange
between the hawks and the doves drinking at the bar.

It started off slowly with drawled sarcastic fencing, the
opponents tossing barbs over shoulders with laughing snorts.
Then suddenly it flared into angry shouting between two men,
one wanting to wipe all those goddam Vietnam gooks off the
face of the earth, the other calling for a lot more people to raise
hell along with all the college students down there in front of
the capitol in Washington if those stupid bastards down there
don't get our boys out of there goddam quick and bring them
all back home here where they belong. The people want it to be
over. — The communists want it to be over. — Are you calling
me a communist, you stupid sonofabitch? — Step outside, we'll
see who's the stupid sonofabitch!

The bartender leaned over the bar and stuck his head
between the two angry faces. I told you guys before. No more

arguing about that in here. Talk about sports. Talk about sex. Talk about cars. Talk about football. But the war is out, goddamit.

That prompted a laugh.

The bartender pointed at the colored TV screen. See, the sports is on. They call that football. Now talk about that, you stupid bastards, football. Pointing at the screen: See, he dropped that pass. Now argue about that. And leave the other out on the street. I say that's butterfingers. What do you say?

That forced a feeble response from the other end of the bar. That's no fingers, he never touched it. And then there was a lot of light ribbing that continued back and forth about the different plays and players as the highlights from the college football games played earlier that day were shown one after another on the colored screen.

Through it all Big Ben kept his mouth shut. He wanted to say that they better get his kid brother Tommy the hell out of there before they dropped any goddam atomic bombs, him and a couple hundred thousand other American soldiers. But even though the cut of the coat of his Sunday suit — his only suit —and the fit of the pants, and the white socks, and the soft collar of the white shirt, and the careless knot of the tie, and the way he carried himself, all told the others at the bar that he was one of them, he still was the stranger here.

The chili hit the spot. Not having any other place to go, he nursed the beer, stretching it out. Maybe take in a movie and then turn in. It did not appeal to him. He tapped the bottom of the empty beer bottle lightly on the bar. The bartender brought another. Is there a hockey game in town? He could yell himself hoarse there. Maybe develop some excitement. Like the time he piled down onto the ice and traded punches with a player who had cursed him and thrown his hockey stick up at him. The bartender picked some coins out of the change in front of Big Ben. We got a good team, but tonight they're playing up in Toronto.

Two girls, hair set for the night out, faces powdered and painted, came in and went to a booth. The bartender wiped off their table. Big Ben picked some change off the dollar bills lying on the bar in front of him. He walked past the girls. Standing where they could see him, he slipped a coin into the jukebox. He looked up as two men walked in and headed for the booth. Big Ben went through the motions of studying the titles of the records: *Honky Tonk Woman (Rolling Stones)* — *Suspicious Minds (Elvis Presley)* — *Get Back (The Beatles)*. The two men sat down in the booth with the two girls. *Aquarius/Let The Sunshine In (The Fifth Dimension)*. Big Ben concentrating on his important decision, pressed the button for that one and went back to the bar.

The bartender picked up a couple of empties and refilled them. Big Ben caught the bartender's eye. That's from that big music show hit, *Hair*. The flower children. The actors take off all their clothes, bare ass front and back, the guys and the girls. The bartender lifted his eyebrows and moved away. The music stopped. Big Ben picked up his change, made a small gesture in the direction of the bartender, and went back out onto the street.

Back at the hotel he told the desk clerk something had come up and he had to get back home. Without complaint he paid for the night.

The big clock on the corner showed one minute past ten when he drove his 1961 jalopy out of the parking lot. Eight years old with eighty-seven thousand miles registered on it before he turned it back to fifteen thousand, the heavy Buick was in better shape inside than it appeared with its rusted and battered exterior. He had rebuilt the motor and tuned it up to its utmost potential.

He saw a long clear stretch ahead and he tried to get the speedometer to move above the ninety mile mark. Ninety, ninety-one, ninety-two, ninety-three. Ninety-three. Ninety-three. That was the limit, though he kept trying to get it up to one hundred. Driving this fast required every ounce of his attention. One slip meant death. Some day he would like to drive in the auto races.

Mike's Bar was across the creek from the machine tool factory where Big Ben worked. A sign hung out from the corner of the two-story frame building. Men's Hotel. Rooms.

Big Ben parked the old Buick in front of the bar and sat there, trying to make up his mind whether to go in or to go around to the side entrance and upstairs to bed.

He was parked directly across from the entrance to the iron bridge with its two empty traffic lanes spanning the creek. The second shift quit at midnight and Big Ben unconsciously registered that the batteries of machines across the creek were all silent now in the dimly lit brick buildings with skylight roofs that stretched away from the tall administration building up front and disappeared off into the darkness beyond the trees and small cottages, formerly boathouses, lining his side of the deep narrow stream, its perpendicular banks reinforced with concrete and rock.

A figure moved in the shadows alongside the administration building, heading toward the guard shack up next to the sidewalk at the other end of the bridge. Except for the plant guards making the rounds to punch their clocks, the only people Big Ben knew who would still be working over there now in any of the buildings were the engineer and fireman in the boiler house.

He got out of the car and stretched his stiff legs. He couldn't see through the front store windows to find out who was in Mike's Bar without walking up the front concrete steps that ran the full length of the front of the tavern. He stood there, undecided.

It was a clear autumn night. He took in a deep breath, enjoying the swelling feeling in his chest, glad that tonight the wind was not blowing in the rotten chemical smells from the factories to the north. And with the roofing and paint manufacturing plant on the other side of the creek not working over the weekend, there was none of that heavy brown smoke that sometimes came from there.

Some men and women working at Mackenzie Machine Tool and living close enough to walk to and from work said they were lucky that this, one of the largest factories in town, is a metal fabrication plant, not a foundry or chemical works. It is nice that you can come out during a rest break or during lunch period to where there is neatly mowed grass in the narrow space running between the buildings and the creek, with flower beds and trees, and even park benches, all provided by the company. They have a gardener working fulltime just to take care of that.

A locomotive whistle sounded at a nearby crossing.

Big Ben could hear the freight cars squealing along the spur line, but they were behind a mask of trees and he could not see them. He listened but could not hear any sounds coming from Mike's Bar. The lights were on and he knew there were people in there.

Outside there was no one in sight except in an occasional car driving by. Most of the frame houses that crowded one another along the street were dark. A lot of men and women who worked in the plant, especially old-timers, lived in the immediate neighborhood. Many of these small houses had two and sometimes three or more families squeezed into them. There were some front lawns, not very big, and there were some trees and flowers and bushes.

An outsider living only ten or fifteen miles to the south inside the sprawling central city — ringed by industrial villages and towns and even small cities like this one — might drive through this neighborhood directly across from the Mackenzie works, not thinking about the chowder picnics, volunteer firemen meetings and parties, industrial softball leagues, church suppers, bingo games, card parties, bowling leagues, roller rinks, baton twirling competitions, high school football rivalries, baseball little leagues, and the labor battles and fierce arguments about what the company and/or the union is doing, or is not doing, and all the sexual intrigues, and all the taverns that serve as gathering places (their country clubs) for the working people living nearby, and the local politics in which anyone can heatedly participate, self-righteously tearing to pieces the political jackasses he just elected to office — and, driving through that way, if any outsider had never worked in a factory or lived in a neighborhood like this, he might see these homes as grubby places from which those who lived out their unhappy lives there wished desperately to escape. But right now Big Ben was touched with a tinge of regret that he was not going to end up tonight in one of those little homes instead of his room above the tavern.

The hell with it. Big Ben sauntered in as if he had not been away. At the bar there were some men and women dressed up for a night out. And a few men from the shop, still in their working clothes, were playing cards. Big Ben shortly greeted those he knew and continued on back to the rear end of the bar. He perched himself on a stool there.

Old Frank brought the usual. A shot of whiskey and beer chaser. Old Frank had retired from the shop across the creek. In return for room and meals and a few dollars spending money, he tended bar after midnight and mopped up the place in the early morning hours.

"Thought you were driving to Cleveland to see the football game."

"Just got back."

He had been given his opening and he went on to tell about the game and how fast he had driven on the way back. He got in a brief oblique reference to the adventure with the girl he had taken back to the hotel. But then he heard himself and the sense of pleasure in the telling turned dead and empty. In the middle of the sentence he stopped talking. Old Frank went back to the front of the bar and resumed his work, rinsing out dirty glasses.

Big Ben, scowling, drained the beer with a few long gulps. He hit the neck of the bottle sharply against the edge of the bar, breaking it off. The sound brought heads up, worried faces turning his way as Old Frank hurried back to him.

"No, Ben, not tonight."

"Here, somebody broke this."

Big Ben went upstairs and without pulling the string to turn on the light bulb hanging from the ceiling he undressed and brushed his teeth at the sink in the corner of the room and went to bed.

Chapter 2

Near lunchtime on Monday morning the men and women working in the machine shop walked out. A wildcat. Time study had set a tight rate on a piece to be turned on the lathes. This piece was part of a new hoist assembly designed by the engineers for the production line in the motor division of an auto manufacturer in Detroit.

The walkout began with four lathe operators, all men, walking off the job. They marched back and forth in front of the main entrance to the factory. This was at the top of the short stairway leading from the sidewalk in front down to the path that ran between the muddy creek and the brick administration building and the series of squat structures housing the machine shop and other departments of the Niagara Division of Mackenzie Machine Tool Corporation.

As part of the tooling for new auto models there had been a lot of overtime work. Pay checks had been good and the people in the shop did not feel pressed by their creditors. Also, since the two youngest of the lathe hands, both in their twenties, had recently returned from their tour of duty in Vietnam, one with a Purple Heart for his wounds, there was a great deal of sympathy for them combined with guilt, also respect for their instant readiness on the slightest pretext to tell the company to go shove it up their ass.

Responding to the impromptu picket line out in front, men and women streamed out of the factory buildings, clogging the path beside the creek, climbing the short stairway to the bridge level, then crossing over the creek, heading toward the meeting hall.

Within minutes after the four wildcatters started their march the grapevine spread the word through all the buildings. The four men, keeping up their ridiculous little parade back and forth before' the entrance until the factory buildings were emptied, did not even bother to make any sign to announce their purpose. Their bodies out there in front instead of back there at their machines told the story.

"Everybody over to the Labor Hall! Find out what it's all about and take a vote!"

Big Ben, walking with others from the machine shop, shouted it out. Others joined the shouting. There was a feeling of fun to it. A good break in the dull, daily routine. Some of the women whistled at Big Ben. He waved good-naturedly.

"Let's take the day off, girls, I got my room right over here at Mike's place."

It was a beautiful day. Early fall. The sun shining. A clear blue sky. It was like a picnic, leaving the shop this way. There was a lot of laughter and joking.

Venison stew, Ben!

The Labor Hall was only four short blocks from the Mackenzie Machine Tool plant grounds. As they walked, the women kept to themselves. About one third of the work force were women. They worked in most departments. The majority were on light assembly and inspection. And the chain department was all female, except for the foreman and two truckers.

Jamison Langner believed in hiring families. If he had a married man in his factory he gave preference to that man's wife to fill a job opening. Both earn money at this factory. They are more satisfied with their total pay than if only one works here. Go out on strike they cut off all their income.

Using much the same reasoning he gave preference in hiring to other relatives. Families in the shop, with brothers and sisters and husbands and wives on different sides of the fence, in supervision as white-shirted foremen, or working on production, blur the line between management and workers. Wipe out the separation. At least make it a little less sharp.

Jamison Langner headed the Mackenzie Machine Tool Corporation. His grandfather, Rip Langner, had headed it before him. Under Jamison Langner the corporation was expanding tremendously. New facilities had been built and acquired all over the United States and Canada, in South America, and most recently in Europe, Africa, Asia, and Australia. The newest factory, still partially under construction, but already starting to produce, was down in Virginia. The oldest facility was this Niagara division, headquarters for the entire corporation. With expansion of production overseas Jamison Langner had considered shifting his headquarters to New York City or possibly even to London. But for the time being he decided to keep things as they were.

His roots were here. He was a major force here.

Several hundred white collar people manned the offices of the corporation headquarters in the brick administration building. One of these offices was Jamison Langner's. He was a soft-spoken man in his late fifties with a slight build, who wore inconspicuous gold-rimmed glasses that went well with his small features and thinning sandy hair. He looked like a shy, well-dressed bank teller. His office on the second floor had been done by his wife, a professional interior decorator with a good family background. He was pleased with the feel she gave to the room. The gray wall-to-wall carpet was quiet and went well with the simple mahogany desk and swivel chair and with the leather couch and matching easy chairs. The series of hunting lithographs she hung on the walls gave the office an unpretentious genteel quality he liked. On his wife's suggestion he had the maintenance department send up a bricklayer and helpers to break open the outer wall and then install a big picture window extending almost from the floor to the ceiling.

Through this main window Jamison Langner looked out over the factory yards. Any time he looked up from his desk he could see huge piles of steel bar and rod stock, and coils of wire, and big overhead cranes shifting material back and forth. He could see his people at work. Over a thousand production workers out there. Jamison Langner enjoyed the sight of their activity. Without even consciously looking, he watched big trucks maneuvering to unload and load at the shipping docks. Without consciously listening, he heard boxcars moving in and out of the yards, their metal wheels squealing against metal tracks.

Jamison Langner was in his second year at Princeton, his father's alma mater, when that gentleman, learning he had a terminal cancer, stuck a pistol barrel into his mouth and pulled the trigger. Rip Langner, his grandfather, told Jamison to finish school and graduate. He did, and then joined the firm at the top as president of the corporation. His grandfather moved over to chairman of the board.

Though he liked his grandfather's gutsy, crude manner, Jamison Langner made no effort to ape his style. It was not him. Rip Langner called himself a brawling, two-fisted pug-ugly. He boasted about starting as a worker in the shop. And about the way he had made it to the top.

"With one punch I flattened this guy who started to organize a union."

For this service Old Man Mackenzie rewarded him with the job of plant superintendent and then plant manager, and later with his daughter. Rip Langner lived in Florida now, a drooling idiot, shrunk to nothing. But until his first stroke he continued to get out into the factory, calling men and women by their first names, stepping in to overrule a foreman in front of his subordinates, giving hell to any worker he thought was laying down on the job, personally booting out to the gate anyone who dared talk union.

Jamison Langner did not believe in getting drawn this way into details of production. You hire men for that and you fire them if they don't deliver.

During some very serious bull sessions with his roommate during his last year at Princeton, the conviction developed in Jamison Langner's mind that banking is more important than manufacturing.

"The most important factor in any economic system is money. Money is power. Control money you control people and the entire manufacturing process."

When he took his place as president of the corporation he seemed to be wholly occupied with expanding its manufacturing and marketing facilities. But he was keeping his eyes open for the chance to move. At the right time he spoke to Frederick Clark, chairman of the board of Central City Traders and Trust Bank. A few months later, after all his firm's financial business was transferred to that bank, Jamison Langner was named a member of its board of directors.

Unaware this morning that the lathe hands had stopped all production at the factory, Jamison Langner was on his way to meet Frederick Clark at the City Club downtown in Central City. Sitting next to his driver in the front seat of the company car, a medium-sized Oldsmobile, he noted almost without seeing them that several more corner traffic signs within less than a mile from the factory had been altered with white paint. Once, not too long ago, you saw that only in neighborhoods in Central City where the State University students lived. That you never see anyone adding those two words is what is so disquieting. Overnight they just appear. And he was concerned that Frederick Clark is very slow to understand and to act in response to this and other signals of this kind. — Another one. Against the red background of the traffic sign, the big white "STOP" — and added beneath that with white paint, "THE WAR."

The friendly rivalry between Jamison Langner and Frederick Clark strangely enough centered primarily in the area of the arts, both competing to establish themselves as the leading force in guiding the direction of the arts in Central City and the villages, towns and small cities surrounding it, a highly industrialized metropolitan area of about a million people, surrounded by farm country.

Though he would not say it to anyone except his wife, Jamison Langner thought Frederick Clark's motive was self-aggrandizement. The man is a strutting little peacock, essentially an illiterate, who loves public recognition of his contributions to the arts.

Jamison Langner does not want his name in the newspapers. His interest in the arts has a much more serious intention than that. Having read Plato, he agrees that poets (artists of all kinds) have magic and they can be, often are, a real danger to the state.

The two men have many things in common. Both had grandfathers who had acquired and passed on to them large homes on sprawling estates out in the country. Both are good horsemen, keep stables, and ride after the hounds, fashionable foxhunts run off every year on the grounds of tremendous estates of some very old families who are vocally proud that their forbears led the revolution to free the country from the tyranny of the British, families equally vocally proud in accepting their responsibility to stop the radicals from making another revolution.

Thus far, despite the rivalry, Jamison Langner has been able to persuade Frederick Clark to work closely with him to make sure that they and others like them hold onto that which he believes is as important as control of money and control of the production process, perhaps in the long run even more important than either of these in determining the texture of their community and their country — control of the magical mixture, the arts.

This mixture in their community is centered in the

symphony orchestra, the art gallery and the community theatre, each controlled by a board of directors whose most influential posts are held by members of prominent families, including many who serve in similar roles on the boards of the local banks and business and manufacturing corporations.

Jamison Langner, deep in thought, staring unseeingly through the front windshield of the company car, rehearsed how he could explain the thing he wanted to talk about in such a way that he would allay any fear Frederick Clark might have that this was an effort to encroach into that territory of the arts which was his to reign over. During the period of national unity to defeat Hitler he had agreed to Frederick Clark's suggestion that they appoint a few local labor leaders to boards in charge of the magical arts mixture, although he was skeptical then that this somehow would translate itself into getting union members to work harder at their machines to produce for victory. In any case, when that war ended those labor leaders were not replaced by their own kind as they died or lost their positions in the labor movement or transferred to other territories. And while they did serve on the boards they had been window dressing, carefully chosen for their readiness to stand aside and let others who knew what it was all about make any meaningful decisions concerning the direction of the arts.

But this time a new and unexpected impetus toward making a link between the arts and organized labor is coming from someone who can upset the situation which has quietly existed for many years now in the arts in the community. The country is entering a new period. There was the Korean War. And that ended. And then the Vietnam War. And now the Nixon administration in Washington, reacting to public agitation and protest, is scaling down that war. No other choice but to end it, honorably. And Nixon will have to move immediately to control the internal situation which the country will then face.

Though he served with Frederick Clark on the local Committee to Elect Richard Nixon and contributed heavily to the committee, Jamison Langner recognizes that in the context of the shrinking world even a conservative Republican president cannot prevent tremendous echoes to the crash of one country after another into the arms of socialism. At the same time the country is in the throes of a great technological upheaval linked to the merging of the entire world into one tightly interlocked producing and consuming entity. This volatile situation will inevitably echo into our community. And it is this which makes it so extremely worrisome, that one of the Old Left, the man he thought he was done with, is now worming himself back in, using the arts as his vehicle.

Jamison Langner, sitting with Frederick Clark at a table in one corner of the spacious dining room of the City Club, was still unaware that the lathe hands had stopped all production at his factory. His lieutenants back there had already contacted the union's business agent by phone and hoped to be credited with getting the men back to work before the return of the Old Man, their somewhat affectionate title for their boss.

For almost an hour, with hardly any interruption from his companion, Jamison Langner spoke intensely, explaining why he thought the time had come again to get some labor leaders involved in the arts. Both men were in a position to easily do something about this. The governor had recently appointed both to a Committee on the Arts, with Frederick Clark as chairman.

Big Ben's name is brought into the conversation. Personnel man Dick Penfield had told Jamison Langner something that morning about Big Ben, a new development that introduces a note of urgency into the situation. Jamison Langner decided it was necessary to loop back to explain that what had happened was related to something that began back in the early Forties when several CIO unions tried to organize the Niagara Division of his firm.

"The Steelworkers led off. But we easily defeated them. We had a Labor Board election and our people voted no union. Shortly after that a group of our employees met in the lunchroom and adopted a constitution and by-laws establishing an independent union. Two days later we signed a contract with them, giving most of the items the Steelworkers had listed in their leaflets. Paid holidays, paid vacations, call-in pay, and seniority. But on seniority, while length of service would be a guiding factor we kept control by making everything subject to the employee being able to do the job satisfactorily in the opinion of the company."

Jamison Langner lifted his hands from the table to make it easier for the waitress to set down the basket of hot rolls and the silver butter dish.

But he went right on, explaining that the most important item raised by the Steelworkers in their leaflets had been a demand for automatic progression within rate ranges, with specified wage increases at specified time intervals, from minimum to maximum of the rate range for each job classification. In its contract with the independent union the company had retained its right to give merit increases to those employees who deserved them.

"An employee," said Jamison Langner with conviction, ignoring the big ears of their buxom waitress, "must always understand he is an employee working for an employer, and his advancement depends upon the goodwill of his employer."

It took less than an hour for his words to travel from the dining room of the fashionable City Club to Mike's Bar across the creek from the Niagara Division of Mackenzie Machine Tool.

In his intense analysis of the situation, his voice lowered, his head bent forward over the small round table in the corner of the City Club dining room, Jamison Langner linked another name to that of Big Ben Hood.

The waitress, busily moving back and forth between the table and a nearby serving area where she had rested her tray, placed lunch plates in front of the two men. And that night Dave Newman received an anonymous phone call, a man's voice.

"You don't know me, Dave. I thought you'd like to know this. Jamison Langner and Frederick Clark were talking about you today at the City Club."

"Thanks. What was it about?"

"I don't know. But you were mentioned and I thought you'd like to know."

"Who is this?"

"Just a good union man."

"Thanks."

"You're welcome."

Jamison Langner enjoyed unravelling for the benefit of Frederick Clark the complications connected with his relationship to Dave Newman. "He first came to my attention shortly after we signed our contract with our union. He's Jewish, you know. His parents ran a small dry goods store here

in town. When he graduated from high school he went to work
in a factory. Two years later he quit that job and went to New
York City and became an actor. The next few years he did
fairly well as an actor, but then he gave it up and returned
home. He had started writing and had written several plays.
Some short ones done by radical groups. And he gave that up.
When we met him he was writing leaflets instead, leaflets
given out at our plant gates by the communist UE, the United
Electrical Union, which back then was still affiliated with the
CIO. Dave Newman was in charge of the organizing
campaign."

Jamison Langner dealt briefly with his effort to shift
direction to ward off the new threat posed by the radical union.
"We preferred our own union to the Steelworkers. But this was
a new situation and the executive board of our union, with our
blessing, recommended affiliation to the Steelworkers. But the
people voted it down. Dave Newman had the shop and we had
to go into a Labor Board election which his union won."

Impatient though he was to get to his main point, Jamison
Langner saw that starting this far back and filling the other
man in was achieving his objective. He had caught Frederick
Clark, had him listening intently.

"We went into a strike situation and we had to grant
automatic wage progression and a tighter seniority clause.
Temporarily. Until Dave went off into the army. That was
sometime early in 1944. While he was away we got our people
back into leadership inside the UE local. When he came back
about three years later they tried to bar him from participating
in negotiations. A communist. But the membership backed him
up and we had to deal with him. He's honest. But tough. And
we had some long strikes. Fortunately, he wasn't with the
union much longer. After the CIO kicked out the communist
unions — when the Left backed Henry Wallace against
Truman, and Senator McCarthy was exposing the communist
conspiracy — we got some of our people to push to pull our
local out of the communist UE. There was a lot of fighting over
that for the next few years. But Dave weathered it. And then in
1956, to get rid of the split this fighting was creating within
the ranks, Dave and his people led all the UE locals in this
area into the Machinists Union who were part of the newly
merged AFL-CIO Federation. And then there was a little

doublecrossing. To be a business agent, which is what they call
the representatives in the Machinists Union, you had to be a
member of the union, and Dave was given membership in the
Machinists local lodge at our factory. We had a conversation
with some of the Machinist leaders in the district here and
then the officers of the local filed charges to expel Dave. And
that's when our Big Ben first entered the picture. I first became
aware of him."

"The same Big Ben who's there now?"

"The same one who's now interested in theatre. He carried
the ball from the floor, attacking Dave Newman. Still a young
kid fresh up from the hills of Pennsylvania. They told me he
shouted and swept the meeting. Stand up and be counted.
Drive out the Reds. And they drove out Dave Newman.
Expelled him."

Jamison Langner, becoming aware that the waitress was
hovering nearby with ears extended a mile, dropped his voice
to little above a whisper.

"Dave disappeared for a long while. He had to pay attention
to his own potatoes. Make a living. And now just recently he
unexpectedly moved in a new direction and caught us
completely off guard. He went back into acting and writing
plays. There was an open casting call at the Arena Theatre. He
appeared and read for a part in Ibsen's *Hedda Gabler*. He read
well and the director picked him for one of the leading roles.
After that I started attending board meetings there. And now
we're changing to a professional company, casting from New
York and Toronto."

"Too late," said Frederick Clark with a sympathetic grin.

"Did you see the play?" asked Jamison Langner. "He was
Judge Brack."

"Yes — and he was very good."

"Unfortunately, yes. And our Big Ben is interested in
theatre. He went to see the play and saw our radical friend
perform.

But it had not been only his interest in theatre that
prompted Big Ben to go to see the performance of *Hedda
Gabler*. When the name of the former union organizer was
listed as a member of the cast in a newspaper item about the

Arena Theatre production Big Ben heard some men talking about Dave in the smoking area in the machine shop.

"He's still on the shit list. No American company will give him a job. He's selling life insurance for a Canadian company."

It was true, as Jamison Langner told Frederick Clark at their lunch in the City Club, that Big Ben had shouted for the expulsion of the Reds at that union meeting. But after tearing Dave Newman apart Big Ben had taken the floor again to shout for the union organizer to be given the chance to reply when others tried to deny him that chance. — "Let him speak! Let's hear what he's got to say!" — The passionate appeal made by the organizer for his right to his own beliefs shook Big Ben and he took the floor. "Everyone certainly does have a right to his own beliefs. But not if he's acting as an agent for a foreign power." — The organizer took the floor again. He gave a flat denial that sounded sincere. Big Ben remained seated. The organizer went on. "Name one time when I did not carry out whatever was voted by the membership even when I disagreed with it." — Several voices out in the hall called out, "That's right." — Big Ben remained silent, but listened intently as Dave Newman spoke about his conduct in negotiations, his handling of grievances, the gains won. — "Tell me one thing I've done against the best interests of this membership!" — Big Ben did not rise to ask the question which immediately formed in his mind. *Yes or no, are you a member of the Communist Party?* But his motion to expel the communist was still before the house. A voice vote. It was a time of fear in the country and there was silence when the chairman asked for those opposed to openly declare themselves. The ayes have it, unanimous. Although Big Ben had been part of it, the bad taste it left with him soured him on the union.

"Department steward? Not me, no part of that fuck'n shit."

But the people he worked with in the machine shop treated him as their rank-and-file spokesman. He had demonstrated he could hit that floor and talk good and loud and clear. And although they kidded him about reading books, they respected him for it. Big Ben joined in the pinochle and cribbage games in the smoking area during rest periods and lunch breaks, but every so often he passed up the card games to read a paperback book, usually one he had already started on company time in the shithouse. — "What are you reading, Ben?" —"Another cock book."

His reading included a wide range of fiction and non-fiction. Best-selling novels and long-hair stuff. Mathematics, science, philosophy, religion, anything that caught his eye on the paperback shelves in the stores. If the book did not hold his interest he traded it in at the secondhand bookshop without finishing it. And on the floor of his room above the tavern, beside his bed, there was a small pile of worn paperback collections of poems. He had accumulated them over the years, never brought them into the shop. Most of them were school textbooks traded in by college students. Every night, before pulling the string to switch off the single bulb hanging from the ceiling, he tried to remember to read at least one poem, folding over the corner of the page if he really like it, and then he would lie there in the darkness, thinking about it until he fell asleep.

When Dave Newman appeared as Judge Brack in the Arena Theatre's production of *Hedda Gabler* it was surprising to Big Ben how many clippings from the local newspapers, items about the cast and reviews and other material about the play, appeared on the bulletin boards in different departments in the shop, the dangerous name usually underlined, sometimes with a red pen or pencil.

Big Ben, so far as personnel man Dick Penfield could find out, was the only person in the entire shop who went to see Dave Newman act in *Hedda Gabler*. It was reported to him that while playing cards in the smoking area the next morning Big Ben casually remarked to the others in the game, "I saw Dave Newman last night. Acting. He was great. The play was great. He said to say hello to all you stupid bastards. After the show I went back and congratulated him."

He did not tell the other card players that he had also apologized to their former union organizer. Sorry I shot my big mouth off way back then. I didn't know what it was all about. I should have kept my big bazoo shut.

"Dave said he heard about us giving up automatic progression. Moving backward instead of forward."

No one commented on that. The men concentrated on their card game. Too many stoolpigeons around. Somehow anything said in the shop gets back to the front office. The card game broke up and the men went back to work.

About ten minutes later Dick Penfield, hurrying from the personnel office, walked into the machine shop. He stopped at the desk of the foreman and spoke briefly to him, then walked down the aisle between the noisy machines. He stopped beside Big Ben's giant drill press. He raised his voice above the noise.

"I hear you saw Dave Newman."

"Acting in a play," Big Ben said, almost shouting to be heard. "*Hedda Gabler*. By Ibsen. He was good."

"Was he?"

"Damn good."

"Maybe I ought to go see him."

"A damn good actor."

"I've seen him act. Very often. But never in a play."

It was shortly after this that Dick Penfield reported the information in an offhand way. Big Ben out there in the machine shop went to see Dave Newman act in that play down at the Arena Theatre. He was surprised at how intently the Old Man questioned him. And the next day he was asked to find out if anyone else in the shop had gone to see the play. No one, only Ben. That seemed to be something the Old Man was pleased to hear. But it was what this might eventually lead to, Big Ben in touch with Dave Newman in connection with theatre, that Jamison Langner was still thinking about when the company car drove out of the parking lot, at the very moment when four lathe hands left their place of work in the machine shop to start their little wildcat parade back and forth in front of the main entrance to the factory.

At the City Club, having filled in the background for Frederick Clark, Jamison Langner let his coffee become cold while he told why it was so urgent that they take steps immediately to block Dave Newman from becoming any kind of focal point for labor involvement in the arts.

"He's writing plays now. And I'm told they're not bad. He mailed out a news bulletin to all the unions in the area announcing he's written a play about *factory and working class life*. His language. Now unless we start our own program in that direction we let it go to him and his group by default."

At that moment Big Ben was standing in the rear of the Labor Hall, squeezed in there with a crowd of men and women from the shop, listening to the youngest of the two Vietnam

veterans, the last of the four lathe hands to speak. A shrill
appeal, coming through the bearded face of Purple Heart,
demanded that the union *do* something. There was a loud
shout from behind Big Ben.

"Hey, somebody get on the phone and call Dave Newman."

"You can call down there at the theatre," yelled Ben, and
added above the laughter and joking retorts, "he's a big man
on the stage down there now."

"Tell him," someone shouted, "we got a damn good play
going on out here for him to star in."

Chapter 3

Before the meeting ended Big Ben was asked to leave the Labor Hall. But that was only after he lit a fuse to a stick of dynamite with one of the women there. Baldy George Walters came running. President of the union, his face was red. Ben, get her out. Big Ben was unperturbed. You get her out. When this argument developed sometime well into the afternoon it gave Ben the opportunity he wanted. Thinking quickly, he ingeniously used the situation to get the union president to do what Ben believed should have been done hours earlier.

Like Big Ben, the largest single group of workers in the Niagara Division of Mackenzie Machine Tool came up out of the Pennsylvania coal mining country. Theirs was a militant tradition, reinforced recently by the death of coal miners' union leader, John L. Lewis, and the reminiscing that that death prompted about battles fought back in the mines. If anyone empties the bucket up on the surface, no one goes down the shaft into the mine. Pouring out the water means the strike is on.

If even only one man — and he not necessarily a veteran of the Vietnam War — had put up the picket line at the entrance to the Mackenzie Machine Tool plant grounds no one would have kept on working. That was the tradition. Shut off the machines and put away tools, everybody. Over to the hall and talk about it.

The president of the local, chairing the meeting, made no effort to buck this tradition. But George Walters knew Dick Penfield would refuse to discuss the grievance until the union got everybody back to work. That was company policy. And if two veterans of the Vietnam War had not been involved this time George himself might have tried to wave the flag and make a patriotic pitch. Get back to work. There's a war on. He knew what Dick Penfield would argue. The time allowed for the job has to be rechecked. You can't do that if they're not working.

George had been in office since the switch from the UE Union to the Machinists Union. Instinctively, he followed up the shrill demand of the bearded young Purple Heart for action

with a long emotional speech of his own, working in a few sobs
as he neared the climax. It was nothing new for the people in
the hall to see bald-headed George take out his handkerchief
and wipe away the tears. A few people snickered, winked or
nudged their neighbor. But no one ventured to speak out. Cut
the crying and do something, for chrissakes. On the other
hand, some people seemed to be truly affected by this display
of emotion. And some who might otherwise have scoffed let it
go by, because of a brief reminder by their leader of the dire
threat looming above them which required his continued
presence in office as their protector. It was a parenthetical
interjection he invented on the spur of the moment with just
the right emphasis. He had tried to reach the business agent
already. (He had not.) But that good brother was meeting with
other union officials from the skilled trades.

"The colored people down there in Central City are raising
hell. Picketing. Demonstrating down at city hall in Central
City. They want jobs in the skilled trades. Apprenticeship
programs. Preference in hiring. Special quotas. Superseniority
to make up for past discrimination. *Down there in Central
City.*" Baldy George repeated it. "*Down there in Central City.*
They may have to give them something — *down there — down
there in Central City.*"

Everybody knew what Baldy George meant. He was still
standing guard with the company to keep pure the sea of white
at Mackenzie Machine Tool. They better keep him in office to
preserve the dam that encloses the 45,000 whites living in the
city of Niagara. When the occasion demanded it Baldy George
whispered it around quietly in the shop, that only one of them
got in here to live. Blame Dave Newman for that. Back early in
the second World War he got the company president and the
local union officers there to bring them into the plastics plant
up on the north side. Almost a hundred of them still working
there. Then one moved his family into town. And for a whole
year he got a special welcome: light bulbs filled with paint
busting up against his house, shots fired every night through
the bedroom windows at two and three in the morning, and
enough other little tricks to get the message through to the rest
of them working up there. They still keep driving every day
back down to Central City where they belong.

Having gained what he wanted with his quick reminder that

he stood in the way of a black invasion that would threaten their jobs and their property values, Baldy George now instinctively sped off in another direction. His voice rose to an excited girlish pitch. "Our boys over there in Vietnam. Some giving their lives. Others coming back home to their mothers and fathers in a basket. Still alive, but God forgive me, maybe better off dead than the way they are. All making the supreme sacrifice. To keep communism away from us. Away from our own shore. And now having served our country so well, those fortunate enough to return in one piece, or almost one piece, they deserve better than they're being given over there now in that shop. Because what do we see now? — What do we see now in that shop over there?" — Baldy George's voice trembled with emotion. He was ready to tear the culprits apart. — "We see the same sneaky tactics our boys faced over there in Vietnam. Time study men sneaking around behind their backs. Time study men hiding with their little sneaky watches hidden in their little clean hands. Sneaking behind the backs of all you boys and girls in there. Hiding behind machines. Taking sneaky time studies. Cutting time allowances. Speeding up these boys on the lathes the same way they're doing to a lot of you boys and girls on other jobs in there. — You deserve better than that. And I am going to see to it that my boys and girls get the fair treatment you all got coming to you."

Big Ben deliberately remained silent and out of it, standing in the rear behind the packed rows of men and women sitting on folding chairs. There was a smirk on his face. The same old horseshit. Willie the weeper up there. Crying for my boys and girls. Hell, the two older lathe operators were somewhere near sixty. Same as Baldy. The sonofabitch, crying for his boys and girls while half the shop knows he's got his tongue a yard up the company's bughole.

There was a hand raised. — "Mr. Chairman." — Big Ben saw that it was Don Mayer, the rugged old timer whom he had finally needled into taking on the job of chief steward and chairman of the grievance committee, replacing one of Baldy's yes-men. He had the machine shop ready now to run Don for president against Baldy in the next election. He waited for the fun, ready to drop the role of amused spectator and pitch in to help. Don Mayer would tell it to Baldy straight out the same way he would. Cut the crap. Tell these lathe operators: okay,

we did this, we walked out, we supported you. The company
knows we're all backing you. Now get back to work in there. So
we can meet now with Dick Penfield and try to settle this.
Otherwise, they won't start talking and we all lose money now
for no reason. Once we meet with the company, and if we don't
get anywhere, that's a different story.

But the chairman made believe he did not see the hand
raised. Instead, with a slap of the gavel he quickly announced
that he was going to recess the meeting to try again to get hold
of their business agent. Big Ben grinned. The sonofabitch, he's
going to let the business agent do it. Smart bastard. Let the
B.A. be the one to tell that hot little Purple Heart kid that he
and his buddies got to go back to work.

Baldy George invited the chief steward and the other
members of the grievance committee to join him in the think
tank.

"You listen while I phone and tell him to get off his fat rear
in the office down there in Central City and get out here quick
and earn what we're paying him."

Everyone there including Big Ben knew what it meant when
the grievance committee and the four lathe hands went
upstairs to the think tank with Baldy George. It involved a
tradition that Baldy himself had started more than ten years
earlier — back when the executive board of the local met in the
think tank to decide what course of action to take regarding
Dave Newman.

It had been the same Baldy George, heading the United
Rank-and-File Caucus for a Democratic Union, who got the
motion passed there that no matter what differences exist
between spokesmen for the warring caucuses within the local,
before they emerge from that small conference room on the
second floor in the rear of the Labor Hall, no matter how long
it takes to arrive at a decision — and it had taken them from
early morning until late that night to recommend the expulsion
of Dave Newman — the minority is obligated to join the
majority to make the decision brought back to the membership
unanimous.

Everyone in the think tank is sworn to secrecy, never to
disclose how anyone in that room voted. Baldy got the idea
from the labor priest working with his caucus to get rid of the
communists. The voting is done that way when they choose a

new pope. It was the same priest who took Baldy along when he flew to Rome a few years later to humbly plead with Pope John. We beg you to rescind your encyclical, Mater et Magistra, allowing Catholics to work with socialists and communists. It is opening the door for the communists to get back into the union. Baldy reported back that Pope John smiled and thanked them. Period.

While Baldy and the grievance committee and the four lathe hands argued it out in the think tank on the second floor, the rest of the people milled around in the main hall on the first floor and spilled down into the smaller meeting room in the basement. The bar and cooler were down there. With cases of beer in the cooler. Locked in there. Intended for refreshment after the regular monthly meetings.

Someone jimmied open the lock on the cooler door. The beer flowed. People had brought their lunches from the shop. Paper bags and tin pails were opened. Food was pooled and exchanged. There was beer and music and dancing. And shouting and laughter.

Self-appointed messengers went upstairs to listen outside the door of the think tank. They came back down and reported they could hear some angry yelling going on between Baldy George and Don Mayer.

An hour passed. Some women said they were going home for the day. Catch up on house-cleaning. Some men left to catch up on painting and carpenter work around the house. Other men invited their friends. Nothing's going to happen today. Let's go fishing.

The noise in the hall became louder. The dancing became wilder. The teasing and joking took on a sharper edge. Men and women who had obeyed all the polite amenities in relation to one another earlier that day in the shop, now made lewd remarks and lascivious gestures. Hey, get your hand there up a little higher. That's something nice you got under there. How would you know? *Put your ump against the wall, here he comes, ump and all, bye bye, unh-huh.*

The less venturesome women quietly slipped out. Don't go in there, it's getting too wild.

The gaiety in the hall included unrestrained abuse aimed at both company and union officials. When the union's business agent finally appeared he was greeted with good-natured booing. Where the hell you been? Go home, it ain't settled yet. Oh, no, another sellout. Him, we're licked.

The business agent smiled and appeared undisturbed. He had taken his time getting there. Let them get the heat out of their system. Blow off steam. Now he wove his way through the thinning crowd, all in their working clothes, men and women standing, some sitting in groups, others still dancing. He went upstairs to join the men in the think tank up there. His disappearance up the steps was a signal for quiet to hear what change his presence might bring.

The music stopped. Some men and women climbed partway up the flight of stairs in the hall, listening. There were a few minutes of quiet up there in the think tank. Then the shouting up there swelled a while and then it subsided.

The music and dancing and loud chattering in the main hall picked up where it had left off.

Almost an hour later a man came down from the second floor on his way to empty his bladder in the toilet in the basement. He was eagerly pumped for information. And the latest report travelled quickly from one mouth to another through the hall. Dick Penfield talked to Jamison Langner at the City Club and got his orders. No change in company policy. Don't discuss any grievance until the people go back to work. And the lathe hands say no work until the grievance is settled.

A beer can in his hand, Big Ben wandered about between the clusters of people on the first floor and down into the basement and then back up again to the first floor. He danced several times, with different women. He was enjoying himself tremendously.

A man from his department tapped him on the shoulder. "What do you think we should do, Ben?"

"Get it settled."

"Stay out until it's settled?"

"Is that what you want to do?"

He moved away, starting across the floor, looking for another dance partner. There was Queen Lila, dancing alone.

He watched and grinned at the provocative way she was moving her broad shoulders, bobbling her big breasts and shaking that curvy ass. While most of the women wore slacks or jeans with a sweater or blouse, Queen Lila wore a thin cotton dress, like a smock, dark gray with white trim, buttoning up the front. She had a flower, bright orange, pinned with a brooch to her collar. The dress hung loosely on her, outlining her body underneath, including the bulge at the stomach.

She was almost as tall as Big Ben with shoulders almost as wide. A strong woman.

As she undulated her big body from side to side in time to the music, dark eyes showed between half-closed lids above the high cheek bones, peering out of a face tensed as if she were in pain. She had let down her long black hair and it hung loosly to her shoulders, swishing back and forth as she moved.

Big Ben started toward her. Then he stopped and got rid of the empty beer can, tossing it along the floor to come to rest beneath a pile of folded chairs. He started toward her again, then stopped within a few feet of her and watched.

She was supposed to be close to fifty. He had been told that despite her age she was a nymph. A nymphomaniac, she'll fuck anybody. But the man in the machine shop who told him that did not personally know anyone who had actually done it. Big Ben had looked at her in the shop many times and wondered about this husky Indian woman who operated a small drill press at the far end of the department. Several times he thought he caught her looking at him. He had been told she had an Indian mother and a white father, and she was born on the reservation up north of Falls City.

She knew he was watching her now. He could see that. She kept moving with the front of her facing him. The sweat glistened on her round face and her broad nose. Her skin was flushed and her thick lips were parted, showing big white teeth clenched together.

Now she saw him coming toward her. She threw her head back and laughed, her mouth wide open in welcome. There was a brief glint of gold showing back there somewhere in the upper teeth. Her arms reached out to him and he smelled perfume as they grabbed and locked together.

It was like coming home. Big Ben yelled and whirled her away. Others quickly cleared a space for them. Everybody stopped dancing and formed a ring and cheered them on. A good match. Both big and both raucously yelling and laughing, both beered up and having a helluva good time. Worth watching. Something to envy. That raw expression of desire in the way they were holding each other as they moved, fast at first, and then more and more slowly. Both now gripping both arms tightly around each other's waist, both pressing their bodies into each other.

Big Ben abruptly broke his hold and took Queen Lila by the hand and led her off the floor. Where you going, Ben? Paying no attention to the hecklers, Big Ben led Queen Lila into the small office in the rear of the hall. He closed the door and snapped the lock and backed her up against the desk.

He came out of the office alone. Who's next? One man went in and the line formed outside the door. All the women remaining on the first floor in the hall quickly fled, some retreating down into the basement, the rest going outside. Ben got another beer, then Baldy George came storming down from the think tank up on the second floor.

"What the hell's going on? Ben, get her out of there. Get her out of the hall."

"A union member, she's got a right to be here."

"Word gets back home to the wives of these men there'll be hell to pay."

Big Ben sipped his beer, calm in the face of the other's anger. "Get this settled with the men on the lathes and we'll all go home."

"Get her out of there."

"*You* get her out of there."

"You took her in there — you get her out of there."

"The hell I will." Big Ben smiled and drank his beer.

The union president shifted his approach. He pleaded. "C'mon, Ben, please." To this Big Ben was receptive. He enjoyed this power he had unexpectedly acquired.

"You want me to get her out of here? I'll make a deal. You stick your neck out and tell those four meatheads upstairs to agree to this. Everybody back to work tomorrow morning while the grievance committee goes in to negotiate a new rate. By noon if they're not getting anywhere the whole shop out again, officially on strike and no more fucking around, shit or get off the pot."

A quick conference up in the think tank and the union president returned. "Her driver's gone. Will you drive her home."

A handshake. "A deal."

Big Ben pounded the door with his fist. Get that woman out of your room. He kept pounding until a man emerged, checking the zipper on his trousers while he swore. Jesus Christ! Big Ben was not disturbed. The place is raided. He stuck his head into the office. Queen Lila, sitting on the edge of the desk, her dress pulled down, smiled at him, welcoming him back. Big Ben beckoned to her.

"C'mon, I'm driving you home."

They walked out of the Labor Hall together. "I have to get my car from the parking lot back at the plant. You want to wait here?" She went with him.

"Can we stop somewhere for coffee?"

"Get it at home."

"I'd like to stop somewhere and wash up."

"Wash up at home."

They walked into the parking lot together. He held the car door open for her. After he started the motor he turned to her.

"Where do you live?"

"I have to stop somewhere first and clean up."

"Why," he asked as he drove out of the parking lot, "afraid of your husband?"

"My kids, by now they're home from school."

"Afraid they'll tell your old man?"

"I'm not married."

"Divorced?"

"No."

"Whose kids?"

"Mine."

There was Mike's Bar. She could clean up in his room over the tavern there. But he had already driven past it.

"You said you're not married."

"I'm not."

"Where'd you get the kids?"

She enjoyed playing with him. "I birthed them. Three different fathers. Three children. Two girls and a boy. He's my oldest."

Big Ben, not knowing what to say, glanced at her. There was a faint smile on her face. She was amused by his reaction. A man doesn't have to be married, he can father all the kids he wants, but a woman must be married, or she's supposed to be filled with shame and under a cloud — if she's nobody and her children are illegitimate. The hell with you.

"I could have married," she said. "Every time I was pregnant I could have married the father." She looked at him and saw that his blank countenance radiated skepticism. "Why should I marry someone like that, someone I didn't know any better than I know you? I wanted the kids and I had them. We're a very happy family, happier than most. We really love each other."

"What if you get pregnant now?"

"I'll have another child. We got a good, happy house with ourselves. Lots of love. Why should we ruin it, bringing in a stranger who wants everything to center around him? I earn good money. We do fine. No thank you, no husband."

"Kids need a father. A family without a father, the kids get all screwed up."

"Not necessarily. With a lot of fathers you and I know back in the shop they'd be in real trouble."

"Kids need a father."

"A male image? I got my younger brother. He loves the kids. He's married, but no children of his own. The kids love him. Frankie, my eldest. He's slow. When he was born there was some brain damage. The bus picks him up in the morning and brings him back in the afternoon. A special school. My neighbor keeps an eye on him. And the girls are there to put him on the bus and meet him when he comes home. Frankie loves his uncle, my brother. He takes Frankie fishing and they get along great."

"What the hell do you tell the kids?"

"Everything. The truth. That's the way we are. And there's love in our house. Enough to take care of everything. It's a lot better this way. The kind of world we're living in now they'll grow up able to take care of themselves. You're intelligent. Ain't it better this way than to stick them with a father I don't love? You can't fool kids. Maybe they can't say what it is, but they feel what it's like in a home. My kids are very happy. That's what counts. Come over and you can see for yourself."

Big Ben was not prepared for this. Not after what had happened back in the Labor Hall. This was something entirely new to him and it attracted him though he did not understand why.

"We'll go back to my place. A bathroom down the hall or

you can wash up in the sink in my room. I got a hot plate. I'll make some coffee."

He had been driving aimlessly up one street and down another. Now he drove back to Mike's Bar and parked the car in front of the family entrance on the side street. She followed him into the hallway. On the left there was the stairway leading up to the rooms on the second floor, and on the right the door leading into the backroom of the tavern. She followed him up the stairs.

He closed the door to his small furnished room and started picking up dirty clothes. The place smelled of disinfectant. A bare dump. And with her there, it had never seemed so small and dingy as it did now beneath that bulb hanging from the ceiling. His eyes took it in, seeing it as she saw it — the hot plate on the scratched dresser, the badly painted chair, the pipe-iron double bed, the torn linoleum on the floor, the tattered and dirty window shades, and the wood pole nailed across one corner of the room on which hung his suit, some shirts and ties, and the winter coat. There were his books, mostly colored paperbacks, stacked in an old apple crate standing beside the bed. He had just discovered the dizzily fascinating world of the beautiful people in Scott Fitzgerald's novels. *This Side of Paradise* and *The Great Gatsby* and *The Beautiful and the Damned,* all secondhand paperbacks, were lying on top of the apple crate with a worn-out copy of *The Complete Poetry of Robert Burns* his high school teacher had given him. He tossed the armful of dirty clothes down so they fully covered the books on top and partially covered those inside the apple crate. And with his foot he shoved his poetry books lying on the floor to where they were out of sight under the bed.

Half-smiling, she stood with her back against the closed door, watching and waiting until he turned and spoke to her. The bathroom's down the end of the hall. She motioned to the small sink in the corner. A sponge bath's good enough. He gave her a bath towel and washrag and sat on the bed and watched while she undressed. Did you ever see a fat woman with her clothes off? He replied by cupping his hands. I like big breasts. Something to hang onto. She used the washrag to soap and rinse herself, piece by piece. When she was rubbing herself dry with the bath towel he reached for her. She backed away. He followed after. She pulled his hand away. The kids will be wondering what happened. He tried to push aside the outstretched hands which were fending him off. She was strong. He laughed and wrestled with her. She punched him on the arm. He slapped her across the face, leaving a red mark. She swore. You bastard. She grabbed his hand and pushed it away. Don't. Each time he reached for any part of her she was strong enough to keep him from getting firm hold. He backed away.

"What the hell's the matter with you?"

She did not try to explain. She reached for her brassiere. He got it first. Come over here or I'll push you out in the hall, bare-ass naked. But he did not interfere while she stepped into her underpants. He sat down on the bed, holding the brassiere. She grabbed an end. He held onto the other end. She let go rather than tear it. He reached her dress before she could get to it. Then he played with her, walking toward her, slowly, letting her back away, relentlessly keeping after her, but allowing her to stay out of his reach. She kept talking as she backed away.

"The children are waiting for me. I want you to meet them. The boy's thirteen. The girls are ten and eleven. Peggy, my younger girl, plays piano. She'll play for you. A secondhand piano I bought her. Jody is my artist. She'll show you her paintings. She's in sixth grade. Her teacher says she has talent. Come over and eat supper with us. Nothing fancy. Beans and hamburger. I made the meat patties this morning before I went to work. You'll like the hamburgers. My own recipe. Egg for body and finely chopped onions and a touch of garlic. Please. You're a nice guy. My kids are worrying about me. I should be home, cooking supper. You don't want to hurt them, do you?"

He tossed the brassiere and dress. "We'll stop on the way and buy ice cream for dessert."

Lila Redbird lived in the smallest cottage on the block, in a working class neighborhood within hearing of the railroad, switching of boxcars going on day and night, and within sight of the dirty old freighters moored along the bank of the wide river where they unloaded their cargoes of iron ore, sand, lumber, wood pulp, and other things brought from all over the United States and Canada and the rest of the world by way of the Great Lakes and the St. Lawrence Seaway. It was the same

river into which the creek flowing past Mackenzie Machine
Tool emptied itself. With the factories close by, most residents
on the block found it a disheartening experience, trying to keep
their houses looking clean on the outside. Too much grime
spewing out of factory chimney stacks lined up along the
horizon down beyond the end of the street. But Lila had talked
her landlord into providing her with paint, and her younger
brother helped her do the work. The one-story frame cottage set
flush up against the truck-travelled street, with only a narrow
sidewalk in front and not even a pretence at a lawn, was the
brightest little crackerbox on the short block. Fresh green paint
screamed: Hey, look at me.

"A little bright, but we like it."

"Cheerful," said Big Ben.

"At least it's painted."

Big Ben watched her kiss the three children, one after
another, her hearty hug matched by the energy of the hug each
child gave in return. Driving there, he had tried to find out
more about the relationship between the children and their
fathers.

"Do they contribute to their support?"

"No. I'm selfish. This way they're all mine and I don't have
to share them with anyone."

"Do the kids know their fathers?"

"No."

"Don't they ask about them?"

"I tell them everything except their father's name."

"Some day you'll have to tell them."

"By then it won't matter."

"The fathers know they got these kids?"

"One does. He's got money and he wanted to divorce his
wife and marry me. No thank you."

The children swarmed over Big Ben while Lila went into the
kitchen to cook supper. What's your name? Where did you meet
Mother? Where do you live? He grinned, enjoying their
attention, and seriously replied to each question.

Looking at the children he wondered about Lila. Did she
really reject the idea of marriage with their fathers? Is it being
a man that raises doubt about that? Did she really tell them all
to go to take a fat shit for themselves? He didn't know why,
but that tickled him. How much more pleasant, being here,

rather than alone back in his room.

He was still answering questions for the children in the small front room when Lila brought a tall whiskey and water for him and one for herself. He was sitting on the long, stuffed sofa. She told him to stay there and talk to the kids and she went back into the other room to make supper.

Peggy, the ten year old, climbed onto Big Ben's knee. Her sister, Jody, one year older, brought Big Ben two crayon drawings. A bird singing and a tree with leaves falling. These I did today in school, I'll show you more. She ran out of the room and quickly returned with a pile of crayon drawings. She went through the pile, showing one at a time. He praised each one. She glowed.

"Would you like to have them?"

"You don't want to give me all of them?"

"Yes, I do."

"Don't you want to keep any?"

"I'll make more, it's easy." She started through the pile from the beginning again, giving him one at a time to look at and keep.

Frank, the thirteen year old boy, hovering around Big Ben and the two girls, occasionally darted in to touch Ben's knee or arm, quickly retreating before Ben could touch him in return. Then he brought his catcher's baseball mitt and put it on top of the drawings Jody was placing on Big Ben's free knee. Jody gave the mitt back to him. Wait your turn. Ben took the glove from the boy. Do you like baseball? The boy's head bobbed rapidly and he left the room and returned with his fishing reel. Where did you get that?

"His Uncle Earl," said Jody, impatiently demanding that Big Ben look at the next drawing she had set on his knee.

"He promised to buy me a gun to go hunting," said the boy, speaking to Ben for the first time.

"When you're older," said Jody, showing another drawing.

The boy leaned against Big Ben's leg. Uncle Earl takes me fishing and hunting. A drawing waved in front of Big Ben's eyes. Ben looked and praised the drawing, and smiled at the boy. I hunt with a bow and arrow. Do you want to come with me some time? The boy vigorously nodded.

Peggy, the younger girl, jealous of the attention being given her brother and sister, hopped off Big Ben's other knee and ran to the piano. Listen to me. She struck the keys, a loud chord. Jody screamed to her mother. Peggy's interrupting me showing my drawings! Big Ben held up his hands and silenced the yelling. Two more drawings and then the piano.

Jody showed two drawings and the concert began. The audience settled on the sofa, the boy on Ben's left, with his catcher's mask ready to be shown, Jody on the other side, impatiently waiting to resume the showing of her art. Ten year old Peggy, taking center stage, proudly struck the keys. My teacher comes to the house and she gave me this to practice.

The concert was interrupted by supper and then the two girls helped Lila clear the table and straighten up the kitchen. The men were told to sit in the front room and watch television. On the sofa Big Ben put his arm around young Frank's shoulders and the boy rested against him.

The two girls ran in and wrestled to get close to the other side of Big Ben. Lila brought in another tall whiskey and water for Ben and another for herself. She sat in an easy chair and joined in watching the news on television, planes napalming an enemy-occupied village in Vietnam, with comment by a reporter who was flying overhead above the flame and smoke in a helicopter.

"How many they killed over there today?"

"If the figures were true they killed enough already to win it a couple times over."

His sarcasm drew a quiet grin, Lila acknowledging she knew what he meant about the military grossly inflating body counts of enemy destroyed to make things look better than they were. While the two girls squeezed tight against his right side, Big Ben told Lila about his brother Tommy over there with the Air Force. Ground crew. Should write him, but my mother writes the letters. The two girls were nudging each other and whispering and giggling back and forth. Then ten-year old Peggy, apparently elected to speak, interrupted. She held her hand to her mouth to suppress the titters long enough to be able to get some words out.

"Mother, can I sleep with Jody tonight?"

Lila sipped her drink and quietly laughed and moved her head from side to side. "You kids."

"Can I?"

"Do you really want to?" asked Lila, smiling secretively

after a long look.

"Yes!" both girls squealed.

Lila laughed quietly again and was silent. The girls repeated their plea. Lila looked at Big Ben, catching his inquiring eyes. Then he remembered. Before sitting down to supper in the kitchen he had been taken on a short tour of the other rooms in the cottage. The boy's room was small, like an oversized closet, but big enough for a narrow cot, a small dresser and a wooden box filled with sports equipment. Then Jody showed off her room, a little larger than her brother's, but not large enough for anything other than the single bed it contained. The only double bed was in Lila's room and Peggy said she slept there with her mother. Big Ben was very much aware of Lila watching him. He surprised himself, feeling the hot blush coming to his cheeks.

"Are you married?" asked Jody, a shadow coming across her face, as if the thought had just occurred to her. She waited for his answer.

"No," he said.

The shadow disappeared and the little face was young and eager again. But he saw that the boy was still silent, watching with an anxious squint. He could feel the tenseness in the boy's shoulders. The boy might be slow on some things. But not on this. The two girls took it for granted that their mother was granting their wish. They whispered into each other's ear and giggled and tittered.

Lila watched the increasing evidence of Big Ben's embarrassment as he concentrated on watching the report by the weather man on the television screen. Her thick lips smiled and she quietly motioned to the two girls to cut it out. Jody couldn't stop giggling. She tried several times to talk and finally through a burst of laughter completed the sentence.

"Do you like cereal for breakfast?"

"Oh, shut up!" screamed Peggy, laughing, and she shrieked and covered her pink face with both hands, and then Jody shrieked along with her.

The weatherman had finished his report and Queen Lila turned down the volume on the television set. Trying to change the subject, she handed Big Ben the newspaper which she had brought in from the front porch. "Take off your shoes and make yourself comfortable."

"I'll take off his shoes," screamed Peggy, reaching.

"I will!" giggled Jody, trying to push past Peggy.

But Queen Lila firmly told them to let Big Ben take off his own shoes. It was an order. They knew it and they obeyed. Untying the shoelaces himself, Big Ben joined in the silliness of the girls. "Do you mind if I take off my socks? My feet stink, but I like to wiggle my toes. *I wiggle a damn mean toe!*" The girls screamed with laughter and hugged each other as he went on to remove both his shoes and his socks and then rapidly wiggled the toes of both feet.

Jody struggled to control herself long enough to burst out, "Do you carry your lunch to work?"

"Why?"

"Do you want me to make it for you?"

Big Ben saw that they were all waiting for his decision. "We'll see."

A moment of quiet disappointment and then Peggy jumped up. "Do you like to read in bed?" He warily nodded and Peggy said, "Mother, can I show him?" Lila took a long draw on her cigarette and sensuously breathed two thin streams of smoke slowly out through flared nostrils. "Mother, please."

"He doesn't want to see that."

"Please."

"He's not interested."

Caught, Ben asked, "What is it?"

"Books," said Peggy.

"I'm interested."

"See?"

"All right," said Queen Lila.

The three children led him into their mother's bedroom. Peggy opened the closet door and pushed aside the clothes hanging there, revealing an old book case with shelves of worn volumes. Big Ben slid out one book and opened it. The pages were yellowed. *World's Great Literature.* Walter Scott's *The Heart of the Midlothian.* He put it back into its place and ran his finger along the line of titles and authors. Sophocles. Thucydides. Flaubert. Chekhov. Shakespeare. Big Ben's breath expelled noisily. Jesus Christ!

"Where'd your mother get these?"

"Uncle Jeffrey."

Big Ben touched one volume after another, with his finger

beneath the name of each author and title. He wondered if
Uncle Jeffrey stayed overnight and got cereal for breakfast and
a lunch to take to work.

"My library's over here," said Peggy, showing him about a
dozen books stacked between two metal bookends on the
dresser.

"Mine's in my room," said Jody. "My own bookcase."

With Frank tagging after them, the two girls led Big Ben
back into the front room. He sat on the sofa again and picked
up his drink. There still was that look of secret amusement on
Queen Lila's face.

"Quite a library."

In reply, her lips broadened the quiet smile and she lifted
her glass to her mouth. The television was still on: a game
show. Lila seemed to be the only one there who was watching
the screen. Big Ben kept glancing at her, while the children
prattled on to him about school and homework, about their trip
to visit Uncle Earl on his farm in Canada, and about school
and play and other things, chattering on and on.

At one point when the children ran into the kitchen to get
some coke and potato chips Lila turned her head and stared
directly at him. He shook his head. You floor me. She laughed
noiselessly.

"Why the hell do you hide the books?"

"I know where they are."

"Why hide them?"

"Nobody else has to know."

"It's nothing to be ashamed of," he said, forgetting that to
keep her from seeing them back in his room he had pushed the
poetry books under the bed.

"I'm not ashamed."

"Do you read them?"

"No, I keep them there to look at." Heavy sarcasm.

"Jesus Christ, how many have you read?"

"Some."

"Many?"

"No, I fall asleep too fast."

"Which ones did you read?"

"Most of the novels."

"*Jesus Christ.*"

The children returned and it was almost another hour before

they went back into the kitchen for a new food supply. The television was still on: a western drama with cowboys.

"Why did you do that this afternoon?"

It came at Lila out of nowhere. She didn't know what he meant. Big Ben jerked his thumb in the general direction of where they'd been that afternoon.

"Back there in the Labor Hall."

She shrugged and her face said nothing. He scratched his cheek and stared, waiting until she had to speak. But her impassive expression walled him out.

"You were there."

"I don't get it. That and this. And who the hell is Uncle Jeffrey?"

"My oldest brother."

"Oh."

"He's a judge in a small town across the border in Canada. Like our Justice of Peace over here."

"You, I don't figure you out. That back there this afternoon."

"It bothers you?"

"Hell, no. It's none of my business."

Later, after Lila had finally hounded the children off to bed, she and Ben talked about the books and many other things. He told her about the play he had seen and Lila tried to analyze why Hedda Gabler practiced with the pistol until she became a crack shot, and then she tried to relate that to what Big Ben told her about his interest in archery. She said the pistol and the bow and arrow amount to the same thing.

They got into Freud and penis-envy and fear of sexual inadequacy, dredging up forgotten childhood sexual experiences they had never told to anyone else. It was a rare moment of honesty and confidence in which each opened up vulnerable areas they had never risked opening before.

Big Ben said he hoped they could be really good friends and Lila said the key to a good friendship is a good sexual experience. Start with a sexual experience and it opens the way to develop a' good friendship. Ben thought a good friendship should precede the sexual experience, with the latter being the final culmination of a period of getting to know one another well and finding much in common.

Lila flatly disagreed. Sex first. That opens the way to be honest and open, like with us. Then you can become really good friends.

They talked a long while about this, not resolving their difference, until Lila warned Ben that it was past midnight. We better get some sleep if we're going to get up in time for work. Big Ben was silent.

Queen Lila left the room and in a little while Big Ben heard the shower running in the bathroom. Queen Lila returned, wearing a loose, flannel nightgown, patterned with faded roses. She stood in the doorway, in her bare feet. Big Ben had not moved from the spot on the sofa where he had been when she left. She stood there, looking at him, waiting. A long silence.

"I don't know," he finally said.

Another long silence, which she finally broke, asking, "Is it that you're afraid what they'll say over there in the shop?"

The skin at the corners of his eyes crinkled. "You're a smart cookie."

"You're not being honest."

"Why?"

"You're just as responsible as I am. You told the others. Not me. You sent them in." He was silent while she let that sink in. She went on. "I didn't think about it back then, but thinking about it now I'd say you really wanted it to happen exactly the way it happened. Maybe that way you were not the only one and so you were not especially connected to me in any way."

He thought that over a while. "But it still hurt that I wasn't enough for you."

"That wasn't it. I didn't owe anything to anyone. If I did, I wouldn't do that. Not if we meant anything to one another and if I thought you didn't want me to."

This was followed by a series of long searching looks into one another's eyes, attempts at expressing what each was feeling, but inability to find the words to properly express what each was feeling. They ended up smiling sadly at each other, admitting their inability to handle what they were in. Big Ben sighed loudly and stirred on the sofa and lifted his big body.

"I'll go take a shower."

Early next morning in the machine shop the leadman on the punch presses greeted Big Ben. Did you get it disinfected, Ben? And Big Ben did not even look up from the metal table on his drill press. The leadman stood there. Get it disinfected, Ben, or it'll drop off. No answer. That old Indian whore, you got jumping syphilis by now. Big Ben picked up a big wrench and rose and gently placed the end of the greasy tool against the leadman's chin.

"You keep your fuck'n mouth shut about her, you shitty sonofabitch, or I'm going to use your fuck'n teeth to part your fuck'n head right through the middle right down through to your dirty fuck'n asshole."

The grapevine exploded that little speech throughout the entire shop and although there was a lot of careful whispering and some hushed joking the new development was welcomed. It eased the waves still tossing in the shop and in the homes. Big Ben had taken over. Queen Lila was his. And every home was safe again.

After work Big Ben moved his things from the furnished room above the tavern to Queen Lila's cottage.

Chapter 4

Within a half hour after the leadman felt the cold wrench pressing against his chin, the plant manager and machine shop foreman were given the opportunity to report what they had heard about Big Ben and Queen Lila to Jamison Langner in his office in the administration building. They had been summoned from the shop by Dick Penfield. The Old Man wants to talk to you about the lathe operators.

It was in the small talk preceding the discussion of the grievance that the plant manager briefly mentioned that he had heard in the shop that there had been a wild party the day before over in the Labor Hall. Big Ben Hood and that Indian woman from the machine shop.

Despite his suit and white shirt and tie, there was a touch of awkwardness in the plant manager's speech, his dress and movement that still reflected many years of hard work in the shop where he had climbed slowly up through the ranks, starting with bull work on the labor gang during the second World War. Comparatively new to his position, having recently replaced the chief steward's brother who had been transferred to Virginia to start up the new division down there, the plant manager was careful not to go on any further about what happened in the Labor Hall until he sensed the reaction of the boss.

But the machine shop foreman had not yet learned to put his toe into the water to test it before stepping in. Casimer Kowalski — Casey — was only a few months removed from his previous role as union steward in the machine shop. He assumed his present position gave him the right to a confidential familiarity in this relaxed moment with his superiors. Led on by what the plant superintendent had said about the wild party in the Labor Hall, he reached to get credit for telling Jamison Langner more.

"Big Ben put the blocks to this Indian woman who works in my department. Then he lined her up for others to go in and pump her." He shook his head. "A few days off would teach her the company don't approve of that kind of conduct."

Silence. Jamison Langner blankly looked at him.

The foreman hurriedly reversed his field. Fumbling to avoid the words Big Ben had employed, he quickly told what had just happened with the leadman. "So if now we punish her we'll have Big Ben to deal with. We might start another walkout."

"Let's begin," said Jamison Langner, deliberately turning to Dick Penfield.

But he did make a mental note to think later about what effect this new information might have on Big Ben's ability to serve as the link to channel in the right direction whatever interest in the arts might be generated among the people in the shop.

Eating lunch later in his office, he took the opportunity to ask the secretary who had come over from The Dance Center what she thought about it. His company contributed the money to pay the secretary's salary and all other expenses of this new project he hoped to develop into an important part of the magical mixture of the arts in the community. Dance, silent dance, rather than spoken drama — that could be useful.

He had asked Betty Lyons to bring the The Dance Center mail to his office and on the way to pick up a sandwich for him. She brought tuna sandwiches and milk for both of them. Jamison Langner at the window called her attention to the men and women streaming out of the factory buildings. An emergency meeting in the yard during lunchtime. A problem we just settled. He did not bother her with the details: an interim adjustment of the incentive rate involving the four lathe hands, with a retroactive date to which any subsequent adjustment after the job had been re-timed would apply. The union is recommending it to their membership.

He respected Betty Lyons' judgment and he wanted to get her reaction to his thoughts about using Big Ben. Betty Lyons was a dark-eyed moppet with short hair and a ready smile, with a somewhat stiff body of medium height, dressed simply to perfection. Jamison Langner knew her as a highly sophisticated person, a divorcee, with a quick mind, who in her thirty-five years had accumulated an impressive knowledge of the arts. She had lived in Europe and traveled all over the world, had done some dancing herself, and seemed to have the ability to be relatively at ease talking to people in the lower as well as the upper income brackets. She was a real asset to The Dance Center.

Through his window Jamison Langner could see part of the crowd of workers standing in the yard. They were looking off toward where he knew someone was speaking for the union committee. He could not see or hear the speaker. There was Big Ben strolling across the yard, his arm around the waist of a husky woman, her jet black hair tied up in a bun on top of her head. The Indian woman. She seemed as tall and broad-shouldered as Big Ben. An impressive pair.

He pointed out their backs to Betty Lyons and briefly explained their connection, leaving out the most lurid details of what had happened the day before in the union hall. Feeling an urgency to pour something in quickly to fill the dangerous vacuum he had uncovered, he moved toward asking Betty Lyons what she thought about using someone like Big Ben to bring the arts to factory employees and their families.

"Are they ready at The Center with that number with all those metal props?" he asked.

"This week they start dress rehearsals."

She passed the sandwich and milk to him and waited. Jamison Langner, unwrapping the sandwich, began to explain to her why and how he wanted to use someone from the factory in connection with this particular dance they were developing at The Dance Center. He himself had suggested the theme of the dance. Something to capture the essence of the complications created in the lives of factory workers by the rapid technological advances in industrial production.

He quickly gave some background for his thoughts about needing a factory worker to put it over. "Three years ago the AFL-CIO unions in town named a man to supposedly get their people involved in the arts. Fortunately, he was hand-picked by the labor priest to make sure they would not get a communist. Or someone too ambitious in the wrong direction. But a high school English teacher, he knew nothing about how to go about it. He still nominally holds the title, arts administrator for the unions, keeping anyone else out of it. And he's back to teaching. A stranger to factory life, he accomplished exactly nothing, which is what they intended here, the way they went about it. I think our Ben can do the job if now we decide we really want it done."

Through his office window, Jamison Langner, his sandwich eaten, saw that the meeting in the yard was breaking up. The

people were going back into the shop. A minute or two later the
phone rang and he picked up the receiver. Send him in. Dick
Penfield entered and reported.

"A lot of shouting and accusations from the lathe men. But
they went along. Big Ben made the motion."

"Our Big Ben?" Betty Lyons was amused by that.

"Seconded by his girlfriend."

"Good."

It was a matter of fact comment that in no way indicated to
Jamison Langner and Dick Penfield that Betty Lyons was
fascinated by the darkly complex relationship she imagined
was there between this unusual factory worker and the Indian
woman. Jamison Langner lifted a hand to fix Dick Penfield's
attention.

"Have you ever checked out Big Ben? Any ties to the Left?
Any subversive organizations? Subversive friends?"

"So far as I know he's not political," said Dick Penfield,
curious, but not daring to ask the purpose behind the inquiry.
"But he's a headstrong guy. Impetuous. Unpredictable. With
Ben anything can happen, and usually does."

Jamison Langner turned to Betty Lyons. Did she think Big
Ben's relationship with the Indian woman would damage his
ability to interest people in the shop in the arts. She thought a
while before replying, very seriously. He made that motion and
they supported him. It may be that he can do what that high
school English teacher couldn't do. It might take someone like
him to interest other factory workers to come and watch
something like ballet and modern dance. — And now that
Jamison Langner had opened up the subject Betty Lyons felt
free to inquire further.

"What's he really like?"

"What's Big Ben really like?" Dick Penfield's hoarse chuckle
included a note of lechery. "You really want to know?"

"Yes, I'm curious."

Dick Penfield was flattered by this opportunity to engage in
an intimate conversation with this attractive woman. A stylish
woman, he called her later when he reported the conversation
to his wife — a stylish woman who must be up there in the
sophisticated four hundred set. He giggled like an embarrassed
schoolboy while he supplied Betty Lyons with tidbits about Big
Ben's sex life. He savored the chance to underline the difference

in age between Big Ben and Queen Lila. Like mother and son, incest.

"Oedipus Rex," said Betty Lyons, and added for Dick Penfield's benefit, "the Greek tragedy where the son made it with his mother." She could not resist an impish glance at Jamison Langner. "That started it, and it's been going on ever since."

"Ben's no Greek," said Dick Penfield. "But he's a handsome guy. Rugged. He has to carry a baseball bat to beat off the women."

"He must have something," said Betty Lyons, and then she blushed and touched her hand to her mouth, and sheepishly added, "I guess he has."

The two men laughed in a friendly way at her embarrassment.

"Whatever it is," leered Dick Penfied, "the women seem to want it."

Betty Lyons turned away from him, to Jamison Langner, "This older woman, is she beautiful or just fantastically sexy?"

Jamison Langner nodded to his personnel man, telling him to answer.

"Queen Lila? Not beautiful and not ugly. Big and heavy and for me too fat to be sexy. A bawdy creature. Bawdy as all hell. A free spirit. When it comes to sex she does what she damn well pleases and plenty of it, from what I hear."

"So does he, doesn't he?"

"Ben? Yes, I guess so. Yes, definitely. I think it's one way he tells everybody to go to hell."

"It makes him somebody different."

"It certainly does."

It fascinated Betty Lyons that this was the same man who Jamison Langner thought the most likely person to get the people in the shop interested in ballet and modern dance.

"Why don't we arrange for him to see a dress rehearsal at The Dance Center and get his reaction?"

Dick Penfield looked skeptical, but Jamison Langner was receptive. "It would be a good test."

"Then we can decide where we go from there."

"Be careful you don't make this Indian woman jealous," Dick Penfield warned. "She might peel your scalp."

Betty Lyons showed her long manicured nails. "I wield a

mean tomahawk myself."

"She eats nice girls like you for breakfast," said Dick Penfield.

"I'm not that nice," said Betty Lyons, cutting him off and turning back to Jamison Langner. "Why don't we ask him to bring her along? Indians have a great tradition in the dance."

"She can show them how to do a war dance," said Dick Penfield, a remark the other two ignored.

Jamison Langner mulled it over a moment and then shifted forward in his polished armchair. "Let's start with Ben."

"Fine," agreed Betty Lyons.

"First we have to find out if Ben is interested."

"I'll talk to him," volunteered Dick Penfield.

"On this," said Jamison Langner, "I'd like to be there to see his reaction."

Leaving Betty Lyons waiting behind in the office to hear what Big Ben would say, the two men went into the machine shop. On the way there they picked up their white hardhats, the same kind worn by foreman Casey Kowalski who hurried across the gray cement floor to meet them. Wearing white hardhats in the shop was compulsory for supervision and visitors. Colored hardhats, blue for the machine shop, were available but not compulsory attire for all others working out in the factory itself. In practice anyone in the machine shop who ventured to suggest wearing one was subjected to heavy ridicule. They don't make square ones to fit your head.

A quick exchange between the two executives and the foreman took place in the wide aisle that cut the department in two. Men and women working nearby made a point of not seeming to be aware of this invasion from the front office. There was intense activity around the lathes, the milling machines, the shapers and the large drill presses along the aisle. The men and women working on these machines seemed to be too completely absorbed in what they were doing to look over to see what was going on. And in response to this intense concentration, the loud humming of machine motors and the grinding and squeaking of metal against metal seemed to grow even louder, and the burning oil smell coming from coolants used to keep cutting tools from burning up seemed to become even more pungent and biting to the nostrils. The operator of a gas-powered truck, a heavy woman stuffed into tight jeans and a sweater, with a baseball cap set rakishly on her head, honked the horn and deliberately forced the trio to move over to let her crawl by with a load of wood pallets and trays of metal parts. The three of them, briefly conferring, still seemed to keep their ears cocked to listen to the horn squawker overhead as it buzzed out its hoarse signals one after another, call numbers summoning different executives and supervisors, engineers, foremen and maintenance men to phone in to the switchboard and get urgent messages.

Jamison Langner and Dick Penfield broke away from the foreman. Matching steps, stiff in their tailored business suits, the personnel man properly one pace behind the boss, they passed by Big Ben's large drill press. Big Ben, seeing them there, bent over the machine's metal table and checked the bite of the drill. He was very much aware of their presence, consciously ignoring them. He examined the slowly turning drill and the thin curl of metal it was eating out of the large casting. He felt a tap on his shoulder and he looked up. Jamison Langner beckoned to him to step away from the noisy machine. Moving out into the center aisle, Ben wiped his hands with an oil rag. He glanced back at the large drill which was still turning, slowly boring its way into the metal.

Jamison Langner had to lean forward and raise his voice to be heard. "Ben, they tell me you're interested in theatre." He stopped and gave Big Ben a chance to react to that, but Big Ben stolidly stood there, face immobile, and patiently waited to hear the rest. Jamison Langner had to explain. "At The Dance Center we're working on something. Not a play. It's a dance in which they're trying to embody the feel of our highly industrialized society. I think you might enjoy it." He waited again, and again Big Ben's immobile silence forced him to go on. "We're anxious to get the reaction of someone like yourself, someone who'll be honest and tell us what he really thinks. You'd be doing us a great favor if you'd come to rehearsal and look at it. I know the dancers will be very grateful."

Big Ben looked directly into Jamison Langner's face as he thought it over, evaluating quickly whether or not he could handle it with his fellow workers, if he agreed, and then he grinned.

"Why not?"

"I'll have my secretary from The Dance Center check the

rehearsal schedule and get in touch with you."

Jamison Langner moved on, and Dick Penfield who had been waiting fell in behind him. Without a word between them they marched out of the department. Once the pair were out of sight, catcalls and shouts came from the men and women at machines up and down the aisle, all directed at Big Ben. Even the foreman laughed at the furor which suddenly broke out. Voices raised above the noise of the machines yelled to Big Ben. One shout topped all the rest.

"Ben, what did the Old Man want?"

Big Ben cupped his hands to his mouth and yelled loud enough to be heard by Queen Lila who was standing next to one of the small drill presses at the far end of the department, looking toward him with an expectant smile.

"He wanted to dance with me — I told him to go get his music."

Chapter 5

Friday at Mike's tavern across the creek from the plant. Payday. Big Ben cashed his check, downed the shot of whiskey Old Frank put in front of him, emptied the tall glass of beer with a long gulp, picked up his change, called goodbye to Old Frank and started for home.

He walked. Queen Lila had taken his old Buick and gone ahead to get supper ready. She had wrecked her own car in a collision a few weeks back and since she had been at fault and since she had originally paid only three hundred dollars for the car and had not bothered with collision insurance it didn't pay to have it repaired and she didn't have enough money saved yet to buy another one.

It was only a brisk ten minute walk from Mike's Bar to the cottage and after being pinned down to his machine all day in the shop Big Ben would have enjoyed the exercise in the fresh October air, except that he had not yet figured out how to tell Lila he was going away for the weekend.

In a way it was fortunate he was going, because before he cashed his check at Mike's Bar the bartender gave him a message to call Dave Newman. Remembering that backstage after the performance of *Hedda Gabler* he had asked the former organizer for the United Electrical Workers (UE) to let him know if he ever was going to be in another play, he went to the pay phone. It was not that. We're getting together. A few people from the university and some union guys. We're trying to get them to do something together. Tie in with the big demonstration against the war down in Washington. Big Ben did not want to say no. He still owed Dave something. But he was not ready to get mixed up with that. Not with the radical young college nuts. Sorry, Dave, I'm going out of town tonight.

The three children were playing catch out in front of the house and Big Ben yelled to them. Peggy threw the ball to him. He had to jump to snare it. And then they were all over him. The boy climbed up on his back. The two girls grabbed him around the waist with their arms, each gripping one of his legs with their feet. Grinning, continuing on as if the three children were not loaded on him, Big Ben plodded heavily to the steps leading up to the small side porch outside the kitchen. The squealing animals ran as Lila opened the door for Big Ben and yelled at them to get off him. Big Ben unbuttoned his gray work shirt and he crossed through the kitchen.

"I have to catch a plane to go visit my sister in New York City."

Lila was too proud to question him. He had told her a lot about himself during the past week but he had not told her there was a sister in New York and this being Friday, payday, with Saturday and Sunday off from work, she had expected they would go out together to the tavern later and get a little drunk and dance and raise some hell, blow off the pressure that had piled up while working in the shop that week, and then come back and have a crazy time together in bed. Tonight there would be a three-piece group playing ear-splitting country music at Mike's place. She did not let Big Ben see her disappointment.

"Supper's ready. It'll be on the table by the time you clean up."

In the bedroom, undressing, Big Ben continued a mental process he had begun when he got the phone call from his sister. It was a process he was to continue throughout the weekend. Sorting everything into two piles. What he would tell Lila. And what he would *not* tell her. What she did not know would not hurt her.

That was what she herself had said the night before. Their warm bodies snuggled together in bed, they had talked briefly about love, agreeing it was something you can't define and not necessarily a part of their relationship. The terms of their arrangement, in addition to payment for his room and board, seemed to include a sort of understanding that he was free to wander to other pastures as long as it was done in a way that would not be abrasive to her personal dignity. For herself, while she seemed to waive this privilege, she did sharply question him.

"How do *you* see it, our relationship?"

"We're providing each other with companionship."

"Better than sleeping alone," she said, seeming to accept that as the way she also saw it. "It's a helluva lot nicer with another body to keep you warm. Especially after sex, instead of just getting up and walking away. It gives you the feeling you've been in deep communication with another human being. It's a lonely damn world out there. Dog eat dog and each for himself when it comes to making a living." Then she gently patted his relaxed penis. "This helps to make it easier." They both laughed.

Stripped down to his jockey shorts, he opened the kitchen door. Queen Lila at the kitchen stove did not turn around. She knew he was there. He hesitated. Going to visit his sister must sound phoney. But that was the real reason. That, and to see a play. — His sister's roommate? That was something *not* to tell Lila. He crossed through the kitchen to the bathroom to take a shower.

On his way back to the bedroom, fresh and clean, with only a towel knotted around his waist, he saw Queen Lila standing there, waiting for him. Her face was grimly set. Then, on impulse, without any change in that grim look on her face she made a playful grab at the towel. He cried out in mock fright and pulled back out of reach. The tension gone, they laughed and embraced and squeezed with all their strength.

"What we were talking about last night. Love. The way my sister feels about me and the way I feel about her, I'd do anything for her and she'd do anything for me. I trust her more than anyone else in the whole world, and she feels the same way about me."

While he dressed he kept moving back and forth from inside the bedroom to the kitchen doorway, talking to Queen Lila, trying to dispell any resentment she might still feel about his going away. "Mary Lou, she wanted to go to college. Back then daughters of coal mining families went to high school and got married. Or got pregnant and got married and quit school. Babies and washing clothes at sixteen and seventeen. And clean and cook. Fit her life to some joker breaking his dumb ass on shift work down in the mines while she waits at home alone at night in a couple rooms in a little old shack. She didn't go for that."

"Want your highball?"

"A tall one," said Big Ben, and rushed on. "She's like you. Maybe not your nerve to go ahead and get kids without a husband. But maybe yes. If she wanted it. Built like you, like a brick shithouse, big and nice and warm, big-hearted and full of holy fuck'n hell. And no shrinking violet. Shit, she told me when her girlfriends were all getting pregnant and hurrying to get married quick before the little bastard popped out she laid it right on the line to any sonofabitch who wanted to screw her, a rubber or no dice."

Talking honestly and earnestly this way about his relationship with his sister made Ben feel better about keeping his sister's roommate in the other pile of something *not* to be told. It created an atmosphere of intimacy with Queen Lila which she was aware of as she made the two highballs and handed him his.

"She always wanted to get away," continued Big Ben. " 'See some of the world before I settle down and die.' — When she told my old man she was going to New York City he told her you ain't going nowhere. Fight? Screaming and crying? Shouting? Yelling? Christ, you never heard anything like it. The neighbors thought somebody was getting murdered."

Lila silently laughed, urging him to tell how it came out.

"My old man, the stubborn sonofabitch, he locked her in her room and she went on a hunger strike. My old lady let that go on for just one day and then she stepped in and delivered her two cents and there was a compromise. We got an uncle in New York City, my old man's brother, a motorman on the subway. My old man wrote him and Mary Lou went to live with him and my aunt until she got a job and could afford a decent place of her own where a nice young working girl could safely live. My old man was against her living alone. Shit, a girl living alone in a city like that gets into all kinds of trouble. It's lonely and loneliness is dangerous. Dirty old bastards and dirty young bastards all over the place looking for the chance to take advantage of lonely young girls. Until she gets a job and makes friends and finds a nice roommate Mary Lou has to live with the uncle and aunt."

The children came running in. We're hungry, when's supper ready? Lila gave them buttered rolls and sent them out to play another five minutes. I'll call you. Big Ben sat down next to the kitchen table to slip on his socks. Lila started to pour another shot into his glass, but he put his hand over the glass. She put the bottle back up on the shelf.

Ben reached for his shoes, and went on about his sister getting a job by looking up the address of the Bartenders Union and talking to the business agent. From a good union family, where could she get a job back of the bar or waiting on table? A place where she'd feel at home. Working people. Nothing fancy.

"She laughs about it now. In back of her mind she had some idea about meeting some guy there she might like. Some halfway intelligent bastard who once in a while would use his mind for something else more than only talk about automobiles and sports. She's got a brain. She reads The New York Times. Started that back in high school in the school library. She's the one who opened my mind and got me feeling the way I do, that I can take just so much of that fuck'n stupid shit in that shop. Then I got to get away."

Without breaking his monologue, Big Ben placed his drink down on the table and went into the bedroom to get another clean shirt, one not frayed at the collar. Lila poured another shot of whiskey into his drink and added half a shot to her own. She went back to the stove, frequently glancing back from there to let Ben know she was still listening. And with only the passing assurance to himself that anything he might do with Mary Lou's roommate while he was in New York would have nothing to do with what he enjoyed here, he ran on.

"All my archery equipment comes from her. Her pay is nothing, state minimum, but she makes it up on tips. And she keeps a special bowl back of the bar down there at The Green Shamrock. All the dimes and nickels and pennies she gets. Into the bowl. Her mad money. Her horse money. All her customers get a kick out of her. How we doing? And she gives the latest poop. What she won or lost. Any time she makes a killing, there's a present for her kid brother. He's the one who keeps me lucky."

"Did she find the guy she was looking for?"

Her question was put quietly, and Big Ben wondered if this was going to lead to him having to tell her about Mary Lou having a roommate.

"She met this guy there. He worked at the postoffice and he kept dropping in there with the other guys for a quick drink. And one time he asked if she wanted to see the fights. Mary Lou's the kind who enjoys seeing a prize fight and she enjoys seeing a serious play. Not only a fight and not only a play. Both. I get that from her."

The phone rang. It was on the wall in the kitchen beside the

door to the bedroom. Big Ben answered while Queen Lila
stirred the pot of stew on the stove. It was Don Mayer, the
union's chief steward, calling from home. His wife just spoke
on the phone long distance to their sister-in-law down in
Virginia, and she let slip that his plant manager brother is
having labor trouble in the new plant down there. "She
wouldn't say what. She asked the wife not to tell me. You
heard anything?" — "No, nothing." — Don Mayer said he'd try
to find out more.

"What happened to your sister?" prompted Queen Lila, after
Big Ben quickly told her the substance of the phone
conversation.

"This same guy, he took her to see a musical show up on
Broadway. Right after he took her to the prize fight! That did
it. He proposed and she accepted. They got married and they
moved into a small apartment over on Eighth Avenue not far
from where she worked. She kept working there and it was
good she did. She found out this guy was great on baseball
scores and lousy in bed. Slam bam, thank you, ma'am, and
leave her hanging up in the air, ready to cut her throat. A
month of that and she decided she didn't commit no crime, she
didn't have to serve no life sentence. She phoned and asked me
to come down, and she paid my way with her mad horse
money. She could move her things herself but she wanted me
around just in case he tried to get rough. But he took it nice. He
really wasn't a bad guy. He helped me get her things out and
we moved her into an apartment over on 23rd Street with one
of the girls she worked with."

Lila interrupted to ask him to call in the girls to set the table
so he could eat before he had to leave for the airport. Ben did
not want the kids around if by further questioning she was
going to push him into any kind of pissing match about the
roommate. Give me the dishes and silverware. He started
placing them around on the kitchen table.

"This week she won almost three hundred bucks on the
daily double. And one of her customers in the theatre business
gave her two tickets to see *The Great White Hope* tomorrow
night. One of the top plays on Broadway, it won the Pulitzer
prize. She said it's about this colored guy, the world
heavyweight champ, Jack Johnson. He marries a white woman
and all the white bastards go out to get him. Find a great

white hope to knock the shit out of him. My sister knew I
wanted to see a Broadway play. And she wants to see her kid
brother."

Ben hesitated, not wanted to give an outright lie. But then,
well, the hell with it.

"My sister's shacking up with this other guy now. She
divorced the first. This one's from the postoffice too. She's got a
thing for the postoffice. The girl she works with moved out and
this guy moved in. The same apartment over on 23rd Street.
She's got a couch there that opens up into a bed. Where I'll
sleep.

His sister did have a boyfriend who worked in the postoffice.
And the couch in his sister's apartment on 23rd Street near
Eighth Avenue in New York City did open up into a bed. And
that was where Big Ben did sleep that night. With Donna
Colangelo, his sister's roommate. The boyfriend was up in
Canada for the weekend, hunting.

Mary Lou had prepared the way for him and before Donna
even saw Big Ben she had already said that if the younger
brother was half as nice as Mary Lou said he was he certainly
was not going to have to sleep on any cold floor.

He took a taxi from LaGuardia Airport to The Green
Shamrock. But not before there was some excitement that held
them up at the airport terminal. He marked it down as one of
the things he would tell Lila when he got home. They were
giving out leaflets out in front of the building. Get our troops
out of Vietnam. National mobilization in Washington or
something. A whole crowd. Not all kids. Some gray-haired old
ladies. All blocking traffic. And the cops tried to push them
back up on the sidewalk. A pushing match and they were
yelling at the cops. *Pigs! Off with the pigs!* The cops had to
send for help. Women right up there with the guys. *Hell, no, we
won't go!* When the cops got them back up onto the sidewalk
they marched right into the building. *One, two, three, four, we
don't want your fuck'n war!* Ben got one of the leaflets to bring
back to Lila. He reached through the open window of the taxi
to get it from a gray-haired old lady dressed like a young kid,
blue denim jeans and jacket.

Traveling light, he had only a small canvas bag with him in
the taxi. His toilet articles and a clean pair of socks and a
shirt. The noise and rushing traffic and the tall buildings in

midtown Manhattan all lit up against the darkness exhilarated him. He relished the excitement of New York, with all the people out on the streets, two streams of pedestrians hurrying in opposite directions on 34th Street near Eighth Avenue when he got out of the taxi in front of The Green Shamrock. But now, after dark, you don't wander off onto any empty sidestreets alone. You'll get mugged and robbed.

Mary Lou and the other waitress were wearing the same uniform, white shoes and a black dress and black stockings, showing off a lot of leg. Good thing they got nice legs. Mary Lou kissed him. This is Donna Colangelo. I told you she's going with you to the play, I'm working tomorrow night. The other waitress shook hands with him. A young kid. He didn't get a chance to say anything to her because Mary Lou swung him around to face the bartender. This is my lovely brother. Ain't he beautiful? His only trouble is he can't leave the women alone. But they don't seem to mind.

Ben sat at the bar. He had to wait for the girls to finish working. He felt at home, reading the little signs stuck up there on the walls: "Work, the Curse of the Drinking Class" — "Saloon Closed for Hanging" — "Dirty Old Men Need Love Too" — "Work Fascinates Me, I Could Sit And Watch It For Hours." They had signs like that back at Mike's Bar.

He put a ten dollar bill down and the bartender in shirtsleeves pushed it back at him. Your money's no good here. Ben asked if they got Canadian ale on tap. We got everything. The bartender kept his glass full, and by the time the girls were through working, several hours later, he was slightly drunk.

Mary Lou had shoved some coins into the jukebox. She came over to get Ben, whispered to him that she had it all fixed up for him with Donna. Dance with her. Be nice and you're all set. From his vantage point at the bar he had already given Donna a thorough going over. Eighteen or nineteen, skinny, dark complexion, tits kind of small, nice smile, looks like a serious, intense kid. He put his arm around her and felt her ribs.

They danced and talked. Where you from? The Bronx. Her mother still lives there with her boyfriend. Parents divorced. Father in New Jersey. Works at a plastics plant there. Mother's a beautician in a shop on Madison Avenue. She lived with the mother and the mother's boyfriend. Until the boyfriend got strange ideas about three in a bed. Two in bed's company, three's a crowd. She moved out. She's still friends with her mother.

"Have you seen many plays?"

"This will be my first real one outside of school."

"Living right here in New York? No kidding?"

"It's too expensive and I never felt like I'd belong there."

"The hell with that."

"Back in school in English class we read plays. And poetry. My teacher give me a book of Emily Dickinson's poems. That was the prize for a poem I wrote."

Mary Lou had told him she wrote poetry. You'll find her interesting. You two have a lot in common. He asked what the poem she wrote was about.

"About giving myself to Christ. It was a Catholic high school and my teacher was a nun. I loved her and I was thinking of becoming a nun just like her and then she quit the order and took a job teaching in a public school. She told me she'd get a good pension teaching in a public school." Donna shrugged. "She was a person, I guess. Like anybody else."

In honor of Big Ben, the cook had prepared thick steaks and an enormous salad for them. They had a little party at a table in a dim corner of the empty lounge. Big Ben asked if Mary Lou had heard anything about their kid brother. Yes, a phone call from their mother. She's worried. Tommy wrote her that everybody over there's into drugs and sex and all the prostitutes have venereal disease. She thinks that's his way of telling her he's into that himself. She's worried about when he comes back. About his sanity. Will he be able to adjust back to a normal life over here?

"What's a normal life here?" said Big Ben. "Drugs and sex and booze and the clap with a running dick."

Mary Lou ignored that. "He's learned electronics, repairing planes. Maybe he can get a good job and get himself together when he gets out."

While they ate there was a kind of relaxed understanding that after this little party in the tavern they would go back to the apartment and Big Ben would shack up with Donna. Big Ben said he had forgotten to bring pajamas. Mary Lou touched his shoulder. In my drawer in the apartment there's just the thing for you. A present some screwball customer gave me. A black sheer negligee with lace fringe. Big Ben swallowed his big mouthful of steak. I'll take you up on that. Mary Lou tossed her head.

"You do and you're no brother of mine."

Ben tried to fix that cute quip in his memory along with the great steaks and the great salad, the late supper for *two* with Mary Lou — the way he would tell it to Queen Lila.

Back at the apartment Donna showed Big Ben the book of Emily Dickinson's poems her English teacher had given her. Big Ben flipped through several pages and handed it back to her. Read one, out loud. Donna lit two candles and turned off the lights. The right atmosphere. She would read one, then Ben read one.

Before she could start, Mary Lou stopped her. Let's get comfortable first. The girls changed into their pajamas in the bedroom. Big Ben went into the bathroom and stripped down to his short-sleeved undershirt and drawers. For a bathrobe he used his sister's trenchcoat. His arms were bare almost to the elbow. Mary Lou got three bottles of beer out of the refrigerator. Donna pulled open the couch. Her bed. Big Ben slipped in beside her. No one questioned it. They sat upright, arms touching, covers pulled up over their legs. Mary Lou sat in an easy chair, relaxed with her beer and cigarette, smiling, watching them. She had already whispered into Ben's ear that in a little while she'd sneak off to bed.

With a thin voice, reaching higher and higher to sound dramatic and poetic, Donna read one of her favorites:

I shall know why — when Time is over —
And I have ceased to wonder why —
Christ will explain each separate anguish
In the fair schoolroom of the sky —

He will tell me what "Peter" promised —
And — for wonder at his woe —
I shall forget the drop of Anguish
That scalds me now — that scalds me now!

Pressed by the two women that it was now his turn to read a poem aloud, Big Ben put them off by telling a story about one of his favorites, deliberately introducing his own special brand of vulgarity to offset the queazy feeling he often got because people might think he was an effeminate kind of guy, liking poetry and stuff. — *To A Coy Mistress,* by Andrew Marvell. He didn't remember the exact words. Sometime back in the 1600's, which only proves that it's been going on for a helluva long while. This guy's trying to get this dame into bed and she's playing hard-to-get. And he says cut the shit. We ain't getting any younger. Wait too goddam long and I ain't going to be able to get it up. And the worms are going to be eating your snatch. So let's hop into bed and let's get cracking. *"Thus, though we cannot make our sun stand still, yet we will make him run."*

Big Ben put the last two lines from the poem together with a dramatic flourish that drew a laugh from his audience. It encouraged him to go on.

"And then another one I come across. *The Lost Leader,* by Robert Browning. There was this sonofabitch poet Tennyson — the queen or the king or some big shit over there made him into a knight or lord or something — appointed him chief poet of England — and they give him some money. And he turned and thumbed his nose at his old radical buddies. Give them the old boot. So this Browning poet give the finger right back to him. *Just for a handful of silver he left us, just for a riband to stick in his coat."* Ben deliberately prounounced it *rib-band.*

"What's a rib-band?" asked Donna.

"Just what they asked in the shop. It's a ribbon. I think maybe they tie a colored ribbon across the chest or stick a small one in his coat lapel. I don't know. And then they hit him on the head with a sword. I now knight you Sir Shit! I told them that's our Casey in the machine shop. Jumped the fence. From union steward to foreman. For a handful of silver he left us, for a rib-band to stick in his coat. A white hat on his head. They run all over the shop yelling it that day. Some guys, laughing. Yelling loud as they could. *For a handful of silver he left us! And a rib-band! A white hat rib-band! — A white hat band-rib!* — It was funny."

Mary Lou finished off her beer and pulled herself to her feet. "My eyes won't stay open. Good-night."

Big Ben got two more bottles of beer from the refrigerator and returned to his place beside Donna. They took turns reading Emily Dickinson's poems aloud until they both finished their second beer. Big Ben took the empty from her.

Want another? No.

"Would you mind if we really go to sleep? It's been so nice

and I'm so tired I can't keep my eyes open. I don't want to take
a chance and spoil it." She stopped his arm when he raised it
and reached to embrace her. "Tomorrow night. I promise.
Please."

He hesitated, wondering if his manhood demanded he try
further.

"Please," she said.

"Okay."

"Don't be angry."

"I'm not angry."

He slipped off his sister's trenchcoat and dropped it onto the
floor and stretched his upper torso and head out of bed to
where his mouth was near enough to the candles to blow out
the flames. They slid down under the covers. She rolled onto
her right side facing away from him and he kissed her neck
and embraced her loosely with his left hand. They dozed off for
a short while and then he awoke and wakened her by making
love to her.

The next day Donna had to work the lunch at The Green
Shamrock. But she and Big Ben were up early, and she went
with him to the Metropolitan Museum.

Big Ben discovered the museum on an earlier trip. Each time
he came to New York he liked to drop by and wander through
with the rest of the crowd, looking at paintings and statues
and old-time furniture — though not for too long. There was too
much to see. He planned on seeing a little of it at a time, for
the rest of his life. Each visit he always took a little look at the
work of the sculptor Rodin. His people were so true to life. *The
Kiss*. It was only a small copy of the original. But he liked that
one best.

Donna stood with him, holding his hand, while they looked
at the man and woman in the act of kissing. Big Ben asked if
she identified herself with the naked young woman there in the
arms of the naked young man. He was thinking how warmly
receptive the woman was, how great it would be to find a
woman like that to make love to.

When they left the museum he took Donna across the street
to a nice outdoor cafe he had found the last time he had been
in New York. Sitting under the awning at one of the small

tables, having a late morning beer, they watched the heavy
auto traffic, including all the yellow taxicabs, speeding south
on Fifth Avenue. And they gaped at the well-dressed men and
women walking by. He wondered if they all came from the big
fancy apartment houses in the neighborhood.

"It must take a lot of money to live around here," he
whispered to Donna, not wanting to be overheard by people
near them at other tables. "Where the hell do they get it all?"
She didn't know.

He put her into a taxi to go work the lunch at The Green
Shamrock and then he walked down Fifth Avenue, alongside
Central Park most of the way, then past the stone lions in
front of the Barbizon Plaza where he looked enviously at a
young couple with two children who were driven by in a horse-
drawn sightseeing carriage.

He wandered through the open areas between the massive,
tall buildings that made up Rockefeller Center, enjoying a
game he played with every well-dressed woman he met,
confronting her with a direct stare, eye to eye, a challenge to
climb into bed with him. In his boasting back at Mike's Bar at
home he had little respect for age or marital status. ("Nothing
under ten and nothing over ninety.") And he said that any
woman, married or not, if approached in the right way and at
the right time in the right place, could be had. He had laughed
at Queen Lila when she suggested that his sex drive, like hers,
had at least some of its source in his deep feelings about
emptiness, and about being nothing in this world, with all the
bigger powerful people who control what you do giving you this
feeling of emptiness, which makes you go to a play and think
about writing something, a poem or a short story or a novel or
a play, that all these vague feelings, frustrations and tensions,
compulsively find their way out in the sex hunt.

He *was* drawn this way to the search and the chase, despite
some feelings of guilt when he slept with a married woman
who happened to be the wife of a friend. Maybe it *was* all an
effort to get a feeling of having some kind of power in a world
in which you are nothing but a peanut being cracked by the
big guys whenever they want to call the signal. Maybe that
was why there was some crazy kind of sense of importance and
power, about having an affair with another woman behind the
back of the woman who thought she was his only bed partner

even if only for that day. That he had slept with Donna Colangelo did not change his relationship with Queen Lila but it did add something. And if in his wandering through the courts and streets of the Rockefeller Center complex he was fortunate enough to run into something with one of these well-dressed women it would have nothing to do with Donna, nor with Queen Lila. But it would add something he seemed to need.

He stopped in at a small bar on the corner of 49th Street and Avenue of the Americas (Sixth Avenue) and had a beer and watched the baseball game on the television screen. Baltimore Orioles playing the Minnesota Twins to see which team would go into the World Series had knocked out the usual football broadcast. From the conversations around him and autographed photographs hanging on the walls he guessed this place was a hangout for people working in the television studios housed in Rockefeller Center. A man's bar. Only a few women, and they sat at tables with male escorts. Not one woman on the loose. He left and wandered over to Seventh Avenue where he gawked at all the prostitutes, most black, a few white, who openly courted him as he passed by. That was something to tell Queen Lila when he got home. And he would tell her about the bare-breasted go-go girls who took turns shaking it up on top of the bar in the crowded Brass Grille where, while he drank a beer, he divided his attention between watching the girls and watching the rest of the baseball game. The Baltimore Orioles were beating the Minnesota Twins.

When the game ended he walked back toward Rockefeller Center and then down the Avenue of the Americas to 42nd Street. New York around there seemed like a dirty, worn-out city. But the old buildings were being ripped down and skyscraper office buildings were going up.

He enjoyed the street parade, registering the things to tell Queen Lila later. A lot of kooks out on the street. A lot of beads and a lot of blue denim. Everybody's a worker now. Wearing some pretty fancy overalls. Fitted to them by their tailor. Crazy clothes and crazy people. And every so often some poor bastard telling his troubles up into the air. Talking to himself. And more beards and long hair than you ever saw in your whole life. The barbers are going broke. And you see mixed couples everywhere, colored and white. Down there nobody pays any attention to them.

Back at the The Green Shamrock late in the afternoon
Donna took him to a table in the corner shadow in the
backroom and Mary Lou waited on them. They went back to
the apartment and hopped into bed for a quick screw before
Donna got all dolled up to go to the play. He wore the same
suit he had been wearing all day, but put on a clean shirt, and
then the same tie.

When they got to the theatre Big Ben had an attack of cold
feet. Comparing his own clothes and those of Donna with those
of the men and women pouring into the lobby, not only the
clothes but the whole look of them, some in fancy evening
dress getting out of limousines and taxicabs, he said something
to Donna about skipping the play and going to a bar.

She waited for him to move. He silently watched the people
going into the theatre. They could have a few beers somewhere
and then go back to the apartment. But his yearning for
something to fill the emptiness he could not yet identify won
out and he touched Donna's arm and they moved into the
lobby. Damn few colored people there to see a play about a
colored guy. They went inside and he was glad they stayed to
see the play. The performance grabbed him and lifted him
completely out of himself. The magic temporarily wiped out the
ache in him. Donna's interest matched his own.

Between acts they went out into the lobby and smoked
cigarettes. Big Ben kept shaking his head as if bowled over by
the wonder of it. Great, great, Jesus Christ, an experience I'll
never forget. He told Donna about *Hedda Gabler* and Dave
Newman and about Jamison Langner wanting to use him to
test how a workingman would react to a dance performed by
his group at The Dance Center.

"He invited me to go look at a dress rehearsal."

Donna was properly impressed.

When the play ended they were feeling very uplifted and
they clapped their hands hard as the cast lined up for curtain
calls. The audience rose to their feet, still applauding. And for
the first time in his life, joining in with the others, Big Ben
yelled, *"Bravo! Bravo!"*

It was an experience which he enjoyed again when he told it
to Queen Lila.

"Standing there in the theatre with my *sister,* both of us

yelling along with everybody else. — *Bravo! Bravo!"*

Queen Lila was stiff when he returned late Sunday afternoon. He gave out presents. Colored neckerchiefs with NEW YORK printed on them for Lila and the two girls. And a make-believe front page of a newsaper with a bold headline: HOORAY FOR FRANKIE! And also for Lila, some anti-war leaflets, and a copy of The Black Panthers newspaper and Worker's World he had picked up down in Greenwich Village. Radical papers.

Before telling about his trip he wanted to know if Lila had heard anything more about what was happening down at the new plant in Virginia. No, nothing. He stroked her cheek. Smile.

"Let's go over to Mike's Bar for a quick drink. Maybe they know something."

Lila somberly agreed. "We'll be back soon, kids. Stay inside the house."

There was only Old Frank and one other man there at the tavern. They had heard nothing about Virginia. Old Frank, sensing that Big Ben and Queen Lila wished to be alone, left two whiskies and two beer chasers and went back to talk to the other man. Big Ben pressed his shoulder against Queen Lila's shoulder. No response. He started to tell her about the trip, the great meal at The Green Shamrock the first night with his *sister,* the visit to the Metropolitan *alone,* the sights in New York City, the baseball game, and then a long summary of the play, how much he and his *sister* had enjoyed seeing *The Great White Hope,* yelling bravo with the rest. — Queen Lila listened, appearing to be very interested, but still somber, holding back.

"Here's something maybe you can figure out," said Big Ben, trying to loosen her up. "My *sister* had her idea about what it is. Let's see what you think."

He went on to tell about the crazily dressed people they saw when his *sister* took him down to the Village. "The streets crowded. People with all kinds of crazy costumes on 8th Street. Like they were going to a Halloween party. One long-haired kid with an old army coat dragging to the ground, and a droopy mustache like some old Chinese character, and waving a wooden sword. And fancy expensive clothes too. One girl dressed like she's playing a scene with the shiek of Araby, fancy knee pants and colored stockings and a veil across the

lower half of her face. A lot of old granny dresses. Even some
cowboy hats. And Chinese button-up-to-the-neck Chairman
Mao jackets. And all the blue denim work pants you ever saw,
more than we got here in the shop. And a couple of sons of
Zorro with black hats and black capes and cord whips. And
there were old derby hats. And stovepipe hats. And a German
helmet from the first World War. And a couple of college
raccoon coats like back in the old flapper days. Jesus, you never
saw anything like it."

"Somebody fiddling while Rome burns?" she guessed.

"Smarty."

He pressed his shoulder into hers and this time she pressed
back, and when he touched her cheek with his she returned the
pressure.

"Vietnam," she said.

"Yeah."

"Back during the Middle Ages, the black plague, the people
who picked up the bodies at night dressed up in costumes and
sang and danced while they tossed the dead bodies into the
wagon."

"No shit?"

"I read that somewhere."

Big Ben went on to tell about some of the other places his
sister had taken him to in the Village. A fairy joint and a
lesbian joint and a nutsy Gay Nineties madhouse and all the
bars until they were both drunk.

He and Lila left the tavern with their arms gripped around
one another's waists. At the curb he kissed her. Missed you.
She kissed him back. Me too. Ben had enjoyed the telling about
it here as much if not more than he had enjoyed the doing
down in New York. They kissed again, hard, before each bent
over to get into the front seat of his old Buick.

Back at the house he tried again to reach Don Mayer to find
out about Virginia. No one answered the phone.

Chapter 6

When Big Ben Hood walked into the machine shop Monday morning he was greeted with shouts from all over the department.

"On strike in Virgina!"

Big Ben set his lunch bucket down on the clean metal table of his machine. "Shit, the bastards ain't even got into full production yet."

For many weeks there had been rumors circulating through the plant that the company intended to transfer all conveyor work to the new factory in Waring, Virginia. Machine shop foreman Casey told the people in his department he thought it was because competition for the business in the conveyor field was getting intense and the company could pay lower wage rates down south.

"What did they walk out about?" Big Ben asked chief steward Don Mayer, catching him before the buzzer rang to signal time to start up machines.

The chief steward said he'd phone and find out. He went to the pay phone in the smoking area, followed by Big Ben. Putting in a person-to-person call to whoever's in charge of the strike in Waring, Virginia, he explained the whole situation to the Waring phone operator who volunteered that her husband was a union man.

It took her about fifteen minutes to trace down the man they were seeking. Then she rang back to the pay phone in the smoking area, asked for the chief steward, and triumphantly informed Don Mayer that she had located his party.

The man at the other end of the line was in the phone booth in a tavern less than a half mile from the new factory, the fifth tavern the operator had tried. He had been called in off the picket line.

A slight southern drawl. "We want the same wages you people are getting paid up there. The same wages for the same work. And we're in disagreement on rates for some new automated equipment they put in here."

Foreman Casey stood on a raised platform up in front of the department, watching, making sure everyone had started to work. The buzzer had sounded and there was the loud hum of motors, punctuated by hoarse honking of the autocall as it sounded out its messages. Chief steward Don Mayer, first class repairman on the maintenance crew, started back to get his toolbox which he had left at Big Ben's machine. He stood there, defying Foreman Casey's disapproving eye. Casey looked away.

"They got new automated equipment down there," Don Mayer hurriedly told Big Ben. "A battery of four welding machines and one operator who inserts tapes and presses buttons. The company wants to pay the man handling four machines less than they're paying one of our men up here for operating only one welder."

"We should back 'em up."

Don Mayer agreed.

He got hold of union president Baldy George Walters down in the warehouse. Baldy had asked him to find out if there were any colored working down there. None. Baldy seemed disappointed. It would have been a good excuse for not getting involved. Don Mayer said he was going to pull all the department stewards out to a special meeting to decide what to do. Baldy said he would not sanction payment for their lost time. Don Mayer turned away. He'd take responsibility and get approval later from the membership. Baldy called him back and suggested an executive board meeting in the think tank. Don Mayer walked away. You can do that too, if you want to.

"All stewards punch out and over to the Labor Hall."

Less than an hour later the stewards returned to their respective departments in the shop and spread the word. A special meeting at lunchtime in the parking lot.

Don Mayer, standing on the back of a pickup truck in the lot, addressed the meeting.

"These are recommendations from your stewards council. Full support to the people on strike down there, financial and moral." So move. Second it. "On the motion." A man in a white shirt, without a tie, from shipping. The best way to keep them from moving our jobs down there is to make the company pay the same wages there they're paying up here. The chief steward lifted his arm. "On the motion. All in favor? — Opposed? — Carried unanimous." He read from his notes. "Recommended by your steward council. Two hours pay a week to the strike fund down there." A shout. So move. Second it. A shrill yell.

Amend that to a straight two dollars a week. Big Ben's hand shot up. You cheap bastards! Amend that to four hours pay a week. Don Mayer interrupted, his voice silencing the others. "Those opposed to helping to keep our jobs here by donating two hours pay a week to the people on strike down in Virginia?" — Silence. — "All in favor?" A roar of ayes. "Carried unanimous."

The chief steward read from his notes. "Recommendation from your stewards council. Plant gate collections at other factories around here to raise money for the people down there in Virginia, strike welfare fund." He looked up. "Some day they're all going to face the same thing. Their jobs moved to Virginia or West Germany or Japan or some asshole place in Africa or South America. We need a good triple-threat man to head this committee. A good organizer, a good talker, somebody who can write a good leaflet and do a good education job. All one working-class family and we all better stick together or we all sink together."

"Mr Chairman, why don't you head it up yourself?"

Don Mayer hesitated. The people waited for his decision. — Though not everybody there knew the whole story, they all knew that the strike in Virginia must cause a special problem for their chief steward. He and his brother, Virginia plant manager Bob, had been born and raised on a large fruit farm on the southern shore of Lake Ontario. There, while still young and going to school, working with their father's farm machinery, they developed their skill as mechanics. During the second World War both came to work at Mackenzie Machine Tool. They were loyal to one another, but they were different in a number of ways, a difference each respected in the other. Bob was the older, easier to know, friendly and open, putting himself out to get people to like him. The company quickly found Bob and moved him up to leadman and foreman and night shift superintendent and then plant manager. His brother Don, generally quiet and withdrawn, at times surly, but respected by all for his blunt honesty, developed a reputation as a good union man, a reputation which was enhanced further throughout the shop when it became known that he had refused a promotion to leadman on the maintenance crew. I don't want to be no fuck'n pusher. But until after his brother left to become plant manager at the new facility he had declined every time

Big Ben had nominated him for any office in the union. — The crowd of men and women standing in the parking lot were looking up toward their chief steward. He finally shook his head.

"You know my situation. My brother down there. I'll serve on the committee but someone else better head it."

A hand lifted above the heads of the crowd. The chief steward pointed at the hand.

The voice of Lila Redbird.

"I nominate Big Ben Hood."

"Any further nominations?" Silence. "Ben, you're it."

A sarcastic, laughing shout. "Thanks."

Though the workers at the Niagara plant of Mackenzie Machine Tool voted unanimously to support the strike down in Virginia, even Baldy George raising his hand, the southern workers themselves were badly split. Plant manager Bob Mayer and his management team down there won support with their argument that the northern workers were supporting the southern strikers only because they wanted the work intended for Virginia to be kept at the Niagara plant.

Bob Mayer had his Virginia foremen working the telephones. "They don't care how long you people are out on strike here. The longer the better. They want this plant closed down for good. Starve. What the hell do they care?"

Monday afternoon a management council of war presided over by Jamison Langner in his office at the Niagara facility resulted in the foremen immediately notifying men and women in their departments that until further notice, starting the next day, there would be two hours of overtime work each regular workday and eight hours overtime on Saturday for all workers in the Niagara division.

That night plant manager Bob Mayer had the Virginia foremen hitting the telephones. "You're on strike down here and they're working overtime up north, doing your work. Damnyankee scabs."

The next morning, Tuesday, it was Big Ben Hood who asked chief steward Don Mayer to call a lunchtime meeting in the parking lot. Union president Baldy George did not object. Go ahead. Fall on your face. Big Ben stepped up onto the rear of the small pickup truck, to whose complaining owner Don Mayer had already laughingly pledged payment for all scratches and other damage done during the meeting.

Big Ben presented his motion.

"Nobody here work overtime for the duration of the strike in Virginia."

It was a bomb tossed into the crowd. And Baldy George, standing next to the truck, smiled while the opposition screamed and shouted, and continued to smile when the supporters of Big Ben's motion screamed and shouted in return. — Those opposed argued that the Virginia workers had not refused to accept jobs they knew were going to result in less work up north. "They didn't worry about taking our jobs!" — Those supporting the motion made an appeal for loyalty to their fellow workingmen and workingwomen. "Some day we'll be out on strike and the company will ask *them* to do our work!" — The opposition shrieked: "*And they'll do it, they'll do our work!*"

Big Ben's voice topped the shouting. "Anybody who works overtime now is a lousy scab! And if people are going to officially approve scabbing in this shop you can take this whole goddam union and shove it up your ass. I'm taking my tools out. I won't work with scabs. And I ask every good union member here to walk out with me. You scabs want to work overtime we'll put up a picket line here right now and shut it down. That's your choice. No overtime or strike."

From the crowd a voice cried out, "Secret ballot!"

"You want to be a scab," Big Ben fiercely shouted in the direction of that voice, "be a man and say so! Don't hide behind a secret ballot!"

Chief steward Don Mayer nudged union president Baldy George. You want to conduct the vote? Baldy George shook his head. It's your meeting. The chief steward hopped up onto the back of the truck and took over from Big Ben.

"All those who want a secret ballot raise your hand."

Not one hand showed.

Big Ben yelled: "Run, you rats, run!"

Don Mayer silenced him with a simple gesture. "Motion is: nobody work overtime until the strike is settled in Virginia. All in favor?" The ayes were loud but sober. "Opposed?" Silence. "Carried unanimous."

Loud snickering and some muffled hooting. From the crowd a shouted motion to adjourn. All in favor? Meeting adjourned.

Personnel man Dick Penfield reported to Jamison Langner that it was Big Ben who made the motion to bar overtime work. He resented it that the Old Man was cooking up something special with Big Ben, bypassing him as if he was too ignorant and lacking in that area to take charge of something relating to theatre and the other arts. He expected that the information he brought the Old Man would turn him against Big Ben. But although it did cause Jamison Langner some concern, which he expressed to the secretary of The Dance Center, he finally agreed with her that what had happened was sure proof that Big Ben was a leader in the shop and that if he were put on the right track he might be the most valuable man they could get, to work in the crucial area involving the arts.

It was Betty Lyons' suggestion that once Big Ben tasted deeply of the highly subjective atmosphere embodied in the arts, that once his needs as a person were linked to actually working with the kind of people he would meet in the arts, the future opening before him would keep him from ever giving all that up to let himself be used as a tool by any radicals.

Thursday morning Big Ben told his foreman he would be punching out early and would be in late the following morning. That afternoon he and two stewards who were on his committee walked over to the main gate of the Office Machines Division of Sperry-Rand Corporation. It was about a half a mile away. Oficers of the local union which represented the Sperry-Rand workers were waiting for them.

Together they distributed leaflets to second shift men and women going in to work and to first shift people leaving the factory. Big Ben had written the leaflet. It told about the strike down in Virginia and made a plea for financial contributions to help the people down south win the same wages paid up north. Your dollars will help keep jobs here. Plant gate collection tomorrow. Thank you.

Big Ben reported for work almost a half hour late Friday morning. He passed the word along that a total of $277.89 had been collected for the Virginia strikers from first shift people at the Sperry-Rand plant gates.

He was kidded about making sure he bet his own money when he asked who was collecting the dollars for the baseball pool in the machine shop that day. It was the first game of the World Series, with the New York Mets scheduled to play the Baltimore Orioles in the latter's stadium, and the last half of the ninth inning had been saved for him. Thanks a lot.

"You're wanted on the phone, Ben. An outside call." Foreman Casey, catching Ben in the act of passing his dollar bill to the machine shop bookie, had waited for the transaction to be completed. "On my phone."

Puzzled, knowing that outside calls to employees during working hours were not permitted, Big Ben followed the foreman to his desk.

"Hello." He heard a woman's voice he did not recognize — Mister Hood? Warily, he asked, "Who's this?"

"This is Betty Lyons from The Dance Center. Mr. Langner asked me to call you. Would you like to see a dress rehearsal tonight at The Center?"

Big Ben hesitated, thinking about the second shift plant gate collection at Sperry-Rand. That meant getting home late for supper, and then shave and shower and dress.

"If you're busy tonight we can make it some other time."

"No, no." Thinking fast, he decided not to explain about the plant gate collection. The voice on the other end of the line did not sound like it belonged to anyone who worked in a factory. "Tonight's okay."

"Good."

"Today's my birthday," he said, as an explanation for his hesitation.

"We can make it some other time."

"No, it's okay tonight."

"Wonderful." Her rich voice brightly bounced. "We'll make it a birthday party."

"Great."

His birthday. Thirty-two years old. He did not know that Lila Redbird had already baked a cake for him and with the kids was planning a small surprise party. If he had known, he still would have accepted this invitation, his first chance to meet someone who sounded like she lived and moved around all day up there on that magical shining cloud. A chance to get initiated into that fascinating world. He could not pass that up for anything.

On her part Betty Lyons was equally interested, looking

forward to meeting a different kind of guy from the men she knew. She thought she fully understood the role Jamison Langner hoped Big Ben Hood would play. Very important that this experience, seeing the dress rehearsal of the dance company, be made something this factory worker will remember and want to repeat.

On the way to the theatre Betty Lyons dropped into the florist shop and bought a pink carnation. Then, having started off on this track, she stopped at a liquor store and bought champagne. She had the clerk wrap the bottle in bright yellow paper, and with scotch tape and a red ribbon attached the pink carnation to the neck end of the package.

Dressing earlier, trying to hit the right note to engage Big Ben's attention without overdoing it, she tried different combinations of skirts and sweaters and blouses and jackets. When she arrived at the entrance to the abandoned factory building which had been converted into a theatre by State University she wore a black sweater, black stocking pants, black leather skirt and jacket, and black boots.

She stood at the appointed meeting place and the attention she drew confirmed what she felt. She looked good.

She was early. Only a few young people, university students, were straggling into the massive brick structure. The wide street in front was busy with traffic of both autos and trucks with their lights on. It was already dark outside. The wide area between the building and the street was newly paved over and well-lighted by overhead spotlights attached to the brick wall.

Betty Lyons stood with her back to the building, feeling safer that way. This was the front corner building in a large industrial park covering many acres on the north end of Central City. It was an area that was a mixture of factories and blocks of working-class homes, much like the industrial suburb of Niagara. She knew that what made this seem to be such an unlikely place for a theatre was exactly what Jamison Langner liked about it.

The theatre, named Comus — a State University project initiated by its Cultural Affairs office to form a link between town and gown — was on the second floor of this old brick building. Both Jamison Langner and Frederick Clark were members of the university's board of trustees. And when she was hired Jamison Langner had told Betty Lyons with some pride that it had taken a long time to find exactly the right place they wanted for Comus, a theatre that will give the audience the feel of our advanced technological society with our massive but sophisticated industrial machine. We're about fifty feet from an active railroad spur line serving the factories. During performances people in the theatre can hear freight trains going by outside. A tremendous complex of old factory buildings covering several square miles, an auto manufacturing and assembly plant abandoned after the first World War. This enterprising Jewish real estate firm acquired it for nothing and went out and dug up tenants. Lease, rent or remodel. Big piece or small piece. Any part of it. A building or a floor, or part of a floor. They heard what we were looking for and came to us. The perfect location. The second floor of one of the old factory buildings. Perfect.

Waiting there for Big Ben, her back pressed firmly into the brick wall, Betty Lyons tested her pulse, the fingers of her right hand resting lightly on her left wrist. Her pulse was racing. But that was to be expected. Worrying about it would only make it race faster. She tried to get her mind set for this new experience by thinking intensely about what had come out of the first session that morning with Henry, her new psychiatrist.

Less than an hour after she had phoned into the plant and talked to Big Ben she had met Dr. Henry Luberacki for the first time. She had been sent to him by a doctor in general practice whom she had seen because her pulse had started to race at a frightening speed any time she faced a new experience such as she faced right now.

Dr. Luberacki was an apple-cheeked young man, meticulously dressed, who said he was thirty-three years old and looked like he had just graduated from high school. Somehow during this first session with her he mentioned that his father had been in supervision at Bethlehem Steel. A foreman in the rolling mill. And that immediately tied in with what she was thinking about Big Ben and his interest in theatre and dance. The world was changing, and she was ready and anxious to somehow fit herself in with that changing world.

Dr. Henry Luberacki called her Betty, and she promptly but somewhat defensively said she would call him Henry. He smiled and said that was fine. She wondered if she had convinced Henry that she could be fully objective about her past and that all she needed was occasional reinforcement to help her cope with the panic she sometimes felt when stepping off into new territory like now.

She was not sure about apple-cheeked Henry. In order to help her he had to be told the whole story including the worst. She knew that. And she could tell it quickly. She had told it so often to other psychiatrists.

"Divorced three years ago. Shortly after my husband's family sold their paint-making business to a giant conglomerate which was expanding rapidly from its oil company nucleus and avoiding heavy taxes by plowing earnings into further capital investment. My husband got five million dollars as his share."

Henry did not blink at the casual mention of five million dollars. And his expression did not change when she told about her husband paying Uncle Sam over a million dollars in capital gain tax.

Good for him. Encouraged, she quickly reported that her husband stayed on as president of the paint-making division until a young and eager hatchet man was sent in. Resign or get fired. And her husband, Warren, joined the ranks of the unemployed.

"A work-oriented character, he didn't know any life without work. Sports bored him. The arts bored him. Travel bored him. He drank too much and that bored him. For excitement he deliberately provoked fights with me and then that was followed by days and sometimes weeks of not talking to each other."

She got a good laugh from apple-cheeked Henry when she described the sugar fight. That always got a laugh. It was funny. Another one of the long silences with her husband. And then, facing each other one morning across the breakfast table, Warren threw the bomb at her.

"Living with you I feel dead!"

She had a spoonful of sugar ready to drop into her cup of coffee. Instead she flipped it into Warren's face. He grabbed his spoon and shot back at her with ammunition from his own sugar bowl. The maid stood there, her face caught between a scream and a laugh, while the happily marrieds spooned sugar back and forth across the breakfast table.

"The maid must have enjoyed it. Because she filled the sugar bowls to the brim every morning. It was fun. I'd wait until out of the corner of my eye I'd see the maid and the handyman peeking in from out in the hall. Then the show began, both *delightedly* tossing that sugar back and forth, making a real mess."

When she told Henry she thought she was tainted, he asked why.

"Tainted and driven."

"In what way?" asked Apple Cheeks.

Driven like Hedda Gabler, Ibsen's heroine. Like Hedda, she was an expert pistol shot. Something had driven her and Hedda to that. — She knew the play well, loved Hedda, liked to think of herself as an independent woman ahead of her time, a woman following in Hedda's footsteps. But not as strong as Hedda. Not yet.

"But why tainted?"

"Like the son in Ibsen's *Ghosts*."

"In what way?"

"Syphilis."

Apple Cheek's sympathetic smile did not seem to change while he accepted that the syphilis had been contracted from her seventeen-year-old mother who had died in childbirth. Born tainted. Treated immediately and cured.

"I never saw my father. He disappeared. I was raised by my grandparents. Both dead now. Grandpa was a well-to-do businessman in furniture." — Her husband, Warren? Met him at college. His softness attracted her. — "I proposed and he accepted."

She tried to tell Apple Cheeks how it must have been for her husband. Now, in retrospect, she was sorry for him. Married to a woman who could not let him ever get control over her feelings. A woman who could not permit any man to get into a position where he could hurt her. Sexual intercourse only when she initiated the proceedings. Twice a week. Her duty as a wife. But from the very first week of their marriage and for the next twelve years the culmination of the sexual act did not occur until after her husband had relieved himself and fallen asleep beside her.

It was easy for her to say it now, but she tried to tell it the same way her husband had told it during their first time together in a psychiatrist's office. Unable to sleep. His mind torn apart, trying to sort out his situation after he was fired. Lying awake after they just had sexual intercourse. Motionless. Sounding like he was asleep. Then he became aware of something going on. A slight movement on the other side of the bed. A steady small movement. He said his heart started to beat so hard it pounded in his ears. He reached over very slowly, carefully, not to disturb whatever was going on. Then his hand came down and grabbed there in the crucial spot.

"He caught me just at the start of an orgasm. And he wouldn't let go. I couldn't stop what had already started. And he just wouldn't let me pull away. He held on while the spasms continued." She cried again this morning when she was telling it to Apple Cheeks.

"Masturbation is good!" exclaimed Apple Cheeks, trying to encourage her. "Masturbation is good, it's good!"

She accepted the box of tissues he gave her to wipe her face dry.

She and Warren talked all night, and she cried off and on through the night. But she did not only defend, she attacked. He had established a pattern of only twice a week. Other nights when she got too sexy she had to do something. And it became a habit that carried over. It ran away on her. She didn't mean to hurt his ego. If he wanted her to, she'd go to a psychiatrist. He said they'd both go. And they both went. And with both present, a rationalization based on her history was developed to explain to her husband why she found it so difficult to have an orgasm with him. And then, with the husband waiting for her outside in the reception room, she was told to masturbate all she wanted to relieve her feeling of tension. A normal outlet. No need to feel guilty. But there's no reason to tell your husband. Why disturb him? — Apple Cheeks smiled agreement with that prescription.

Betty Lyons felt her pulse. About 80 or 85 per minute, she guessed. Not too bad. She wondered if that came from thinking about the session with Apple Cheeks that morning or from wondering whether or not this factory worker was going to keep his appointment with her. It was getting closer to curtain time.

She tried to occupy herself by watching the steady stream of students passing by on their way into Comus to see the dress rehearsal. She told herself not to keep obsessing about the first session with Apple Cheeks. She had handled herself well enough, even when she told the story she heard her former husband was telling about her and a girlfriend. The way he was telling it, the girl working for them came in and said she wanted her pay because she was quitting, and he told her to talk to Mrs. Lyons. But she wouldn't talk to Mrs. Lyons.

"Why not?" — The girl wouldn't say anything except she was quitting and she wanted her pay. — "You want your pay you tell me what your gripe is."

So the girl told him. "This afternoon they were there. Both only in their birthday suits. On the bed with her girlfriend."

That episode produced more tears and the decision to break the relationship with the girlfriend by moving to California. A new place. It sometimes is as good as a shock treatment. Shake things up. Make a fresh start. — And Apple Cheeks this morning nodded his agreement with what they had been told then by the other psychiatrist.

Once she got past the masturbation and lesbian episodes, the rest went easy, though she did think she might possibly have tried to make it all sound too matter-of-fact and ordinary for Apple Cheek's benefit. The divorce, she started proceedings. And then showed her husband some recent photographs a private detective had collected for her. Warren wanted his freedom as much as she did. And with community property laws in California, she grabbed half the bundle, almost two million dollars. Enough to get by on. Their children, a boy and a girl, eleven and ten, off to boarding school, to make their own decisions about which parent to visit during holidays and vacations. She agreed that their legal home base would be the father's home, then built her dream house on top of a mountain in an isolated area of woods, a half hour's drive from downtown San Francisco. Smoked pot. An LSD acidhead for a while. Sniffed cocaine. Shot up with morphine. Tried hash, opium, peyote, any shit you could smoke, sniff or drink. Shacked up with a scruffy group in Haight-Asbury for a few months. Financed a Black Panthers cell for a while just for the hell of it and for the cause of civil rights. Played a few sex games: two on one, daisy chain, and ring-around-a-rosy. And just for the experience, tried it for about a month, trick or treat

in a Mexican whorehouse. Picked up a slight venereal disease
there and hopefully gave it back to a few of the customers
before she got rid of it. Learned yoga, Practiced TM —
Transcendental Meditation. And learned karate. Close to
getting her black belt. Picked up a young starlet in Hollywood
and brought her back to the house on the mountain to live with
her. Added a handsome young pool attendant she found at a
hotel bar. Bought a riding horse and a sailboat and a white
Continental roadster. Then got fed up with everything and
decided to try the wrenching shock treatment again. Kicked out
the boyfriend and girlfriend, sold the house and everything
else, and off to London. Then Paris, then Rome, then Warsaw,
Prague, Geneva, Leningrad, Moscow. Tired of traveling. Back
to Paris. Got fed up with all the wisecracks about you ugly
Americans in Vietnam. Went home to find out what was going
on there. And to try to start a new life. Another wrenching
shock treatment.

Apple Cheeks told her she had good reason to be proud of
herself. She was back again in Central City, functioning well,
breaking completely with all that self-destructive past. And she
could be proud she had gained this job on her own merits. A
paying job. Not volunteer work. She would not be a rich,
empty-headed dilettante.

At the Music Hall a grey-haired spinsterish type told her
they did not need anyone there for publicity or promotion, but
suggested she try the Arena Theatre. The nice young man in
the Arena Theatre boxoffice said The Dance Center was
looking for someone to do their administrative and secretarial
work, someone with experience with the dance. She reeled off
her dossier. Performed with a dance company at college.
Familiar with dancers and dance companies all over the world.
Moscow, London, Rome, Paris, even Cuba. They have one of
the greatest ballet companies in the world in Cuba, even with
Fidel Castro. The young man phoned Jamison Langner's office
and made an appointment for her.

"Hell-lo!"

She turned to the effusive greeting, thinking it might be Big
Ben. There was the obsequious young one she had met only the
day before at lunch with Jamison Langner. He was Leonard

Something-or-other and he looked silly now, wearing that black tam on the side of his head. Corny.

"*Hell-lo!*"

He repeated the effusive greeting with an obsequious smile that she recognized as coming from his identification of her with Jamison Langner who had unexpectedly dropped a bonanza into his obsequious, little lap.

"*Mister* Director." — But he did not catch her sarcasm. She dismissed him. "I'll see you inside."

She watched him go on into the building, wondering if she had to introduce him later to Big Ben. She did not like to question Jamison Langner's judgement, but this man's only experience as a producing director had been with a coffee house and now he was not even going to produce the one play he had announced for production there.

An item in the newspaper announcing a casting call for actors to perform in a play about factory workers automated out of their jobs had prompted Jamison Langner to ask her to set up a lunch meeting as quickly as possible with this Leonard Something. Her dislike for him was almost immediate when she heard the obsequious way he apologized for his involvement with this radical who had written the play. He said he did not know this was the same man who once was the union organizer for the union at Jamison Langner's factory. She decided that he *did* know, as she listened to him apologize and explain.

"When I opened the coffee house my only idea was that it would be a place where young people would come to drink coffee and play chess and checkers and talk and listen to entertainment by would-be folksingers. This man came to me with his play. I hardly knew him. He had a plan to raise four hundred dollars to build a small stage and some tiered rows for seats. Forty people contributed ten dollars each and we remodeled the place into a little theatre. But there's nothing in writing that says for that I have to do his play now."

It amused her, the way little Leonard Something leaned forward with that obsequious look on his face to let them see how he was doing his utmost to catch every word uttered about Comus. His head obsequiously nodded too eagerly to register each phrase spoken by Jamison Langner. A new kind of theatre. Multi-media. Total theatre. Simultaneously involving all the senses. A total experience. Back to the beginning. Primal sounds. Primitive emotions. Strip off the plastic, civilized surface. Combine voices, music, dance, film, slides. Work in mass chant, lighting, sound. Everything. Experiment with the new forms. Break away from the sterile naturalism and traditional realism of Ibsen and Odets and Arthur Miller.

The obsequious, round face bobbed its fixed smile in eager agreement. And without even being asked specifically to do so, Leonard Obsequious offered to cancel production of that radical's play. When Jamison Langner asked him if he would be interested in the post of production director at Comus, a Creative Associate on the payroll of State University, starting salary $12,500 a year, he positively drooled, ready to agree to anything. Betty Lyons had no patience with so little principle, especially when someone was so obvious about it. Disgusting.

She wondered if Big Ben might have passed by without her recognizing him. She had seen him only once and then from a distance, when Jamison Langner at the window in his office at the factory had pointed out Big Ben and his Indian girlfriend in their working clothes, on their way to the meeting out in the factory yard. When she had talked to Big Ben on the phone he had asked how he would recognize her.

"Look for a fat woman," she told him. "Short and dark, old and wrinkled, and bald, and no teeth in front."

They both laughed and he said, "I'll do that."

They had agreed to meet in front of the building at the entrance to Comus and both would look for somebody who looks like somebody looking for somebody. But this was only after she refused his offer to pick her up at home. She was not ready to let him see where she lived. He was from a world she did not know and though she was not ready to admit it to anyone except her psychiatrist she was afraid of him.

The big man stopped in front of the sign. Underneath THEATRE, a big finger pointed the way. The big man looked like somebody looking for somebody who was looking for somebody. The attractive woman, stylishly dressed in black, walked toward him with the look on her face of somebody looking for somebody. Not short, not tall, dark skin, a little older than himself, boyish, feathered haircut framing a small face with dark eyes that sparkled. A puckish creature in black leather who looked like she'd been lifted out of a movie. He liked

what he saw and he grinned down at her as she looked up into
his face.

"Mr. Hood?"

"Miss Lyons?"

"Betty."

"Ben."

"*Big* Ben."

"That's me."

She stuck out her hand and he gripped it so tight she
involuntarily tried to pull it away. He let go and apologized.
She laughed and forgave him.

Chapter 7

When Betty Lyons offered Big Ben the bright yellow package with the pink carnation and ribbon tied to it he instinctively backed away, caught offguard, shaking his head. Betty Lyons, too late, wished she had not done this. Bringing him a present was too much.

"Happy birthday."

"Thanks."

Both silent. An awkward moment. She reached out and separated the flower from the package he held. She inserted the stem into the buttonhole in his lapel. She began to chatter brightly. Brittle and false to her own ears.

"Dragging you away from your friends the least I can do is provide a birthday drink."

"What is it?" He juggled the package.

"Champagne."

"Oh, Christ."

"Happy birthday."

"Thanks. How about a drink."

"Not now."

She led him toward the building as she tried to put their relationship back into place. She was Jamison Langner's secretary and she was there because her boss had asked her to arrange for Big Ben to see a dress rehearsal. "After the performance you'll meet the dancers backstage and we'll all drink to your birthday."

They joined the parade of people who were walking, singly, in pairs, and in small groups toward a wide passageway between two old brick buildings. Another sign, with a finger again pointing the way and *Theatre Entrance* crudely lettered above a door. Long-haired young men, with and without beards, some wearing blue denim jeans. And young girls in similar jeans, or short-skirted with legs and thighs sheathed in black and red and purple and brown stocking pants. The stone path was uneven. Betty Lyons touched Big Ben's arm to steady herself.

"Mostly university kids tonight. Formal opening for the public next week."

Big Ben, sliding his hand along the steel railing as they
climbed the stairs inside the building, liked what he saw of her
legs as he followed her. The concrete steps reminded him of
bare stairwells like this out at Mackenzie Machine Tool. Their
footsteps echoed the same hollow way here to give a feeling of
loneliness.

Entering through a steel door to the abandoned factory's
second floor area, now named Comus, he was probably the only
person there that night who immediately saw those steel tracks
attached to the ceiling and he knew at once that in years past
they had been used as overhead tracks for a traveling crane.

Walking behind Betty Lyons he kept glancing up toward the
ceiling. There must have been a craneman up there in the cab,
probably an alcoholic screwball like so many cranemen he
knew who were up there alone all day. And down below on the
concrete floor a daredevil crane follower hooking up material
and machinery to be moved, with hand signals guiding his
partner up there in the cab, strutting and cursing and shouting
and singing, romanticizing the danger he flirted with every
day.

Now all the machinery was gone from the floor. But steel
beams still criss-crossed overhead up into the shadows under
the high roof. And vertical steel beams ran down through the
cement floor. Big Ben knew these beams continued on down
through the first floor deep into the ground.

Taking in what he saw, with a quick look all the way around
the tremendous room which made up the whole floor, it gave
him a feeling of grotesque awkwardness and raw bare strength.
His eyes registered the large open square in the center, with
ball park bleachers on three sides and a platform stage closing
the square. Steel folding chairs, with bright orange plastic seats
and backs, lined up in three rows on wood platforms, each row
on a different level to permit people in back to see over the
heads of those in front. The stage itself cleverly constructed
with large box-like units pushed together like building blocks to
form wide steps mounting far upstage to a height of ten or
twelve feet above the floor.

Betty Lyons led Big Ben to a woman with a deeply lined
faced and a young girl's body. Sad eyes set deep in white
gargoyle face wore a creamy gown reaching to her ankles.
Betty kissed sad eyes on her pale white cheek.

"Good to see you, dear." She introduced sad eyes to Big Ben. "Clever. All the dances, she choreographed them."

Big Ben held the long, warm fingers and looked into sad eyes set deep in white face. He appreciated meeting someone like this, someone competent in a form of the arts about which he knew nothing but would like to learn something. Sad eyes asked them to come backstage after the performance.

They took seats in the first row, directly opposite the stage. Big Ben's thoughts were lewd. All these good-looking, young college girls in the bleachers on both sides of him and some with no brassieres and with nice long legs showing right up into their stocking-pantied crotches. Lovely.

He enjoyed thinking about what he'd tell the boys back in the machine shop the next morning. Fuck'n eating pussy. Shit, just reach out and grab a fuck'n handful. He became aware that Betty Lyons was watching him and he felt guilty. There was an amused, patronizing smile stuck on her face. He tried to pass it off with a laugh.

"It don't hurt to look."

Her lips broadened her smile and she turned her face away. Although part of her was drawn to his blatant sexuality, she was embarrassed to be seen with someone who gawked like a yokel. She had expected him to question her about the dance and about theatre in general so she could fill him in and excite his interest and curiosity in that direction. But he was too busy measuring breasts and legs. For her this kind of crudity added up to being cheap, than which she thought nothing could be worse in a man or woman. Did Jamison Langner know this side of the man? She turned back to him to fulfill her duty as his guide into the arts.

"Have you ever seen a performance of ballet or modern dance before?"

"On television."

"What about plays? Have you ever seen a play live in the theatre?"

"A few."

"Performed by professional actors?"

"One at Arena Theatre — *Hedda Gabler*. Semi-professional."

"Oh, yes," — letting him know she had been told about him going to that performance.

"And one in New York," he added.

"New York? What did you see there?"

"*Great White Hope.*"

In her mind his stock started going up again. "Did you like it?"

"Great. Great play."

"Who took you there?"

"Nobody."

"You went alone?"

"No."

She was caught. He had aroused her curiosity and he knew it and he wasn't going to tell her who went with him to see the play. Not unless she asked. And to her own surprise she was too embarrassed to ask him.

"That's based on the life of a Negro boxer, isn't it?"

"Jack Johnson, the world heavyweight champ. A long string of great white hopes tried to chop him down to win back the white man's manhood."

Betty tried to put him on the defensive. "His girlfriend was white, wasn't she? Does that bother you?"

"Black and white sleeping together?"

"Doesn't it undermine your manhood, give you problems?"

"Not me. It's never given me any problems — not when I did it."

He said it bluntly, directly into her eyes. But it had bothered him. Not the color. But it had been the first time, only fourteen years old, and his friends had kidded him when he came back downstairs at the whorehouse down home and the colored girl laughed, in a friendly way, but had to tell the secret, that she just got this young kid's cherry.

He was boldly staring, ready to pounce upon any spark he might strike in Betty Lyons' eyes.

"There's a lot of equipment up there," she said, turning her head away and pointing to the spotlights strung with thick cables along one of the steel beams overhead.

Glaring lights and deafening factory sounds started the dress rehearsal. Big Ben looked at Betty Lyons and covered his ears with his hands, laughing while he screwed up his face into a picture of mock pain.

Betty Lyons, grinning back at him, nodded vigorous agreement.

The leading male dancer was lowered from the ceiling by a

steel cable. His costume consisted of a form-fitting garment covered with silver sequins. Strips of stainless steel were strapped to his arms and legs. The rest of the company, six men and six women, dressed similarly, their strips of stainless steel reflecting the glare of the lights, waited below, their arms upstretched.

The dance they performed was movement into which Big Ben fought hard without success to install some logical meaning. He attributed his failure to his own stupidity and ignorance about dance.

An expert in his craft usually respects others who are expert in their own craft. And Big Ben, an expert machinist himself, recognized and admired the skill with which the dancers moved. They must have spent years in training.

Concentrating to catch every move they made during the three dance numbers which made up the first half of the program, he tried desperately to create some kind of story out of what the dancers were doing up there. All the beautiful leaping and whirling, and graceful stretching out, and the breathtaking catches, and the muscular strength and tensed balance that movement required, it was all very exciting to watch — *for a while*.

But then, as he found it impossible to make any sense out of what they were trying to get across up there, he became aware that his attention was wandering, and his hard seat was becoming very uncomfortable to sit on. He was aware that Betty Lyons was continually glancing at him to measure his interest and understanding about what was going on up on that stage, and he consciously made himself focus his mind back on the dancing.

There *had* to be sense to it. It couldn't all be just movement, like some skillful boxers or wrestlers. At least with them there's a contest to see who'll be the winner.

There were times when the movement was really exciting, tremendously exciting. One movement was repeated several times by the leading male dancer, a run across the stage and a *leap* that took him up high, to hang there a long, long moment up in the air, and then gracefully drop and recover and go on. Each time he did it, everybody applauded, including Big Ben.

It was the kind of thing that Big Ben would want to tell about back in the shop, but in his own inimitable way. This

sonofabitch took off like a ball of shit that just got shot up
there out of some fuck'n cannon.

And Big Ben might also add to this some crude comment
about the nipples of all the girls showing through, sticking out
like two buttons stuck on their chests. Telling it that way he
would unconsciously protect himself from being kidded about
being some kind of goddam fairy.

But that marvelous leap had to mean something more than
just that it was a *marvelous leap*. Was there a contest here, the
dancer competing with himself? What the hell was it? It had to
mean *something*!

Betty Lyons explained it to him when, during intermission,
she took him into the crowded little room off the main
auditorium where refreshments were being served. First she
gave him refreshment. Non-alcoholic punch in paper cups. One
for you and one for me. Save the champagne for later.

"The movement is deliberately stripped of emotion," she
said, now interpreting the dance for him. "Technical words
were fed into a computer, along with a whole series of possible
individual modern dance movements. The whole thing was
programmed by a brilliant young man who tells everyone that
he'd rather quit the university than have his mathematical
genius become a tool for the war machine of the Establishment
in Vietnam. Of course, if he did quit, he'd be drafted. He knows
that."

"They all know that," said Ben, thinking of his brother
Tommy over there and with a motion of his head taking in all
the young college men here.

"They certainly do," she agreed, lowering her voice as if it
was a secret between them. "Anyway, this young genius says
he's programmed this to be a dance about the computer taking
over. Man's supertechnology destroying human relationships,
empty but perfect machines replacing feelings of imperfect
people, making us turn ourselves into empty unfeeling robots,
as we try to compete with the computers by disemboweling our
emotions out of ourselves."

Big Ben, holding the paper cup filled with punch in one
hand and the wrapped birthday present in the other, wisely
nodded to let her see that he was paying close attention, while
he suppressed the impulse to say out loud the phrase that
sprang into his head:

"No shit?"

But at the close of the performance Big Ben vigorously applauded the dancers. There were three curtain calls and then the predominantly young audience started moving toward the exits. Betty Lyons led Big Ben forward toward the area behind the stage.

"Did you like it?"

He looked at her and said, "It was interesting."

"What about the lighting and the sound?"

"Interesting."

"The dancing?"

"Interesting."

"The setting and the costumes?" — She said it for him. "Interesting."

"If you say so," he said, grinning and showing big, white teeth.

They came around behind the stage and she stopped him before going toward the dancers who were grouped around sad eyes set deep in white face.

"Do you think you could get any people you work with out there at the factory to come to see something like this?"

"Maybe if you told them there'd be free beer," said Big Ben, and not knowing whether or not he was serious she did not know what to say and was silent.

Sad eyes and creamy gown extending down to her ankles was reading her notes out loud to the dancers. Betty Lyons and Big Ben stood within hearing and watched. Betty whispered into Big Ben's ear.

"Tell them you liked it."

He whispered back into her ear. "I did like it.'

She looked at him, trying to read the truth in his face.

He laughed. "I didn't understand it, but I liked it."

She saw he meant it. Good.

He awkwardly bobbed his head, "Anything artistic, even something far out like this, as long as it's artistic long-hair stuff I go for it. I like the challenge it makes to my mind, making me reach in there to try to get what it's all about."

Betty Lyons could not think of anything to say in reply to that which would not seem patronizing. She remained silent and smiled at him, approvingly.

After sad eyes finished her critique Betty Lyons introduced

Big Ben to the dancers. "He liked the performance and he's a factory worker." — Big smiles. Brother worker. — "And today is his birthday."

They sang to him. *"Happy birthday to you, happy birthday to you; happy birthday, dear Beh-en; happy birthday to you."* (But one dancer's voice did not sing his name; instead the male voice, louder than the others, sang: *"Dear factory worker"* with a touch of sarcasm that flushed Big Ben's cheeks.)

Sad eyes brought paper cups and they all drank champagne and the dancers went off to change into street clothes and Big Ben offered to drive Betty Lyons home.

"Thank you, I have my own car and first I have to check tomorrow's rehearsal schedule here. You don't have to wait."

"I'll wait and walk you to your car."

Later, standing beside her new station wagon, they talked for over an hour. When they parted Big Ben was in no mood to go straight back to the small cottage where Queen Lila was waiting for him. He had tasted a different world and the taste of this red apple given him by Betty Lyons changed the eyes with which he saw everything.

He stopped off at Mike's tavern across the creek from the factory and after grunting acknowledgement of greetings from some factory men he knew who lived in the neighborhood he motioned to Old Frank to bring the drink to a corner spot at the front of the bar, a place where he could retreat into himself and shut out the noisy country music that the three-piece band was making in the crowded backroom.

Tonight the shouting and laughter all around him bothered him. He was unable to draw from it the usual warmth he got from being there in friendly territory. He downed two shots of whiskey and then lingered over the second beer chaser, vacantly staring at the busy activity all around him, not seeing or hearing it.

In his head he tried to piece together the world of Betty Lyons, peopling it with super-intellectual high-styled men and women like herself who had the ability to make fascinating conversation. Her wide range of knowledge and experience in areas unknown to him had shaken him deeply, though he thought he had been able to hide that from her. But now, thinking about their conversation while they stood next to her station wagon, the envy and longing for the good life she represented welled up and choked him. She had apologized for place-dropping, but he had urged her to go on.

"I like to hear about those foreign places. This kind of conversation fascinates me. I never get anything like this."

Encouraged by his intense interest, especially since he expressed it with such naive directness, Betty Lyons had allowed herself to range far and wide.

"There was a dancer in Paris who moved like that tall skinny drink of water in the first part of the show." — "That girl with the long black hair coming out of the theatre there, she reminds me of an Italian princess I met in Venice." — "In London we went to see a performance by the Royal Ballet Company. Beautiful. Breath-taking. And then after the performance we sneaked around the corner to a delightful old pub where we ran into some of the dancers from the company and we all drank beer and sang and told dirty stories until they kicked us out and closed the place." — "My finger? It's all healed but I keep a dirty bandage there for sympathy. The bone sticks out and I keep scraping off the skin. I broke the finger when I went sailing in the Mediterranean. The Riviera. I should get it broken and re-set."

What was so great about it was that as she talked, skipping around all over the map, the place itself where whatever she was talking about happened seemed unimportant to her. To be able to move around like that all over the world, oh, boy, what a fuck'n great life that must be. Oh, shit.

"In San Francisco," she told him, "I bought an interest in a Chinese restaurant. Authentic Cantonese. I didn't make much on the investment but I did get free meals and waiters bowing over me." — "The Democratic Convention in Chicago. I was in Paris then and I wanted to see for myself. I flew in and I had a front seat in the balcony and I yelled myself hoarse at Mayor Daley. Go back to Russia, you dictator!" — "Don't dismiss all politicians. You can't run a government without politicians. In Washington those old-time politicians, the Senators, those old men from the South with their black string ties, the ones who chair all the committees, when you meet them you're surprised, their charm, you talk to them and you learn they're really brilliant men."

He kept the wall around him, shutting out the loud music coming in waves from the backroom and fighting off the loud laughter and banter nearby.

He tried to remember all the important names she had mentioned, adding them one by one to the string he tried to hang onto. Freud — Fromm — Adler — Marx, Hegel — Nietzsche — Stalin, Lenin, Trotsky — Picasso, Cocteau — Stravinsky — Toulouse-Lautrec — Cezanne, Degas — and Rodin. And she talked about the Greeks, the Romans — Oedipus —Sophocles, Aristotle, Plato — Classic and Neo-classic —Shakespeare, Ben Jonson and Marlowe — and *comedy-del-art* or some damn fuck'n thing that sounded something like that. And Japanese novels.

His ignorance depressed him, especially here in the tavern with others as ignorant of these things as himself. Having tasted so briefly of this fascinating life Betty Lyons spoke about, he ached to gain admittance to it. Being pinned down to this life here, condemned all day to his machine inside the shop suddenly seemed a drudgery that was almost unbearble.

"Feeding my fuck'n energy every day into a machine at one end of the goddam factory and then at the other end of the fuck'n place, over past final assembly into shipping, it's being crated and shipped out as part of some fuck'n hoist or conveyor. My own body, my own fuck'n flesh and blood, turned into some fuck'n *thing* to be bought and sold, installed, used up, and scrapped — !"

Old Frank put another whiskey in front of Big Ben and pointed to one of the men at the other end of the bar. Big Ben looked down the long line of noisy men and women. Dusty Rhodes, a skinny ex-coal miner who worked on the milling machine over in the shop, leaned forward, waved and then saluted. He had to yell to be heard.

"You look so sad there, Ben, you need another drink."

Big Ben lifted the drink in a toast, thanking Dusty, and downed it.

Dusty called to Old Frank to give Big Ben another. "Get him drunk, that's the only way to cure what he's got."

Big Ben refused this second drink with a friendly gesture. He insisted on buying a drink for Dusty and then turned his eyes and ears inward again.

He thought back, trying to recall if he had ever met anyone even approaching the kind of person Betty Lyons was. No, never, at least not on this kind of personal basis. For the first time in many years he worried about his sexual ability. She had been around and to her he was only a clumsy Joe.

"A woman like that takes you under her wing she can teach you the right way to act and take you to the nice places where you can use your mind and where people talk about things that require some intelligence to talk about them."

But he warned himself about women like her.

"If you let her walk all over you, she'll cut your balls off. To keep the upper hand you got to get her hooked so her tongue is hanging out and she's begging for it. Fuck her so good she'll do anything and give you anything to hang on to you. Get a woman like her on the hook she'll buy you new clothes, give you a new car, slip you spending money, any fuck'n thing you want."

He bent his head down over his empty shot glass, to shut out the noise and activity around him, and let his thoughts run wild.

"Divorced, she's already had a good taste of cock. Without it she's probably starving for it. She needs it, can't do without it."

In the complex fantasy he constructed in his mind's eye he mounted her and pounded her steadily down the home stretch through one climaxing orgasm after another, driving her crazy, enslaving her to a point where to show her gratitude she plied him with gifts, starting with the champagne and the pink carnation and going on to give him one more expensive gift after another.

Old Frank poured another shot for Big Ben and picked up the money from the small pile of change and bills on the bar. Big Ben had glumly held up his hand until he got Old Frank's attention. Now he went back deep into his own thoughts, starting off on a new track, wondering if Betty Lyons would turn in a good report.

"Probably. And Jamison Langner needs a good Judas goat to keep the people in the shop happy. Well, fuck Jamison Langner. Play the game and let him think he's getting his fuck'n Judas goat, and then fuck him."

Big Ben tossed down the shot of whiskey and chased the beer after it. He gathered his change together and slipped it into his pocket. He muttered a curt good-night to Old Frank. The old man waved him out. Dusty Rhodes yelled from the other end of the bar.

"Don't worry, Ben, it'll all come out in the wash."

In the cottage all the lights were out except for a night light over the sink in the kitchen. Queen Lila had given up waiting for him and had gone to bed. There was a note on the table that Dave Newman had phoned. He wondered what the former union organizer wanted now. Probably something to do with Vietnam. He opened the refrigerator. There was the birthday cake. Why didn't she bring it out when they had supper? He remembered how silent she had become when he told her he was going out. Nobody had mentioned his birthday. Not even the kids. There was the cake with one red candle and the red birthday greeting: *Happy Birthday, Ben.* The kids must have felt bad. He'd get some ice cream tomorrow, to go with the cake.

He put together a thick bologna sandwich and poured a tall glass of milk. In the dimness of the kitchen, still leaving only the night light on, he leaned his back against the cupboard. Too much inner turmoil to sit; too many fixed points had become unfixed. He chewed noisily, biting off huge mouthfuls, washing them down with big gulps of cold milk.

A company man? Never. Not the kind who sells out the people he works with. Everybody hates that kind of rat. Even the company. They'll use him, but even they don't like him. But nobody resents the man too much who does it all open and aboveboard, taking an opportunity offered him to hop the fence to become a nickel-boss or leadman or foreman, as long as he doesn't go out of his way to knife the people he works with. It's easy to make foreman if you want it. Run for union steward and then use good sense in handling grievances. There comes an opening for foreman and the company rewards the steward for acting responsible. Half the foremen now in the shop went that route. Christ, now almost every fuck'n union steward in there is bucking for foreman. His old man when he was local union president back down in the coal mines said anybody who jumps the fence is selling out. But that was back in the old days when unions were really unions and not some old ladies' sewing circle. Back then if you got caught playing footsy with the company you got your head busted wide open.

He finished the sandwich and folded his arms across his chest and threw his head back and squeezed his eyes shut.

"Shit, who the fuck wants a cheap pusher's job in the shop?

That's hell, caught between the company and the men. And what do you get for it? Shit from both sides."

And it still would not get him what he wanted out of life. He began to unbutton his shirt. Betty Lyons could be the key. But he would only blow the whole thing if he tried to play the game with her. She was too smart for that. The only way was to be honest with her.

"I'm a working stiff and I don't know my way around in your territory. I'd like to get into that life if I can and I know I need help. I realize maybe it's not for me. Maybe if I try to move up there I'll be a fish out of water and wish I were back here with my own kind where I belong. I won't know until I try it. But I don't want to sell anybody out. If that's what it takes, the hell with it. I want to be honest with you and with the people I'm working with in the shop. That's it. I'm laying it right on the line. I need your help."

In the darkness of the bedroom Queen Lila stirred and murmured. Happy birthday. He slid under the covers and patted her ass to say goodnight. Surprise. No clothes on. Hello, Mother. Happy birthday, Sonny. Later, resting in Queen Lila's arms, feeling at peace with his head pillowed against her big breast, he thought about Betty Lyons and decided not to mention anything to Lila about her.

"That dress rehearsal tonight, that modern dance thing, you would have liked it, I think," he said. "I guess Jamison Langner has some ideas about putting on a performance for the people in the shop. To test if working people will go for it."

Queen Lila wanted to talk about it. She respected this side of Big Ben, the intellectual side. And she always enjoyed this kind of talk. But after working in the shop and cleaning the house and cooking supper and getting the kids to bed and making love with all she could give to make it a good birthday present — she was exhausted. She wanted to say something deep and intelligent. But it took all her energy just to say that she didn't think the people in the shop would go for that kind of stuff.

"Would you like it?" he asked.

"Yes."

"Are you something special?"

"No."

"Then why won't the others like it?"

No answer except a nocommittal grunt. And a moment later
Big Ben heard a snore. He blamed the waves of shattering
sound that followed for his inability to fall asleep. Lying there
in the darkness, staring at the ceiling, with his mind's eye he
again ran through fanciful scenes in the world of Betty Lyons.
At one point, fed up with it, he rolled his head from side to side
on the pillow. Too bad he wasn't married and all settled with a
wife and children to support and a mortgage and a new car
and a washing machine and a dryer and a color television set
and everything else to pay for. Then there wouldn't be much
choice. He'd take the path his father took when he was a young
man back down in the mines. Be a loudmouth for the men. He
loved and respected his old man, but he ached to get the good
life he saw could be there for him, not to be deprived of any
part of it just because he was born into the world a working
stiff.

He obsessed and agonized over this for what seemed like
hours before he finally fell asleep.

Chapter 8

Working at his machine Monday morning, Big Ben waited for Jamison Langner to wander through the department with Dick Penfield and to stop and ask him the question. Oh, Ben, by the way, how did you like that dress rehearsal?

The sweeper came down the aisle and Big Ben stopped him. Is the Old Man in yet? The sweeper was one of the best informed men in the whole shop. He reported that Jamison Langner was on the company plane on his way to Virginia.

It was at the request of the mediator assigned by the Federal Conciliation Service that the mayor of Waring, Virginia, invited both parties to meet in his office "to resolve this dispute which is idling so many workers and cutting into the purchasing power of our community."

And since the mediator had revealed, off-the-record, that it was the business agent of the Machinists Union down there who had, off-the-record, asked him to ask the mayor to call together the interested parties, and since the mayor in making the invitation had, off-the-record, passed on this information, Jamison Langner on the plane made notes and rehearsed what he might say to give the business agent a face-saving way out.

"Men, now is the time when we all must pull together to give this company a chance to get this new facility firmly on its feet and operating efficiently. This is necessary if we are to guarantee that you men will have your job here — now and in the future. And in that future I can see that your demands — your *proposals* — which now might make it necessary to re-evaluate the whole matter of transferring work into the Virginia facility — in the future these proposals might appear just and practical." And then something about how management itself might possibly be willing then to go even further than you men right now are asking. "But right now, men, let's face it. What you are now demanding will jeopardize all the fine plans this company has for this new location and may very well destroy your job now and for the future."

News of Jamison Langner's plane trip to Virginia traveled from Big Ben's area in the machine shop out into the rest of the factory, getting almost as much attention as the baseball World

Series. The Baltimore Orioles had won the first game, beating
the New York Mets, with Big Ben not even getting a chance to
win the betting pool. Baltimore had been ahead at the end of
the first half of the ninth inning and it was not necessary to
play out the second half. Bets were being taken now for the
second game, scheduled for Tuesday at Shea's Stadium in New
York City.

But then an event occurred late that same Monday afternoon
in Mike's Bar that temporarily wiped out the World Series and
Jamison Langner's plane trip and the whole state of Virginia
for the men and also for the women who were working in the
shop. For almost a year the men had been provoking laughter
and all kinds of wisecracks from the women by ooh-ing and ah-
ing over newspaper pictures of a luscious, redheaded young
doll. *She's stacked like a brick shithouse.* What makes her so
interesting, this gorgeous body that invited every man to hop
on and ride, this face of wide-eyed innocence that invited rape,
was that she, dear innocent Mary Magdeline Kelly, had deftly
slipped the sharp blade of a knife between the ribs of her
business partner, a slight accident which disposed of him
quickly and permanently.

It was Wayne Henderson, a lift truck operator in the
warehouse, who got the first look at this lovely doll. An urge he
could not deny had prompted him to park his lift truck on the
shipping dock and sneak over the bridge across the creek to
grab an early morning belt of whiskey. If caught he could be
fired, but he desperately needed it to get through the day. When
he returned to the shop he said the risk was worth it. He had
seen Mary Magdeline Kelly dishing out booze across the bar.

Each time he told the story he waxed more ecstatic and
shook his hands to cool off his overheated fingers. Oh, man,
those big tits floating free. Christ, it was all I could do to keep
from grabbing hold and gobbling a mouthful. The women
joined the men in shouting the name across the shop. Mary
Magdeline Kelly! And their lewd comments made men's faces
turn red with embarrassment. Big Mary the fat lesbian in
Bench Assembly patted young Teddy the fairy who worked
next to her. Don't you go over there, she's mine. He fluttered
and minced. Oh, you can have her but you have to let me
watch. And down in the steamy pickling room Casey Jones with
a wife and six children at home whipped out his cock and

waved it around, yelling to the other men in the department: Meet Mary Magdeline Kelly. One of the other men in the pickling room offered him a crowbar. Here, break it off and I'll take it over and give it to her. Stanley used both hands to cover his cock protectively. How do I know you'll bring it back?

The people in the shop had not lost their perspective. They poked fun at themselves about their preoccupation with this lovely piece of tail that had miraculously appeared behind the bar over at Mike's place. It's wiped out the whole World Series and all talk about what's going on down there in Virginia!

It was a relief they all welcomed. They could chew over the question of her guilt or innocence without worrying about the outome one way or the other. Lift truck operator Wayne Henderson defended her. But some people in the shop said he was prejudiced, because only the summer before he had left his motor boat unmoored at the dock and his wife, a non-swimmer, trying to leave the boat, fell into the water and drowned, very opportunely dissolving a childless marriage that had been a miserable, carping relationship from which Wayne had admitted he lacked the energy and fortitude to escape by way of divorce or separation.

When Big Ben said he'd have to go over and take a look at the new arrival the men around him in machine shop warned him to stay away or *he'd* get a knife between *his* ribs. — "To get off that way she must have laid every guy on the jury." — "The prosecuting attorney must have gotten in there too."

Lift truck operator Wayne Henderson conceded that the accused had admitted killing her partner. "But it was in self-defense. The jury heard the evidence and they believed her. She could fool some people, but not the whole jury."

That reaped him a chorus of hoots and jeers. There were a lot of experts in the shop, men and women who had read every word of testimony that appeared in the newspapers. It was a juicy story and the people in the shop enjoyed talking about it. Through the rest of the afternoon, while working at their machines and on the benches or on the assembly lines, and in the toilets and in the smoking areas and in the lunchroom, they spewed out a steady stream of expert opinion.

"The guy she killed — Lucky Carpenter — was a pimp. They say he was pushing narcotics. He was a stoolpigeon, a fence handling stolen goods, a crooked gambler, a gun for hire. The cops, the judges, the politicians, the mayor, everybody was afraid he'd sell out to some higher bidder. He's one guy nobody will ever miss. They all sent him flowers and said a prayer to speed him on his way."

Another expert:

"They say his friends set up a fund to get him out of town. Set him up in business with a saloon down in Miami. Account of his record there was trouble about a license. So Mary Magdeline Kelly was listed as owner and she hired Lucky to work for her behind the bar. But all the money coming in was supposed to go to Lucky and he would pay Mary Magdeline Kelly to shuffle out the drinks. She testified he tried to make her work in the rooms upstairs. He had a whole crew of hustlers banging away on the beds up there. He wouldn't give her anything but a couple of dollars spending money and when she said she was quitting he beat the living shit out of her. He give her two black eyes and bruises all over her face and body. That's *her* story."

Another expert:

"One reporter who went down to Miami said the scuttlebutt in the bars down there is that Little Mary thought she had Lucky over a barrel and tried to make him live up to the fine print of their phony agreement. She threatened to turn him in if he didn't cut her in fifty-fifty and there was a little argument which ended with unlucky Lucky slapping her across the mouth and this caused a butcher knife to suddenly sprout between his ribs."

Lift truck operator Wayne Henderson, bringing over the news about the new barmaid appearing in the tavern, had been so excited about that that he had forgotten to mention someone else who had unexpectedly put in an appearance there and, surprisingly, seemed to be a friend of Mary Magdeline Kelly. Late in the morning, driving through the machine shop, Wayne stopped his lift truck in the aisle and hopped down to speak to Big Ben.

"Your redheaded actor friend was over there too, talking to the other redhead behind the bar. He said he knows her old lady."

Big Ben turned back to his machine without giving any sign of recognition. The lift truck operator looked around to make sure no one else was listening. He bent over and hoarsely hissed above the loud machine humming and squeaking noises into Big Ben's ear.

"Our old organizer — the guy Jamison Langner loves — Dave Newman."

Sheilagh Kelly was already fifty years old when she gave birth to Mary Magdeline. She rested her hand on her swollen belly.

"A surprise, David. Not that she isn't welcome, seeing as how she's already on the way. But the truth is, David, I thought I was through." In the parlor of her flat she confided this to the much younger redheaded union organizer, while her husband, Jim Kelly, went back into the kitchen to get more beer for the three of them. Her voice lowered even further. "Don't say anything to Jim, David, but if it wasn't that I'm already in so much trouble with the Church I would do something about this." Her eyes lifted in mock horror. "If I added that on top of the rest, my priest would have a fit. He'd send me straight to hell, for sure."

The strange friendship between Sheilagh Kelly and Dave Newman had begun back during the second World War and had continued for more than twenty-five years despite excruciating changes in their beliefs that now put them at opposite ends of the political pole.

The day before he appeared at Mike's Bar, the former union organizer answered the phone and recognized the lilting brogue that always gave him a feeling of good humor. It had been a long time since he had heard from her.

"David, can you drop by the house?"

She believed their phones were tapped. Both yours and mine, David. She first told him this years before when she let him know that *they* were inquiring about him *again*. Be careful, David.

Her second husband, Jim Kelly, had been the first man at the metal smelting shop where he worked to sign up for the union, and the organizer dropped in at the house often after that to talk over the progress of the organizing campaign. Sheilagh Kelly, a devout Catholic, confided to David that the bone in her throat was the Church's refusal to recognize her second marriage by dissolving the first.

"So far as the Church is concerned we're living in sin. Even though my divorce is legal in the eyes of the court. Adultery, that's what it had to be back then. A young girl and two witnesses. And a lot of lies that cost too much money. And the lawyers — the liars — get richer. The liars and the priests, God forgive me. And the people get poorer."

Like many men who work in the shop and do the quiet spade work to get a union started and then slip into the background, Jim Kelly talked only when it was necessary and then very sparingly. To keep in close touch with developments inside the shop, Dave Newman dropped by the house every day. Getting information from Jim Kelly was like pulling teeth.

It was Sheilagh Kelly who did most of the talking, while she drank beer or coffee with the two men. She always asked Dave Newman to stay for supper, and a special kind of relationship developed between her and the union organizer. They instinctively liked and respected one another.

Later, when Dave Newman was called before a Congressional investigating committee — "exposing the communists in our midst" — Sheilagh Kelly phoned and told him she had lit candles for him in church and prayed for him. And once she summoned Dave with one of her mysterious phone calls to tell him she had dreamed about him. "Leading a host of men and women, carrying all the flags of the United Nations, and you out front, David, leading the way, leading all the flags of the United Nations, marching in out of the high waves of the ocean up onto the sandy beach, all safe and sound, the sun breaking through the clouds."

She poked fun at herself for talking so much. "Making up for Jim being so quiet." Every day, having read the local newspaper column by column from the first page to the last, she buttonholed Dave when he came over to talk to her husband and she went through everything she had read, item by item, picking his brain to add to her fantastic fund of miscellaneous information.

After Dave Newman stopped being a daily visitor at the house, she energetically built up a wide range of other contacts with whom she checked out what she had read in the newspapers.

Despite the gap that developed between her and Dave Newman during the period of political reaction (McCarthyism)

following the end of the Second World War — as she swung far
to the Right while he remained relatively steadily aligned to the
Left — her friendship for David and her hate for informers was
so deeply ingrained that she developed a remarkable lapse in
memory when two polite young FBI men came to see her to
inquire about the union organizer.

"Is Dave Newman a communist?"

"Not from anything he said to me."

"Did he say anything that might be termed subversive?"

"Not to my knowledge."

She had been born in County Cork in Ireland and her father
had been a soldier in the Irish Republican Army, forced to flee
to America when he escaped from his British captors during
the troubles in the old country. The man who informed on her
father was tried by a military court of the Irish Republican
Army, found guilty and shot. Sheilagh Kelly inform? Never, no
matter how many Party meetings she had attended with her
husband and Dave Newman, no matter how many copies of the
Daily Worker the union organizer had brought to the house,
and no matter how anti-communist she and her husband
became as the country moved to the Right.

But since the FBI men had seen fit to come to her house to
ask for her help she did not hesitate to frequently telephone the
Special Agent who was in charge of the local office. "This thing
in the newspaper today on the front page of the second section.
This student demonstration. Your people were there, weren't
they? That young blonde girl the police picked up. (I'm not
naming names.) Her mother is working in the shop at
Westinghouse to put her daughter through college. There are
enough rich hippies there to pick up. If I were you I think I'd
pass the word along to leave the sons and daughters of our
laboring people alone. Or you're going to get some trouble from
their parents. For what it's worth you might pass that on to
your boss down there in Washington."

She phoned the chief of police, the mayor, members of the
city council, county supervisors, heads of unions, officers of the
local chamber of commerce, corporation officers, state
legislators, anyone whose name appeared in the newspapers.
She enjoyed the game, giving the impression that she was
trying to help them while she pumped them for information she
could use to carry out her private long-range plan to somehow

undermine the rich and advance the cause of the poor.

When she read in the newspaper about Jamison Langner's idea for The Dance Center, long before it became a reality, she telephoned him at the factory. The switchboard operator put her through to one of the private secretaries and she was given the standard reply. Mr. Langner's in a meeting, can I help you?

"It's a personal matter, I'll call again." The thick Irish brogue exuded mystery.

Every hour during working hours for three days, Sheilagh Kelly telephoned and asked for *Mister* Jamison Langner. The private secretaries could not crack her open to find out what she wanted from him. Finally, out of curiosity, the Old Man spoke to her, as Sheilagh Kelly knew he eventually would, and he had to grin when he heard that thick Irish dialect which she unconsciously thickened, knowing it did delight people.

"*Mister* Jamison Langner?"

"Yes?"

She sailed in and rushed on, not giving Jamison Langner a chance to break in and stop her:

"Your Dance Center, I have a prize for you, a gifted girl possessed of the natural gift of dance, a rhythm and spirit flowing in her veins, a joy to watch, she never walked, ever since she was a child she always danced, never walked, but always danced from room to room in the house, star pupil at Betty's Dance Studio, tap dancing and some ballet and some soft shoe."

She ran on, giving Jamison Langner a good taste of what he was in for if he did not cooperate and then she gave him his chance to break in. "Have you ever heard of Betty? She'd make a good teacher for your organizaiton. Very enterprising young woman. She took over an empty storefront and made it up into her dance studio. A great dancer and a great teacher. A genius. Drop in and look at her work. Tell her I mentioned it. Do you have pencil and paper? This is her address."

Jamison Langner dutifully took the name and address. He found it amusing to humor the eccentric Irish creature who was ordering him around. He promised that when the plans for The Dance Center reached the stage where he would be recruiting dancers for the company Mary Magdeline Kelly would be notified to come in and audition. And he kept his word.

Almost a year later the letter came, inviting Mary Magdeline to come in and audition, but she was already dancing for a living at Ducky's Tavern, with a thin string of beads to keep her warm and with the promise that as soon as there would be an opening she would be promoted to an executive position dishing out drinks and keeping a sharp eye on the girls who were hustling customers for the house. She liked the excitement of the life at Ducky's Tavern and refused to change it for what she sensed would be something much different. Sheilagh Kelly argued with her. But Mary Magdeline was adamant.

"Those people would never even let me in the back door of their house. Why should I dance for them?"

Mary Magdeline Kelly was eighteen when she left home to move into an apartment of her own. Her half-brother, now with the Marines in Vietnam, and her half-sisters, all from Sheilagh's first marriage, had also left home in their teens —to marry and divorce and then all three to quickly re-marry and again divorce and then all three to take up with common law spouses to avoid the future trouble and expense of a divorce. Their trusted conspirator, ever ready to give good advice on tactics when the time came to slough off one partner and pick up the next, was Mom. In a crisis Mom was great. She remained calm and took over and went to work. The more difficult the situation the greater the relish with which she attacked the problem. So it was to be expected that within minutes after the knife sprouted between the ribs of Lucky Carpenter the telephone rang and Mary Magdeline tearfully dropped the problem into Mom's warm lap.

"Don't say a word to anyone until I get you a lawyer."

Sheilagh Kelly knew all the well-publicized criminal lawyers in the city, phoning them often to give advice on how to handle their more difficult cases, advice they sometimes followed with good results, and they in turn frequently phoned to ask her to use her contacts to get them information they needed to defend their clients. She telephoned a fellow Irishman, Mike Sullivan, who had once been chairman of the Democratic Party's county organization and still carried a lot of political clout he could use behind the scenes.

Mike Sullivan really appreciated Sheilagh Kelly. A lively woman. Unpredictable. He told his fellow lawyers about her while drinking with them at the bar across from the courthouse. A character, eccentric as hell and cunning as all hell. She'll steal the gold out of your teeth while she's got you laughing. And her daughter Mary Magdeline, defending a beautiful piece like that brings you the kind of friendship money can't buy. Without hesitation he blandly asked Sheilagh Kelly for a thousand dollars in advance.

"For expenses, Ma."

"A thousand dollars?" she appropriately gasped, mortally wounded. "My God, Mike, where would I ever get that kind of money?"

"Take it out from under your mattress, Ma."

"Mike, I would have a terrible time scraping together even a hundred dollars."

"A thousand to start and a couple thousand more before we even get to trial, Ma, or don't waste your time."

She protested her poverty, but Mike Sullivan blandly repeated his admonition that she take the money out from under the mattress. He had checked her out with commercial credit the first time she telephoned him. Find out for me what kind of a nut she is. And he found out that over the years, by putting down small amounts of money and picking up the biggest mortgages she could cajole from the banks, acquiring one big empty house after another, Sheilagh Kelly had become a rich nut who still paraded as poor.

The rundown neighborhood in which she lived had once been a very nice upper middle class section of the city. Now it was a borderline area between two antagonistic ghettos, one poor black and the other poor white. Sheilagh Kelly had put her clever husband to work. Without pay, doing everything himself, the carpentering, the painting and papering, the electrical work, the plumbing, Jim Kelly broke up the old homes and the big garages behind them into as many small apartments as Sheilagh Kelly decided could be squeezed into the available square feet of space. Every attic blossomed into one or two small apartments.

Sheilagh Kelly shrewdly advertised for tenants in the college newspapers. Those rich hippies want to live near workers so they can peddle their radical propaganda to the poor and be living where they can see colored people and talk themselves blue in the face about civil rights. Their rich parents can afford to pay well to give them that privilege.

Mike Sullivan knew Sheilagh. He threatened:

"Ma, don't take too long to think about it because the more time I have to think about it the more money I think it's going to take, maybe something closer to five thousand to start."

"Oh, my God, Mike, no!"

He had the thousand dollars in cash the next day and demanded and received two thousand more in cash before the end of the week. Move quick, Ma, before it all hardens into place. He used the money judiciously to produce a minor miracle. The trial was shifted back up north to the city in which the accused and the deceased supposedly were legally domiciled. Here Mike Sullivan could use his political clout more effectively. It was a maneuvre that would never have stood up if anyone had ever challenged it.

Congratulating himself in his office Mike Sullivan took a bottle out of his desk and drank a toast to himself. To one of his clerks he explained that the law business is like farming. Spread enough manure around and you grow a good crop.

At the trial he began his questioning of the accused by asking her where she lived.

"I live with my Mom," she replied, her voice truly shaking with fright. It sounded great.

Dave Newman dropped by to see Sheilagh Kelly. He kissed the sunken cheek of the deeply lined face and embraced the bony little woman whose energy belied her fragile appearance. She asked him how old he was now. Fifty-six. You don't look it. He boasted that he was jogging regularly. A mile a day. The body and pulse and blood pressure of a forty-year old. Except for the hair, the red turning blonde with the white creeping into it.

"How are you, Ma?" She must be close to eighty now.

Sheilagh Kelly sighed heavily. "As good as can be expected, David, under the circumstances."

She led him into the parlor. Mary Magdeline said she would like to see you again, David. Her other friends, they've been told to stay away from her until after the trial. She's got good memories of you and Dad, drinking beer and coffee and talking union. But the accused had gone out to do some window-shopping to keep from going out of her mind. Sheilagh Kelly served coffee in the parlor.

"David, you know Mary Magdeline. The newspapers don't tell the whole story. The truth between me and you, this man had an evil purpose in mind, you know what I mean. Mary Magdeline is a decent girl, you know that. No angel and full of spirit, but decent. This man was an animal. He reached out to grab her and he said he was going to tear her dress off her, and she pulled back, sudden, like this. And he lost his balance and fell forward." — Her deepset, faded blue eyes insisted that what she would tell him now was definitely true. "Unfortunately, at that very minute Mary Magdeline was holding this sharp knife in her hand. Like this. She was bringing it from the kitchen to slice some beef for the hot sandwiches for the lunch business. The poor man, this crazed animal, he was his own executioner. He fell right into the knife. David, that's the God's honest truth, I hope to die."

She crossed herself and held up her right hand and she waited for him to tell her what he thought of the story. He sipped his coffee. With a lawyer like Mike Sullivan and a defendant like Mary Magdeline and some money in the right places it might work. He looked into Sheilagh Kelly's shrewd eyes and nodded his approval. But she needed a more enthusiastic response to reassure her. She reached out and grasped his wrist and the delightful brogue rose to a high-pitched urgent whine.

"Mary Magdeline, she wouldn't even know where to put the knife!"

There was an unusual amount of traffic into and out of Mike's Bar when workers left the factory that day at change of shifts, both men and women hurrying over for a quick drink and a look before going on to the parking lot.

Big Ben with Queen Lila at his side turned toward the tavern after crossing the bridge over the creek. Let's say hello to Dave Newman. But he stayed on after Mike told him Dave had already left.

"Wow," breathed Queen Lila, seeing for the first time the golden red hair hanging down to the shoulders, the dark brown eyes, the lovely face of innocence, and the nicely shaped pair of melons jutting over the bar. "Jesus Christ, if I were a man I'd risk a knife in the belly any time for that."

The place was noisy with many hushed conversations about the lovely creature working behind the bar. She seemed to have her ears turned off. The gabbling all around her broke into a hissed dispute over the circumstances that led to her presence in this unlikely place. Big Ben moved to get the answer from the source. He motioned to Mike Staruski and then whispered the question into Mike's ear.

Mike whispered back into Ben's ear. Dropped in off the street and asked for a job. Big Ben turned his head and whispered back into Mike's ear. You're full of shit. Mike laughed quietly and walked away.

Some of the experts along the bar said it was the mob who arranged it. They call the signals here and Mike asks no questions. He was working in the shop on hoist assembly when the old German running this place had a stroke and his wife put it up for sale. Mike talked to the guy who ran the branch bank for the mob in the shop. Give you all the money you want for only an arm and a leg interest. He set it up for Mike to meet the boys. Two characters with the suits with the high shoulders and with the sharp pants and the pointy shoes and that shitty after-shave perfume that smells like a fuck'n whorehouse. They took Mike for a ride to a diner down near the river where they met the iceman. Cold eyes and no fuck'n expression on his face. How much do you need? Shake, partner.

There was agreement at the bar that Mike was happy about the deal. He reached down into a pile of shit and come up with a fuck'n bucketful of money. Two hundred a week salary and fifty-fifty on the profit. Every week high-shoulders with pointy shoes and the whorehouse perfume comes in and orders one drink here at the bar and goes out with a fat envelope shoved up his ass. Last Christmas a contractor showed up from nowhere and fixed up the whole fuck'n joint. Mike never asked who sent him. You don't kick old Santa Claus in the fuck'n balls. As long as the money keeps rolling in good you just roll over on your back and enjoy getting fucked.

Mike Staruski had the sense to keep his mouth shut about the wide-eyed innocent he'd acquired behind the bar. But he suspected there was a bold, sharp mind there. She must have learned early in life that God had blessed her with something special to sell and she was not going to sell it cheap to any stupid bastard who walked by.

Mike knew about Ducky who ran the tavern down by the river. Any girl who started working there was in for a quick education on the facts of life. The girls were quickly moved up from dancing with customers and pushing drinks into the higher classification where they made a better buck by selling what they had heretofore given away. Mike assumed that his wide-eyed innocent had probably gone the whole route. But something about her manner, a touch of steel that occasionally flashed in her eyes kept him from being sure. It was that same touch of steel that flashed when Ducky tried to use a good-looking young stud to hook her. The stud got her into bed and then tried to talk her into becoming a professional. At that point she moved quickly and became the girlfriend of Joe the Romeo, the nicest and youngest of the high-shouldered suits hanging around Ducky's place. Joe the Romeo showed Ducky the bulge in his jacket over the pistol in his holster. Ducky backed up quickly. All yours, pal, nobody else touches her. That was the way Joe the Romeo told the story. But he did not know Mary Magdeline any better than did Ducky. The hard times before her mother had parlayed Jim Kelly's factory wages into good income from property had taught her the value of a dollar. She showed Joe the Romeo her savings bankbook and he teased her about the small size of the amounts she deposited every week. (She did not show him the bankbook for her secret account.) What are you going to do with all your money? Mary Magdeline fluttered her long eyelashes, blackened with mascara. I think I'll buy a house of my own. It was still her dream and taking long walks alone since she'd come home for the trial she'd seen the house she'd buy someday if she ever had the money, a big place on a tree-lined street on the north side of Lake Park in the heart of Central City. It was the same block where Betty Lyons had bought her house a few weeks after she returned from Europe.

To anyone else in Mike's Bar other than Queen Lila it might have appeared that nothing special was echoing back and forth between Big Ben and Mary Magdeline. Sitting on the stool beside Big Ben, drinking her beer, Queen Lila watched and missed nothing.

Big Ben said only the few words necessary to order the first drink and then the second drink. And Mary Magdeline routinely helped herself to the money for the drinks from the paper bills and silver coins Big Ben put down on the bar and left there. When Big Ben finished the second drink he picked up the money remaining on the bar and started toward the door. Queen Lila followed him. Big Ben silently flipped a quick wave of goodbye to Mike over the heads of the people still lined up at the bar.

"Drop in again."

It was Mary Magdeline. She hardly raised her voice, but it cut through the noise in the place and made Big Ben stop and look back.

"I will," he said and moved on toward the door.

Queen Lila tagged along, letting Mary Magdeline see her staying close to Big Ben. When they reached the car in the parking lot after a silent walk from Mike's Bar she stood aside and watched him unlock the door of the car.

"That's a nice piece of ass back there."

"How the hell would you know?" asked Big Ben, getting into the car and sliding across the front seat.

Queen Lila sat beside him and pulled the door of the car shut. "Wipe the drool off your lips."

Big Ben reached for her and she grabbed his hand and pushed it away. He reached again. She held his hand away from her. He put it back on the wheel.

"Jealous?"

"Why should I be jealous?" she snapped.

He started the car. "You're way ahead of me."

"You're so damn obvious," said Queen Lila, "it's pitiful."

Chapter 9

Mary Magdeline Kelly drew Big Ben back into Mike's Bar that evening. And there was the other redhead, his red hair turning blonde with the white in it. Dave Newman had used the same magnet as his excuse to return.

The day before, on Sunday afternoon, Sheilagh Kelly had served coffee to the former union organizer. The faded blue eyes of Mary Magdeline's mother measured her visitor. She was not sure of the role into which to cast him. He was known out there where her daughter would be dishing out drinks, known and respected for what he had done for the people out there when he was a union leader.

"If you could get out that way on your insurance travels, David," she slyly suggested, "it would be nice for her to see at least one friendly face."

"When they get word over into Mackenzie Machine across the creek, Ma — she'll get more friendly faces than she can handle."

"Do you think so, David?"

"A beautiful girl."

"Isn't she though?"

Her visitor grinned. "Takes after her mother."

"Perhaps when I was younger," Sheilagh Kelly conceded, boldly accepting the compliment as justified. Then she got right back to business. "But drop out there if you can, David. After all Mary Magdeline has been through, a friendly face and a friendly word would be appreciated. And pass the word if you can. It will help her if they think she's bringing more business into that place out there."

Dave Newman needed no urging. He had not been back in Mike's Bar for several years, not since the time Mike Staruski had bitterly invited him to stay out after he had too vigorously argued there against the country's involvement in the Vietnam War.

But Monday afternoon it was Mike Staruski himself who was the first to hurry over and grab Dave Newman's hand and pump it. Where you been, stranger? We missed you. Don't stay away. Dave asked about Big Ben. Mike said Ben might be dropping in after work. But Dave couldn't wait. He had an insurance appointment back down in Central City where he lived. He told Mary Magdeline and Mike Staruski he might be back that evening. Some insurance calls in the neighborhood.

It was about a half hour after Dave Newman returned that evening that Big Ben arrived. He wore a bowling jacket and carried a bowling ball in a canvas bag. *Machinist Union — Mackenzie Tool,* the golden words sewed on the dark blue background of his bowling jacket reflected the equal split of the cost of the garment between the union and the company. Dave Newman had already noticed that he himself was the only man in the tavern wearing a suitcoat, his insurance salesman uniform. All the other men wore sweaters, flannel shirts, bowling jackets, or windbreakers of some kind that zipped or clipped together. Mike Staruski wore a heavy sweater that buttoned up the front.

Big Ben, not immediately seeing Dave Newman, walked right past him and found a space down further at the bar and leaned forward to look down the line toward the back of the room. What the hell you doing back here tonight? There was a swift retort from lift truck operator Wayne Henderson. Same as you, stopped back for a quick one.

Big Ben showed his canvas bag with the bowling ball in it. Bowling, need refreshment. Lift truck operator Henderson hooted derisively and jerked his thumb in the direction of the curved back of Mary Magdeline who was busy dishing out drinks to the unusual Monday night turnout. Big Ben shook his head and held up his right hand. I swear, going bowling.

Seeing Big Ben arrive, Dave Newman hurriedly put away his pack of small index cards. Ostensibly, he was using the polished surface of the bar as his desk to make notes about his insurance calls. But actually these were almost illegible reminders of bits of dialogue and other information scribbled down rapidly for use later in connection with his writing. When Wayne Henderson, the lift truck operator, walked in earlier and told him about the furor over in the shop that afternoon caused by the appearance of Mary Magdeline behind the bar "the whole fuck'n place went wild" — that piece of dialogue was jotted down to be filed away later in the large manila envelope labelled *Wayne Henderson.* There was already information there about the peculiar way Wayne's first wife

had died, also new information gleaned that afternoon about
Wayne's forthcoming second marriage to a school teacher: does
the second wife know the way the first wife died? The
information about the shop going wild over Mary Magdeline
would also be filed in the large manila envelope labelled *Mary
Magdeline Kelly,* already fat with newspaper clippings and
scribbled notes. Those two manila envelopes were stacked away
back home in his workroom, in a cardboard carton filled with
many such envelopes including the one labelled *Big Ben Hood*
— to be used some day to write a play or novel.

"Hey, Mike." Big Ben made a sweeping motion to take in the
long line of men at the bar. "What the hell brings all these
stupid bastards out here on a Monday night?"

"The good whiskey," said Mike. And he pointed to Dave
Newman. "A friend of yours here. Looking for you."

"Dave!"

Big Ben moved over to shake Dave's hand, and Mary
Magdeline who had been about to serve him in his first place
at the bar, followed him. She put a shot of whiskey and a glass
of beer down in front of him, the same thing he had ordered
that afternoon. Big Ben put down a ten dollar bill, with a
knowing smile: you remembered. A gesture toward Mike and
Dave. Whatever they're drinking. Out of the corner of his eye
he watched that luscious body as she moved away. Squeezed so
nicely into that tight dress. — Dave Newman was talking to
him.

"I tried to reach you here and they gave me another number.
You weren't home."

"I know," said Big Ben and, anticipating Dave Newman's
intention, he tried to channel the conversation into a different
direction. "Are you doing any more acting?"

"Not since *Hedda Gabler* closed."

"Are they going to do your play down there?"

"What play is that?" Mike Staruski's face showed surprise.
"Did you write a play?"

"He's a playwright now," said Big Ben, and he tossed off
the rest of the whiskey in his shotglass.

"No shit — ?"

The phone rang, interrupting Mike. He hurried to the phone
booth. Dave Newman slipped an official-looking envelope out
of his pocket and showed it to Big Ben. Something interesting

here. He took the letter out of its envelope and gave it to Big
Ben. The stationary heading also looked official: *Central City
— Office of the Mayor.* Addressed to Dave Newman. Thank
you for your helpful suggestion. Signed by the mayor. —
"Election time. This woman running against him. Making hay
on the race issue. Opposing school integration. Against
bussing." — Dave Newman accepted the letter which was
quietly returned to him. "We went to high school together years
ago. Me and the mayor. I dropped him a note. Break up the
ethnic line-up against him by making a public statement.
Support the National Mobilization against the War. He did it."
— Dave Newman saw Mike Staruski coming out of the phone
booth. "Wednesday there's a candlelight vigil, round-the-clock,
in front of city hall in Central City. Some union guys will be
there. If you want to come along — ?"

"What's that play about?" said Mike Staruski, rejoining
them.

Dave Newman gave his full attention to Mike. And Ben was
silent.

"It's about some guy who works on one machine in a factory
most of his life and then he's automated out and hangs around
the tavern and gets drunk every day."

"We got 'em," interjected Mike.

"From then on," continued Dave Newman, now trying to
include Big Ben in his audience, "he's bottom man on the
totem pole wherever he works. Moves from one job to another.
Knocked off each place. Coming apart. Becomes a real drunken
piece of shit. Schlobbered day and night. — The play starts
there. It's about the fight he makes to re-establish his
relationship with his daughter. She was taken away from him
and put into a foster home. It's about his fight to regain his
self-respect."

"Does he make it?" asked Mike.

"Yes and no, depending on how you look at it."

"What's the name of it?" asked Big Ben, his voice
surprisingly somewhat cool. He had changed his mind a great
deal about the war, but he did not like it that Dave was
keeping after him this way. A phone call Friday. And another
while he was away. And now coming after him in the tavern.
He was for ending the war. What stupid sonofabitch wasn't?
But he could still understand why some of the people he

worked with felt the way they did about leaving there with our tail between our legs, defeated by some little horseshit country like that when, if we wanted, we could blow them right off the fuck'n map with just a couple of atomic bombs like we did so easy with Japan. Maybe like somebody suggested, we should just announce now that we *won* the war and then get the hell out of there.

"Right now," said Dave Newman, answering Big Ben's question, "I'm still calling it *Empty Hands*. But I'm trying to think of something less obvious.

Big Ben motioned to Mary Magdeline to bring another round of drinks and then asked again if Dave Newman had any chance of getting the play done at the Arena Theatre. The playwright shook his head. Big Ben had a good idea what it might be. But he wanted to hear what the playwright would say.

The playwright shrugged. The director there read the play and liked it. First play he's ever read about factory workers written from the inside. Real people instead of propaganda. That's what he said. A nice guy, liberal in politics, a homosexual but that's his business. (Every man to his own religion, said Mike.) He gave the play to Jamison Langner to read. Chairman of the board down there. And he told Jamison he thought doing the play would bring a whole new audience into their theatre. — Big Ben interrupted. What did Jamison say? — The playwright's lips twisted into a narrow grin. The director says Jamison Langner told him they can't risk the financial loss doing a new play by a complete unknown.

"Horseshit," said Big Ben, "that ain't it."

"What do you think it is?"

"You," said Big Ben, "they still got the gun out for you."

"I know," said Dave, showing his big teeth with a kind of forced laugh that made Big Ben momentarily feel sorry for him, — "I know, and my only chance of getting it done anywhere, I think, is to get some union to do it in their union hall. — What about you guys?"

That caught Big Ben flatfooted. He had been intending to tell Dave at the first opportunity about the rehearsal he'd seen at The Dance Center, to get his reaction. But now he thought that Dave was not the one to whom to mention anything like that to do with Jamison Langner. And he didn't think it would

be possible to do anything with the play, not with Baldy
George still the president in there. Baldy would scream. That
UE commy with his commy play, keep him out!

"Who'd act in it?" he asked Dave Newman.

"There are four characters. Get four people from the shop."

"Who'll direct it?"

"If I have to, I can do it. But it might be better to get
somebody else not connected with the old fight between the two
unions."

"Is the play political?"

The heads of the three men were close together as they tried
to separate themselves from the surrounding activity and noise.
Big Ben and Dave were seated in front of the bar. Mike was
standing back of the bar. And Mary Magdeline was standing
nearby, washing glasses and leaning their way, doing her best
to overhear the conversation. She had caught the word "play"
and that interested her. She knew Dave had become some kind
of a writer.

"Is it political?"

It was the playwright who repeated the question that had
been asked of him. He could answer that it *is* political,
everything is political, and that would be the end of it —
because Big Ben would say there was no chance to get the play
done. He did not want to lie to Ben.

"It's completely working class, if that's political," It was
deliberately evasive, and the other two men knew very well
that he was being evasive, guessed why, and allowed it to
remain at that. "I'm shooting to give a sense of pride in being
working-class and to develop in other people an understanding for
some poor bastard who's knocked himself out on a machine
all his life and now gets drunk because he doesn't have a
machine any more."

"That sounds like you're telling it like it is," said Mike.

"Would you like to read it?"

The question was addressed to Big Ben. — Yes. Why not?
Sure. Then he could talk it over with some people in the shop.
See if there's any interest in putting together something.
Maybe in the Labor Hall. Dave took out his pen and asked for
Big Ben's home address. He would drop off a copy of the play.
Big Ben glanced at Mary Magdeline, she was wiping glasses,
and listening. Drop it off here. Leave it with Mike.

"Dave," piped up Mary Magdeline, "are there any women in your play?"

"Not in this one."

"I thought maybe you'd let me star in it."

"You got star billing here behind the bar," said Mike. "Keep that good act going right here."

Mary Magdeline drew two glasses of beer and took them down to the far end of the bar and returned and rang up the money on the register and went back to rinsing glasses, as she looked over at Dave.

"Why don't you write a musical, Dave, with a dancing part for me?"

Do you dance?" asked Big Ben, picking up the cue.

And Mary Magdeline did a quick tap step behind the bar prompting Big Ben and some other men to applaud.

"Do it up there on the bar where we get a better look at the way those things bounce," lift operator Wayne Henderson down at the far end of the bar called out. Mary Magdeline tossed a withering smile in his direction.

"Watch the big mouth," Mike sharply warned, and there was a tense moment of quiet which Dave Newman eased by resuming the conversation with Mary Magdeline.

"We might work something in. *Empty Hands* is a one-act play. A couple dances and maybe a song before the play could fill out the evening."

"Set her dance numbers *after* the play," said Big Ben. "And nobody gets into the Labor Hall to see her dance unless he's already inside there watching the play."

Mary Magdeline threw him a smile of thanks for that. She wandered off and then returned, trying to remain in the conversation between Big Ben and the former union organizer. Mike Staruski served drinks for a while in her place. Dave Newman earnestly explained to Big Ben how he had come to his present view about theatre and working people, the need to utilize the theatre to help give working people a deeper insight into who they are in the existing social-historical complex that is our country and our world at this time. At one point Mary Magdeline shyly touched his forearm.

"This is the way you used to talk to Jim." She turned to Big Ben. "He talked to my father like this. I loved to listen. It was an education for me."

Big Ben had not known this side of Dave Newman before.
So far as he knew, except for the fact that Dave Newman had
acted at the Arena Theatre in *Hedda Gabler,* the man had been
a hardnosed union organizer interested primarily in union,
union, union — fighting grievances, getting the membership
involved in union activy, organizing the unorganized, talking
politics — a hardline, politically-oriented, Lefty union
organizer. It was as if this was another man here now when he
talked about theatre and its role in society — the need to
develop a vital theatre being contingent on finding an artistic
way to get the deep conflict between classes existing in the
basic structure of society onto the stage as it reveals itself in
the personal conflicts developing in the superstructure that
builds upon and interacts with that changing basic structure
as the world moves from one economic system of production
and distribution into another. The difference was evident.
There was a hardness there when he spoke about doing things
political, like when he spoke about this demonstration thing
against the war. But the minute he started talking about
writing and the theatre his voice changed, he seemed to think
more carefully, to speak more slowly, haltingly, feeling for the
words as if he wanted to be sure that in talking of artistic
things of that kind he was sure he was telling it with exact
truth as truthfully as he could dig into it and put it into words.
He apparently did not have many people to whom he could talk
this way and several times, embarrassed by how much he was
talking, he tried to break off the conversation. He had to go
home. His wife was expecting him.

And each time he tried to break away Big Ben ordered
another drink or threw in another question. And it was Mike
Staruski who yelled out to give him another drink and started
things going again on another round of drinks and talk when
the former union organizer pushed aside his stool and said he
definitely was going home now. No, Mike. — Sit down, you old
redhead, shut up and sit down and have a drink on me. —
During this brief argument Big Ben had a quick whispered
exchange with Mary Magdeline.

"How come you're putting in such a long day?"

"Some people I've got to see in the morning" — a soft,
intimate aside to Big Ben — "and I can't come in until late
tomorrow."

Mike Staruski won the argument with Dave Newman, and Big Ben had to wait for another chance to ask Mary Magdeline if he could drive her home. The actor and playwright eagerly picked up where he had left off. He didn't want to leave the impression he thought he might have given, from the questions asked, that there had to be a split between union activity and the arts. As he talked he was so absorbed in this effort that he missed the underlying byplay developing between the luscious redhead and the big man from the machine shop, both of them still seeming to be intensely interested in what he was saying. He misinterpreted their exchange of looks and smiles at the outset, as he told what it had been like when he had worked with the local union presidents to put out shop papers and to get people from the shop to write poems and short stories. But then he did catch their intense interest again, because telling about his experiences stirred up deep memories for him and colored his voice with an excitement that compelled their full attention. Mary Magdeline had to step away several times to serve drinks, but each time she quickly returned to listen to him talk. His excitement infected his listeners.

"A writing class, a labor writers' workshop, with people writing about their own experiences in the shop and at home and in the union hall. We mimeographed their poems and short stories and gave them out at the plant gates, like leaflets. That way the people took them in to work with them and they talked about them all day. And for stewards classes we wrote short dramatic sketches about grievances, writing the dialogue right into the middle of the confrontation between the steward and the foreman, breaking it off there, leaving it to the actors — the stewards themselves — to improvise the rest on their own. Some of them were born comedians. They had us laughing so hard we were literally rolling out of our seats."

It had happened before Big Ben was working over there, before the UE local moved into the Machinists Union. Big Ben shook his head. Sounds great. None of that over there now. — But Mike remembered. He was over there in the shop then. That show after the wage conference. In the ballroom at the Niagara Hotel. Tell him, Dave.

"Sunday afternoon. Delegates there from all our local unions in the area. Dry speeches and discussion from the floor all day about contract clauses. Then refreshments. Sandwiches and beer. And then entertainment." — (Listening, Big Ben tried to visualize the performance back then, trying to compare it with the dance performance he had seen with Betty Lyons, trying to measure the difference, why that one at the wage conference had affected the people there in a way he was quietly certain, not that he would ever say it directly to Betty Lyons or Jamison Langner, that it was very unlikely they would be affected by that thing at The Dance Center.) — "And then entertainment. One of the girls from the shop did a tap dance. Another girl sang a couple of songs. And some guy did an Irish jig. And they had their own orchestra. These were all people who worked in the shop. And then came two comedy sketches the stewards had worked out about some of the grievances in the shop. The best sketches that had been developed with improvisations in the stewards classes. — Christ, the people literally screamed with laughter. — One sketch was about a man who had been given a pink warning slip for spending too much time in the toilet and the other was about a man who had been laid off as the result of his own twenty-five dollar prize-winning suggestion on how to improve production efficiency in his department. The people made them do both comedy sketches all over again. Made them repeat them right then and there, both sketches. And the second time the people out in the audience, men and women out there, yelled out new lines for the actors to say, and the actors said them, and people from the audience ran up on stage and joined them in the act. — Talk about audience participation, I've never seen or heard anything like it. And when it was over the people talked about it, and talked about it, and talked about it, the loud chatter in the hall so loud you could hardly hear. They were so stirred up and so exhilarated they stayed there and drank beer and talked until past midnight, and when the hotel people kicked them out in the early morning they piled into cars and drove out to an all-night ginmill. They didn't want to let go! — It was as if they sensed that this was a high water mark they had touched, as if they sensed that it couldn't last, as if back then they saw into the future, how all the beautiful hope opening for them that night for a richer inner life, the beautiful possibility for a new dimension to be permanently added to their lives, was about to be wiped out, as it was during the immediate years ahead, their union to be attacked by the government, raided by other unions, destroyed as being too radical to be permitted to survive. They talked all night, trying to hold onto the feeling they had, and a lot of them didn't go to work all the next day, staying there all day in the ginmill, talking and talking and talking, not wanting to let go. It was a great experience for me. As long as I live I'll never forget it."

Listening, Big Ben was himself so caught up in the excitement created in the telling by the former union organizer that he had not noticed when Mary Magdeline on signal from Mike Staruski slipped away. She was already near the door, calling out good-night, with the cab driver waiting in the doorway, when he became aware she was leaving. Her sing-song *Good-night everybody* provoked a choral shout of *Good-night* back to her. She joined in the laughter that provoked.

"Don't forget to come back, dear," shouted someone.

"With bells on, honey," she flashed back over her shoulder, and she went through the door with an energetic tap dance step that provoked brief applause.

The door closed behind her and the lewd remarks were shouted after her, each sally producing another flurry of laughter. But with the star attraction gone the tavern quickly cleared.

"Drop the play off here with Mike and we'll see what we can do with it," said Big Ben, after tossing down the remains of his shot of whiskey and beer.

The playwright, face flushed and brain a little fuzzy from too much whiskey and beer and talk, put out his hand.

"Good-night, pal."

Chapter 10

While Big Ben, his bowling ball his excuse for being there, played the game with Mary Magdeline at Mike's Bar and spoke to Dave Newman about his play, three executives alighted from the company's private plane at Niagara airport. The driver, waiting with the company car, opened the door and the three men entered in order of rank, Jamison Langner first.

Early the next morning Big Ben and Queen Lila, walking from the parking lot to the long low brick building housing the machine shop, caught up with the night shift crane operator who had slipped out for a quick snooze in the back seat of his car. Walking with them along the towpath beside the creek, he told them that personnel man Dick Penfield and Tom Watson — the fuck'n assistant to the president — had been burning the midnight oil half the night with the Old Man in his office.

"The strike's still on down there in Virginia."

The sweeper came by Big Ben's machine early that afternoon. Questioned, he gave an up-to-date report.

"A big meeting getting underway in the conference room upstairs in the main building. The company car's bouncing up and back to the airport bringing the big boys in from all over the country."

Big Ben sent the sweeper back to take another look. He returned later and pushed his wide broom down the center aisle, pausing briefly beside Ben's machine.

"The Old Man's there at one end of the table with Tom Watson and Dick Penfield on each side of him and there's a whole bunch of big shots there."

He vigorously swept, pushing his broom ahead of him, moving out of the machine shop as foreman Casey approached with a stern look. Big Ben kept his eyes on the revolving drill biting its way into the big casting. The foreman returned to his desk up front.

During the smoke break the sweeper returned with his broom and reported to the pinochle players that while Dick Penfield seemed to be doing a lot of talking up there it looked like Tom Watson was chairing the meeting for the Old Man. Big Ben nodded, registering this latest battlefield communique, as he

144

dealt the cards. The sweeper pushed his broom out of the department after promising to be back with further reports.

While they violently slapped down their cards and scooped them up again, rapidly going through the deck, dealing and going through the deck again, and again, and again, the pinochle players argued about the relative status of Jamison Langner's two most immediate aides.

"During the second World War," said Big Ben, "that sonofabitch Watson was the Old Man's executive officer in the fuck'n artillery."

Queen Lila who had been watching and listening moved away and joined the other women. Not that she minded the language the men were using now, but she didn't feel it right for her to be the only woman there when that kind of language was being used. Big Ben went right on.

"The Old Man is Number One and Tom Watson's his fuck'n Number Two. Dick Penfield's a smarter bastard any time, but he has to eat Tom Watson's shit and smile and say it tastes good."

"He's a good-looking guy."

"Who?"

"Tom Watson."

"A fuck'n ass-licking piece of shit."

"He's got the women eating out of his hand."

"A fuck'n muff-driver. He eats it, the fuck'n bastard."

"You're jealous."

"Sure I am."

For the next minute or two Tom Watson was amiably and brutally dissected by the card players, each adding his little tidbit to what went before. "Without Jamison Langner he ain't nothing but shit." — "He lives there in that big fuck'n house in the country with the Old Man." — "The Old Man bought him that red fuck'n sports car." — "The stupid sonofabitch saved the Old Man's life during the war." — "He ran a fuck'n small shit of a grocery store up in Maine before he was drafted into the fuck'n army. His ex-wife still runs it." —"The lucky bastard tripped into a pile of fuck'n shit and come up with a shitpot full of roses." — "Jealous? You're fuck'n well right I'm jealous."

The card players then gave Dick Penfield his share of this same fond attention. — "Him? He's the worst shitty bastard they got up there. The sonofabitch, he's nothing but a born fuck'n strikebreaker." — "He was born in Macon, Georgia, the fuck'n asshole of the south where I did my fuck'n basic training as a fuck'n shitass buck private." — "No wonder he's such a fuck'n shit." — "They wouldn't let him into the damnyankee Institute of Technology up in Massachusetts to study engineering, not until the fuck'n sonofabitch learned how to wear shoes and put in for his fuck'n citizenship papers." — "That's how that bastard got promoted here. He used that fuck'n damnyankee engineering degree he stole up there." — "That's before you were here, Ben. The bastard was working here in engineering. We had a real bitch of a strike going here. The company wouldn't meet with Davey Newman on our fuck'n negotiation committee, not until he signed a fuck'n non-commy affidavit, and our union convention had gone on record instructing all officers and organizers to refuse to sign any of that fuck'n shit. We shut down all production. But the whole fuck'n office and engineering was going in." — "At the start we let 'em in, the bastards, and then we heard that some smartass sonofabitch by the name of Penfield took a bunch of engineers down into machine shop. They were running our fuck'n machines down there, doing our work. We got up a mass picket line next morning and kept them all out, office and engineering, everybody." — "Not for long." — "Dick Penfield the bastard went over to the police station and come back with a whole shitting army of cops. Nobody got really hurt. Only a few punches tossed, some sore ribs and a few shins kicked in, but they got in." — "He did it, broke the strike." — "Dave Newman said the committee should go in without him and talk to the company. They left Dave out and went in, and there he was, shit-eating Penfield, the fuck'n strikebreaking bastard, promoted on the spot, sitting across the table next to Tom Watson." — "Ever since then he's the shitty sonofabitch Jamison Langner sends in any time he needs somebody to be fuck'n tough and say no for the fuck'n company."

Up in the conference room on the second floor of the main building Jamison Langner sat stiffly in his armchair and watched and listened as his two subordinates conducted the meeting. He intended to say as little as possible now. He was still angry with himself for what he now thought was his mistake in meeting with and talking to the union committee down there in Virginia. Bad judgment on his own part. Now it's necessary to take firm action to regain the ground that's been lost. Employees at all levels throughout the corporation must be made to see that refusing a final offer brings them nothing but trouble.

Especially at this critical moment there must be resolute action taken or the forces already unloosed by the rejection of the final offer may endanger the safety of everybody on board the whole ship. He made his feelings clear to the two subordinates on his top management team in this same room during their long nighttime conference. As he expected, his personnel man Dick Penfield more than welcomed this hard approach. He jumped to agree. Rap their knuckles down there. Let them know they're due to pay a heavy price for rejecting the final offer. A good lesson not only for them down in Virginia but for our people right here. And throughout the rest of the plants. Treat it as an opportunity.

Tom Watson presented the plan to the enlarged management committee in the conference room. Jamison Langner's idea was to give them all a chance to discuss this approach. Let's find out right now what kind of men we've got out there running our plants. We need people with enough iron in their backbone to take this back and apply it in their own divisions. An opportunity here to separate the men from the boys in our own ranks.

They were plant managers, plant superintendents, and personnel men, and they were all dressed in business suits, ties neatly knotted, hair cut properly short and carefully combed, and they listened, without saying a word, waiting until they would be asked to speak. They all knew that what was being presented to them for their consideration already had the Old Man's approval, even though Tom Watson sincerely explained that this was a suggestion that came from the Number Three Man, Dick Penfield.

One by one Tom Watson polled them on the plan of action. Agree or disagree? No one disagreed.

Number Three vied with Number Two for Number One's approval.

Dick Penfield: "The union will undoubtedly file an unfair labor practice charge with the Labor Board. They'll make charges and countercharges. Wild statements to the press and hysterical leaflets. Believe nothing, say nothing, do nothing, unless you hear directly from us."

Tom Watson: "No matter what happens the Virginia facility is being closed out. That's all you know."

Dick Penfield: "Irrevocable."

Tom Watson (a disarming smile on his handsome face): "Anticipating your agreement Mr. Langner has already released a statement to the press which should be in the early afternoon edition down there and also up here, an announcement that all our real estate and buildings and machinery in Virginia are up for sale."

Dick Penfield: "Don't be surprised if you hear that some local businessmen and politicians down there decide to set up an impartial citizens committee to act in the situation."

Tom Watson: "You men just sit tight and wait and keep your eyes posted for trouble in your own locations."

Dick Penfield: "We're optimistic on the situation here. Closing Virginia keeps the work here and we're confident that within two weeks they'll be fighting one another here for overtime."

The meeting in the conference room was still in session when people reporting for work on the second shift brought in the early afternoon edition of the Niagara Daily News. Chief steward Don Mayer got hold of a copy and brought it to Big Ben. On the first page of the second edition, a box enclosed with thick black lines contained the statement released by Jamison J. Langner.

"Conditions beyond our control regretfully necessitate immediate and permanent shutdown of all our operations in Virginia. Our land and buildings and machinery will be sold."

It was near the end of the shift. Operators were already cleaning up. Heated shouting began. Foreman Casey left the department rather than admit his inability to keep the people quiet. The loudest loudmouths and hottest hotheads yelled back and forth across the rows of machines.

"No work here on anything moved back from Virginia." — "Get the president to call a special meeting and go on record." — "The hell with that, they took our work down there in Virginia, didn't they?"

"What does the constitution and by-laws provide?" a woman

yelled.

It was another woman who screamed back at her. "You know what you can do with that constitution and by-laws, where you can put it!"

And it was another woman who yelled, "Right up your ass!"

"Girls!" screamed Big Ben in a high-pitched voice.

"Well, if they want a special meeting," replied the woman who had yelled last, "let them get the twenty-five signatures required by the constitution and shut up."

The quitting buzzer rang. The people throughout the shop dropped all activity connected with putting away tools and cleaning around their machines and raced to punch out at the time clocks. No one stopped to draw up any petition or to go after signatures. Not then, or later.

After eating supper in the kitchen with Queen Lila and the children, Big Ben went into the front room to listen to the sports announcer on television and watch excerpts from the World Series game. It was the third game, won 5-0 by the New York Mets. He heard the news commentator report that as many as a million demonstrators were already pouring into Washington for the October 15th demonstration there against the war.

The phone rang in the kitchen. For you, Ben. Queen Lila passed the phone to him. One of your girlfriends wants to talk to Mister Hood.

"Hello." And he heard a woman say hello in return and he recognized her voice. "What's up?"

"I thought you might be interested in a conference they're having tomorrow afternoon at the Arena Theatre. They're kicking off the annual subscription drive and they're trying to reach out to a new audience. The main speaker will be Richard Becker. Have you heard of him?"

"No."

"A big shot in university theatre. He edits Modern Theatre. A very *avant garde* magazine. A controversial guy. It should be very interesting. Would you like to go?"

"When?"

"Tomorrow afternoon."

"I'm working."

"I explained to Mr. Langner that if you went you might be able to come up with some worthwhile ideas on building audience. He'll arrange for you to get off and still be paid."

"Great. What time does it start?"

"Four-thirty. Drinks and hors d'oeuvres."

"Do I have to wear a tuxedo?" He was only half-joking.

"Wear what you wore last time. That was fine."

"Okay."

"I'll pick you up at three o'clock in front of the main office building. We'll go in my car."

Queen Lila put the last of the dirty dishes quietly into the electric washer. The two girls, moving on tiptoes, finished straightening out the table and chairs. Big Ben hesitated only a moment before speaking into the phone.

"If I can leave the shop at two o'clock I'll have time to go home and shower and shave and change into my clothes and get back there to meet you."

"No problem. I'll pick you up at home. Where do you live?"

He kept his eyes on Queen Lila's averted face and said, "Back in front of the main office is okay."

He told Queen Lila it was some more of that theatre stuff that Jamison Langner was experimenting with, that the Old Man wanted him to look at something down at the Arena Theatre and he probably would not be home in time for supper the next day.

First thing next morning in the shop the grapevine had it. Big Ben's getting off early to go to a fancy fuck'n cocktail party today. Make sure you get all that grease out from under your claws, Ben. Spray your deodorant under your crotch. Hey, Ben, line up some of that fancy high society snatch for me. I hear that's great fucking, Ben. Tell the director you want to star in his next stag movie.

"You ignorant uncouth bastards, go fuck yourselves!"

During the first smoking break Big Ben sought out Queen Lila. You got a big mouth. A surprised look. Not from me. Big Ben passed the question from bench to bench and machine to machine. Within thirty minutes the grapevine brought the answer back to him. A young girl in payroll in the front office picked it up from a girlfriend in personnel and then she passed it on to her father, a maintenance electrician who freely moved around out in the factory.

Before noon the grapevine carried the word across the creek to Mike's Bar and at lunchtime, when Mike Staruski handed

Big Ben the play Dave Newman had left for him, Mary
Magdeline came hurrying over. We're not drinking that cheap
stuff today, not when we get fancy mixed cocktails free.
Replying to her in kind, Big Ben tried to keep his gaze up above
the cleft between her big breasts. Watch your language there.
She reached back for the whiskey bottle. He started for the
door. No time now.

Coming out of Mike's Bar, he looked across the creek.
Through the second floor windows of the administration
building they could see him. He stuffed the bound manuscript
inside his gray work shirt. Back inside the shop he stopped off
at his locker. He looked around. No one looking. He slipped the
play under the towel up on the shelf and slammed the metal
door shut and locked it. When he left the shop at two o'clock to
go home and change clothes the play was inside his work shirt.

In the bedroom in the cottage he only had time to flip
through the first few pages of the play. But even this quick
glance at the cleanly mimeographed lines of dialogue
impressed him.

Back to the first page. *All action takes place in a tavern
within sound of noises from the factory across the street.*
Mike's Bar? His heart beat faster in anticipation. Christ, he
wished he could read it now. But hardly enough time to shower
and shave and dress and get back there to meet Betty Lyons.
He slipped the play underneath his shirts in the dresser
drawer.

Betty Lyons tapped the horn as she drove her station wagon
across the bridge over the canal and saw him. Big Ben was
dressed in his Sunday best. His blue serge suit and white shirt
with soft collar and loosely knotted tie held in place by a gold
pin. His car was in the parking lot. He had told Lila not to take
it, to leave it for him for later. She'd have no trouble getting a
ride from someone else.

As he moved away from the brick wall of the administration
building toward the curb he waved goodbye to the office girls
sitting near the windows close by. They waved back. The
station wagon stopped in front of him. Big Ben reached for the
door handle, but Betty Lyons slid over toward him and cranked
down the window.

"You drive."

Disregarding the giggling office girls at the windows, trying to act as if this was nothing unusual, Big Ben circled behind the vehicle and came around and took his place at the wheel of the new station wagon. The car moved away from the factory.

Betty Lyons chattered lightly. "Sick and tired of driving. Nice to have someone else drive. Someone else take responsibility for dealing with traffic. Go straight ahead. I'll tell you when to turn."

Big Ben obeyed her directions. He sensed that his relationship with this woman was in process of changing and he was afraid he might say or do the wrong thing and spoil his chance. But he concealed his fear behind his silence. What did she expect of him? A woman. No different from any other woman. The best way was to treat a lady like a slut and a slut like a lady. He had read or heard that somewhere. But face to face now with this real *lady* lady he wondered. Would he ruin everything if he reached over and grabbed hold and said let's fuck? Or would he ruin everything if he gave in to his fear of her and did *not* reach over and grab hold and say let's fuck? He had to decide. He did not want to lose his chance here to get into the kind of life he wanted. His mind worked overtime on this, but in all his thinking, while silently driving to Arena Theatre, obeying directions, it never even once occurred to him, not even in fantasy, that he might be able to establish a relationship of any depth and permanence with her, so deep was the gulf he unconsciously placed between them.

In the large greenroom backstage at Arena Theatre the main speaker was introduced by the skinny executive director, and Big Ben rememberd that this was the homosexual guy that Dave Newman had mentioned to him back in Mike's Bar. He seemed to be all right, except he did seem to be hanging onto Richard Becker's elbow a little too long.

Richard Becker removed his dark glasses and said he could see better with them off but he liked his image better with them on. He put the dark glasses on and Big Ben, enviously aware that the speaker was about his own age and beautifully, though carelessly, dressed, refused to join in the burst of friendly laughter from the group gathered in the room.

"Written plays," proclaimed the speaker after a few introductory remarks, "are a thing of the past. They may still be performed but as some kind of historical thing. A written play cannot possibly reflect the chaotic complexity of our existential way of life in our modern world."

Big Ben squinted and thought it sounded like a lot of long-hair horseshit. But this guy should know what he's talking about. Silent, intensely interested, leaning forward in his seat, Big Ben listened to the speaker go on to describe a *happening* he had staged with students at the university where he taught in the Drama Department.

"Eight cameras projecting simultaneously on all four walls. Pictures and sound. Thousands of ping-pong balls. The walls alive with them. Crackling sounds. Wood paddles slapping against ping-pong balls. The din, the noise, rising, louder and louder, until it becomes almost unbearable. Then, unexpectedly, with no warning, dumped down on the heads of the audience below. *Ten full barrels of ping-pong balls!* Pandemonium. Shrieking and yelling. Everybody joining in. Throwing ping-pong balls at each other. Tossing them against the wall. Stepping on them. Cracking them flat. All spontaneous. A fresh dramatic experience for everyone there. Alongside that all written plays are stupidly dull and outmoded. From now on the playwright is outmoded. A thing of the past."

A hand raised from the front row. The speaker pointed. A tall beanpole awkwardly unfolded his body and rose to his feet. He stammered, as he probed.

"Theatre must have a social purpose of some kind, don't you think? What social purpose can there be in bombarding an audience with ping-pong balls?"

The speaker, as if touched on a sore spot, flared back, "You don't have to tell me the theatre must have a social purpose! Modern theatre must reflect the chaotic death struggle of capitalism! I'm a *socialist!*"

The beanpole, flattened into silence by the flushed speaker, folded his body down into the seat in the first row, and Big Ben, sitting next to Betty Lyons, wondered what special kind of radical this guy was that made him welcome here while Dave Newman said he was having trouble.

Richard Becker went on, disdainfully addressing himself directly to the beanpole. "We're taking this *happening* on tour to college campuses all across the country."

The beanpole, speaking as he rose, again unfolded. "Then you must have a written script describing what was done at the first performance, so it can be repeated. That means you have a play, and whoever wrote it is the playwright."

The speaker briefly gave that some thought, cocking his head to one side, and then testily conceded, "Once you write it down I suppose you could say we're on our way to having a play and possibly a playwright. So at each performance you have to find a way to renew the spontaneity. Otherwise those who saw it will tell it to those who've not yet seen it. And if you allow the critics in to write about it you kill it completely."

The beanpole, satisfied with the speaker's retreat, looked around, letting his gaunt face be seen, and then folded back down into his seat.

"Abe Lincoln," hissed Big Ben out of the side of his mouth.

Betty Lyons turned her head and made a face showing her distaste. "No relation to Abe Lincoln. Roy Gwylie, a spoiled overgrown brat with too much money."

They were seated in the last row. When they arrived Betty Lyons tried to get him to come with her to sit somewhere closer to the front. Big Ben hung back. You go up front. He sat down on the aisle seat in the last row. The program had not yet started. Betty Lyons said she had to say hello to Mrs. Chandler. She's in charge here. The Women's Committee. (Mrs. Harrison Chandler — Mrs. President of Niagara Trust Bank.) And Big Ben's face shows he is impressed in spite of himself.

She joins Mrs. Chandler up front. Big Ben can see the two of them, politely chatting. Her eyes meet his. She is watching him, looking back across the rows of folding chairs. There are about fifty people seated, most of them women, including three nuns wearing long black habits. Only seven men. By his dress and manner, the whole look of him, Big Ben stands out from the others. She wonders if he feels ill at ease here. Normally he would still be working back at the factory now. She tries to read the meaning of the smile set on his face. He looks like he can take care of himself. She sees that the women nearby are aware of him and she wonders if Big Ben is giving all of them the once-over so openly in order to impress her with his sexuality. Ending her meaningless chat with Mrs. Chandler she goes back to join Big Ben.

"Back here is fine."

Richard Becker, continuing his lecture, makes Big Ben feel very ignorant as he goes on from talking about *happenings* to touch on the experimental work being done by Cafe La Mama, by The Living Theatre, by The Theatre of Cruelty, by the Theatre of the Ridiculous — very rapidly sketching in different directions modern theatre is taking as part of what he labels as Theatre of the Absurd. The language he freely uses surprises Big Ben. The four-letter words pour out in one sentence after another, not quite as freely as they do in the shop or in the ginmill when factory guys get together. But in this place it seems to be even more freely, because this is not the place where Big Ben expects to hear this kind of language. And in this he is not alone. One of the nuns raises her hand. Richard Becker stops speaking and points, recognizing her.

The nun has swallowed *shit* after *shit* after *shit*. But *fuck* is just too much for her. A thin woman, tight-faced, she's about fifty, or maybe younger.

"You may feel it necessary to use four letter words to express yourself. But there are some of us here who find this offensive."

Shocked silence during the moment it takes Richard Becker to recover from this unexpected criticism. He flushes and then angrily retorts.

"This is good Anglo-Saxon language."

The nun firmly replies, "But this is not the place to use it."

Richard Becker looks around for support, but finds none. No one else is ready to agree or disagree. All eyes on him, waiting for his reply. Not apologizing, he speaks directly to the nun.

"We're here to talk about creating the theatre of today! If you want to suppress the language people actually use in real life then you don't belong here."

The nun reddens and sits. Big Ben leans toward his companion. A hissed whisper. "He's a rough sonofabitch." Then he adds, to prove his own integrity, "But I agree with the fuck'n bastard." He is pleased when Betty Lyons, looking straight ahead, pressing her lips together, smiles and firmly nods.

Down in the front row the skinny beanpole slowly unfolds upward. A thin voice emerges. Pronunciation slow and precise. Occasional taut pauses, a struggle for the right word.

Big Ben suddenly catches on. He stutters! Betty Lyons brings her mouth close to his ear. He's afraid he *might* stutter.

Beanpole speaks slowly, intensely shaping each word. "This is not — the New York — scene. You have to give these people — time — to catch on and develop — and to — understand —

these new trends."

But the speaker, offended, angrily snaps, "Something of this kind, the inherent sensibility and emotional equipment, the sensitivity to know instinctively what is honest and what is dishonest in art, in theatre! You can't cultivate that kind of understanding! Either you have it, you're born with it, or too bad, you just don't have it!"

At this point Big Ben, sneaking his hand over to where it rests against his companion's thigh, is glad to hear Abe Lincoln tell the speaker that this is about the most stupid remark he has ever heard. He gradually increases the pressure of his hand against the firm thigh, while Richard Becker, flushed again, launches into a tirade aimed at the beanpole. (These fucking establishment people are so full of shit with their Vietnam War and their racism they can't adjust to the new society being created by the students and the Blacks.) Some snickers from the audience, while Betty Lyons shifts away and Big Ben's hand follows her. Her hand blocks his. Both look straight ahead, listening to the heated exchange cool off and then die of repetition. Big Ben slips his hand under hers, palm against palm. Their eyes meet. Her feelings are masked off from him. But he holds the stare and it is she who looks away. And though she does not try to disengage her hand from his tight clasp he worries now about where he stands with her. She makes no effort to pull her hand free until the session ends and then she firmly withdraws it from his grasp. He rises from the seat with her.

"We can stay here for cocktails and talk," she says, turning to him, still masking her feelings behind her regular features. "Or if you prefer we can drive out to Jamison Langner's place in the country. He's giving a party tonight. Good food and good booze. And he said he'll be anxious to talk to you to get your reaction to this."

"I'll take the ride out into the country."

Having gone this far with her he has to make the crucial move. He dreads it, fears what it might do to his hopes. But there is nothing else to do now except to make it or break it. There is no joy in the challenge lying ahead. He feels absolutely miserable and there is no escape.

They have over an hour, she tells him, before it will be time to start a leisurely drive out to Jamison Langner's home. Do

you want to go out and get some fresh air? Or do you want to
stay and drink? He has the fleeting thought that it might be
interesting to walk over to city hall and get a look to see how
many people are demonstrating in the candlelight vigil against
the war over there. Not dark enough yet for the candles. Maybe
see Dave Newman there. But he doesn't know how Betty Lyons
feels about the war. He self-consciously takes light hold of her
elbow, barely touching her, as they emerge onto Main Street
and begin their walk, going in the direction opposite to that
which would bring them closer to city hall.

"Who's the skinny guy who took him on back there?"

Before replying Betty Lyons reaches over with her free hand
and takes Big Ben's arm and pulls it through hers so their
arms are firmly linked.

"That's Roy Gwylie. We may see him later at the party. He
was an actor in New York for a long while and then he came
home to start his own theatre here. He set up his own group
and he teaches acting and he directs. He's got money."

"That helps."

"His father went to work years ago at the Buren Hosiery
and Knitting Mills in Falls City and he worked his way up into
management and finally made it as president of the whole
corporation. He built it into a world-wide outfit. And when he
died a few years ago he left Roy and his brother and sister a
bundle tied up in a foundation to cheat the government out of
taxes. Roy and his brother and sister are officers of the
foundation and they're paid to spend money to encourage the
arts. They do a good job encouraging themselves, setting up
their own little non-profit entities to request money from the
foundation. They run a theatre, an art school, and other
miscellaneous artsy-craftsy ventures. Very cozy, and very
legitimate. And, I suppose, it does some good."

"Lucky bastard."

"No talent. Lots of money, but no talent."

"I'll trade."

Betty Lyons presses his arm more firmly against her. "Don't
you trade anything. You've got what he'll never have. You'll do
fine on your own."

Big Ben wants to ask what he has, but he is afraid to make
any waves that might disturb the calm.

It is already dark when they leave the city and start out into the country. Big Ben is at the wheel of the station wagon. They drive about twenty minutes in comparative silence, while Big Ben, his face wearing a worried expression, keeps glancing over at his companion. She seems completely relaxed, speaking only to give direction.

There are very few houses along the road now. And not many lights. Traffic thins out.

"Okay." Big Ben speaks to himself, lifting his foot off the gas pedal as he sees a road ahead that branches off to the right. It has to be done. If it works out, he is in all the way. If it doesn't work out, then the hell with it, nothing ventured nothing gained.

The station wagon slows and turns onto a paved side road, and then a few minutes later turns off onto a dirt road. Big Ben is alert for a protest. He has turned without any direction given by her. But she remains silent. Encouraged, he parks the station wagon in dark shadows between two trees. He switches off the motor and the lights. Not a word from his companion. Her face is still turned to the front as he sits looking at her. Her regular features mask her feelings from him.

It is a difficult decision to make, with no joy in it. He shifts his body over next to her and touches her shoulder. Tense. No other outward reaction. Still looking straight ahead. Nothing to indicate her feelings. He reaches under her dress and touches her. No movement and no change in her expression. He reaches higher. No underpants. And still no reaction from her. He goes on, apprehensive, expecting a verbal cut from her that will destroy him, but still advancing, step by step, stopping after each small move to give her the chance to react and let him know how she feels about it. But there is nothing to encourage or discourage him except that this nothing compels him to go on, while still suspecting it may flare into a trap that will blow up everything. It is like fucking a statue.

Later, still without a word having been spoken between them since he turned off the main highway, he straightens up behind the wheel and adjusts his clothing. She makes one gesture, a swift movement pushing down her skirt. Nothing else. He doesn't know what to say, so he says nothing. He starts the motor, backs the car onto the road, and turns back to the main highway.

"Turn right?"

She does not answer. The station wagon turns right. No
protest from her. He's sure now that he has ruined his chances
and she is trying to think of the best way to get rid of him.
She'll do it when they get to Jamison Langner's place, and if
she does, then fuck her, the hell with it. He is prepared for a
scene of painful humiliation in the presence of the Old Man. He
is not even certain that she had an orgasm. At one point he
thought something was happening there, but now he wonders.
They drive for several miles in silence. Then he hears a throaty
chuckle and he is not sure what it means.

Chapter 11

Big Ben was impressed, completely awed, by Jamison Langner's big, white, two-storied, wood frame, Colonial-style house. It was set in the middle of an open expanse of green lawn surrounded by thick woods, with a driveway leading from the main road to the clearing on top of a knoll. With its white pillars in front, the house reminded him of something he had seen in the movies. Later, inside, on the second floor, he had his chance to look through the windows and even though it was nighttime he could see for miles out over the countryside. What a sight!

A manservant wearing a dark suit and a black tie opened the door and admitted them into the foyer. Big Ben heard music. An orchestra. Dancing. He turned to Betty Lyons.

"Sounds like a mob in there."

She only smiled, and she turned back to the waiting manservant. "We'll just wander."

The manservant left them. Big Ben looked to his companion for guidance. What was going on behind those small, fine, regular features in which he could read nothing? He was acutely aware that except to give him the minimum directions she had not spoken to him since he had pulled the station wagon off the highway and parked it under the trees on the side road.

"Are you hungry?" she asked.

"I'm starved," he said, with anxious eagerness, hoping this meant forgiveness.

"So am I," she said.

She led him into the large dining room where food was set out on silver platters on a long table. At the far end of the room a bartender in a bright red vest was handing drinks across a makeshift bar. The room was filled with knots of people, eating and drinking and talking.

Big Ben fell behind as Betty Lyons moved toward the table. She glanced over her shoulder, stopped, and waited for him. She looked into his face and took his hand and squeezed it. Are you all right? Big Ben nodded. She put her lips near his ear. Don't be intimidated, they're all stuffed shirts, Jamison does

160

this once a year to clean up his social obligations. Holding his hand, she led him to a spot near the table.

"I'll fix a plate for you." She returned shortly with two plates of food and gave Big Ben one.

"Thank you." She still puzzled him but his confidence was beginning to return. He greedily stuffed the delicious food into his mouth and he didn't seem to care how his tremendous bites and bulging cheek might look to others in the room. He hoped that she had decided to simply pass by without comment what had happened in the station wagon.

Then he saw the gaunt beanpole standing alone, holding a plate piled with food, also stuffing his mouth with hoggish delight. He turned to Betty Lyons.

"Ain't that him?"

"Roy Gwylie."

"Do you know him?"

"Not really."

"I'd like to meet him."

"Introduce yourself."

"Just like that?"

"Why not?"

Betty Lyons followed Big Ben as he walked around the end of the table to the other side of the room and stopped in front of the beanpole.

"We heard you tell off that joker with his ping-pong balls," said Big Ben. "Good job."

The beanpole did stutter a little. Thanks. What's your name? Big Ben stuck out his hand. Ben Hood. And this is Betty Lyons. The beanpole shook hands and bent his head. Roy Gwylie.

"Ping-pong balls," said Big Ben, "Jesus!"

"Are you connected with the theatre?"

"Nothing but audience."

"Without audience there's no theatre."

The beanpole welcomed his allies. He talked about Richard Becker and his *happenings,* and repeated his view that *happenings* inevitably develop into written plays. "And usually, after the surprise of the first presentation, *bad* plays."

"I know nothing about it," said Big Ben, "but I think you're right."

"How did you happen to be there this afternoon?" asked the

beanpole.

Big Ben asked Betty Lyons if it was alright to tell the beanpole. She shrugged. Why not?

"The truth is that I work in the machine shop out at Jamison Langner's factory. He's got some bug in his ear about getting working people involved in his theatre stuff. Betty here is his secretary at The Dance Center. She brought me there this afternoon. They think maybe on the same stupid level like the rest of the people in the shop I might come up with some idea on how to get them to come and take a look at a long-hair play."

Roy Gwylie nodded in a way that indicated strong interest. He spoke, starting stiffly, with difficulty shaping the words. "To get working people to come to the theatre — you — have to do — plays that relate to their lives. Do something —something important enough — and close enough — to a factory man and woman — to pull them away — from a television set."

"Where do you get plays like that?" asked Betty Lyons, as if what the beanpole had said was intended to be critical of Jamison Langner.

"Oh, there's a — playwright — in town — who writes that kind of stuff. He used to work in a factory — and then he was a — a union organizer."

"Who's that?"

"Dave Newman. Do you know him?"

"No." said Betty Lyons.

Big Ben silently hoped he would not be asked if he knew the former union organizer. Fortunately, the beanpole was more interested in the fun he was going to have with Betty Lyons.

"Dave Newman," he said to her, and then, enjoying the subtle needling, he added "he's a communist."

Betty Lyons' voice took on an acidly sweet tone. "A play about communism — great."

"*Empty Hands,* a play he wrote about factory workers and automation. Very human and very timely." The beanpole, talking seriously now, did not stutter or falter. "In a year or two when we get more firmly established we might do it in our place."

Recalling now that this was the same play that Leonard Something-or-other was supposed to have done at the coffee house he abandoned to take over as director of Comus, Betty

Lyons felt the need to defend her boss's leading role in community theatre and the related arts. She instinctively sensed that doing a play of this kind *might* reach out and pull into Roy Gwylie's theatre the very audience Jamison Langner was most concerned about. And with the wrong kind of play. She knew Jamison Langner's concern, that with the terrible restlessness developing in the country, automation and factory shutdowns and job layoffs and unemployment, and along with that the anti-war demonstrations getting out of hand and the Blacks angry and wanting jobs and equality NOW — it was important to engage the attention of the working people, the country's work force and to keep them away from ideas which they would not see in their proper perspective. She sharply questioned the beanpole and learned from him that he was looking for a vacant, small movie house he could convert into a legitimate theatre.

"Are you planning to have a permanent acting company?"

"Maybe."

"An Equity company?" She turned and explained to Big Ben, "That means they'd all belong to the actors union. Professionals." Big Ben nodded. His mind was racing.

The beanpole answered her, still enjoying himself, knowing he was shaking her up. "A nucleus of Equity actors from New York and Toronto to play the leads, and cast the rest locally."

"That's the present policy at the Arena Theatre."

"I know. Competition, it'll be good for them."

"It might kill everything." Betty Lyons was annoyed with the beanpole's offhand manner. "You're going to do a radical play written by a communist. And then what other plays will you do?"

Big Ben, keeping himself out of the developing duel, listened, putting things together. He really enjoyed hearing this kind of talk. And Dave Newman's involvement made it more dangerously enjoyable.

Beanpole and Betty Lyons seemed to agree that the restlessness developing among working people had to be recognized and channeled properly or it could get out of hand. Beanpole was strong for bringing the fights off the streets onto the stage, as was already being done with Black theatre. But Betty Lyons just as strongly opposed that kind of theatre which is primarily concerned with giving a message. It underestimates the potential of working people. They can be trained to enjoy the same kind of theatre enjoyed by people in the upper classes. Both cited examples of plays and directors and theatres to back up their arguments.

While the other two ranged far and wide, verbally fencing, Big Ben kept jabbing his fork into the delicious food on his plate, stuffing his face. His inner voice kept up a running commentary to himself, related to what he was hearing from the two duelists. Money, it takes money and the free time you buy with money to accumulate all this they know about plays, actors, kinds of staging and direction, and about playwrights, and different styles of playwriting. Just to see all the plays they mention must have cost them a fuck'n fortune. And the fare to go back and forth to New York every damn time they go there to see plays. How can a working stiff make it, competing with them? A head start, they know so fuck'n much already about every goddam thing about the whole fuck'n theatre. Shit, what chance does a guy have who has to bust his balls every day all day in the shop? Jesus Christ, listen to them go. Sophocles and Shakespeare — Nietzsche and Kierkegaard and Tolstoy — Chekhov, Ibsen, — Goethe — Balzac, Stendhal, Scott — the Frenchman Moliere and the Englishman G. B Shaw. Aah, shit. And there's Americans Eugene O'Neill and Arthur Miller. And Brecht the German red. Go red up your ass. Christ, it'll take a whole lifetime to learn what the fuck these sonofabitches already know without hardly trying. Lucky fuck'n bastards. Shit on them both.

Cleaning his plate, leaving nothing that could be speared or shoveled up with his fork, he listened, still fascinated, as the other two argued on, now on the subject of the responsibility of community theatres. Should they do bad plays written by local playwrights, however sincerely written, in order to help them learn how to write good plays? He agreed with the beanpole. Yes. From Betty Lyons an emphatic no. Then into an argument over the relationship between the play and dance and lighting and music. How much can a director pile on without burying the basic idea of the play, destroying its heart?

"What's more important?" demanded Betty Lyons, with a fire Big Ben had not suspected in her, a strong feeling for something, a trait he instinctively respected whenever he

encountered it. "What's more important, some nice intellectual
theme in a play badly written and badly staged? Or to hell
with being intellectual if by use of all available techniques,
with good, clever, highly professional craftsmanship, with
dance, lighting and music, with brilliant direction, you hold the
interest of your audience and make them think there's
something damn important up there on the stage even if there
really isn't? As long as they're entertained! Showmanship! —
Craftsmanship! — Art! — The highest form of entertainment!"

As the beanpole leaned forward and earnestly answered her,
ticking off his arguments on his fingers, Big Ben reached over
the back of a chair and put his empty plate down on an end
table. He now felt stupid and out of place and awkward. And
dumb. Ignorant as all hell. Listening, feeling incapable of
saying anything that could fit into the high level of significant
opinions so confidently exchanged between the two ardent
debaters, he kept his shit-eating smile hanging on his face. His
heart became heavier and heavier, and the stiff smile became
even more set, as the other two criss-crossed opinions, touching
some of the things mentioned by Richard Becker earlier and
expanding beyond those — Theatre of the Absurd, the *avante
garde,* Theatre of Cruelty, Theatre of Ideas, mime, improvs,
Second City — the two of them tossing off one famous
director's name after another to exemplify different styles of
direction which the other knew that name represented without
any elaborate explanation, and both reeling off names of
producers and plays and playwrights and actors. Names,
names, names. Each standing for something significant in
relation to theatre, to styles and content. And he was lost,
didn't know what the hell they were talking about. You lucky
bastards, you don't know how fuck'n lucky you are.

"True," said the beanpole, breaking into Big Ben's private
thoughts by reaching and gripping his forearm to bring him
into the argument, asking his support, "Dave Newman is
probably a communist in his politics. Maybe as a writer he
even has communist ideas in his head he thinks he's
expressing. But I read his play *Empty Hands* from beginning
to end twice, and I can't find anything in it I'd call communist.
I'm a capitalist, and I read the play, and to me it's a human
play about human beings, and it fully engages my sympathies.
So it should be done, it should be seen."

Big Ben wondered how they had come back to Dave Newman. He had been so lost in his own thoughts he had stopped listening for a few moments. Now he alerted himself. He was not going to trip into a situation where he had to say he knew Dave Newman. Maybe he'd work that in later, after he had some better idea on where this was all going. He kept his expression vacant, as Betty Lyons, vying with the beanpole to get his support, looked directly into his eyes.

"Do you think a community theatre should do a play written by someone like that, even if this one play itself is not communist?"

Not a flicker of agreement or disagreement from Big Ben. Neutral, fuck you, neutral. The set smile hung on his face, motionless. Only his eyes moved. To the beanpole. Your turn. The beanpole spoke.

"Your Arena Theatre did a play by Berthold Brecht, an avowed card-carrying communist."

"That's different."

"Why?"

"A red writer, but in East Germany, not a traitor in our own midst, in our own living room, in our own kitchen."

"One of our own, a member of our own family, a writer in our own house, right here, let's be as nice to him as we are to a total stranger, a communist stranger." The beanpole turned to Big Ben for agreement. "Don't you think so?"

It was a direct appeal, hard to refuse, but the smile set in front of Big Ben's face only stretched a fraction wider. Ask me no fuck'n questions and I'll tell you no fuck'n lies.

"Much more dangerous," insisted Betty Lyons, jumping into the moment of silence. "This one's here to follow up his play with his own communist presence. The play opens the way for him. The less communist his play is the more dangerous it is because the more likely it is that it will make a good firm sounding board for him to speak from later as a political communist."

Big Ben, thinking of the copy of *Empty Hands* back there under the shirts in the dresser drawer, turned his smile to the beanpole and back again to Betty Lyons. Nothing either of you two fuck'n smartasses say is going to make me open up my fuck'n mouth.

"Before you do anything with that play," said Betty Lyons,

"I would talk to Jamison Langner."

Startled a moment, thinking Betty Lyons was talking to him, Big Ben was glad to hear the reply come from the beanpole.

"Why do I have to talk to him?"

"A matter of courtesy!" Her face reddened. "No one else in this community has done more to encourage the arts. Before doing anything that might undermine what he's done you owe it to him to talk to him."

"Competition," drawled the beanpole. "Isn't that what makes this country great?" This, said directly into Big Ben's face, produced no change there.

Betty Lyons took Big Ben's arm. Excuse us, coldly tossed at the beanpole. Leading Big Ben out of the room, rubbing shoulders with him. Upstairs, let Jamison Langner know we're here. Big Ben, relieved at leaving behind the talk about Dave Newman and his play, dropped the set smile from in front of his face. Race you up the stairs. She did not let go of his arm. Together they scampered rapidly up the carpeted flight of steps, Big Ben's laughing bringing its echo from her.

The ballroom, its hardwood floor polished to a shine, seemed enormous. Except in the movies he had never seen anything like this in a private house. More space here than in the big room the local union met in over at the Labor Hall, even when they cleared away the folding chairs there for wedding parties and dances.

He squeezed Betty Lyons' hand. Christ, look at that.

The high ceiling was clogged with hundreds of toy balloons, all bright colors, layers of them bobbling about up there, covering all the ceiling area above the two tremendous chandeliers made up of glinting cutglass. A balloon vendor, his gas tank set up in the far corner of the ballroom, was blowing up balloons and tying them off with string as fast as he could, passing the end of each string to the nearest outstretched hand of a guest, and when no hand quickly grabbed hold of the string he let it go, the balloon rising to join its fellows overhead. Playful adults were touching cigarettes to the swollen blobs of color held by others, the loud plops almost completely drowned out by the loud chatter from the many guests and the dance music provided by the five piece orchestra. The balloon vendor, skilled at his trade, had an audience. He blew up balloons much faster than the guests were exploding them.

Betty Lyons worked her way over to the vendor and returned with two red balloons, passing one of the strings to Big Ben. One for itty bitty girl and one for itty bitty boy.

She skipped across the polished floor in the corner, jerking at the string to make the balloon bob up and down, and then she turned and skipped back to Big Ben. He shoved his red balloon inside the front of his jacket and reached for hers. She slapped his hand. Don't be vulgar. But she was laughing. Then she stopped laughing and reached to pull the balloon out from under Big Ben's jacket. Here comes Jamison Langner.

"Hello."

Jamison Langner had seen what Big Ben had been doing with the toy balloon. The thought flashed through his head that it might be better not to talk to him now. But then he saw that Betty Lyons had seen him. Nothing to do but say hello. Having delivered his warm greeting, he stood there, gripping his hands together. Too late he decided he never should have asked Betty Lyons to bring a man from the shop to something like this. He's not ready. Tomorrow morning, inevitable, he'll sit in the smoking area in the machine shop, enjoying his role as the center of attraction, telling dirty stories about the conspicuous consumption here, jokes about the rich boss thinking up ways to spend the money you stupid bastards make for him with the sweat off your balls. And he'd say it much more vulgarly than that. Jamison Langner occasionally read the verbatim quotes reported by security in the shop. The language used out there by some men and even by some women could curl your hair.

He could imagine how Big Ben would be talking next morning. And the people he works with will pick up what he says and embellish it, telling about this big house, the ballroom, the balloons, the dance orchestra, the guests, especially those in evening dress, even more especially the flambuoyant garb of the two willowy homosexual partners showing off with their dancing out there now. Big Ben sees them and he's marking them down for some filthy jokes in the shop in the morning.

In that brief moment of quick exchange of smiles and greetings Jamison Langner saw his home and his gathering of guests through the eyes of one of his own factory workers and it was a thought too unsettling for him to linger over it.

"The balloons cost nothing, only a few dollars a thousand and minimum wage to the man blowing them up."

He had not intended to apologize this way for spending his own money as he wished, but as he heard what he had said he realized that is what he had done — and he blamed the slip on his generally disturbed feeling connected with the news reports. Anywhere from 500,000 to over a million people converging on Washington, marching against the war. That kind of unrest was not something you could turn off like a faucet once the war was ended. The longer this went on, the more necessary it would be to get something going to get away from making it so easy to bring people out into the streets for direct confrontations of this kind.

He smiled at Big Ben, thinking it would be a waste of time to give explanations about what was going on. No matter what he said now it would be translated tomorrow into colorful shop language. Two bars, one on each floor — that's the way he'll tell it in the shop tomorrow. Two bars loaded with booze, and bartenders wearing fancy red vests, maids in black and white uniforms. — ("Two fuck'n bars loaded to shit with booze, and bartenders, the sonsofabitches wearing fancy fuck'n red vests, and some fuck'n maids in fuck'n black and white fuck'n uniforms with little white aprons covering their snatch.") — Ben might even know some of the extra people working here tonight. Some might even be here from the machine shop at the factory, moonlighting on second front jobs.

In another unsettling flash of insight Jamison Langner wondered if he was surrounded, the enemy having infiltrated his camp, reporting back to the people in their own camp.

Too late to do anything now but welcome Big Ben. Maybe take him around and help him to feel at home and enjoy himself, so at least he reports back to the people in his camp that the boss is a regular guy even though he's a rich sonofabitch who's pissing away the money he squeezed out of the sweat off the balls of you stupid monkeys. But if he introduces Ben around indiscriminately there are some people here who, when they recognize his social unsureness, might try to bait him and have fun by making a fool out of him. That would be risky. If he catches on that one of our clever beautiful people is making an ass out of him he might haul off and throw a punch. Worse, he might start to throw a punch and before it lands on the target he himself might be flattened by someone like the skinny half of that willowy couple on the dance floor who happens to be an expert boxer.

"Tell me, Ben," said Jamison Langner, his voice coming out warm and sincere as he smiled, "how was it there at the Arena Theatre — did you enjoy yourself?"

Answering for Big Ben, Betty Lyons chit-chatted an unfavorable report on Richard Becker, punctuated by nods of agreement from her companion.

And Jamison Langner then sounded like he was taking Big Ben into his confidence. "Not exactly the kind of man for us to invite to give a lecture to our people out there in our plant cafeteria."

It was said so directly to Big Ben he was forced to grin and give a reply.

"He might start out with a big audience, but he'd end up awful lonely."

Big Ben's easy humor made Jamison Langner feel a little more relaxed. "That dress rehearsal you went to with Betty, the dance program at Comus, how much interest do you think there would be if we were to present a sample of that in our cafeteria out at the plant?"

"I don't know."

"Given a taste of that, free of charge, on each shift during lunch period, do you think any of our people would buy tickets to bring their families to a Sunday night performance over in the theatre at Comus?"

"Some might," said Big Ben. "The only way to find out is to try it."

At that moment Jamison Langner abruptly reached out and grabbed the arm of a man passing by.

"Dr. Tanner."

"Hel-*lo!*"

The man was dressed like a fop, his clothes highly styled, and Big Ben thought he moved his long, thin arms and legs a little too gracefully for a man. Jamison Langner pulled him over and introduced him.

"*Professor* Tanner — he teaches at the university."

"This year I'm not teaching," Dr. Tanner pleasantly

corrected him, speaking with a tone of voice and clipped diction
that made Big Ben wonder even more about him.

"Oh, yes, this year he's acting chairman of the Music
Department. Normally he teaches in the English Department.
His speciality is James Joyce. But right now he's one of our
most distinguished directors on the board of our theatre at
Comus."

"Not," said Dr. Tanner with a slight laugh to round off the
sharp edge, "that I have much to say there. More important,
that you or any of your associates pay any attention to
whatever I do say." He turned to Big Ben and Betty Lyons.
"Window dressing to give the appearance of democracy, that's
my role there."

Big Ben could not figure the man out. He dressed like one of
Jamison Langner's beautiful people and he spoke with an
exaggerated diction that sounded like someone imitating an
English accent. His voice was pitched high like a fairy. But his
wife joined him right after he had been grabbed by Jamison
Langner, and Dr. Tanner affectionately gripped her hand and
held her to him while he introduced her.

"An unusual combination," said Jamison Langner,
answering the question he assumed might be there in the
minds of Dr. Tanner and his wife. He was referring to Big Ben,
explaining his presence there at the party. "One of our skilled
machinists at the factory who's interested in the theatre, a very
unusual guy."

"Unusual only here in our backward country," said Dr.
Tanner, grasping Big Ben's hand warmly. "In most of Europe
the factory people are a basic part of audience in the theatre.
In the Soviet Union and Eastern Europe they are most of the
audience."

Jamison Langner made a quick defensive thrust to parry Dr.
Tanner's statement before it might influence Big Ben in a
radical direction. "But what great plays have they written
there with their proletarian dictatorships?"

"Beside the point."

"The central point."

Dr. Tanner continued, unperturbed. "Have you ever asked
yourself why we can't get our working class from the factories
and the stores and the offices to fill our legitimate theatres?"

"We're filling our Arena Theatre almost to capacity every

Friday and Saturday performance."

"With pretentious snobs who delude themselves into thinking they like the plays you're doing there because they think this marks them off as being aesthetic and superior to others. Any real basic working class people you do lure into your place, with few exceptions, are ashamed to be identified as working class. They go there to your theatre, not to enjoy the plays, but to do something they think raises them above their own class and separates them from it."

Jamison Langner took the opportunity presented to him to undermine the influence the professor might be having on Big Ben. "That's what he thinks of you, Ben."

But Dr. Tanner did not allow himself to be sidetracked from keeping after the main target. And Big Ben, listening to him, surmised that the professor was a good agitator. The way the professor said sharp things with a sweet smile aroused both appreciation and envy in him. When you can handle yourself like Dr. Tanner you can say things you otherwise could never dream of saying to someone as important as Jamison Langner. The professor, told that Big Ben had seen a dress rehearsal performed by the dance company at Comus, congratulated him on his interest, but immediately turned back again to the main target, Jamison Langner.

"The company's dancing is very competent, occasionally even exciting. But the material they're doing is not sufficiently relevant to factory people to get them to pass up a bowling game or a hockey match or a chance to hunt or fish. The weak stuff you're doing there now can't even pull them away from their church suppers." Then, after a quick grin aside to his wife, he said to his host, "Of course, dear sir, if they're still going to church suppers and to bingo games you don't need to lure them into your theatre. The minister and the priest are doing the job for you. It's only when they start turning their backs to the strawberry festivals on the church's green lawn and the bingo games in the church's damp basement that you start to worry. That's when you want them to come to Comus to watch a dance performance instead of getting themselves involved in something you think might lift their level of working class consciousness. The age-old principle of the safety valve."

It came as a real shock to Big Ben that these people knew so very clearly what they were doing. The safety-valve principle. Jesus, we're so fuck'n ignorant, we stupid bastards. He was thinking of himself and the people he worked with.

Dr. Tanner put his arm around his pretty wife's waist and continued, smiling pleasantly at Jamison Langner, obviously enjoying the game he was playing for the benefit of the only representative of the factory working class present.

"Of course, you're still doing fine with your football. Your baseball is a little shaky except for your World Series, but it might come back. And you've got basketball. And your hockey is coming in strong. And to take care of Sundays for those with children you provide your zoo — charging the suckers a small fee. And there's your parks for picnics. And to take up the slack in the factory districts and working class neighborhoods — to fill up those empty evenings and week-ends — and afternoons and mornings for your shift workers — you've got at least one saloon on every block in the heart of the working class neighborhoods. — But we must look to the future. Automation. Less work and more energy. More fornication and adultery will dispose of some of that. But there might still be some surplus energy that might seek an outlet, heaven forbid, in some kind of intellectual fulfillment. Heaven forbid, some of your factory workers might start thinking, '*Who am I and where the hell am I going and is it worth it, goddamit?*'And then you're in deep trouble."

He was chuckling out loud now, amused by the sick smile on Jamison Langner's face. He turned and spoke directly to Big Ben.

"The theory is that if we provide the right things in the arts within the system you factory sheep will follow the Judas goat down the garden path. You won't be susceptible to those damn message plays that breed class revolution."

Then becoming unexpectedly serious, but still enjoying his self-appointed role as mentor of this representative of the factory working class, he explained, as Big Ben listened, appreciating this attention, "Comus is a State University project, supposedly geared to doing something for the community. But as a State University project it does have to be a theatre of innovation where we seek to create new trends, new forms, new kinds of writing, new combinations of the different aspects of the performing arts. That is its true function. It is not a place for the old kind of traditional theatre that flourished back in the Thirties with its simplistic form of realism."

Big Ben saw that Jamison Langner liked that, liked it very much.

The professor conceded a smile to his superior on the board of directors. "Agreed, Comus must not do the simplistic socialist realism crap like they're doing in the Soviet Union, with Joe the happy factory worker marrying Sadie the drill press operator because she's fascinated by his superbly swollen production record on the assembly line instead of his big balls and superbly swollen prick."

Now he turned back to Big Ben, explaining in a warm and friendly way, "Like our own agit-prop plays back in the Thirties. They were intellectual, abstract, and so damn righteous, and so very little in them about the real truth of the human condition. There was a depression and unions were needed to right the balance between classes. But that's in the past. Unions are not what they were. Back then they were a leading force for change. Now union men and women are fat and complacent and defenders of the status quo. They are working and making a lot of money. Probably too much for their own good. The force for change in our country has shifted from them to the Blacks and to other minorities and to the young people, the third force, the third world standing between capitalism and socialism. There is the future, and the arts must find their way in that direction. That is the true function of Comus."

Jamison Langner, smiling and nodding, patted Dr. Tanner's arm. "Enough lecturing, professor. Now give Ben a chance to enjoy himself."

Betty Lyons led Big Ben out onto the dance floor and turned to him. He put his arm around her and squeezed. Hang on tight, baby. He whirled with her across the ballroom's polished floor. Whee-ee-ee!

Chapter 12

Big Ben drove the station wagon into the factory parking lot. The graveyard shift was already at work. From the sounds he could hear he recognized different machines the night shift people were operating inside the brick buildings. There were not many cars in the lot for this shift. He knew most departments were working only one or two shifts. But the big machines, most of them in the machine shop, were too costly to be left idle for any part of the day.

He reached for Betty. She might expect it of him. But she blocked the move with her hand. It's late and we both have to get up early. Her face was stiff. She had second thoughts now about what had happened earlier.

She was beginning to realize that there must be much more going on in that head of his than she had given him credit for. A very complicated guy, nowhere near as ignorant as he makes himself out to be.

It was during the exchange between Dr. Tanner and Jamison Langner that she first sensed a reticence on Big Ben's part that did not seem to fit his image as a naive and very open and simple kind of guy. Thinking that over during the ride from the house in the country, something like a suspicion, if it can be labelled something that definite, crept into her mind. Instead of he being the subject that Jamison Langner and she were shaping to use to achieve their objective, could it be that Big Ben had some Grand Design of his own?"

She, of course, assumed that unlike the radical playwright with his play, Big Ben's objective was wholly personal. If he only wants to get out of the dirty factory there's nothing wrong with that. *But* if he has some childish fantasy about using her, she does not intend to be used by anyone, especially by someone who still has to be taught a lot to really get to know his way around in the sexual department.

During the ride back she studied that face, trying to make up her mind about him. But his easy grin and amiable eyes were too difficult to break through and it was this challenge that saved him.

Big Ben was not an easy one to put off once he made the

move, especially when he felt that a determined effort might be expected of him. Betty Lyons protested and struggled. Not saying a word he forced her hands aside and grabbed her groin under her dress. She tried to pull his hands away while sharply telling him to stop it.

He silenced her by kissing her hard on the mouth, and went right on, working on her, massaging away. Despite herself she was reacting. But while being swept along, her body defying her mind, she was able to pull her head to one side away from his lips, freeing her mouth.

"Meat!" she taunted. "Meat! Meat!"

That hoarse cry, reeking with contempt for his lack of sensitivity as a human being, was magic. It stopped Big Ben cold. He pulled his hand away and straightened up and reached and opened the door on his side.

In the bluish white light coming through the factory windows to illuminate the parking lot she saw his face. She spontaneously reacted to reach for his head to hold him while she tried to kiss him. He pulled free. Go to hell, you bitch. But her lips brushed one of his eyelids and confirmed the wetness she thought she had seen there. Good-night, darling.

He did not look back. He got into his car and slammed the door. The motor roared. The wheels spun and then the tires squealed as the big old Buick swung around in a tight circle and headed for the street.

The house was quiet and dark except for the night light in the kitchen. He looked at the electric clock on the wall. Five minutes past two. He had to get up at six. Shit.

He went to the door of the bedroom. It was opened a small crack. He listened. He could hear Lila's deep breathing. He carefully felt his way into the room and undressed down to his shorts. He bumped into a chair.

Lila stirred. Did you enjoy yourself? She was not fully awake. He whispered. Yes. The mattress spring creaked and then he heard her deep breathing again. His eyes were used to the darkness now. He closed the door and stood there at the foot of the bed, looking and listening.

He slipped off his shorts and slipped into bed and reached for her. Without fully awakening she turned to him and responded with grunting sounds as he angrily muttered filthy obscenities and drove on into a violent climax. Then she said something he did not understand and she collapsed into deep sleep.

When he returned from the bathroom, his shorts back on, he felt his way to the dresser in the darkness. He stuck his hand into the drawer and reached under the shirts for the play. Not there. His heart pounded. Cold sweat broke out on his face. He reached further into the drawer. His hand touched something. Boy, oh boy, Jesus Christ, how did it get the fuck that far back in there? Lila? No. My imagination, nobody's touched it.

He carefully slid the drawer shut and tiptoed out of the room, closing the door carefully behind him, the play in his hand. He switched on the overhead lights in the kitchen. Almost three o'clock. He stood there, next to the kitchen table, holding the play, listening. No sound except some night-creaking in the walls and a drawn-out train whistle somewhere outside and the muffled clank of machinery from the rolling mill down across the field at the end of the street.

Wide-awake. Three hours to get-up time. The hell with it. The fuck'n party's still going. That bastard Jamison Langner's still hosting out there and he won't come into the plant until late morning or early afternoon, the lucky sonofabitch. So why break my holy fuck'n ass to get in by seven-thirty? Only that lucky bastard don't punch no fuck'n clock. And he gets paid anyway. Fuck it — too sick to work — the party last night was too fuck'n rich for my weak shitty blood.

And the truth is that he is sick. His throat is choked. His head feels like some tense lump is pressing outward behind his eyes.

Anyone raised down in Pennsylvania and West Virginia coal mining country (down there some still call it fuck'n John L. Lewis country, saying he brought union conditions down into the mines) has a tremendous thing pulling at him. While the coal mines birth out of their bowels their fair share of informers and stoolpigeons and strikebreaking scabs, these are a different breed from those bred elsewhere. It's the coal dust in their lungs and in their blood. It's there forever. And when one of these special breed sells out his brothers and sisters he does it in a special kind of tortured way of thinking that includes as part of the betrayal a deep hate for those who are paying off, the coal dust in his lungs and blood affecting the brain so that it twists and turns the mind into convincing him that he is maneuvering those who think they are maneuvering him and what might be mistaken for betrayal by those who don't know how complicated these things really are on the inside is actually a damn clever plan, a brilliantly conceived tactic, the only way you can ever get away with it, to sink those who think they have bought your soul. It's this coal dust still working in Big Ben's blood that does not let him forget the phrase used by that Dr. Tanner at the party.

That fuck'n safety-valve principle. If that's what they want, fuck 'em, we'll give 'em their safety-valve, bugger it right up their fuck'n bughole.

Hungry, he headed for the refrigerator. Working very quietly on the kitchen table not to wake anyone, he made a tremendous sandwich, putting three slices of swiss cheese and four healthy cuts of liver sausage and several crisp lettuce leaves between two slices of rye bread. With that and a cold bottle of beer in front of him, and with matches and a pack of cigarettes ready, he sat at the kitchen table and took hold of the black manuscript cover of the now excitingly dangerous play and opened it, revealing the title page.

Empty Hands by David Newman.

He began to read, rapidly flipping the pages, his eyes running swiftly down each page, his lips mouthing the lines. Four characters: three guys from the shop and a bartender, shooting the shit with each other in the ginmill across from the factory. It sounded like the talk in Mike's place. But he recognized what the author had done. It only seems like this is the way they talk in Mike's Bar. But this talking has been lifted to a level above everyday speech. All the stupid shit has been cut out except where leaving it in makes a point. There's still some of what you might hear in Mike's place, a touch here and a touch there, but nowhere near like you'd hear there with no women around when every other word could be fuck or shit or piss or prick or cunt or some highly ingenious combination. And he's done something to the language so that there's a real fuck'n poetic rhythm in the way all the sonofabitch'n characters speak. And behind what seems to be only a helluva lot of loudmouth horseshit there's some real fuck'n deep stuff.

Reading half aloud, his lips moving, again and again he was struck by some subtle touch that put it exactly the way it is to someone working in that shop over there and he burst out with a satisfied laugh of recognition that he immediately muffled to keep from waking Lila or the kids.

Reading on into the center of the play where the gut confrontations begin to tighten in he had a flash of insight that deeply pleased him because it meant he was not as stupid about these things as he often feared he was. He recognized that the play would mean one thing to the people he works with in the shop and something much different to people like Betty Lyons and Roy Gwylie and Professor Tanner. Hell, even Jamison Langner knows factory life in a way much different from the way the people who work for him know it, and he can't possibly have the same feeling for the alcoholic wreck who is the central character in this play as will the people out in the shop who work on the machines and on the benches and on the assembly line, who know from day to day that fuck'n threat that they might be automated out of *their* jobs and be tossed onto the scrap heap without enough solid structure left to the rest of their lives to keep them afloat. He was proud of that thought.

Fascinated, caught in the developing web of conflict, swept into the emotional excitement of the characters, Big Ben could not keep from punctuating a line here and there aloud with an "Oh, Christ!" or an "Oh, shit!" or an "Oh, fuck!"

Never in his whole life had he read anything that touched his experience so specifically where it really counted and, therefore, nothing he had read before had ever penetrated so deeply into his heart and mind and moved him so much.

It took him less than an hour to read the play. He closed the manuscript and let his folded hands rest on top of the black manuscript cover. For a long while he sat there at the table in the kitchen, motionless, staring into space, putting together with his mind's eye the scenes that stuck with him. Then he flipped open the front cover of the manuscript and started to read the play again.

This time he enjoyed the dialogue and incidents even more, relishing the way each detail of speech and incident contributed to what was to follow. Oh, Christ. He shook his head, marvelling. Tight as a drum. Like some fuck'n hotshit toolmaker working to some goddam fuck'n tight tolerances with everything fitting together perfect. Reading this the second time, it's like final inspection going over a complicated hoist assembly before it's shipped out, recognizing and admiring the perfection of each detail, instinctively knowing what a helluva lot of sweat and fuck'n good craftsmanship went into this whole fuck'n thing.

The dawn stretched a strip of graying light behind the factory chimneys on the horizon down beyond the end of the street as Big Ben, with the playscript still in his hand, stood and stared out through the kitchen window. The frantic feeling engulfing him, fevering his mind, preventing him from even thinking of going to bed now, is — *envy*.

Enraged at his lot in life — he sees himself strapped to his machine back in that damn factory while he dreams that Dave Newman is destined to soar up into the glittering and glamorous world of the stage and movies and television. He could write as good a play, even a better one, if he could only learn how to write up his own experience. And then, suddenly, another flash of insight of which he is proud. Hell, until now he had never even thought that his own personal experience, his own life, had enough importance to be worth writing about, to put it into plays, novels, movies, the whole fuck'n works. Now he understands why Jamison Langner is afraid of this kind of play. It is what it might start, or help to start.

Still staring out through the window, but no longer seeing the factory chimneys which are even more clearly outlined now against the early morning horizon, he grapples with the question of tactics.

Maybe pass the script on to some of the worst agitators in the shop. Drop a little word here and there to the wild ones and get them going. Get some loudmouth like that Purple Heart lathe operator to yell at union president Baldy George, "What the fuck, you fuck'n bastard, why don't you put on this fuck'n play over there in the fuck'n union hall — you company suck!"

But then Jamison Langner would inevitably find out who is really behind it. With the glimmer of an idea shaping in his mind, Big Ben turned away from the window and went back to the kitchen table and sat down. He does not know enough of the world of the labor spy to jump quickly into recognizing and naming the role he is creating for himself. If he did he might reject this role of a — *double agent*. But to withdraw and be nothing is intolerable. The only way to be more than a zero now in his own eyes is to advance into the center of the storm with its promise of excitement and intrigue to give a real flavor to what otherwise would become a dull and furiously frustrating kind of life.

He talked to himself, rehearsing the complicated approach, feeling it out. Tell Jamison Langner that I've been approached by Dave Newman to help him get his play put on in the union hall — and tell Dave Newman that I've been approached by Jamison Langner to help him get the people in the shop involved with his Comus dancing shit. And then tell Jamison Langner I decided to play the game with Dave Newman to find out what the hell he's really after — and tell Dave Newman I'm going along with Jamison Langner to find out what the hell *his* game really is.

His ingenuity pleased him. He grinned. Hang on, brother, we're in for a helluva fuck'n wild ride.

He sat there at the table in the kitchen, holding the play, thinking out possible complications in the developing situation and different ways to handle them. The alarm clock sounded in the bedroom. Time to get dressed for work. He hid the play on the top shelf in the broom pantry and opened the bedroom door as Queen Lila swung her bare feet over the side of the bed and placed them flat on the floor. He tossed a silly grin at her.

"And good morning to you, dear."

He made breakfast for Queen Lila and gave her his car keys.

"If anybody asks, the old man is home — sick."

He cooked breakfast for the kids and herded them off to school. The house was quiet again. He went to the phone and dialed. A woman's voice. Hello. "Is Betty Lyons there?" A southern drawl, the maid. Who's calling please? He hung up.

Feeling tired, he went to the refrigerator. No sleep — eat a lot to keep up your energy. He stuffed himself with two oranges, a bowl of corn flakes and milk, four scrambled eggs with six slices of bacon, and four pieces of white toast with butter and strawberry jam, washing it all down with three big mugs of coffee.

Still clad only in his shorts, he went to the broom pantry and retrieved the play and went into the bedroom. The mussed up sheets looked like they were still warm from Queen Lila's ample body. He dropped the play onto the floor next to the bed and slid under the covers.

He was awakened by the sound of voices from the kitchen. He saw the play lying on the floor and quickly reached for it and stuffed it under his pillow. He looked at his wrist watch. The girls were home from school, making their lunch. He was quiet, hoping they would not look into the bedroom to see if he was still home. They giggled and jabbered and yelled so long he wondered if there was no school in the afternoon. Then the door slammed and the house was quiet again.

He dressed and went into the kitchen and made another cheese and sausage sandwich and ate it, washing it down with big gulps from a tall glass of cold milk. Still hungry, he made another sandwich and wolfed it down, along with a second glass of milk. His intense concentration seemed to have developed an enormous appetite in him which renewed itself as he satisfied it. He finished off the lunch with a banana and another glass of milk.

Holding the play in one hand, he paced back and forth from the front to the rear of the house, his head bent, thinking, trying with difficulty to map out specific tactics far ahead. But he realized that it depended upon what happens each step along the way. Main thing — don't panic. Don't get your shit hot. Let *them* do the worrying.

Restless, feeling that he had to get out of the house into the open air, he put the play back under his clean shirts in the dresser drawer and went outside. The sun was shining.

He breathed deep. A great day for a walk. He briskly moved along. Too late to report in for work. Reporting pay clause in the contract says four hours pay if you report in and the company doesn't give you at least four hours work. But he recalled that the contract also says that if there isn't four hours working time left on the shift the company retains the right to refuse to let you start work. So the hell with that. But he continued on toward the plant.

What if someone in the front office looks out the window and sees him.

He passed over that quickly, not wanting to seem too cocksure of himself and thus invite trouble, but the thought did flash through his head that Jamison Langner was not going to let him be penalized for missing a day's work when he had spent the night before at Jamison Langner's home and when the Old Man himself is probably missing the same day's work for the same reason.

But Jamison Langner had been awakened early by a phone call from his assistant, Tom Watson. And at ten-thirty in the morning he was already in his office at the factory to meet with his assistant and personnel man Dick Penfield. There were new developments down in Virginia and an important decision had to be made.

Tom Watson gestured to personnel man Dick Penfield. Bring the Old Man up to date. Jamison Langner seated himself in the swivel chair behind the desk and faced his aides. Sit down, gentlemen. They pulled chairs closer and sat. Dick Penfield extended his pack of cigarettes to the other two men and after they shook their heads he lit up and began.

"They're waiting down there now for our decision. A citizens committee has been formed by the commander of the American Legion post. He works in our accounting department down there. The chief steward of the local union down there is also on the committee. Yesterday the committee issued a press release, a public statement, asking us to reopen the factory and asking the national office of the union to call off the strike and send all employees back to work."

Tom Watson leaned forward to interject, "I had a long talk with the Special Agent in charge of the FBI down there and he spoke to the Chief of Police who happens to be the brother of this Legion commander in our accounting department. That's how we got this thing started."

Dick Penfield, after a nervous pull on his cigarette to conceal his annoyance at the interruption, continued. "They've circulated a petition to decertify the union and take away its bargaining rights. They've filed it with the Labor Board. Signed by fifty-two percent of all eligible employees. The union's lawyer argued that the Board can't entertain a decertification petition because at the hearing on the unfair labor practice charge that the union filed against us our lawyer argued that the factory is permanently closed — and if that's true then technically there are no employees there for anybody to represent or bargain for, and nobody's eligible now to vote in any kind of election, certification or de-certification."

Tom Watson, again to Dick Penfield's ill-concealed annoyance, interrupted. "And he argued that in any case no action can be taken on the decertification petition until the unfair labor practice charge is disposed of — which *is*, apparently, an established rule of the Board."

Sulking, Dick Penfield remained silent until Jamison Langner nodded, a signal for him to resume, and then he impatiently ground out the burning end of his cigarette before speaking.

"They're all meeting right now in a room at the motel at the Richmond airport — an informal session set up by the Labor Board examiner. Our people phoned us — it's deadlocked and they're stalling until we tell them what to do."

The Old Man had had only about four hours sleep, but he did not look tired. Probably it helped that everything was going so well down in Virginia. He asked his lieutenants their opinion on what should be done. He thought it over for only a moment after both had expressed their views. They were in agreement. His decision was to accept their suggestion.

"Tell them to go ahead down there."

Dick Penfield went to the phone and put the call through to one of their lawyers who was waiting in his room at the motel. "Plead guilty on the unfair labor practice charge — and tell them plans to close the factory have been changed. The factory will be open in the morning for all employees who wish to work — and any employee not reporting for work tomorrow will be considered a voluntary quit and will be permanently replaced."

Within the hour there was a phone call from their lawyer down in Virginia. They were waiting for it in Jamison Langner's office. Dick Penfield grinned and nodded at the Old Man and Tom Watson while he listened to the report from the man at the other end of the line. Victory.

"The union is calling off the strike and instructing its members to report to work in the morning."

A few minutes later another phone call came through from Virginia, this time for Tom Watson. He recognized the voice of his undercover man on the union's strike committee.

"Mr. Watson?"

"Yes."

"I just got this. The union's going to circulate a petition of its own. The lawyer from their national office told us we're officially still the bargaining agent — until we're decertified by the Labor Board. But he wants us to get the people who signed the decertification petition to sign again, with a later date after their signature, on a new petition *for* the union. He says that can block the Board from setting up a decertification election."

Jamison Langner shook hands with his two assistants. Good job, good job. Tom Watson shook hands with Dick Penfield. That's it. To get support down there now the union will have to tell their people they won't be going back out on strike again. Dick Penfield turned to Jamison Langner. We can start all over now, start talking fresh about wage rates —begin from the beginning. The Old Man laughed. No, no, we've got what we wanted — let it alone.

It was at this happy moment in Jamison Langner's office in the administration building that the phone rang again and the switchboard operator said there was a call for Dick Penfield from the guardhouse at the front plant gate. Dick Penfield took the phone and received a report he welcomed from the plant guard.

"Big Ben Hood didn't come in to work today — and now he's over in the tavern across the creek — drinking and trying to make time with the new redheaded barmaid over there."

Chapter 13

The plant guard at the gatehouse waved to Big Ben and laughed. You taking the day off? Big Ben returned the laugh. Don't want my big head to fall into my machine.

"Watch out," the guard warned, dropping his voice as he nodded in the direction of the administration building, "Dick Penfield's up there."

"Fuck him," said Big Ben, cheerily, walking on into the parking lot where Queen Lila had left the car.

The guard waved goodbye as Big Ben drove his car out of the parking lot. But the car did not go far. It slowly moved across the bridge over the creek and then came to a halt at the curb on the street where it could be seen from one of the windows in Jamison Langner's office. Big Ben emerged from the car and went into Mike's place. The guard shook his head and swore aloud.

"Dirty bastard — he can't resist the smell of cunt."

He glanced across the creek at the offending vehicle. If only that sonofabitch had the sense to drive away out of sight. Now what if some fucker from the shop goes in there and big tits behind the bar shoots off her mouth and the whole shop knows this wise bastard didn't come in to work and then he had the fuck'n nerve to come and get his car from the parking lot and park it right in front of the fuck'n ginmill where the whole fuck'n front office can see it? — Then who'll be left holding the bag?

And having justified doing what he would have done anyway the uniformed guard went into the shanty and picked up the phone. When the operator told him personnel man Dick Penfield was meeting with the Old Man he took a chance and said his message was urgent. He feared that Dick Penfield would raise hell if he wasn't told now when he could look out the window and with his own eyes see the car still parked there in front of Mike's Bar.

The plant security system at Mackenzie Machine Tool is modeled after the standard counter-intelligence network Jamison Langner and his executive officer Tom Watson had once set up in their artillery outfit. While the purpose of this plant security system is given out to be to prevent thievery and to guard company secrets most of the men employed for it are workingmen with a union background — supplied by a plant protection agency — and they have no illusions about what they are hired to do. Hours before the plant guard phoned him Dick Penfield knew that Big Ben had not shown up for work and that Queen Lila had driven in alone that morning in the Old Buick — and that the women working with her in the machine shop had been needling her with lewd remarks about wearing out her boyfriend and leaving him too weak to work. But he also knew that Big Ben had been at the party the night before at Jamison Langner's home to which he himself had not been invited. And he knew that the Old Man still had this cockeyed idea about using the cultural arts to fill up time outside work for the people in the shop and keep them out of mischief. He couldn't see it. Hockey, football, baseball, boxing, and other sports — yes. But some fancy kind of modern dancing and plays? All you do there is help open the door for some smart radicals like Dave Newman to work their way in with their radical propaganda about the war and all that other radical stuff.

Through the friendly contact he maintained with the local FBI office Dick Penfield knew that Dave Newman still met frequently with a handful of radical-minded factory workers to exchange ideas and to work out specific projects around which to rally working people in the area.

He had been told that at one of these meetings recently in his home Dave Newman talked about using theatre to develop a sense of unity and pride — a feeling of class — among working people and their families in the western part of the state, a feeling that would make it easier to get across all the other things they were trying to put across.

A few days after getting that warning a phone call came to his home from one of his security men, an oiler planted in the maintenance group where as part of his job he could wander freely anywhere in the factory. He was in the pay phone booth over at Mike's Bar. — "Dave Newman and Big Ben are over here at the bar." — What are they talking about? — "Some damn thing about a play." — About an hour later the phone rang in the same pay booth from which the oiler had made the previous call. Mike Staruski answered the phone. Dick Penfield questioned Mike about the conversation between Dave Newman and Big Ben. — "Dave just mentioned some play he wrote. He said he'd give it to Ben to read." Mike did not reveal that he himself had also asked to read the play.

Dick Penfield had not yet passed on this information to the Old Man. He was waiting until he could make it definite: "Big Ben has this play written by Dave Newman." After talking to Mike he put his men on Big Ben's trail. Only the day before he had received a report very late in the afternoon — "There's a rumor down there that Big Ben *did* bring the play into the shop." But no one had actually seen the book. He sent a man down to the machine shop to pump Big Ben. But it was too late. Big Ben had already punched out to go with Betty Lyons to the meeting at the Arena Theatre. Big Ben's locker was searched during the. graveyard shift and this morning Dick Penfield on entering his office found a short note, unsigned, on his desk blotter. "Nothing there." A few minutes later a maintenance electrician, silently rehearsing his line — ("Hey, I hear you're reading Dave Newman's play.") — entered the machine shop, but he found that the actor to whom he was to deliver his well rehearsed speech had missed the cue to make his entrance that morning.

Leaning over the bar, in the tavern on the other side of the creek within sight of the administration building where Dick Penfield and Tom Watson and Jamison Langner were at that moment deciding his future, Big Ben peacefully monitored the bobbling movements of the two big melons belonging to Mary Magdeline Kelly.

When he walked in and took his place at the bar she came over to him. "Aren't you supposed to be working?" — "Taking a day off." — "Don't they mind?" — "Why should they mind?" — She brought him his shot and beer chaser. He glanced through the big store window up front, looking toward the guardhouse across the creek.

No guard in sight. That fuck'n bastard — on the phone already to Dick Penfield. He'll shit, but Jamison Langner will cool him off. Look the other way, pal. Forget it.

Big Ben is unworried — since he has no way of knowing about the complicated fear deeply rooted in Jamison Langner which is now being fanned by his aide. But Dick Penfield knows that while the Old Man is quick to talk about all of us being one big happy family in the shop and all of us pulling together, the truth is that to Jamison Langner his factory is a battlefield where his employees carry on continuous guerrilla warfare, from one minute to the next, conniving to grab more and more money for doing less and less work. Yet, despite this, and giving little clue to the conflict it embodies, the method of payment for production workers in the shop might be described in exactly the same way — except for a variation in use of profanity — by both Big Ben and Jamison Langner. Dick Penfield made this point one time when, having referred to the bonus system in a conversation at the dinner table with his wife, she asked him how it worked.

"It's measured day work. We have our time study people check production operations with a stop watch. And they allot so many minutes for each operation in making each part and for each step in assembling the parts. There's no bonus earned or paid for the first basic sixty minutes of timed production per hour. That's four hundred and eighty minutes of production work, the equivalent of the work that should be produced by the employee in an eight hour day."

His wife strained to hang onto that, as Dick Penfield went on.

"The employee is guaranteed his minimum basic hourly rate of pay even if he doesn't average at least sixty minutes per hour of timed production that day."

His wife nodded She got that. He went on.

"To get the employee to increase his production and earn bonus for producing more than sixty minutes of timed production in sixty minutes of actual time, the carrot must be placed close enough within his reach to get the employee to voluntarily extend himself rather than to take it easy and bring home only his guaranteed hourly wage floor."

She nodded. She got it. He relaxed. It was usually not grasped that readily.

"This is very similar to a piece work system where the rate is so much money — instead of minutes — per piece or per operation. And, as in any piecework shop, there naturally is a constant tug-of-war going on between the time study men and the people on the machines or on the assembly lines, the people working on the job naturally trying to get a loose timing so they can then easily speed up their work pace and make a lot of money, and the time study men naturally trying to set time allowances as tight as they can, while still giving sufficient incentive to get the people to reach out and grab for the carrot.'

Dick Penfield also explained to his wife that Jamison Langner and Big Ben would probably agree that the majority of grievances in the shop involve complaints about *rates* set by time study. — "*Rates* is the way men and women in the shop refer to time allowances, in their minds automatically transposing time allowance per piece or operation into its equivalent in money." — But from there on those two will disagree as to the causes of the war waged around the rates, Jamison Langner generally finding fault with the people working on the job, Big Ben generally finding fault with the time study men.

But then, even though Dick Penfield is aware of something of that nature, he does not know how deeply Jamison Langner is haunted with the feeling that he is at the head of a small band under siege and keeping at bay a horde of greedy barbarians, knowing he and his lieutenants are far outnumbered and fearing that if the men and women working for him out in the shop ever lose their sense of discipline, anarchy will erupt with disastrous consequences. Dick Penfield had been present at a recently unpublicized gathering of industrialists — assembled by the Industrial Relations Committee of the Central City Chamber of Commerce — to discuss rising unrest among factory workers and their increasing disregard for no-strike, no-slowdown, and no-walkout clauses in labor-management contracts, at which meeting Jamison Langner, as the featured speaker, told of three specific instances within the past eighteen months where employers in this area permitted slowdowns and walkouts in violation of their contract with the union to go unpunished — "*liberal* employers who also allowed excessive absenteeism to go unpunished on the grounds that an employee is free to choose to work or not to work since he is not paid if he does not work — and from these seeds of laxity grew a monster, the employees acting with less and less restraint, disrupting production at will, and ultimately raising labor costs to a level where the employer, his competitive position destroyed, had to consider as the only alternative course — to close his doors and go out of business, wiping out the jobs of all his employees."

At that time Dick Penfield had registered for future use, the way Jamison Langner's voice rang with a sincerity stemming from absolute belief in the truth of what he was telling his colleagues. "Once the rigid discipline is relaxed it is difficult, if not impossible, to reverse the process! The only cure once you've gone that far, the only way to pull back from the brink, is to summarily discharge *all* violators after fair warning that this henceforth will be the punishment meted out without exception. But even that can be too late. When one of these three employers tried to reverse the process this way he only brought on himself another vicious round of walkouts and sickness absenteeism — which ended only when he threw in the sponge and sold his entire manufacturing operation to a hard-hearted, absentee-owned, conglomerate corporation. — They immediately laid it on the line. Cut it out — or we close this place down and consolidate the work done here into one of our other manufacturing facilities elsewhere."

Now, ever alert to this danger in his own house, Jamison Langner needs little prodding to act at once in the situation created by Big Ben. Anxious though he is to use Big Ben to test the effectiveness of an arts program in capturing and channeling the developing intellectual restlessness among working people — which he attributes to the swift technological changes breaking up old production structures that form the base of society — he immediately agrees with Dick Penfield.

"Yes — we can't permit anyone to get away with that."

If Big Ben had had the common sense to stay out of sight, then he might accept the fiction that the man was absent from work due to illness. But the way it is it's necessary to set an example that will mean something to everybody else in the shop. He is aware that his two aides are waiting for him to set the penalty.

"Give him a week off — and a warning that next time it happens he's fired."

In Mike's Bar, the only customer there in the mid-afternoon, Big Ben is trying to take advantage of the opportunity he had hoped to find. Mary Magdeline is on duty behind the bar. Mike is not there. The buxom redhead allows Big Ben to buy her a vodka and coke. She taps the rim of her glass with the tip of her silvered fingernail. If Mike walks in, this is straight coke —he don't want me drinking on the job unless he's around to keep a sober eye on the register. Big Ben puts a quarter into the jukebox. He dances back to the bar, his arms out to Mary Magdeline. Dance, baby. She does not budge from her spot behind the bar. Mike finds us alone dancing — he'll think we're cooking up something else besides dancing. Big Ben leers and grabs the chance to widen the breech she's presented. What else? She moves away as if she had not heard him, going to the sink behind the bar, bending over it to rinse glasses she has already rinsed a few minutes earlier. She looks up into his leering stare.

"Did you read that play yet?"

"Yeah."

"Did you like it?"

"Yeah."

"Are you going to do it over in the Labor Hall?"

"I don't know."

"I want to play the part of the bartender."

"Okay."

"Don't laugh — why not?"

"That would get all the guys to come to see the play — but they'll leave the old lady at home."

"They won't —" But she smiles, thanking him for the compliment.

The second shift men enter and come to the bar near Big Ben. What the hell are you doing here? Why ain't you working, you horny bastard? — Big Ben, grinning, puts a finger to his lips. Watch your language, you sonofabitch, there's a lady present. — The offender turns a blank face to Mary Magdeline. Excuse me, lady. — More second shift people come in, including two women wearing slacks and bulging sweaters. They all order drinks. — A man's loud voice: "The boss didn't invite *me* to *his* house." — "Jealous?" — "You're damn right I'm jealous." — Prompted by needling from the curious men and women gathered at the bar Big Ben breaks the resolution he made to keep his mouth shut about the party. He simply can't hold it in. There is too much enjoyment to be had in the telling.

"*Christ* — what a shitful of food and booze! And a whole sonofabitch of an orchestra for dancing. A fancy ballroom — a private dance hall — up on the second floor. The whole room filled to the ceiling with a whole shithouseful of balloons. And there were two sonofabitch'n fairies — dancing together on the floor and nobody paying no attention. A goddam high society real shit of a party — and you, you stupid bastards, get the hell over there to work now and pay for it."

Only a few hours later, hearing some of his words quoted back to him verbatim, Big Ben frantically tried to recall the faces that had been around him when he was shooting off his big mouth back at the bar.

But for the present he is still holding forth in Mike's place. He sends word in to Queen Lila with one of the second shift women, to tell her that he has taken the car from the parking lot and will pick her up after work at the corner light on the tavern side of the bridge over the creek.

When Mike shows up Big Ben catches him off guard. A round for the house in return for a dance with the little girl behind the bar. Mike moves behind the bar. You're on. After downing the free drinks the rest of the second shift people leave, going across the creek to punch in and get ready to start work, and Big Ben feeds another quarter into the jukebox and replenishes the supply of money he left on the bar. When Mike puts on an act complaining about his hard life (This expensive help making the poor boss work —) Big Ben pushes his empty shotglass forward to be refilled. Stop crying, you bastard —you need a truck every Friday night to carry your money to the bank. He dances Mary Magdeline into the backroom. Even though he's supposed to pick up Queen Lila in a few minutes he suggests that they slip out the family entrance and go for a ride. She breaks away.

"I can't leave now — I'm supposed to be working."

"When are you through?"

"Eight o'clock."

"I'll be back."

"I have to go right home. Old Frank comes in at two in the morning to relieve Mike — and he stays all night pushing out drinks and mopping floors. I have to get in early to relieve him." She is trying to get past Big Ben but he won't let her through. "I have to get back there to the bar."

"I want to ask you something about Dave Newman." He seems serious and she waits for his question. "Some jokers over there in the shop say Dave's still a communist." He pauses only momentarily, trying unsuccessfully to read an answer to this in her face, and then adds, "I said if you got proof let's hear it — if not keep your big mouth shut."

"If he still is — whatever he is," said Mary Magdeline, accepting the change of subject and liking the chance to talk more seriously, "that's his own business." She went on without any hesitation to say, "My father was once a member of the Communist Party. He's against them now — because he says during the world war they sacrificed the fight for the American workingman just to help the Russians get strong. But he won't argue against Dave. My Ma says Dave's a man who believes in the working class of people — and he paid his dues, so you respect him even if you don't agree all the way with him."

"That's what I told them over there. — Look, I'll pick you up at eight o'clock."

"I have to go straight home — my Ma's expecting me."

"I'll be back and I'll drive you home. On the way we can talk."

It was only a few hours later that Big Ben was finishing supper with Queen Lila and the kids in the kitchen, dawdling over his second cup of coffee — when the phone rang. Laughing, pushing aside Queen Lila and the kids, he scrambled to reach the phone first. Hello. He heard a woman's voice and recognized it. He motioned to the others to be quiet —serious business. What's up?

"Were you over in that tavern across from the factory this afternoon?"

"Where's that?"

"At Mike's something-or-other."

"Why — ?" he asked, able to tell from the tone of her voice that something was wrong. He wondered if someone had told her he was fooling around with Mary Magdeline. — "I might have been over there — why?"

"Did you say over there that there was a whole shithouse-ful of balloons at the party last night?" His heart sank. She sharply asked him, "Did you say that?"

"I don't remember what I said." His heart beat rapidly — sweat cooled his forehead as he listened to Betty Lyons quote more of his own words back to him. She questioned him and he stubbornly sidestepped, refusing to affirm or deny. Then he became aware of Queen Lila and the three children soberly watching him. He made his funny face at them and grinned.

But he felt sick. Betty Lyons told him she had left Jamison Langner only a few minutes before.

"He says you know this man who wrote that communist play. How well do you know him?"

"He used to be the organizer for the union over at the shop."

"Stay away from him."

He tried to laugh — "Is that an order, sir?"

Betty Lyons talked rapidly for about five minutes, not permitting him to inject a word, coldly reminding him in detail of the great opportunity awaiting him, sharply warning him that Jamison Langner hates communism and will not tolerate anyone in the arts program who in any way associates with communists.

"Is there anything else you wish to tell me, sir?" asked Big Ben when he could get a word in — and his voice was ice. If he had apologized and backtracked she would have swarmed all over him and destroyed him. But his independent rejoinder — especially his tone of voice — was exactly right. She immediately apologized for sounding so bossy and aggressive, the warmth flooding into her words.

"It's that I'm worried about you — don't want you to lose out. You now I'm very fond of you. You're different from most men I know and I don't know how to handle you. But that's good. I like that. So forgive me. — I'm very tired — feeling pushed — so little sleep last night. I'm going to bed early tonight and we'll talk about it tomorrow."

With Queen Lila and the kids listening, he could not say much. The conversation ground to a halt. She interpreted his reluctance to speak as anger — that she had offended him — and she again explained her concern and asked his forgiveness. She'd get hold of him as soon as she found out anything further from Jamison Langner.

When he put the phone down Queen Lila and the three children waited, their faces expectant. He was too disturbed to be able to think of what he should tell them. He moved toward the bedroom door.

"I'm pooped, I'm going to lay down."

"Bad news?" asked Queen Lila, trying to stop him.

"Some stupid jerk over at the shop. Some stupid goddam grievance. Instead of going to the union — I don't know why the hell he bothers me?" He opened the bedroom door. "I got to grab some sack time, I'm pooped."

He sat on the bed and stripped off his shirt and undershirt, took off his shoes and socks, and stretched out flat on his back. The coolness of the bedspread under his bare back felt good. His hands gripped his face and squeezed hard and then with his clenched fists he massaged his eyes. An almost inaudible groan came out between clenched teeth — "Oh, shit."

He blew air out between his lips, deflating his chest, and then inhaled and exhaled several times. No use crying. Don't panic. Figure it out. Move — do something — quick. Take the offensive. First thing tomorrow morning step into that ball and hit it a whole fuck'n mile. — How? How? How the fuck how? Dick Penfield must have heard about the play. And he must have passed the word to Jamison Langner. — Now how the fuck do you handle that? — You've got to take it for granted they know you've got the play. Now what the fuck do you do about that? What? — He wracked his brain in one direction after another, following through the possibilities. And then he hit it. — Confess! Confess! Before they tell you they know you have the play — you tell them you have it. Phone Dick Penfield or Jamison Langner at home right now. No, no, wait. Not too fast. Take it easy. Relax, slow down, don't panic. — Go through the chain of command over there — during regular working hours. Dick Penfield — give Dick Penfield something good to take to Jamison Langner. Get him on your side. Make him a hero. — Big Ben swung his feet around and set them down on the floor. He sat up on the edge of the bed, thinking. With his mind's eye he staged the scene for the next morning.

He saw himself entering the factory, punching in at the time clock, going to Dick Penfield's office, facing the personnel chief, man to man. Dick, something very important. You know Dave Newman. He got hold of me in Mike's Bar and he asked me to read a play he wrote. I didn't know what the hell to tell him. If I told him to go fuck off and then word got around in the shop that he spoke to me about his play I'd be blamed for it up here in the front office even if I hadn't done a fuck'n thing — you'd still hold it against me and think I was hiding something maybe. So I decided I better find out what the hell it's all about before I shoot my stupid mouth off one way or another. I got his play. He gave it to me to read. I'd like you guys to read it and tell me what you think of it.

As he went on, testing it out, his forehead smoothed and a touch of a smug smile replaced the intensely sober set of his mouth. Going through the scene again, rehearsing it in his mind, he gained confidence and began to enjoy the anticipation of the inner excitement he would feel in the morning when he played out his role in the personnel office. He rehearsed it through again several times in his head. Satisfied with himself, confident he could handle it well, he whispered aloud a husky paeon of triumph — "Fuck you, Brother Penfield, you fuck'n smartass sonofabitch — fuck you!"

He heard a stealthy, heavy step outside the bedroom door and he hastily swung his feet up and stretched out flat on the bed. The door opened. He could hear it. A moment of silence. Then a soft whisper.

"Ben — "

He kept his eyes closed and breathed regularly and deeply. A long moment of quiet. Then the door was carefully closed.

He felt a pang of regret. Playing this kind of lone hand is awful fuck'n lonely. He wondered if he should confide to Queen Lila. He decided against it.

Chapter 14

Less than an hour after Big Ben left Mike's Bar and picked up Queen Lila to drive her home for supper a middle-aged man with a briefcase under his arm entered the tavern. The business suit fitted his present occupation.

"Hello, Dave," Mary Magdeline greeted him.

The former union organizer, now blacklisted into becoming an insurance salesman, seated himself on a high stool at the bar. Draw one, please. He took off his shell-rimmed glasses and used the lower end of his tie to wipe the lenses clean. Mary Magdeline served the glass of beer. Dave put a dollar bill down on the bar. Mary Magdeline brought his change. Dave lifted the beer.

"Big Ben Hood been around?"

"You just missed him."

Dave Newman put down the beer and fished a business card out of his coat pocket. "Will you do me a favor? When he comes in again please ask him to phone me."

"Is it about the play?" asked Mary Magdeline, taking the card he held out to her.

"Yes — please tell him it's important."

"I'll tell him."

At eight o'clock the big battered Buick is parked outside the family entrance to Mike's Bar. Mary Magdeline gives Big Ben the business card and the message. He sticks the card into his shirt pocket. Tomorrow. He drives toward the nearest entrance to get up onto the expressway. Mary Magdeline, getting cigarettes out of her purse, looks up when they turn onto the ramp leading to the elevated highway. Wait, where are you going? — Big Ben steps on the accelerator. Nowhere, my favorite joint for a quick drink and then home. — Mary Magdeline puts a cigarette between her lips. A damn quick one.

It is only a short drive on the expressway to the bridge across the wide river and over that to Horvath's Dock, a dimly lighted saloon hidden near the river. This is a place like Mike's Bar. It is a favorite oasis for working people when they go fishing. But it is off the beaten track, and Big Ben thinks it very unlikely that on a midweek night anyone he might see here will carry the word back to Queen Lila or Betty Lyons.

"Did Dave say what he wanted?" he asks, shortly after the Buick settles onto the expressway.

"Something about the play — important."

"Did he say what it is?"

"No — and I didn't ask." She puffs on the cigarette, and then since silence makes her uneasy she goes on to fill the gap. "A woman should play the part of the bartender. I told Mike and he agrees — a woman bartender would bring sex into the play. It needs sex."

(Who did you tell that I have the play?) He thinks of asking her that, but doesn't. Take it for granted she shot off her mouth in the ginmill and somebody took it back to personnel man Dick Penfield. He has tentatively figured out the way to handle that. Dick Penfield will want to read what is in the play —

"To warm up the audience before the play I'll do my dance," offers Mary Magdeline with a smirking laugh, interrupting his thought.

"With or without?" leers Big Ben.

"With or without *what*?"

"With clothes — or bare-ass?"

"A little something in the essential places — please."

"Essential to who?"

"To me," trills Mary Magdeline.

"Start practicing."

He continues to respond this way, with forced joking with Mary Magdeline, trying to concentrate on her. But the situation with Dick Penfield and the play pulls his thoughts elsewhere. And despite the danger of falling between two stools and breaking his neck, or *because* of the danger, he draws deep satisfaction from the double direction he is developing. It is fascinating to be planning two courses of action which are almost exactly the opposite of one another.

The story he will tell Dick Penfield in the morning takes shape in his mind and he keeps going over it, making whatever adjustments seem necessary. Chasing down some information yesterday about Dave Newman and his play, he stopped off at Mike's Bar to see this Mary Magdeline the barmaid over there

— found out that her old man and Dave Newman were good friends — both were old radicals, Old Lefties together. She had already phoned me before when I was still home and still hung over from the party the night before at Jamison Langner's joint — she told me that Dave Newman had left me a message — she got my phone number from one of the outside truck drivers — she did that after she sent word across for me to drop over and get the message Dave left for me — and the word came back to her that I was home — that I was sick —

He parenthetically interrupts his thoughts to make a mental note to print some kind of short message on the back of the business card — so he can show it to Dick Penfield in the morning to substantiate his story. He again goes over his explanation for his presence in Mike's Bar when he was supposed to be sick at home, checking it carefully with his mind's eye and ear to see how it will sound to Dick Penfield. —It sounds phony. Christ, phony as all hell. But fuck it, it's an excuse for being there. If Dick Penfield and Jamison Langner want to go for something like playing along with Dave Newman to find out what's really cooking there, it don't matter how phony the story sounds, they'll let it go.

In Horvath's Dock with Mary Magdeline, feeding money into the tavern's jukebox, dancing with her, drinking one boilermaker after another with her, he keeps practicing, refining and improvising his story, checking it through again and again to see how it will sound to Dick Penfield the next morning.

Mary Magdeline, warning him that no man has ever been able to drink her under the table, matches him shot of whiskey for shot of whiskey and beer chaser for beer chaser.

An hour goes by quickly.

Mary Magdeline glances at her wrist watch. She stands up, unsteadily. Time to go home. He rises, as unsteadily as she. Let's go.

In the car he tries to pile on top of her. She pushes him off. Wait until we get to my place. With that promise dangled in front of him Big Ben stops fighting to get his hands past her defenses. He starts the car and rolls down the window. He is dizzy and is anxious to get the car moving with the window wide open, hoping the breeze will clear his head.

Driving with his left hand on the wheel he gropes toward her with his right hand. She takes the hand and grips it tightly. To build a moat to keep him out she chatters on about her apartment and her mother, having led into this by telling him where she wants him to drive her.

"On the West Side in Central City, just off Main Street. My apartment's in the cottage behind my Ma's place. The carriage house years ago. She's on the first floor in the big house up front. A window peeper, day and night at the window, peeking between a slit between the curtains — she don't miss nothing. The minute I switch on the lights in my apartment she'll be over for coffee."

"We better not switch on any lights."

She lets the carrot stay out in front of him. But when he parks the car and switches off the lights, getting ready to go into the house with her, she tries to leave without him. It's too late and I'm too tired. He pulls her back before she can open the door. She lets him kiss her, but she pulls her head away when he tries to force his tongue into her mouth. Okay, good-night. Her weary tone is a challenge. His hands move all over her above her waist. She makes no effort to stop that, letting it go on for a while, then — "Okay, good-night." — the same weary tone. His hands move below the waist and she grabs them and holds on with a strength surprisingly equal to his own — or close enough to equal to keep him from getting a firm hold anywhere. "Okay, good-night."

"You lousy cockteaser, I'll slap you across the mouth!"

"You . . . better . . . not."

Her icy threat reminds him of the fate of business partner Lucky Carpenter and he lets go. "You dirty bitch, getting me this way, then leaving me high and dry. You cockteasing bitch!"

He grips the steering wheel and hunches over it and glares through the front windshield at the cars parked ahead on the street. Then he feels her hand fumbling down the front of his pants and she bends her head down over his lap. He is surprised and when it is quickly over he doesn't know what to say or do. No good-night kiss, thank you. She is neat and efficient and distant. She turns down the window on her side and sticks her head through and spits out onto the sidewalk. He is still occupied with straightening himself out when she gets the car door open and scrambles out of reach. Good-night.

She does not look back. He sees her disappear into the shadows between two houses.

After Big Ben drove away, there was a stillness on the block for about a half a minute. Then the angelic face of Mary Magdeline emerged from shadows between the two houses and peered around the corner of the front porch. She briskly walked to the corner and turned toward Main Street.

About fifteen minutes later a taxi pulled up in front of a high-rise apartment house further down into the city. Redheaded angelic face paid the driver and headed toward the canopied entrance. Only a few people entered and left the apartment house during the next hour. Then two taxis arrived together and parked at the curb in front of the entrance.

A stout man with a swarthy face, wearing dark glasses and holding the elbow of his female companion, emerged from the apartment house. He was well-dressed with a hat and topcoat. He kissed redheaded angelic face good-night, put her into the first taxi, handed the driver some dollar bills, and waved goodbye as the taxi pulled away.

Early next morning this same stout man with the swarthy face removed his dark glasses and stuck his hand across the conference table, warmly thanking the man accepting his hand for being kind enough to talk to him.

Jamison Langner graciously smiled and squeezed the man's hand in return. He had planned on being in his own office at the plant this morning while Dick Penfield spoke to Big Ben Hood. But the night before he had received a phone call from his firm's chief legal counsel. A very attractive proposition for you if you're interested and act quickly. He explained that the president, of a conglomerate which was successfully gulping down one small firm after another in the area wished to meet with Jamison Langner.

"The people heading their corporation are of Italian descent — good, honest people born and raised right here. But with all the wop names on their board they're being called a front for the good old Mafiosi. A washing machine operation to clean up dirty money. This is getting them into all kinds of embarrassing situations with the banks."

While these negotiations proceeded at the lawyer's office in the bank building downtown in Central City, the portly businessman explaining how his financial proposition would make it very inviting for Jamison Langner to bring himself and a few of his friends with attractive Anglo-Saxon names onto the board of directors of the conglomerate, Dick Penfield stiffly sat behind his desk in his office at the factory, impassively listening to an intense Big Ben explain his previous day's absence from work and his presence across the creek in Mike's Bar.

Big Ben had come in and lined up with others in work clothes, ready to punch in at the time clock, only to find his time card pulled from the rack. In its place was a pink slip with a brief typewritten message directing him to report immediately to Dick Penfield in the personnel office.

The grapevine quickly flashed it through the machine shop and out into the rest of the factory. Cocky Big Ben, the smart sonofabitch, is going to get holy hell from Dick Penfield for not coming in to work yesterday. Too sick to work, the bastard, but well enough to shoot the shit with that cunt behind the bar over there.

Since Big Ben was tied up with Dick Penfield he could not shield Queen Lila from the unmerciful ribbing directed at her by the women working with her back in the rear part of the machine shop. Proper ladies, most of them married and good churchgoers, possibly jealous of the dark relationship existing between Big Ben and Queen Lila — they stabbed at her with obscene thrusts, piling one on top of the other, the remarks becoming more and more degrading and insulting to her as the female drill press and punch press operators and inspectors across the aisle from her tried to outdo one another. The ladies started by shouting shrilly above the noise, then quickly ducking their faces behind their machines or benches, embarrassed by their own words. But seeing that each was not alone they became more and more bold and soon stood there, erect, shrieking directly across the aisle at their unfortunate target who at first bent over her work on the drill press table and tried to ignore them.

"She can't keep her boyfriend away from that Irish fish smell." — "He likes the taste of that Irish stuff." — "He laps it up like a hungry kitten." — "He's tired of eating that smelly old Indian taste."

At this point Queen Lila quietly walked from her work place to the woman seated on a high stool at a punch press across the aisle. This poor woman, a widow, in her early forties, had four children and she was very active in her Catholic parish's campaign to prosecute all neighborhood store owners who permitted sale in their establishments of magazines and newspapers and books dealing explicitly with sex — pornography. She was vocal all over the shop about her commitment, the need to keep innocent minds of young children from being inflamed. But as one of the loudest of the mouths this morning she had *cunt*-ed and *fuck*-ed and *prick*-ed at Queen Lila in a way that would have made any foul-mouthed truck driver flinch. Her head was turned away to some of the other women as she laughed out some newly contrived obscenity about the Indian Queen. At this moment a hand reached over the poor widow's shoulder and grabbed her under the chin, at the same time as another hand grabbed her hair and pulled her head back to make her face a perfect target into which Queen Lila spat a big fat glob. It landed in the center of a startled wide-opened eye, and a blood-curdling scream promptly sounded through the department above the noise of the machines, followed by a frantic flailing tussle between the two women, both grabbing and pulling hair, tearing clothes, punching, slapping, scratching, kicking, both crying and screaming as if each was being murdered, interspersed with exchange of the filthiest swear words they could bring to mind, shouting these at the top of their lungs, while the men in the department marvelled to one another — oh, shit, listen to them.

Fortunately, foreman Casey was out of the department and before he returned the other people had a chance to pull the fighters apart and hold them where they could not get at one another. The fight over, the two combatants quietly sobbed. But except for a few superficial face scratches neither had sustained outward physical damage. They were released and permitted one at a time to go into the ladies room, first the spat-at, and then the spitter.

The scrappers were both back at their work places, both too upset to actually do any work, both still dabbing away to sop up leaking eyes, when foreman Casey returned. Nobody could find out later who told him. It could have been any of the several asslickers among the men or one of his few female favorites in the department with whom he had a relationship similar to that between a pimp and his prostitutes — he was their big daddy. It was less than halfway through the morning, and Big Ben was still closeted with Dick Penfield in his office, Jamison Langner was still meeting with the portly businessman in the attorney's office in the bank building downtown, Mary Magdeline was riding to work at Mike's Bar in a taxi, and Betty Lyons was sifting mail at her desk in The Dance Center — when foreman Casey, wearing his white hardhat, emerged from his glass-enclosed, inner office at the front corner of the machine shop and gathered up Queen Lila and the widow and led them back into his windowed cell. The rest of the people working in the department watched and saw but could not hear the emotional scene reenacted behind glass for the benefit of the white-hatted foreman. The matter was quickly settled. Both fighters were sent home for the rest of the day. While both women silently accepted the punishment when it was meted out to them, both secretly glad they had not been discharged — the punishment specified in the contract for employees fighting inside the shop — they both later bad-mouthed the union's chief steward Don Mayer for not joining them in the foreman's office to argue for an even less harsh penalty: "If it had been two men caught fighting, he would have come in and put up an argument."

Meanwhile, in his office up front personnel man Dick Penfield made no effort to challenge the validity of the contrived explanation Big Ben offered for the previous day's absence from work. He gulped down the bait, reacting just as Big Ben had expected. Dick Penfield wanted that play that Dave Newman had written: *Empty Hands*. A triumph for him if he alone, without Tom Watson, discovered and reported to Jamison Langner this attempt of Dave Newman to work his way back into the union situation.

"This was why I stopped at Mike's Bar yesterday," said Big Ben, showing the short printed note on the back of the business card. "He asked me to phone him."

"Did you phone?"

"Not yet."

"What about the play — did you read it?"

"Not all of it," lied Big Ben.

"What you did read — what do you think of it?"

"I didn't read enough to be able to tell."

Under further questioning Big Ben admitted he had brought the play to work with him. It was locked in the glove compartment of his car out in the parking lot. Maybe Dave wants to get hold of me to give back the play. Dick Penfield said if he could have the script for about an hour he could duplicate the pages on a copying machine. Big Ben said he would go get the play out of his car. But what about my time card? He now expected that what had happened the day before would be overlooked. Dick Penfield said this was something he would have to talk over with Jamison Langner.

"How about if you take off the rest of the day without pay?" — Big Ben's silence said it had to be something better than that if he was to go out and get the play. Dick Penfield went on, as if he had only paused after what he had already said. "Then later on we'll work out some overtime — enough to make up whatever you lose today."

"Sounds good," said Big Ben, maintaining a quiet and serious demeanor.

"I'll get hold of the Old Man and clear it with him, while you go get the play."

On the way to the parking lot Big Ben detoured through the machine shop to report on the situation to his friends there. It looks like the rest of the day off without pay. Dick Penfield's trying to get hold of the Old Man. Would he file a grievance? He shook his head. The hell with it. He looked around. Where's the Queen? While they were telling him what had happened, he saw the white hardhat, foreman Casey, watching him from a position in front of his office, apparently knowing what was going on and waiting to see what Big Ben would do about it.

Big Ben headed for the front of the department. He stopped in front of the white hardhat who gruffly asked what he wanted. Both knew the whole department was watching. Big Ben looked straight into Casey's face and then spat on the floor at his feet and turned and started away.

"What the hell's that for?" the white hardhat called out to him, after deciding that with an audience he could not let this go unchallenged.

"What's what for?" asked Big Ben, turning back and showing a face of sneering innocence.

"They know they're not supposed to fight in here — I have to protect my neck."

Big Ben sniffed at that and walked away. He left the department and the foreman made no effort to stop him. When Big Ben returned from the parking lot a short while later he could have bypassed the machine shop. He didn't. He deliberately detoured through the department again with the play wrapped in newspapers under his arm. Foreman Casey moved over to block his path. Where the hell do you think you're going? Without even bothering to reply, Big Ben brushed past the white hardhat and continued on his way.

The personnel man had not been able to reach Jamison Langner but when Big Ben did not pass over the package he said he would take the responsibility himself to clinch the deal. He unwrapped the script.

"Wait here, I'll get it duplicated."

"Hurry up, I got to call Dave Newman."

"It won't take long."

But Big Ben waited only a minute or two and then told the secretary he'd be back soon. He triumphantly marched down the center aisle through the machine shop, shaking hands right and left with people at their machines. See you tomorrow, you slaves, they told me to go fishing the rest of the day. The white hardhat went into his windowed office and bent his head over his desk and concentrated on studying some papers there until Big Ben left the department.

Mary Magdeline was at work behind the bar. She placed the shot of whiskey and the glass of beer in front of Big Ben. He tossed down the shot, sipped the beer, pushed the empty shot glass forward to signal for a refill, and went into the pay phone booth and called home.

"Hello, slugger." When Queen Lila asked where he was he told her he was still at the plant waiting for Dick Penfield to reach Jamison Langner. "Looks like I might join you for the rest of the day. Keep the bed hot." She was silent. "What the hell was the fight about?"

"Nothing." She knew he had already been told.

"I'll be home soon as I get straightened out here — okay?" She did not answer. "Dig out the boxing gloves, I'll teach you how to protect yourself."

"I can protect myself," she said, "I don't need lessons from you."

He asked, "Are you all right?" And he sounded as if he was

genuinely concerned. She softened.

"I'm all right."

"You sound funny."

"Do I?"

"Not your happy self."

"Ha ha," she said flatly.

"That's better," he said. She did not speak. "I'll be home soon," he added.

"Take your time," she said, keeping her voice as empty of feeling as she could.

When he arrived home that afternoon Queen Lila was not there. There was a note on the kitchen table. Gone to the grocery store. The play was safely locked away again in the glove compartment of his car. Big Ben phoned Dave Newman and told him he had finished reading the play and liked it.

Dave Newman began to explain why he had asked Big Ben to phone him. The Drama Department of State University works along with this theatre they call Comus. Big Ben interrupted to say he had been there. One of my girfriends dragged me to a rehearsal of some dance thing there. Dave Newman was too intent on advancing his own project to question this. He explained that he had approached the chairman of the Drama Department about doing his play at Comus and the chairman had stalled him off.

"Then one night last week when I was out chasing insurance I made a cold call on some guy I used to know when I was with the union. He's an inspector now at Chevrolet — the motor division out on River Road — and he told me his son Jimmy is a sophomore at the university who wants to teach drama when he graduates. He's a member of some student drama group out there and he said some of the students on campus who are seriously interested in theatre and want it to be more meaningful don't like the things they're doing at Comus. He read the play and liked it and gave it to the president of their drama group. Yesterday morning we met out at campus and it turned out that their president — he's a graduate student in the English Department — is the son of a couple I know very well. They respect me because one of the black guys still working there at the plastics plant in your town is married to their maid, and she told them he says I'm the one who got him in there. — Anyway, this college kid is excited about the idea of doing the play with you guys out there."

Listening to Dave Newman explain what the college students offered to do to get the play put on, Big Ben began a mental process very like what he had done when he took his recent trip to see *The Great White Hope* and sorted everything into two piles, what he would tell Queen Lila and what he would *not* tell her. Now it was what he would tell personnel man Dick Penfield and what he would *not* tell Dick Penfield. He listened intently to Dave, wondering whether or not to pass it on to Dick Penfield that Dave said the students wanted to produce the play, would do the dirty work, make the set, take care of the lighting. If we want them to, they'll provide the director to stage it. And they'll provide the actors for any parts we can't fill with people from the shop.

He might tell Dick Penfield he expressed some objections to Dave about getting involved with these university students now: What about the news report that the students had occupied the administration building out there at the university? What the hell do they want? And Dave said they were demanding some more voice in deciding what courses would be taught — about revolution, about urban studies, about Blacks and the Third World. They want the army reserve guys, ROTC, kicked the hell off campus. And all corporations selling stuff used in the war not to be allowed to send representatives in to interview students about jobs. And all that. And the administration was calling in the Central City police to clear the students out of the building — Dick Penfield would like to hear that.

If he handled it the same way he had handled it with the Queen there was no reason why he should not be able to do just as well, if not better, with Dicky-boy Penfield. For the first time Big Ben thought it might really be possible to actually get the play done and he could continue to play his game with Dick Penfield and Jamison Langner and come out on top. — Dave's got these college students who are all ready to do this play for him. That's what it is.

"We'd like to do it out there in the union hall, if possible."

Leaning his big frame against the kitchen wall, Big Ben pressed the phone receiver to his ear. Dave was waiting for his reply. He tried to think how it might be done. And then it came to him. Jamison Langner and Dick Penfield wouldn't like it. The union president Baldy George wouldn't like it. But without sticking his own neck out in front he should be able to needle someone to blow up a storm for the students to be allowed to rent the hall just like anybody else. Chief steward Don Mayer. Or even Queen Lila. They rent the hall to other people! Meetings and parties! Weddings and such! As long as their money is green, why not them? — When he answered Dave his real feelings broke through the cloak of caution he had gathered around himself.

"Why not? They rent out the Labor Hall to anybody. Your students rent it. Nobody's business where they get the money. — That would be great!"

Dave Newman suggested that they all get together as quickly as possible, if possible sometime this weekend. Big Ben had been planning to drive down home to Pennsylvania to pick up his archery equipment. He had taken it down there for safekeeping when someone broke into the room next door to his, back over at Mike's place. The bow season on deer would start this Monday, but he didn't plan to go hunting until the next weekend. However, he needed at least a week on the archery range to strengthen his arm again and get the kinks out. Well, he could go hunting the week after that. No hurry. The bow season would last three weeks before the shotgun season started, when about ten or twenty percent of the men in the shop would take off from work to join all the other shotgun hunters, their cars and small trucks clogging the main highways going south, bumper to bumper in the early morning dark, worse than the crowd driving to the football game.

"In the afternoon," he suggested, agreeing to get together the next day, Saturday, at Mike's place. He could tell Dick Penfield he went there to find out what they would say.

After supper that night, trying to make up for the tough time the women had given her in the shop on account of him, Big Ben asked Queen Lila if she wanted to go over to Mike's Bar and do some dancing. The orchestra's there tonight. She said no. She was not talking to him except when necessary. He thought it might help if he told her about Dave Newman's phone call. But then he decided that for the present it was smarter to play a lone hand.

The children had gone to bed and it was late. Ben was

watching a murder mystery on television. Lila got ready for
bed. She asked Ben to turn off the television and go into the
bedroom or the kitchen. She was going to sleep on the couch in
the front room. He said he would sleep on the couch, she could
have the bed. It's your bed. She accepted that without comment
and went into the bedroom and closed the door. He switched off
the television, and stayed up late, drinking one beer after
another, pacing the floor in the front room — thinking,
thinking, thinking —

When Lila came out of the bedroom in the morning he asked
her if she was going to stay up. Yes. He got up off the couch
and went into the bedroom and undressed and slipped into the
warm bed and slept until almost noon. He made his own late
breakfast. The two girls had gone to visit some friends on the
block. He went out with young Frank and played a simple
game of touch football with him in the lot down at the end of
the street, with make-believe roughhouse, careful not to hurt
him. When he brought the young boy home he told Queen Lila
he was going over to Mike's place to play cards. She did not
answer him.

He found three people waiting for him in the backroom and
he winced inwardly when Dave introduced him to Jeffrey
Simon who was president of the drama group. The English
Department graduate student had wavy, dark brown hair that
hung down below his shoulders and a ludicrous beard all over
his face and a handle-bar mustache with the ends drooping
down below his chin and he wore gold-rimmed spectacles.
Later, when Big Ben went through the front room on his way
to the toilet, Mary Magdeline motioned to him. He went to her.
She leaned over and spoke softly so the few people nearby
watching the college football game on television could not hear.

"Who's your new girlfriend with the long hair?"

"They're both college students," said Big Ben, making
believe she was referring to the blonde girlfriend Jeffrey
Simon had brought along.

"I like her wavy black hair."

"It's cute, isn't it?" said Big Ben, embarrassed but hiding it,
and he went on into the toilet.

"Kiss her once for me," said Mary Magdeline when Big Ben
passed through again.

"I dare *you* to come back and kiss him," said Big Ben and

continued on into the backroom. Mary Magdeline called after
him that she'd be back there later.

To Big Ben it seemed that Jeffrey Simon was a nice young
guy, amiable, with a sharp mind and a witty way of talking.
He had the kind of intelligence and knowledge that Big Ben
respected. The long hair didn't bother Big Ben too much. There
were young fellows in the shop now with hair almost as long
but they tied it up behind in a pony tail like the pirates used to
do — the company made them do that or else they had to wear
a hair net, because of the machines with their moving parts.
The blonde girl Jeffrey Simon had brought along was a senior
at the school. An anthropology major. But she was also active
in the theatre group. She told Big Ben she asked to come along
because she wanted to meet a factory worker who was
interested in plays. What we need more of, students from
campus to establish friendly contacts with workers in the
factories. — "This is exciting. Here I am, sitting in a real
working class bar, talking to a real factory worker about doing
a proletarian play."

"Touch me," said Big Ben, holding out his arm, pleased by
her rosy-cheeked honesty.

"This is a first for me," she confessed and then questioned
him. What department did he work in? What kind of work did
he do? How did he get into factory work? And she was
fascinated when he told her in a quick offhand way about
growing up in a coal mining town in Pennsylvania, how when
he finished high school he went down into the coal mines and
how his daddy blew up one day and kicked his ass out of there
and told him it was no job for a kid with clean lungs, how he
made a deal with his daddy for both of them to quit the mines
and come to work up here, except his daddy moved back home
a year after and went back into the mines.

"That's marvelous," she said, beaming at him, and in the
face of all that naked admiration Big Ben glowed and felt very
important.

Dave Newman brought them back to their purpose for being
there. Do you think the people in the shop will like the play?
Will they come to see it? Will they bring their families? What
about the language in the play — do you think there's too
much swearing? Do you know any people in the shop we could
get to act in the play? — "What about you?"

"Me?" asked Ben, stalling, thinking there is little chance he can do that.

"Would you want to act in it?"

"I don't know, I'd have to think about it?"

They questioned him further. How many performances? How would they go about putting it on in the Labor Hall? If not able to do it there, should they rent the neighborhood movie house? Should the students provide the director? Big Ben listens with his forehead deeply wrinkled and his eyes intently focused on each person speaking, letting it be seen that he is trying to catch every single precious word. His replies come slowly, after long silences during which a mass of chaotic thoughts quarrel in his head. Ordinarily, he would have been bubbling over with ideas, ready to respond with an excited rush of words to this opportunity for intellectual conversation. But since meeting these students he has had second thoughts about working with them. Their presence reminds him of the attitude of many people in the shop toward college students, especially since Jamison Langner has been bringing in college students to work during their summer break between semesters. You can always count on some students to speed up and kill every job they work on. In any fight with the company they always take the company's side, try to keep working when everybody else walks out, make all the money they can make in a few months and the hell with what that does to the people they work with.

Big Ben was torn. He himself wants to grab this chance to work with these lively students from the university and to put on a performance of *Empty Hands* with them for the people in the shop. But even if the people in the shop go along with the students, Dick Penfield is sure to find out who is connected with it. Dick Penfield is not that stupid. Yet here is the opportunity to make what has been only a vague and unlikely possibility into a real and immediate actuality. The possibilities he senses stir up a feeling of exhilaration which requires a conscious effort to try, unsuccessfully, to curb and conceal. He tries to divert them away from pushing him to a firm and specific commitment.

"Sometimes I'd like to see what it's like out there at the university."

"We need people like you to see what we're doing out there."

said the graduate student. "We're trying to change the reactionary policies of the administration. They favor the middle class. Discriminate against working class."

"Sometime I'd like to go to one of your radical meetings there. Hear what they got to say."

But when the two students promptly urge him to come with them the next night to a meeting on campus sponsored by Students for a Democratic Society, a rally against the war and also against the university president for bringing city police onto campus to break up the student occupation of the administration building, he remembers he still has to decide how much he will tell Dick Penfield about what's going on in this session in the backroom — (Dicky-boy will certainly hear about it) — and he lamely mumbles that he has to go somewhere else tomorrow night and then, in contrast to his brief flash of enthusiasm, he sits there, seeming to have suddenly grown dull in his reactions to the excited talk he has provoked. Then the way he thinks he can handle it comes back to him and he speaks again, fumbling along to find a solid path through the maze.

"There'll be some big problems getting a play like this put on out here."

His seriousness compels their silent attention. Haltingly at first as he gropes his way into it, then speaking more and more fluently as his foundation is set firmly into place, he gives a detailed account of what has happened thus far in Jamison Langner's effort to use him to sound out the possibility of getting the people in the shop interested in the company's idea about the arts. He tells them about the dress rehearsal of the dance program at Comus, mentioning Betty Lyons, describing her as Jamison Langner's secretary at The Dance Center, leaving out the details of his personal relationship with her.

His voice is low and conspiratorial as he leans over the table, taking them into his confidence. He acted receptive to Jamison Langner's approach because he hoped he might be able to get something started that could lead later on to doing things that would really appeal to the people in the shop.

"Something like Dave's play — something really on the side of the workingman."

He believes what he is saying and the students and the playwright believe him. He has to be careful how he proceeds now. They agree. If he starts working openly for getting *Empty Hands* performed in the Labor Hall, then Jamison Langner might think he is doing it deliberately to undercut his dance program. But the dance program will flop by itself anyway. Meanwhile he does want to do what he can to help start the wheels going in the shop to get *Empty Hands* put on in the Labor Hall. But Jamison Langner will be sure to hear about it if he does anything. He puts his solution to this dilemma on the table for them.

"Rather than wait until some stooge goes in and blows the whistle on me I think the wise thing is for me to go in myself and tell them up in the front office that I've been approached by you people about working out something with Dave's play. I'll tell them I told you I'd see what I can do. If I closed the door you'd only find somebody else in there and go ahead without me." — He could see that they were ready to go along with anything he said. — "So let the company think I'm working for them. For Jamison Langner and his dance program. Meanwhile I'll get what information I can from them on anything they do to try to stop us from doing the play."

His listeners do not need much to convince them. They accept it as a fact that Big Ben will have difficulty concealing his association with them if they start working together on a production of *Empty Hands*. They understand how difficult it is for Big Ben, a working guy in the shop, to get out of seeming to go along with the boss, Jamison Langner, on *his* program.

Later, back on campus, the students talked to their friends about the native ingenuity of a real working class guy like Big Ben Hood. He figured out such a *marvelous* way to survive by seeming to go along with the boss while cutting the boss's throat.

Big Ben, talking to the two students and Dave Newman, knowing in his heart that in the long run where it really counts he is wholly on the side of the workingman, is completely at peace with himself. He is being realistic, recognizing the facts of the situation, handling them well in the interest of both himself and the people in the shop. When the other three shake hands with him and leave by way of the family entrance Big Ben goes up front to the bar. Mary Magdeline serves him his shot of whiskey and beer chaser. He toasts her. He thinks he knows where he is going now and he has it all under control.

Mary Magdeline pours another shot for him. Will she meet him later? No, she has to go right home. He doesn't press her. He downs the second shot, chases a gulp of beer after it and takes off.

He goes straight home, on the way planning to straighten things out with Queen Lila. But she will not talk to him during supper time and he doesn't make anything out of it because the children are there. He takes the three kids out to bowl. Open bowling Saturday night. They stop for ice cream on the way home. It is good fun. A relief from the pressure he is feeling.

The children go to bed and the house is quiet. Queen Lila is reading in bed. A book from her library in the closet. Big Ben undresses, stripping down to his jockey shorts, and gets into bed. No protest from the Queen.

"If I can find some place to buy them tomorrow, I'll get those wood panels and start putting them up." — He had promised her he would put wood panelling in the kitchen. Lila does not look up from her book. A cool thank you. — What are you reading? No answer. He looks. *Cousin Bette.* Who wrote it? No answer. He slowly slides his hand under the book until it is gently resting palm down on the mound bumping up between her thighs. Without looking up from her book she takes his hand and tosses it away.

He grins and let's it go. Leave her alone and she'll get over it. More important business right now — to figure out how to handle the new situation when he gets back into the shop, what he'll say to chief steward Don Mayer and union president Baldy George, and what he'll say to Dick Penfield and Jamison Langner. He lights a cigarette.

Sitting there in bed beside Queen Lila, easily sucking in and expelling smoke from the cigarette, he has a feeling of well-being come over him as he thinks about the bigger world into which he is entering. He will handle it in such a way that it will be for the benefit of all the people in the shop and not only for himself. He is confident he can do that and keep it that way.

He is ten feet tall and walking big as he reaches for the paperback resting on the chair that serves as his night table. *The People, Yes!* A book of poems by Carl Sandburg he had picked up at the airport newsstand in New York City on the way back home after visiting his sister there.

Chapter 15

But a new development at work Monday morning tossed Big Ben's neat plans up into the air. He had been so busy juggling Jamison Langner, Dick Penfield, Dave Newman, Mary Magdeline Kelly, Betty Lyons, and Queen Lila that he had misjudged the situation involving the four lathe hands who were still carrying on their own private war in the machine shop.

He had been aware ever since the walkout that the four lathe operators were not satisfied with the new time allowances set by time study for the operations involved in turning out the controversial metal piece that fitted into the mechanism on Hoist 2X397D. But he had not correctly assessed the degree of their dissatisfaction. This could have been because of the puckish sense of humor of the Purple Heart. This bearded young man, one of the two Vietnam War veterans in the quartet, developed a clowning routine with which the four lathe operators expressed the reason for their dissatisfaction.

Big Ben, seated in the smoking area during a rest break the day after the walkout, asked the Purple Heart how it was working out. Are you guys satisfied? They were not. Why not? The Purple Heart had prepared for this moment. He gave the cue. And the two young men and the two grey-haired old timers — the newly trained Lathe Operators Quartet — put their heads together and their arms around one another's shoulders in imitation of a barber shop singing group. To the accompaniment of laughter and jeers from both men and women gathered in the smoking area, they recited with no prompting the full contract clause in question, chanting and humming out the phrases with a mocking stacatto rhythm.

"When there is a change in the method — the operation or operations involved may be retimed (yeah, yeah!) — in which case a new rate shall be set — so that by expending the same amount of effort — on the revised operation or operations (yeah!) — that the operator or operators expended on the operation or operations prior to the revision (yeah!) — the operator or operators shall earn an amount equal (yeah!) — to the average earned rate (yeah!) — earned on the job (yeah!) —

217

prior to the revision (yeah, yeah, yeah!) — !''

For Big Ben and all others working measured day work, this one sentence — by itself it made up a full clause in the contract — defined the obscure and constantly shifting boundaries of the battlefield within which the serious struggle in the shop went on every minute of the day, the company trying to get more work put out for the same or less money paid out in wages, the people working in the shop trying to get more pay for putting the same or less energy into the job.

The quartet's ridiculous rendition was greeted with friendly booing and Big Ben mockingly summed up the problem involved, lowering his voice to let the women nearby know that his choice language was not meant for their ears.

"How the fuck do you measure effort expended so you set new time allowances requiring exactly the same fuck'n effort to produce the same fuck'n earnings as was earned by previous effort expended prior to the change in the fuck'n operation —Christ!"

Everybody in the machine shop took it for granted that on Hoist 2X397D prior to the revision on one of the operations the lathe men had been turning out the work as fast as they could — to make their earnings as high as possible. But the Purple Heart, speaking for the quartet, charged that while now there had been a slight change in only *one* lathe operation on only *one* piece of the hoist mechanism the company had adjusted *all* the timing taken by time study to force them to work on *all* lathe operations on *all* parts for Hoist 2X397D at the speedy rate they had developed over a period of time on the job prior to the change — as if this were now the normal pace.

Not satisfied with the new rate proposed by the company after their walkout the four lathe hands refused to exert themselves on *any* work on *any* parts destined for assembly into Hoist 2X397D. Since by contract they were guaranteed a minimum rate of pay per hour no matter how much work they turned out, they hoped by turning out as little work as possible to penalize the company for its failure to revise time allowances to their satisfaction. They were in a position to slow down the assembly of Hoist 2X397D to a trickle and they hoped customers would soon be frantically phoning in. Where's Hoist 2X397D? Meanwhile, there were wild arguments within union ranks over the grievance, and both sides reported to Big Ben, trying to win his support.

"I agree," local lodge president Baldy George Walters said he had told the Stewards Council, "the contract says earnings of the four men when they work at incentive speed should be at least one-third more than their minimum guaranteed day rate — there's no argument on that — but they're supposed to work at incentive speed."

"But," angrily rebutted the bearded Purple Heart, speaking for the lathe operators and backed up by chief steward Don Mayer, "if there isn't sufficient fuck'n incentive to work at incentive speed — if what the fuck money we make by working at incentive speed isn't high enough to lead us on to want to keep working at that fuck'n speed — that in itself proves the goddam fuck'n time allowance has been set fuck'n well all wrong."

That point was being argued back and forth across the entire shop when Big Ben was approached in the smoking area by the bearded Purple Heart and union president Baldy George and chief steward Don Mayer. — What do you say, Ben?

"You dumb bastards, what the hell is a time study setup for? The whole fuck'n thing is supposed to be set so the time allowance they tag on the job will be a fuck'n carrot hanging close enough to the front of your nose to make you lazy fuck'n stupid bastards break your fuck'n ass chasing after it. If it doesn't do that, then the fuck'n rate is wrong!"

Personnel man Dick Penfield, on orders from Jamison Langner, told machine shop foreman Casey Kowalski to back up the time study men. The time allowances were originally set too loose and the lathe operators deliberately outwitted the time study people. Yes, the contract provides that time allowances on incentive work are to be set "so that an operator working steadily on the job and performing satisfactory work should earn at least one-third above his guaranteed hourly base rate." And yes, in actual practice time allowances are usually set so the operator can make this one-third bonus so easily he will be pulled along into going after fifty and sixty percent bonus.

"But you stupid bastards," Big Ben bluntly and blandly told the four lathe hands, "you killed the fuck'n job — eighty and ninety percent — holy shit!"

The four lathe hands would not admit that it had been the high bonus they had been knocking out on the job that had flagged it for the front office, prompting time study to bring down a minor change from engineering as the excuse to retime all lathe work on Hoist 2X397D.

As for Dick Penfield and the time study people, they had expected their drastic move to create a storm. Any cut in time allowances provokes a protest, usually followed by the filing of a grievance and a tug-of-war. By making the cuts more drastic than what they hoped finally to get away with, they left room to maneuvre and to give liberal concessions to the men after giving them a chance to blow off steam. But the four lathe hands carried on in a way that made it impossible to give concessions without encouraging more of the same throughout the shop.

Their barber shop quartet performance during the morning rest break disturbed no one. But that same day, during the afternoon rest break, the four lathe hands caucused in the same smoking area and decided upon a new tactic in their guerrilla war. They said it was to keep both the company and the union honest in dealing with their grievance.

"Like pissing into the wind," chief steward Don Mayer confided to Big Ben, describing how far he got by trying to reason with the lathe hands the next morning when they brought in a small radio, a card table and a fresh deck of cards, four folding chairs, a reading lamp and a box of comic books and magazines — and made themselves comfortable. Not enough incentive there to break our ass to make incentive pay.

The following morning, Friday, they brought in a rocking chair and an overstuffed armchair, handing them over the back fence and carrying them through the warehouse. In their living room in the immediate area of their lathes they announced open house for visitors.

On Monday morning, the same day the people down in Virginia started their strike, one of the women working on a punch press down the aisle from the lathe hands brought them a handwoven throw rug to put down on the concrete floor. Other workers in the department, both men and women, vied with one another, deeply enjoying the game, bringing in house plants, lamps, books, an electric hot plate with a long extension cord, a coffee pot with all the makings to brew coffee, and dishes and cups and silverware.

In the midst of all this fun there was one jarring note that only intensified the determination of the lathe hands to get satisfaction. Some anonymous critic, on the night shift, knowing that the Purple Heart would react to connecting him to the late president of North Vietnam, put up a sign in the makeshift living room: *Ho Chi Minh Memorial Hall.* When the bearded hot-blood saw the sign the next morning, he used a black crayon to angrily print in the names of the three American leaders who had been recently assassinated, changing the sign to read: *Ho Chi Minh-John F. Kennedy-Martin Luther King-Robert Kennedy Memorial Hall.* The next morning the sign was gone, and no one in the shop spoke about it again, except for a few whispers attributing the original sign to some fuck'n stooge of personnel man Dick Penfield or union president Baldy George.

At another time the company would have precipitately fired the four lathe operators for engaging in an illegal slowdown. But with the workers out on strike in Virginia the decision was made to avoid the possibility of provoking another unauthorized walkout at the Niagara facility. Jamison Langner decided to look the other way, especially since personnel man Dick penfield did not think the lathe operators would hold out very long. One of them will soon get greedy and break ranks and produce. Also, the very audacity of the idea amused everybody. Executives from the front office brought down salesmen in their business suits to look and laugh and exchange pleasantries with the lathe hands who politely invited them to sit and visit a while. One of the older lathe hands neatly set his comfortable bedroom slippers beside his machine. He had the stem of his unlit pipe clenched between his teeth.

The slowdown dragged on day after day until the strike down in Virginia was broken. Then Dick Penfield and Tom Watson conferred with Jamison Langner and they sent for the plant manager and then for machine shop foreman Casey. And Casey reported on the general sentiment as he saw it. Some people are beginning to squawk because the slowdown on the lathes is holding them up, cutting *their* earnings. The decision was made to give the lathe hands still a few more days to hang themselves.

It was the Monday morning when Big Ben was planning to

tell Dick Penfield about Dave Newman and the students. The personnel man and his young assistant were preparing to meet again with the union grievance committee. *Once we get Virginia rolling we'll put an end to this kind of blackmail.* Dick Penfield told union president Baldy George and chief steward Don Mayer that he had been instructed by Jamison Langner to tell them there would be no further talk about the complaint of the lathe hands until the four men involved resume normal work — "So we can retime lathe operations on parts for 2X397D."

Baldy George and Don Mayer visited the lathe hands in their living room and conveyed to them the message from the company.

The Purple Heart was not in any mood for compromise this morning. He had had a drawnout argument over the weekend with the young woman with whom he was living. She had a job as an aide at a nursing home, and one of the nurses there had convinced her to go to college. The Purple Heart had not objected because he expected she would not make out with her grades and she would drop out. He knew she had not done well in high school and had not attended any classes for a number of years. But she was doing very well now in her first semester and she liked it and she was making friends there at the college and he was afraid he was going to lose her. She insisted that she still loved him. But he was afraid he was not equipped to talk about the things she wanted to talk about now that she was attending classes at the college. And he argued with her that continuing with college this way would surely result in a split between them. They were already having big arguments about the things she was learning there. In response she offered to marry him immediately. And now, goddamit, he didn't know what the hell he wanted to do. — This was his state of mind when he held a brief caucus with the other lathe hands to decide what response to send back to Dick Penfield.

"Tell them to shove it up their ass!" he reported back to Baldy George and Don Mayer.

There was a loud argument there in the middle of the machine shop. Men and women working nearby joined in, some berating the lathe hands for their stubbornness, an equal number defending their militant stance. Union president Baldy George yelled across the aisle to Big Ben. *C'mere, Ben.*

"That's your sonofabitch'n headache," shouted Big Ben, laughing at the predicament of the grievance committee and refusing to leave his machine to help them. He was waiting for Dick Penfield to be free so he could talk to him about Dave Newman and the students with whom he had met on Saturday afternoon at Mike's Bar.

The four lathe hands, with Baldy George and Don Mayer insisting on a formal answer they could take back to the company, caucused again in a corner of their living room and then brought back a written statement to be given to Dick Penfield. But so no one in their group could be accused of being the ringleader the statement was written in the center of a sheet of paper and all four men signed it three times, in three different places, to form a ring of twelve signatures encircling the statement.

It read: "No work at normal incentive speed, whatever that is, until the company gives us a signed guarantee in writing that there will be no change in time allowances on any lathe work on any part of Hoist 2X397D where there has not been a specific change in the method or operation, and that then the time allowance will be changed only for that portion of the method or operation which has been changed, and that the new rate will be set so that with the same effort expended previously the lathe operators will earn the same money they earned previously."

Dick Penfield precipitately rejected this demand for a new written commitment from the company. We're going in circles. This is already covered in the contract. A rate was set. The lathe hands disagreed with the rate. Their recourse was to file a grievance through you men, their representatives. They filed the grievance. Now they have to work at normal incentive speed so we can re-time the job and check whether or not the time allowances to which they object are proper and fair — as we think they are.

Union president Baldy George and chief steward Don Mayer went back to the lathe operators' living room in the corner of machine shop. The lathe hands stood firm. Tell them we worked at normal speed before and the fuck'n company set rates that were too fuck'n tight and the sonofabitches even changed the fuck'n rates on operations which hadn't even been changed. So fuck them — we want it in writing now so we

know we're not going to get that same fuck'n shit all over
again! Baldy George and Don Mayer went back to Dick
Penfield. He stood firm. Work at normal speed or there's no
way to check the time study.

Foreman Casey, caught between the men on the machines
and the bosses up in the front office, made a personal plea to
the lathe hands. Resume normal production so the work can be
re-timed and I promise I personally will fight to get you a good
rate. — "Will you fuck'n well put it in writing that you
guarantee a better rate?" — You know I can't do that. — "Then
let them sweat it out up there the same way we're sweating it
out down here — the bastards, fuck 'em!"

Casey had an ulcer. It was acting up again, his stomach one
big burning pain. Unfortunately, adding to his troubles in the
shop, he had been having an acute problem with his wife. She
had not come home the night before. She had phoned. Her
sister was ill and she was going to stay there overnight. He
phoned a half hour later and his sister-in-law answered. From
her conversation it had been easy to conclude his wife had been
lying. He tried unsuccessfully to trace down his wife. He called
relatives, police, and hospitals. He went out on the town and
checked all the ginmills. This morning, before leaving for work,
he phoned his sister-in-law again. He was told his wife was
there but he could not speak to her because she was asleep. He
insisted. Wake her up. His sister-in-law tried to explain but she
fumbled too much. Casey had come to work but he was
distraught and ready to explode at the touch of a match. With
great effort he had set aside his personal problem to approach
the lathe hands and ask them to trust in him. Turned down by
them he returned to his place at the front of the department
and stood there, his white hardhat firmly set in place and his
arms folded, staring into space, his mind turned in again upon
his own situation with his wife. He was torn out of this bitter
reverie by a scream from the bearded Purple Heart who mistook
the foreman's stare into space for a pair of eagle eyes glaring
down his throat.

"You sonofabitch!" the young hot-blood screamed at the poor
man wearing the white hardhat. "Who the hell do you think
you're staring at?"

Shocked by this unexpected attack Casey reacted like a man
out of his mind. He shrieked back, pouring forth upon the

luckless lathe operator all the suppressed venom generated by his tortured feelings about his wife. His face was ghostly white and his voice hoarse and hollow by the time he topped it off with a final shot.

"Get the hell out — you're fired!"

And that wiped out any possiblity that Big Ben might speak to Dick Penfield that day about Dave Newman and the students and the play. The four lathe hands led the march of men and women from the machine shop through the rest of the plant.

Big Ben and Queen Lila, side by side, went along with the others. He took her hand and squeezed. Friend? She squeezed in return. Friend. They rubbed shoulders as they walked.

The line of men and women snaked through one department after another, with shouts to people at the machines and on the benches to come over to the Labor Hall for a special meeting. — Get out the bow and arrow, Ben. *Venison stew!* — Machines were turned off as power switches were pulled in one department after another. In the plating room an eager foreman tried to stem the spreading stoppage. He threatened to fire any of his people who walked out. That threat guaranteed that everyone in his department immediately walked out. A few reluctant dragons were informed by their fellow workers, jokingly, but there was no mistaking the threat behind the laughter — "You better get the hell out of the plant or you'll get your teeth kicked down your throat!" When one husky young man had the nerve to ask *who* would kick his teeth down his throat a quickly formed education committee, made up of three men over six feet tall and each weighing over two hundred pounds, let him know who would kick his teeth in. He volunteered on the spot to join the education committee. Belying the nervous tension beneath the surface the workers laughed and called back and forth to one another, joking as they shut off machines and put away tools and gathered together lunch pails and other belongings.

A loud yell rang out at one point. "Take out your toolboxes!" — "What for?" — "It may be a helluva long time before you come back to work, stupid!" — Like brushfire it rolled through the shop: "Take out your toolboxes!" and it caught up with those who had already left their departments and they turned back to get their belongings.

John Riley, a pipefitter, was one of those who did not have the message catch up to him until he had already gone out beyond the factory gates. He was the first to turn back. The guard — the same one who had turned in Big Ben only two days earlier and who had been personally thanked for that good deed by Dick Penfield — confronted pipefitter Riley. "Where are you going?" — "To get my toolbox." — "No, you're not." — Pipefitter Riley, six feet plus four inches and two hundred and twenty pounds of muscle and beer belly, looked down at five feet plus seven inches and skinny one hundred and fifty-four pounds in gray uniform.

"What — did — you — say?"

The guard repeated himself. He had a pistol in a leather holster attached to his belt. Fortunately for him he did not reach for it. But he did not retreat. You can't go back in there. The pipefitter offered to flatten the guard's nose. Either that or step out of the way, sir. No move. I'll give you one more chance. Will you step out of the way, sir? No move. Six feet plus four inches and two hundred and twenty pounds lifted five feet plus seven inches and one hundred and fifty-four pounds and tossed him into the muddy creek.

The guard could swim. Wet but unhurt he climbed up onto the grassy bank. The pipefitter had gone on into the plant to get his toolbox. Others had followed him. The guard went into the shack and phoned Dick Penfield. He was told the matter would be taken care of. Go change into dry clothes.

When two detectives from the police department arrived at the Labor Hall their intent was to sit in their unmarked car parked at the curb until the meeting ended. They were men who had once worked in factories in the neighborhood. One had been a union steward. Both had relatives working in the Mackenzie plant. Their friends were officers in the union. The husband of the switchboard operator at Police Headquarters was a union steward in the fabrication department. The information which had raced ahead of the detectives might have come from either of these sources or it might have come directly from someone in Dick Penfield's office or from one of the plant guards who had once worked on production and was still friendly to the union. As the vehicle with the two detectives in it approached the Labor Hall there were shouts greeting them. Here they are, the bastards. Go home, men. The large assembly of factory workers had overflowed out of the Labor Hall onto the porch in front of the building and out across the field alongside the hall up onto the nearby railroad embankment. The proceedings going on inside blared out through loudspeakers temporarily hooked up over doors leading into the hall.

As the detective behind the wheel of the car switched off the ignition, he and his partner having agreed to wait until the meeting ended before making any arrest, the people inside and outside the hall roared out a tremendous "Aye!" And with loud cheers encouraging him to grin and wave to well-wishers, pipefitter Riley emerged from the dirty frame building, the crowd parting to let him through. He walked directly to the vehicle parked in front of the building. Hundreds of men and women from inside and outside the hall surged along behind him to surround the police vehicle. John Riley bent over and spoke through the opened window to the two detectives. Put on the handuffs, men.

The meeting was over. The Mackenzie Machine Tool workers had just voted unanimously to keep the plant shut down after instructing union president Baldy George and chief steward Don Mayer not to start talks with the company until all charges against pipefitter John Riley were withdrawn. The motion to end all bickering by taking this decisive step had been shouted from the floor by Big Ben Hood.

No one there was more surprised by this action than Big Ben himself. No sooner had the hot words involuntarily burst from his mouth than he wished he could swallow them back. Something within him — the coal dust still in his blood from his time down in the mines — instinctively rebelled against all the shilly-shallying and wishy-washy talk from union president Baldy George when he was informed of the imminent arrest of pipefitter John Riley.

"Cut the horseshit! None of us back to work — no meetings with the company — not until they withdraw all charges!"

"Second the motion!" a hoarse voice yelled in support of what had not been phrased as a motion.

From all over the hall came shouts. Call the question! Question! Call the question! The chairman had to put it to a vote. Baldy George slammed his gavel. All in favor signify by saying *Aye*. A loud roar. All opposed? Silence. The gavel

slammed. The *Ayes* have it. A voice moved to adjourn. A
motion to adjourn is always in order. Chairman Baldy George
hit the gavel. All in favor? A loud *Aye*. Opposed? One weak
No. Meeting adjourned!

Stunned by what he had set in motion Big Ben stopped
listening. His mind worked furiously. He thought of Dick
Penfield and Jamison Langner and Betty Lyons. Jesus Christ,
what now? Shoved along with the rest of the people, pushed
through the doorway out onto the porch of the Labor Hall and
down the steps to the sidewalk and out into the street, shoved
against the car of the two detectives, he could not immediately
think of a way to rectify the damage done. He knew that
stoolpigeons must already be rushing the word to Dick
Penfield.

As the detectives drove away with pipefitter John Riley in
the back seat of their car there were shouts and catcalls from
the crowd, and then a shrieking, laughing, scrambling race
down the street back to Mike's Bar. Men and women playfully
pushed and shoved and tagged one another. — *Venison stew,
Ben!* — Big Ben lost Queen Lila as he ran ahead of the pack,
taking long, loping strides, yelling gleefully to keep in spirit
with the others on the surface while his mind went far away.
Breaking into Mike's Bar ahead of the others he called to Mary
Magdeline, slapped a five dollar bill down on the bar and dove
into the phone booth. He had thought it out on the way. It was
risky as hell. Some stoolpigeon inside the plant might get word
out that he had called. But the hell with it. He had to act
immediately to counteract what he had done. He put the dime
in the slot and dialed the number. He heard the girl at the
switchboard and he disguised his voice. Mister Dick Penfield,
please.

Dick Penfield's voice: "Hello." — Big Ben could not reply. —
"Hello." — What could he say? — "Hello." — What, like a
stupid little kid say he didn't mean it? — "Hello." — Big Ben
put the receiver back on the hook. But he held onto it. Maybe
in the confusion at the meeting with so many people yelling
and calling out from the floor the stoolpigeon hadn't been able
to identify who shouted the crucial words which turned into a
motion. Shit, not a fuck of a chance.

He pulled open the phone booth door. Mike's place was
jammed now with men and women who had come from the

meeting. He looked for Queen Lila. She was not there. He went
to the bar. Hey, where's that stupid bastard who got us out
here on strike? They made room for him where Mary
Magdeline had placed his drink and his change. There was
laughter and joking. All friendly. No malice or resentment —
not yet. You had to open your big mouth. Half kidding, half
serious, he put on the big surprise act. Who, me? Not me, I'm
not that stupid! He talked rapidly, adding and adding because
everything he said seemed inadequate. I was only trying to get
the chairman's attention. I was asking for the floor to talk
about it. I didn't think it was right to arrest a man for going
after his own toolbox. It's his toolbox. His property. It belongs
to him. I was against going along with him to be fired. No
negotiating on that. Back to work with the rest of us. With full
rights same as the rest. Someone interrupted him. Drink to
that. They all drank. Someone yelled that the house should buy
one for that. Mike wasn't there. Mary Magdeline said she'd
take it up with him when he came in. She moved up and down
the bar, replenishing drinks and picking up bills and making
change.

Big Ben had a point he wanted to make. "But the other
thing — on the other — the incentive rate — the time study — I
think we should be meeting right now with the company,
working that out."

"The hell with that," the bearded Purple Heart called out
from a table in the corner of the room.

But Ben saw that the rest were listening. They were
receptive. He guessed that they were afraid they had been
boxed into what was sure to be a long strike with both sides
standing pat and refusing to talk. Encouraged, he went on,
feeling his way.

"Somebody ought to get up a petition instructing the
committee to set up a meeting with the company to work out
the time study issue because once that's worked out I don't
think the company will make an issue over Riley and keep the
whole plant shut down. That's what I was trying to get to tell
that big dumbhead handling the chair. But before I got a
chance to get it all out some stupid bastard had to grab half a
sentence and make it into a whole goddam motion. And then
you bunch of stupid bastards stampeded right over the goddam
cliff. A bunch of dumb sheep. Plug up your assholes or your

brains will run out."

He was smart enough to say all this in a joking way, laughing and ready to back off if there was strong opposition. But he could tell that what he was saying was striking a sympathetic chord. He knew that a reaction always sets in after you're swept along by your own indignation and excitement into voting a strike. He knew they all realized now, as he did, that a condition had been set up to which it would take a long time for the company to agree. You yourself, you fuck'n stupid asshole, you put the company squarely on the fuck'n spot by closing off all talk until they agree to drop the charges against Riley and now you got to come up with something great to provide a retreat all around to both parties. He knew he had to come up with it quick. He sweated. Dancing on tiptoe on eggs.

He stayed at Mike's Bar all afternoon drinking steadily while he unsuccessfully sowed the seeds at every opportunity toward getting someone else, on his own initiative, to draw up the petition. There was a lot of heavy drinking being done. Mary Magdeline served round after round as men and women at the bar took their turn to set them up for the others who had bought drinks for them. The normal routine of work had been broken and this was the time to get drunk and blow off steam.

Big Ben also kept his eye on Mary Magdeline, looking for signs of encouragement from her. She was too busy to stop and talk to him but each time she served him he thought there was a little extra smile beyond the laughing sentence or two she normally dispensed to each customer. After a while the drinks began to win out over his tongue and his words stopped spilling out so freely and he withdrew into a shell, surrounding himself with a moat, a vacant air building up about him as he found it more and more dificult to pay attention and grasp what people were saying to him and to answer.

In a vague and fuzzy way he kept trying to talk through his situation to himself. Choking, and doing too much, flying too high, going off in too many directions at once. A decent guy who believes in loyalty to his fellow man. But use my mind. Shit, what's wrong with thinking you've got some fuck'n fairly decent intellectual capacity? That you're not a dumb ox like they fuck'n well make you out to be because you work with your hands on some sonofabitch'n machine in a factory. That's

what's good about that thing, the dance and everything, with
Betty Lyons. Get me in touch with that life where people talk
about theatre and philosophy and poetry and literature. Okay
to talk about cars and baseball and football and hockey and all
the rest of that stupid shit. But not all the fuck'n time —Christ!
Talk about some fuck'n thing else once in a while! But what
about Dave Newman and his play? How long can he get away
with playing him off against Jamison Langner? Neither Dave
Newman nor Jamison Langner are stupid. Somewhere down
the line they'll catch on. Both of them. Then what? Maybe the
only way is to make a clean breast of it to both sides and let
what happens happen — and fuck it. Nobody can kill you for
admitting you did something wrong. I made a mistake. I lied.
This is what it really is. I wanted something so bad I got
greedy.

Though not yet consciously aware of it Big Ben instinctively
sensed already that he might have boxed himself in so deeply
there was no way out except to tell the truth. But he was not
yet ready to accept the painful conclusion which could flow
from telling the truth — surrender of the hopes he tied to
Jamison Langer and Betty Lyons. He did not see any
possibility to achieve the same result or its equivalent by taking
the other path with Dave Newman. He did not think the people
in the shop were ready for that. Or for what Jamison Langner
wanted to do. But if he made the effort with Jamison Langner
and Betty Lyons he would still gain much even though the
program itself would fail. So he agonized on in his clouded
state trying to puzzle out a way to ride two tigers going in
opposite directions.

Mary Magdeline several times urged him to take it easy.
Slow down, honey, you're drinking them too fast. Serving a
round of drinks that had been ordered by Dusty Rhodes who
was a good friend of pipefitter Riley, she skipped Big Ben, only
to be reminded: You forgot good Brother Ben there. Big Ben's
eyes took on a glassy look. His tongue thickened. He gobbled
his words in his mouth. Mary Magdeline told him to eat
something. Big Ben pointed to dried sausage sticks lying in a
basket on the shelf behind the bar. He broke off and gulped
down big chunks of the hard spicy meat. A little while later he
lurched off to the men's toilet. He was discovered there, on his
knees, his head bent over the toilet bowl, heaving up the whole

stinking mess of whiskey and beer and sausage. It was lift truck operator Wayne Henderson who found him. He retreated, holding his nose and howling with laughter at the ridiculous spectacle. There's a ghost dying there in the toilet!

Mary Magdeline sent Wayne Henderson back in with Dusty Rhodes to rescue Big Ben. But no sooner had they dragged him out than Big Ben broke away and rushed back into the toilet. He insisted on staying there hunched over the bowl. There seemed to be no end to it — he retched and retched — his eyes teared — his nose ran — he dirtied his clothes — his cheeks burned — his vision blurred — he felt a terrible pounding in his head — waves of dizziness and nausea repeatedly engulfed him.

In the midst of this terrible state a foggy idea took hold of Big Ben. It came from Mary Magdeline, busy though she was behind the bar, taking time out to try to help him. She came into the men's room at one point — through the fog he remembered that — and she gave him a handful of ice wrapped in a towel and told him to hold it to his forehead. In a fog the foggy idea swelled and he saw it as the answer to his situation. He would go off to California with Mary Magdeline and together they would start over. In the dizzines of his thoughts marriage got mixed up with a job in an airplane factory on the West Coast and developed into a blurred vision of a small cottage in a neat suburb where there would be a little boy and a little girl, maybe two boys and two girls, and this mixture became mixed further with some obscure idea about getting together some factory people out there and setting up some kind of theatre of their own to do plays — and into this he blurred some idea about writing a play — there's a play there in this situation with Queen Lila and Betty Lyons and Mary Magdeline — he'd ask Dave Newman to help him write it.

He was buried deep in these blurred thoughts and visions and completely out of his immediate surroundings when tavern proprietor Mike Staruski, helped by Wayne Henderson and Dusty Rhodes, dragged him out of the toilet and stretched him out on the floor in the backroom. Mary Magdeline covered him with an old raincoat some bar patron had left behind.

Dogs were chasing him and the men were hunting him with bows and arrows. He looked back and he tried to see their faces as he ran from them. Arrows twanged past his head. He ran across a freshly plowed field. The dogs snapped at his heels. He turned and kicked at them. Mary Magdeline let fly with an arrow and it hit him in the throat and bounced away. He choked. The arrow had started internal bleeding. He coughed up blood as he gripped his throat and fell to the ground. He couldn't breathe. His fingers clawed into his bloody mouth, digging into his throat, trying to clear away the red flood welling up and choking off his breath.

Lying there on the floor in the backroom of Mike's Bar, Big Ben awoke. He had just vomited again, all over himself.

Chapter 16

There was an embarrassing confrontation when Queen Lila arrived at Mike's Bar. Mary Magdeline stared, trying to figure out the relationship. Big Ben, seated and bent over a table in the backroom, looked up when Queen Lila approached. His face was white and his eyelids were red. He pushed Queen Lila's hand away when she reached to help him get up. What the hell do you want? She tried again to take his arm. I'm taking you home. He pulled back from her. What home? Mary Magdeline was waiting a few yards away near the door to the front barroom. Queen Lila turned to her. He boards with me.

"My landlady," said Big Ben to Mary Magdeline as he let Queen Lila take his arm.

With Mike's help Queen Lila walked Big Ben to the car. In the front seat of his old Buick, Big Ben leaned his head against the right side window. Queen Lila at the wheel asked if he felt all right. No answer. Go to sleep. She wondered how much went on between him and the redhead.

The thought occurred to her that some day Big Ben would walk in and tell her he was marrying some woman closer to his own age. But until then there was nothing to do but to enjoy this relationship as best she could. She thought she gave Big Ben something he could never get from anyone like Mary Magdeline. The redhead was too gorgeous to ever give herself completely to a man like she gave herself to Big Ben. She was Big Ben's woman all the way and that gorgeous piece can never be that to any man. But when Big Ben gets older, reaches forty and fifty, she herself would be going on sixty and seventy. The hell with it, We'll never last that long together and I'll probably be dead by then anyway from burning the candle too hot at both ends.

She looked over at Big Ben. With every bump of the front wheels his head rolled loosely against the side window. He looked terrible, his face was so white, his mouth was so slack. She thought of other men she had lived with. None as wild as this one and he has the best mind. She really enjoyed the long conversations she had with him — about everything — at night in bed before and after they made love. But look at him now. Ugh!

She helped him out of the car and into the house. The children, already in pyjamas and ready to go to bed, were watching a movie on television. Awed into silence they watched Big Ben. He grinned foolishly as he tried to hold himself steady. Queen Lila stepped into the awkward breech. Say good-night and go to bed. The three children obediently lined up and each gave him a hug and a kiss. The boy gave him an extra hug. Lila was stern. Now you kids get the hell to bed and I don't want to hear one word out of you or I'll split your ass. They disappeared.

Queen Lila switched off the television set and led Big Ben back through the kitchen into their bedroom. He sat down on the edge of the bed. He said he felt bad — "the kids seeing me like this." Queen Lila closed the door. They've seen drunks before. There was the sound of scuffling and the voices of children arguing. Queen Lila opened the door. You kids get back into bed and be quiet or I'll come in there and beat the shit out of you — you hear? There was silence. She closed the door again.

"Lay down." — He did and she took off his shoes and socks and unbuttoned and unzipped his clothes, stripping him down to his jockey shorts. She covered him with a blanket. — "You look like a little boy, a *sick* little boy." — She switched off the light and as she closed the door behind her Big Ben shut his eyes and stretched out his hands and hung on to the bed to keep it from rolling over.

Queen Lila went into the other room and told the children she'd break their necks if they made any noise. Then she went back into the kitchen and cleaned up there. She brought out the ironing board and set it up to iron the children's clothes. The phone rang and she grabbed it to quiet it and said hello.

"Can I speak to Mr. Hood, please?"

"Who is this?" asked Queen Lila, wondering if this could be the redheaded one from Mike's Bar although it didn't sound like her.

"Is Mr. Hood there, please? I'd like to talk to him."

"Who is this?"

"A friend — may I please speak to Mr. Hood?"

"Mr. Hood is not feeling well," said Queen Lila, sure now from the tone of voice and manner of speaking that it was not the redheaded one.

"Who am I talking to, please?"

Queen Lila hesitated only a moment before replying that this is Mr. Hood's landlady. — "Will you give me your address there, please?" the voice ordered, speaking as if to someone lower down the scale. — Queen Lila was offended. Who is this? — "Mr. Hood gave me his phone number and his address, but I've misplaced the address." Queen Lila suspected from the glib way it was put that Big Ben had not given the caller his address. Who is this? — "Can I talk to Mr. Hood, please?" He's not feeling well. — "Will you please ask him if he'll come to the phone?" — He's asleep, give me your name and I'll tell him you called. — "What did you say your address is there?" snapped the voice in a quick thrust intended to provoke an automatic response. — Queen Lila sidestepped. If you'll give me your name I'll have him call you back tomorrow. — The woman's voice at the other end became less officious and explained, "I'm a good friend of Mr. Hood, and if he's sick I'd like to come over there and see if he needs a doctor." — Queen Lila was deliberately harsh and ungrammatical. He don't need no doctor — he ain't sick — he's drunk. And she tried to sound like a tough bitch to frighten off the caller. He guzzled down too damn much happy juice over at that lousy damn ginmill.

After that there was a moment of silence and then the voice at the other end was level but softer, almost pleading. "It's something very important, I must see him. Won't you please give me the address?"

"Tell me who's calling and I'll see if he's awake."

"Tell him it's Betty Lyons — from The Dance Center."

Queen Lila remembered and was more respectful and more careful of her grammer and pronunciation. Betty Lyons was an extension of the power of Jamison Langner. "I'll give you the address, but there's nothing to do for him except let him sleep it off.

"What's the address, please?"

Queen Lila gave it to her, knowing Big Ben would be thoroughly pissed off. Why the hell did you give it to her? On account of Jamison Langner I thought I had to or she'd make trouble for us.

Almost twenty minutes later the station wagon stopped in

front of the cottage. Inside the house Queen Lila was ready and waiting. She had changed into a housecoat, a flowered print, newly washed and ironed. Her hair was combed. She had sprayed herself lightly with cologne. Preparing herself she had the amusing thought that she was more worried about her appearance for this Betty Lyons than she was for Big Ben.

She watched through the front window and saw Betty Lyons getting out of the station wagon. The stylish simplicity of the other woman's clothes made Lila sweat.

Stepping onto the sidewalk in front of the little frame house Betty Lyons hesitated. The cottage looked so small she wondered how people could live in it without feeling choked. The bright green paint outside did not help. She glanced up and down the street at the other frame houses. She felt there were eyes peeping at her from behind curtains on both sides of the street. It was exciting to be here, but also very frightening. In the dimness, with only a few street lights on the block, she had the wild thought that these cottages were crouching to spring at her and knock her to the ground and rob her and hurt her.

She stepped up onto the first step leading up to the porch and peered at the house number to make sure she had the right address. From somewhere in the neighborhood came an ominous whining and rumbling and pounding of metal against metal. The sky flared red only a short distance away and she thought she recognized that as a reflection of steel being poured in one of the factories along the river. Down across the end of the street, she saw some tremendous mounds outlined against the horizon. There was a neon sign alongside the mounds announcing the name of the paper mill and she realized that the mounds were huge piles of logs to provide wood pulp for making paper. Scary sounds poured into the night: metallic and machine motor sounds from the factories nearby, sounds of moving trucks and freight cars.

The clanging of the bell on a locomotive, the squealing of metal wheels on metal tracks and the crunching slam of boxcars into one another ending with a loud thump, and the contrast between this noisy life surrounding her now and the silence in the park-like treed and grassy area where she lived, the contrast between these small cottages crowded together and her large empty house where there was only herself and the woman who came in during the day to clean up and prepare her evening meal fascinated and attracted her as much as it frightened her and repelled her. Could she ever become part of this and live in the middle of it in a little place like this with someone like Big Ben? If she could ever do that then she could feel safe anywhere and she could survive anywhere.

Mounting the porch and groping for the doorbell she was aware of strange odors from the factories and she breathed in and out several times slowly, trying to sort out the smells and remember them In the darkness she could not find the doorbell. She knocked several times and then waited, apprehensive, thinking that the whole of this little house could be put inside her high-ceilinged living room.

A big heavy woman wearing a loose housecoat and smelling of perfume opened the door and Betty Lyons followed Mr. Hood's landlady into the front room.

She could not stop making comparisons: the living room (they must call it the parlor) compared to the size of her bathroom — it is bigger than the bathroom off the guest room, bigger than the bathroom off the foyer on her first floor and the bathroom off the washroom in her basement and the bathroom off the maid's room on the third floor, but just a little smaller than her own bathroom off the master bedroom on the second floor in the rear of her house where she looks out over the trees and bushes and green lawn back there.

She had quickly changed clothes before driving over. Not wanting to feel overdressed in this neighborhood she had put on what she thought was a very simple and casual combination — a tan cashmere sweater, a dark brown skirt, her black leather jacket, and sweatsocks and low-heeled loafers. She did not realize that this studied simplicity spelled money to Queen Lila.

Looking closely at Betty Lyons in the light from the two table lamps in the front room Queen Lila envied and resented her visitor. The thought crossed her mind that if she ever tried to wear clothes like that she would look positively ridiculous, like a fat horse. Before anything else she would have to lose at least fifty pounds.

She tried to set aside the feelings of jealousy as she quickly made a comparison between this new rival and Mary Magdeline Kelly. This one had her hair cut short and it was fluffed loosely, looking as if she had only to run her hands through her hair to make it look natural and fresh. Compared to this stylish lady the redheaded bitch was a fat emptyfaced tramp.

Queen Lila thought she knew Big Ben and what he needed. Lately she had been doing some hard thinking about him. He is a chaser who thinks he can satisfy himself by gobbling down women. But his sex hunger is related to his mind hunger, and that at least in part is the thing that makes something special in their own relationship. She would never forget how deeply shaken Ben had seemed to be the first time he saw all those books in her closet, so much more serious stuff than he had ever read.

She can see that this new friend of his is no simple sexpot like Mary Magdeline, there is an intense intelligent face here, and from the little Big Ben said about her she is a brainy girl full of all kinds of intellectual ideas and with an ability to express herself that impressed him. This is someone to fear in a way she does not fear that redhead.

The three children, hearing a strange voice, got out of bed and came in to look. Queen Lila, careful not to use the warmhearted vulgarity she would have normally used, tried to push them off to bed again. But they took advantage of the presence of the stranger to ask if they could look at television for a little while, wailing that they had been sent off to bed too early, before the movie finished.

Queen Lila, trying to get rid of them without sounding too nasty, said she wanted to be alone to talk to the lady. But Betty Lyons graciously insisted that she would go into the kitchen. I don't want to interfere with their watching television. Lila gave in. Fifteen more minutes and then to bed. She led the way.

"It's a small kitchen," she said, glad that she had cleaned up the supper mess.

"Very cozy," said Betty Lyons.

Queen Lila apologized for a torn section in the rear wall. There was a shack attached back there and Mr. Hood hasn't completely finished off the wall where the doorway used to be. She spoke with pride of the new wood panelling on the other walls in the kitchen, explaining that Mr. Hood intended to put the same panelling on the rear wall where he was still working and to build new cabinets with matching wood to hold the dishes and pots and pans. He'll do it a little at a time, evenings and weekends. Whenever Mr. Hood has time to spare.

She deliberately gave the impression that she was paying for all the materials even though in reality Big Ben was buying everything out of his own pocket after telling her off when she tried to pay him at least for his labor.

She had some kind of vague notion that by talking this way about the work Big Ben was doing around the house she might discourage Betty Lyons' interest in him, that this might make it look like there was a complicated domestic situation here in which Big Ben was already so completely involved that she, Betty Lyons, should avoid it as being too troublesome.

The idea was also to make Big Ben appear less glamorous to the visitor by reducing him to the level of an ordinary working stiff who does odd jobs around the house — and to hint to the visitor that Big Ben plays a much bigger role in his landlady's life than any ordinary rent-paying boarder should play. But Queen Lila knew she had to be careful how she spoke since whatever she said might be repeated later to Big Ben.

For her visitor's benefit she detailed at great length some other projects Mr. Hood planned to do around the house. Mr. Hood's going to do over the other rooms after he finishes the kitchen. And then he'll paint the inside of the house — except where there's the wood panel — he says the panelling will save us money — less to paint. Did this make her seem like she was a cheapskate? Panelling *looks* better than painted plaster, she quicky added; and then she went on to detail another project planned by Mr. Hood. Soon as he can, before cold winter sets in, he's going to scoop out the earth beneath the house with a shovel and a wheelbarrow, dig out a cellar there, then put in a furnace, central heating, and we can throw out these space heaters up here — they're dangerous with children.

She was building up Big Ben's involvement in a part of the world outside that part inhabited by the visitor. And at one point she reached out and moved a newspaper. His union paper. He's a union man. — She would have liked to say it straight out: "You stay where you belong, oil and water don't mix." But the closest she could come to saying that was to obliquely bring to Betty Lyons' attention some things about the lifestyle of a Big Ben which were a far throw from the lifestyle of a Betty Lyons.

If she had only known the true effect of what she was saying Queen Lila would have kept her mouth shut. But she had no way of knowing what was going on in the mind of her visitor. Since Betty Lyons had met Big Ben her own style of living seemed more and more empty to her in comparison with the fullness she imagined in every day of Big Ben's life. He's living in the middle of people, in the heart of bustling life out there at the center, while she — she believed — is falling apart in an isolated and well-kept musty vacuum. The very things which Queen Lila hoped would discourage and frighten off the visitor, including the relationship between the landlady and the boarder, excited and increased Betty Lyons' interest. She knew that her psychiatrist — Henry the Apple-cheeked —would highly approve of her going ahead to make herself completely vulnerable with Big Ben. And she congratulated herself that she had sufficiently sorted herself out to make her ready to accept this challenge. She desperately believed she needed to become involved with the harsh realities of life and all its messy problems in order to become a healthy person, and Big Ben though still very much a diamond in the rough could help her come into this direct contact with these messy realities of life — he could help her learn how to stand squarely on her feet again and get a touch of inner peace in the midst of the chaos of conflicting impulses and pulls haunting her. In return she could give him the polish he needed to make his earthy strength shine.

While Queen Lila talked, Betty Lyons unobtrusively rested the fingers of her right hand on the inside of her left wrist. Good, her pulse was back to normal. A good omen.

The sightseeing tour and the list of handyman jobs indicatd the distance she would have to jump. If she had not talked things out with her psychiatrist Henry Apple-cheeks, she might have been frightened off. But now she thought that even if in the end it did not work out, the effort to make it work could only be good for her — she had everything to gain by going down this road, at least until such time as she decided there was nothing more to gain.

She knew her guide had more than a landlady's interest in the handy man boarder and while she seemed to be looking only wherever Queen Lila directed her attention she was busily checking out every door she could see in an effort to guess where Big Ben had his room and his bed. There did not seem to be enough rooms in this house to go around.

Did he have a room of his own? She tried not to sound awkward, but it came out stiff as a board. "Does Mr. Hood have a separate outside entrance to his apartment?" — Queen Lila indicated the door leading off the kitchen. This is his room. She stepped between the door and her visitor. He's asleep, sleeping it off. Both women lowered their voices to keep the children in the front room from hearing. The muffled sound of the television program could be heard as background to the guarded exchange which began between them.

"How long has he been sleeping?"

Lila tried to ward off the next question by replying, "He'll sleep through the whole night."

The question still came: "Can you wake him?"

"He's drunk."

"I have to talk to him."

"He's asleep."

"It's very important — involving his job."

"What is it?"

"Something personal."

Lila responded by sticking her head into the front room to shout to the children. That's enough television, turn it off and go to bed! And don't give me no back talk or I'll bat your ears in! This was the way she would have liked to talk to Betty Lyons but Ben might be awake in the next room — he might be listening to every word said in the kitchen. C'mon, off to bed, right now! Past your bedtime, never mind kiss and hug, you already kissed and hugged, get to bed or I'll bash in your backsides — quick! The children, intimidated by the sharp tone of her voice and sensing the tension between their mother and the visitor, silently padded off to bed.

At the outset there had been a wary attempt at warmth, with each of the women trying to win the other's confidence. But now this shifted completely to direct antagonism. They kept their attention tightly focussed on one another's stiffening faces. Queen Lila moved to position herself squarely between Betty Lyons and the door to *that* room. She wanted to talk to Big Ben first, when he would be cold sober, a serious talk.

She cautioned herself to avoid any loud or sharp exchange now with her visitor that might wake Big Ben, but even if he

did not awake and recognize the voice of the visitor she did not
want to say anything now which he might be told about later
and consider an insult to his fancy lady friend.

'Why don't you give me your phone number and I'll have
him call you tomorrow when he's sober?"

"It's about his job, I have to talk to him now."

"He's asleep." She shifted a step and again blocked a move
by Betty Lyons to get by her to the door. "He's asleep."

"I'll wake him — I'll take the responsiblity."

This caught Queen Lila flatfooted and she moved to the door
and grasped the knob. "Wait out here." But she did not go into
the room. "I better give him some black coffee first, he'll need
it."

She waited for the visitor to move back and give her room to
get the coffee from the stove and their eyes locked a moment.
Then Betty Lyons silently backed off a few steps, not a full
retreat, but a momentary tense truce while Queen Lila went to
the cupboard and picked out a mug and went to the stove and
poured black coffee from the pot there.

Queen Lila stopped with her hand on the doorknob. "Maybe
I should heat this up, it's cold."

But she did not move back to the stove. She surmised that
her visitor, silently standing there and looking at her, might
not wait much longer and she had to make up her mind now or
her visitor would make it up for her. Should she still try to keep
her from finding out that she and Big Ben occupied the same
bedroom and the same bed? Or should she open the door wide
and switch on the light in there and let her see *all*? Would that
drive this woman away from Big Ben? But then at the same
time she might be driving Big Ben away from herself.

Looking at her visitor, Queen Lila suspected that she was
ready to bust on right into the room if the door was left
unguarded. "Black coffee is black coffee, hot or cold," she said
to Betty Lyons.

But in her thoughts she wavered a moment. In the presence
of this younger woman to whom she ascribed a better set of
morals than she herself possessed in matters relating to sexual
intercourse, the impulse to conceal the truth of her relationship
with Big Ben and to maintain the fiction that it was restricted
to that of landlady and roomer renewed itself. But then the
desire to keep Big Ben for herself and to drive off this outside

interloper rose again and pushed her to do everything possible
to make it look like she had a well-established relationship
with him and that he had been playing this naive competitor
for a fool, giving her the impression he was interested in her
while each night he went straight home from her and rolled in
the hay with his old bag of a landlady.

Okay, open the door wide.

She couldn't.

Instead she released the knob and knocked on the door.

Call out *Ben* or *Mister Hood?*

She couldn't decide. She knocked again, louder, "Wake up,
somebody wants to see you!" No answer and she knocked
again. "Wake up, you got a visitor!" No answer and she opened
the door a few inches and peered into the darkness. She slipped
her hand in, keeping the door as nearly shut as she could, and
switched the light on and off, and carefully closed the door
again and faced the visitor. "He's asleep."

Betty Lyons tried to reach past her to the doorknob, but
Queen Lila raised her free hand and her fingertips touched the
visitor's stomach. They stared, eye to eye, big Queen Lila
glaring down at little Betty Lyons. She deliberately moved the
mug of coffee between them. Betty Lyons took a small step
closer, pushing into the other woman's fingertips. Spill your
coffee, no one's stopping me, I'm going in there. Queen Lila
could read it clearly in the determined gamin face.

"Wait here," she whispered huskily, "I'll wake him." She
reached behind her and opened the door and slipped into the
other room, switching on the light as she entered and closed
the door behind her.

In that brief moment, with the light on and the door closing,
Betty Lyons sees a chair near the corner of a bed. Were those
feminine undergarments lying on the chair? She hears the
woman's voice. Wake up, wake up. Ben's voice with what he
says indistinct, and then the woman's voice again. Wake up,
someone to see you, one of your girlfriends. Ben's voice, a
muffled whisper. The woman's voice, a muffled whisper.

Betty Lyons strains to hear, but the whispers are clouded by
the door. And then they must have lowered their voices even
more because for a while she hears nothing. Why is it taking so
long? The door is unlocked, should she walk right in? Then she
hears the soft snap of the light switch from the other room.

The door opens only wide enough for Queen Lila to squeeze her big bulk sideways out of the dark interior and she closes the door quickly behind her. She speaks weakly, knowing her visitor is beyond accepting what Ben has insisted she try. "Mr. Hood will phone you first thing in the morning, he doesn't feel well enough to talk now." — "Did you tell him this is very important, about his job?" — Queen Lila nods. "I told him." — "Can *I* tell him, I'd like to tell him myself." — Queen Lila looks at her. "Wait, I'll tell him again."

She disappears into the room and the muffled conversation begins again on the other side of the door.

Inside the bedroom Queen Lila and Big Ben look to the door as it opens and Betty Lyons steps in. Ben, lying on the bed, wearing only jockey shorts, shakes his head, and a sickly grin splits his white face. Surprise, he says. Queen Lila reaches and covers his lower half with the bed sheet.

Betty Lyons speaks before they can recover from their shock. "Drink your coffee, Ben, and listen. — I'm risking my whole situation with Jamison Langner by coming here to talk to you. But this is very important to me or I wouldn't act like this."

Her eyes take in everything, an open closet with women's dresses and a man's suit, and a man's ties and a woman's nightgown hanging on the hook inside the door, and clothing for both a woman and a man mixed together and tossed onto chairs and into corners, and his and her shoes, and women's cosmetics on the dresser, and Big Ben's black tin lunch bucket along side a half-empty pint of whiskey on the floor.

"Ben, you're in serious trouble and we have to talk about it, right now, because I want to help you."

Queen Lila looks at Big Ben, expecting him to say something, but he keeps the sick grin painted on his face and he stares back at Betty Lyons, waiting for the blow to fall. He has already guessed what has happened and he can think of no way to undo it.

"This involves Mr. Hood and Mr. Jamison Langner."

Betty Lyons faces Queen Lila, telling her that her presence is not wanted, that from now on this will be a private conversation. Queen Lila looks to Big Ben whose expression does not change. Betty Lyons tries to convey the urgency of what she has to say to him.

"I was with Jamison Langner today, Ben, and we talked about you, a new job for you, exactly what you want, and he agreed you would be great for it, coordinator on a program to bring theatre and the arts generally to blue collar workers and their families, with plays and dance and painting and music, the whole works. It would start off as a part-time thing with you still working in the plant, but every day you'd be given time off with pay to work with me while I train you. I convinced Jamison Langner to go along with everything and we were figuring out what time you would spend with me over in my office at The Dance Center, and then Jamison Langner got a phone call, very important, from Mr. Richard Penfield in charge of personnel.

She stops and the disaster shows on her face and Big Ben groans. "Oh shit." Queen Lila reaches with a towel to mop the sweat and Big Ben takes it from her and wipes his face and gives the towel back to her. "What did that dirty bastard tell him?"

Betty Lyons does not know except what she could put together from what she heard and from what Jamison Langner told her after the phone conversation ended.

"Some problem in the plant and the people all left work and then someone attacked one of the plant guards and the police arrested him, and then, according to Mr. Penfield, a motion was made that no one go back to work until all charges against this man who hit the plant guard are dropped. — Did you?"

The way she asks it she is asking for a denial or at least some explanation she can use in his defense. But Big Ben is silent, his eyes sad now in his sad white face.

"*Did you?*" she asks him again.

Queen Lila speaks up. "Whatever takes place at a union meeting is private, nobody else's business!"

Betty Lyons disdainfully sweeps that aside. "They seem to know everything that happens in your private union meetings." Back to Big Ben. "They're furious, but what I'm more concerned about right now is this. Are you mixed up with that communist writer, the playwright, the one who used to be with the union in there, and are you trying to get him back again in there now into the union?"

Reddening, Queen Lila angrily protests, "He's not trying to

get anybody in anywhere!"

"Aw, fuck!" Big Ben's face is also coloring. "Fuck and shit!"

This burst of anger seems to please Betty Lyons. Smiling at him, she clears clothing off a chair and moves it over to the side of the bed.

"Fuck and shit won't help any."

"Fuck it!"

"Your vocaculary is too limited."

"Tell him to take his job and shove it up his ass! Fuck it!"

Betty Lyons turns to Queen Lila who is sitting on the other side of the bed. All right, we'll play you're his landlady and not his sleeping partner. "Would you mind stepping out of the room, please, so I may speak to Mr. Hood alone about something very confidential?"

Queen Lila looks to Big Ben. Please tell me to stay. Big Ben, sitting up in bed, his muscled and thinly-fatted torso bare, sullenly drains the coffee mug in one long gulp and then rests it against his belly button, and stares down into it. — Betty Lyons quickly presses.

"Ben, you know I respect you, your ability, no matter what you may have done I respect you. More important, I have a great regard for you, a very great regard for you, personally, for you and for the things that are there beneath that vulgar exterior behind which you hide the real sensitive Ben I know is there. I want to help you, and I think I'm in a position where I can help you — I know I can."

She stops and waits. Big Ben's blank face turns to Queen Lila and dismisses her. Queen Lila's hate for the visitor shows. Big Ben intervenes before big Queen Lila takes a swat at the slight woman at whom she is glaring. "Leave us alone a minute." Queen Lila gives him a look of hate (you bastard) and she goes, noisily shutting the door behind her.

Betty Lyons stands beside the bed, looking down at Big Ben who keeps staring down into his empty coffee mug. She wonders if his landlady is pressing an ear against the other side of the door.

"Do you want me to go?"

Without looking up Big Ben shrugs his shoulders. But his insides ache and his throat is clogged. Up shit creek without a paddle, thrown off the fuck'n track by his own fuck'n stupidity, blocked now just when every fuck'n thing was opening up wide. Tears of anger form, but he will not let them come to the surface. All right, you sophisticated bitch, fuck you and fuck Jamison Langner, nobody's going to kiss your ass or kiss his ass, what's done is done and fuck you and fuck him and fuck everybody. He feels the wet on his face as she embraces him. He holds her tight and there is a long kiss. When he slips his hand between her legs she laughs softly.

"What are you laughing at?"

"That's my Ben, you could be dying and as a final gesture you'd reach and grab."

"Why not?"

She takes his hand and moves it away.

"Now be a good boy and get dressed and we'll go out and sit in my car where we can talk with some privacy."

Big Ben obeys.

Chapter 17

While Betty Lyons and Big Ben and Queen Lila played out their little game in the bedroom of the small cottage in the factory district Jamison Langner met with two neatly dressed men who came unannounced to his home in the country. Special agent Rod Maybee and his junior agent followed Jamison Langner into his library study.

"You have a beautiful home, sir, very impressive, the high ceilings, the wide halls, that domed foyer, this wood carving here — hand carved, sir? Beautiful."

The older of the two men, in his middle forties, special agent Rod Maybee polished his black-rimmed spectacles as Jamison Langner turned and opened a cabinet behind his desk. A drink? No, thank you, sir. Jamison Langner offered the box of cigars. No, thank you, sir.

The youthful partner sat back in the leather armchair and let the senior member of the Bureau's team lay out the groundwork for their specific mission. Serious situation, hush-hush, undercover, watching subversives — and then he got down to the business at hand.

"Sir, the Bureau has for many years been keeping a close watch on the activities of a young man you had some business with when he worked for the union. Dave Newman. Right now he's out of the union but potentially he's still one of the most dangerous men in this part of the country."

"Yes!" Jamison Langner exclaims with delight, pleased that at last someone in a position to know agreed with his own assessment. "Do you know if he is still a member of the Communist Party?"

"The information we get, sir, is that Dave Newman has not paid dues to the Party nor has he attended any CP cell meetings since he returned from overseas with the army in 1946."

"But he's still following the Party line, isn't he?"

The senior agent noisily exhaled. Yes and no. Yes, he still associates with members of radical organizations including the CP. But he does not appear to be a dues-paying member now of any left-wing organization. Not at this time. — A friendly relationship with people from other radical organizations, rivals to the CP — people he wouldn't talk to before. But the opinions he expresses privately still do lean towards the Old Left. — Jamison Langner leaned forward, listening intently. The special agent went on, establishing the basis for his visit.

"We know this. Any time there's anything public staged by anyone around here, any protest about the war in Indo-China — Dave's either in it or watching it, somehow connected with it. But more and more into the background. Not in any key position."

"Still I would think you people would be doing something about him."

The special agent smiled politely and adjusted his glasses. "Well, he hasn't violated any law, sir. — We don't have anything we can make stick in the face of the kind of public support he could pick up in this area from union people who still respect him and like him. — But we're watching him, sir."

"I hope so."

Special Agent Rod Maybee glanced at his junior partner and then, seeming to have decided that this was the time to give the reason for his mission, he lowered his voice and spoke very deliberately, his mouth only about a foot away from Jamison Langner's ear. Confidential, sir. Instructions from the Bureau in Washington. Regular reports every three months, quarterly, on Dave Newman's current activities. The skin around Jamison Langner's eyes screwed up and he nodded. Good.

"Which is why we're here sir," continued the senior agent, his voice returning to normal as he straightened up. "Dave's into acting in the theatre now. And writing plays. About labor and politics. — We're looking into that."

At this point Jamison Langner and special agent Rod Maybee exchanged what information they had on the latest activities of this threat to the security of the nation. The special agent did not know who had suggested the latest tactic: Dave's end run around the road block. More dangerous now than when he was only a union organizer. No way to control what he writes and the people in the union remember him as a militant scrapper who got them good contracts and fought hard on grievances and won them a lot of arbitrations. And now here he is, an actor, and a playwright who's writing about *them*, the factory people he knows and who know him. What he's doing tickles them. Any item in the newspapers about his acting or about something he's written is plastered the next day on bulletin boards in a dozen factories around here. The special agent's voice revealed his admiration for a worthy opponent: a nice game of chess, my move, your move.

Leaning forward again, his mouth closer to Jamison Langner's ear again, and the lowered voice again: "Last night a half dozen Old Lefty radicals. Old time union radicals he's known for many years. A meeting at Dave's house. — Dave told them that he has some union people in your plant out there in Niagara who are working to get his play about automation staged out there in their Labor Hall."

Jamison Langner immediately volunteered what his personnel man Dick Penfield had already given him about the play and Big Ben Hood. The special agent did not reveal that he had already been in touch with Dick Penfield many times before and already had this information. When Jamison Langner offered to provide him with a copy of the play, the agent thanked him. He already had a copy. From Dick Penfield? No. — He did not elaborate. — He took out pen and paper to make notes.

"Big Ben Hood?"

"Benjamin Hood, he works in our machine shop."

"*Benjamin Hood.* — We'll talk to him. Do you know where he fits? Is he a radical?"

No, Jamison Langner did not think Big Ben is a radical. *Definitely* not a subversive. Intelligent, but limited by his background. A workingman all his life, from a coal mining family, little formal education, restless, ambitious, but hampered by a pugnacious nature and an anxiety about the people he works with, wanting them to think of him as some kind of devil-may-care kind of fellow who doesn't give a damn what people say about him or think about him, and unfortunately too prone therefore to give in to some stupid impulse to show off how ready he always is to tell off the company.

At this point Jamison Langner told the government agents about the walkout and about Big Ben's motion that turned it into a full-fledged strike. A very confused man who doesn't know what he wants and doesn't know who he is. He doesn't stop to think before he obeys that impulse to act.

"Now he's out there on a limb and we certainly can't ignore what he's done — can we?"

He stopped and waited for an expression of opinion from either of these two men who he believed were trained experts on how to handle situations of this kind. But they outwaited him, forcing him to go on and tell how he had intended to use Big Ben in handling his idea about the arts. Along with this he suggested they call to the attention of their superiors in Washington the developing vacuum in connection with the growing desire of blue collar people for some kind of fulfillment which would be supplied by the arts — very important to do something to prevent this vacuum from being filled by any of the radical element.

They let him know that the Bureau has an excellent theatre division whose job it is to keep an eye on exactly this kind of thing and they assured him that any information he can give them about Dave Newman and Big Ben Hood and the play will be brought to the attention of that division.

Jamison Langner was pleased to hear this and he made another effort to get their advice, telling them about his ideas on an arts program to fill the vacuum.

"We picked Ben as the perfect choice to get our employees and their families involved in this program. But that motion of his to strike is something to think about. We don't want to put ourselves into any position where we are building a Trojan horse."

He paused here to give the men from the Bureau a chance to remark on this, but they had been trained to remain quiet as long as there is any possibility that continued silence promotes diarrhea of the mouth on the part of any person from whom they are trying to get information.

Annoyed at their silence, Jamison Langner impatiently lit a cigar for himself, after again offering the box to his visitors only to have them politely refuse with a shake of the head. They leaned back in their chairs, patiently waiting, and he could not resist this compelling invitation.

"This strike — we told the business agent of the union that we're holding his International Union and its officers responsible for the loss of production and we intend to file suit for damages against them as well as the local union and its officials."

Still hoping he might get some comment on the moves he was thinking of making to force a quick end to the walkout he now reported in detail what he had been told by the union's business agent. "He says the four lathe hands and Big Ben and his Indian girlfriend are the ones most responsible for agitating this walkout and he wants a chance to straighten it out. As soon as he's sure he can put it over he's going to order the people back to work. That means he's ready to declare this strike illegal and *that* means there will be no strike benefits from the International Union. He says he's as much opposed to what's going on there in our plant as we are. He says it only causes trouble for the International Union when you have people like that in there. He's asking that we hold off on any damage suit and when he gets the people back in to work he will not be very angry if those responsible for all this trouble find a slip waiting in the rack at the time clock instead of their time card. A note telling them to report to the personnel office. — *'Your employment is terminated for infraction of company rules.'* — At that point he says he'll have to go through the motions of filing a grievance on their behalf so he can tell the other people to stay on the job while this is handled through the regular grievance and arbitration procedure. But he makes the point that the three-man board of arbitration will consist of himself for the union, our attorney to represent the company, and a third person selected by those two, and this will guarantee a decision that gets rid of the worst trouble-makers. Now that's *his* suggestion."

The special agent abandoned his role of the good listener to ask if Big Ben would be included in the group to be let go. Jamison Langner, happy that he had at last prompted a response, said, "Ben's the man who made the motion." — The special agent asked Jamison Langner if he could hold off. Can you wait until we talk to him? — "We have a costly strike on our hands," Jamison Langner reminded the special agent. — First thing in the morning, sir, promised the special agent, we'll talk to Ben and we'll get right back to you.

This time it was Jamison Langner's astute drawn-out silence which forced the special agent to go on and explain that it would be their purpose in speaking to Big Ben to find out what his intentions are and to what extent he is involved with Dave Newman. How much does he know about Dave's political

history and is he ready to help keep his government posted on
whatever Dave is up to?

Jamison Langner did not need to be told much beyond this
to convince him to try it, believing as he did that something
must be done at once to head off Dave Newman from moving
into the vacuum and that Big Ben was the logical man to do
the job if only some way could be found to guarantee that he
could be kept under control. It seemed very logical from what
he knew about Big Ben that if these secret agents from the
Bureau made the approach they could enlist Ben in the ranks
and make a good believer out of him.

He conducted the two agents to the front door and they
promised again to be in touch with him in the morning after
they spoke to Big Ben.

Jamison Langner returned to his study and sat behind his
desk and smoked his cigar and thought about what might
happen after Big Ben was formally enlisted in the ranks. When
the strike was over it would be possible to fill the vacuum with
a sensible arts program for labor financed by the Regional
Committee on the Arts where, as its chairman, with the
cooperation of Big Ben as administrator of that program, he
could watch closely to prevent any unhappy surprises. He was
confident the government agents would have a strong
immediate effect upon Big Ben. And later when Ben gets a
good taste of the rewards, both financial and social, he should
be the perfect choice — with the mark of the workingman
written all over him, including even that peculiar relationship
of his with that older Indian woman.

In his study, where he seemed to be staring intently at the
intricate patterns carved into the wood panels on the walls,
Jamison Langner puffed his cigar and sipped his brandy out of
a fragile, finely stemmed decanter and thought about the ever-
surprising complexity he was discovering in life. Even himself,
if he did not have the sense to keep his feet on the ground and
check impulses toward such flights of fancy, there are times
when he himself might envy people like Big Ben and his
unusual lady friend. What would it be like to exchange places
for a while? He laughed at his own embarrassment.

It was long after the visitors had left when Jamison
Langner's wife looked into the dimmed study and interrupted
his thoughts. What are you doing alone in here.? He smiled

foolishly and he showed her the empty glass. Drinking and thinking — about this situation out there at the plant.

Chapter 18

The station wagon was parked in front of Queen Lila's cottage, with Betty Lyons in the driver's seat, her hands gripping the wheel. Big Ben sat beside her, looking straight ahead. She made him go over the story for the fifth time. But why did you react so violently? He told her again, ending with an angry outcry.

"They were his own tools — *his*! Instead of arresting him arrest the guard!"

Betty Lyons relented and let his explanation stand. "But in the future think twice before you speak — or you'll be slaving in that dirty factory the rest of your life."

"Those were Riley's own tools!"

"That's *his* problem."

"What if it was *my* toolbox?"

"It wasn't your toolbox. Subject closed."

The quiet finality of her tone almost caused him to break out again. But he remained silent. He was relieved that the painful grilling seemed to have come to an end. Yet he resented that she had forced him to recite like a child his answers to her leading questions. Yes, I want to get into a position where I can enjoy using all my mind as part of my work. Yes, I would like to associate with people with whom I can have intelligent conversations about important things other than what they talk about in the shop. Then, feeling pushed too hard when she asked what important things he would like to talk about, like a wild circus animal snapping at the trainer and refusing to be easily directed to where the trainer wants him to go he cunningly struck back at her.

"Important things like maybe what our union should be doing now to provide these intellectual things for our members instead of treating us all like stupid dummies!"

Frightened, she snapped the whip and drove the snarling lion back into his corner. "Unions are much too powerful now for their own good! The original idea was fine but ever since the war with Germany and Japan ended the unions have overstepped themselves! Now all they want is power! Power for themselves! Power for the leaders!"

Defensively arguing the need of working people to be organized, Big Ben in a very natural and offhand way used the phrase *"the working class"* and Betty Lyons winced and said don't be an ass. She quickly took his left hand and squeezed it between both of hers while she talked earnestly into his stiffened face and she saw his lips press even tighter when she told him he had to *cooperate* now to help straighten things out.

She hurried to explain that by that she meant he had to help her find a way to overcome the bad taste his strike motion at that meeting had generated so far as Jamison Langner was concerned.

"The key to it is that Jamison Langner wants to get the people back to work quickly and he'll be grateful to anyone who can help him do that."

She could see Big Ben's face in the light from the street lamp and what she saw there warned her to back away.

"What we have to think of is something you can do that's completely honorable in every way for you and for the people who are now out on strike there. Nobody wants you to do anything that's dishonorable. But what is the right thing now for those people there? Is it in their best interest to stay out on strike and earn nothing or to go back to work and earn money to support their families? In certain situations a strike might be necessary. But in this situation the union can't even start to talk about the main issue until the side issue of this man Riley is settled. That's because of *your* motion. You put it there and now you have to help clear it out of the way."

Being involved this way in a role where she was dealing with the human core at the center of the production machine was a new and exciting experience for Betty Lyons, a highly satisfying one, as satisfying to her as was the satisfaction Big Ben hoped to find in the upper reaches he was aspiring to. She went on, her warm hands still holding Big Ben's unresponsive paw.

But Big Ben was only half listening. His head ached, but only partly from the hangover he still had from having had too much to drink. *What to do?* His mind could not put his thoughts into good order. Betty Lyons was pressing him, reminding him of what he hoped for, the good intellectual life, the life of the theatre, the life of the mind.

He wished she would shut up a minute so he could think.

Should he cut himself off and surrender to being nothing again
but an ordinary working slob? Up early every morning and off
to work to be run all day by the fuck'n machine? And talk
about who won the fuck'n ball game and which sonofabitch
had his car break down and what bastard put himself in hock
for a new fuck'n jalopy? Sports and cars, and cars and sports,
and shit, and shit, and shit — from punching in to punching
out, and then over to the fuck'n ginmill for a drink and then
home for supper and off to bowling or back again to the fuck'n
ginmill. Or stay home and watch all that stupid shit there
every night on that fuck'n TV idiot box. And then to sleep and
up again early in the morning and start the same goddam shit
all over again — off again on the same fuck'n merry-go-round
— and the same fuck'n thing the next day and the same the
day after that and the same the next fuck'n day until your
fuck'n mind feels so goddam fuck'n useless from not using it
you want to fuck somebody up the ass or kill somebody,
anything to blow up the whole goddam fuck'n shitty
sonofabitch'n — !

Venting an inner inexpressible anguish he squeezed one of
her hands and she let out a small cry and grabbed at him with
her free hand.

"Ouch!"

He let go and apologized.

"Sorry."

She patted his cheek and he moved his head away. She took
his left hand again between her warm palms.

"Let's think together out loud."

He appeared to be listening. But he had already made up his
mind. No matter what she said he would not agree to be a
fuck'n fink, a lousy stoolpigeon. It was now Big Ben the True
versus Big Ben the Shit, and Big Ben the True had to find
some way to kill off Big Ben the Shit and put an end to all this
fucking around.

"What do you really want out of life?" she asked him,
getting satisfaction out of the solemn moment as she looked
into his face and invited him to join with her in serious
thinking on this profound question.

"What do I really want out of life?" he parroted.

"Take a minute before you answer. And don't say what you
think I want to hear or what Jamison Langner would like to

hear. Say the truth. Tell me. *What — do — you — really —want — out — of — life.*"

"How the fuck do I know?"

"Think, and say whatever instinctively comes to mind. Don't shut it off."

He *was* thinking — that right now this is his chance to end the whole goddam ball game. Fuck off, you stupid bitch, and tell Jamison Langner to go fuck himself, and Big Ben the Shit is as dead, as dead, as dead as can possibly be. But he couldn't say it.

"What are you thinking right now?"

"Right now?"

"Don't stop to think of something else to tell me. Tell me what you're thinking. Say it!"

He fumbled his way into it and then picked up steam as his suppressed anger found an outlet. "I'm thinking that with all that's happening right now I'm so fuck'n well confused that I don't know what the fuck I'm thinking and I don't know what the hell it is that I really want. What I do know is that I'm so fuck'n well tired that I want to go to bed and get some fuck'n sleep and get rid of this fuck'n miserable hangover that's splitting my fuck'n head right down the fuck'n middle."

She was silent and he thought that she did not like what he had said. He rapidly alternated between regretting having said it and being glad he had said it. He kept his face open and neutral and waited for the outcome of her long stare. She lifted her hand so her wrist watch caught the light and then she turned back to him.

"Alright, we've been talking out here almost two hours. You go in and get some sleep. I'll be in touch with you tomorrow as soon as I can get to Jamison Langner. Now let's both go get some *fuck'n* sleep and some *fuck'n* rest and then maybe we both can think of some *fuck'n* thing to do to straighten out this whole *fuck'n* thing." She leaned to him. "What would you do if that word was wiped right out of your vocabulary? You'd be left speechless."

She was teasing him, inviting him to be soft and loving. But right now he did not feel like being soft and loving. He had to embrace her and kiss her, but with the struggle still going on between the True and the Shit his lips were cold. Betty Lyons' body stiffened in his arms and her lips hardened. But then she attributed his lack of ardor to worry about his situation. Her lips softened and she tightened her embrace in an encouraging gesture and then let go of him and pulled her head back and smiled into his face. Don't worry too much. Get some sleep. She patted his cheek as if she were soothing a troubled little child. Go to sleep, baby.

He walked back along the side of the house and wondered if Queen Lila was waiting up for him. The thought struck him that she probably had been watching the whole time they were out there, peering at them through one of the curtained windows in the front room. He entered into the kitchen and the night light was on above the sink. He carefully closed the door behind him.

"Is that you?"

Lila's low voice came from the front room and there was dynamite in it. The room was dark except for some light coming through the front windows from the street lamp. A cigarette end glowed and he saw her. She was sitting on the sofa. His eyes adjusted to the darkness and he saw that she had changed into pyjamas. One bare foot showed. The other was tucked under her. Her dark black hair hung down below her shoulders, framing the lighter shaded blob of features making up her face. She lifted something and he saw the glint of light against the glass.

"What are you drinking?"

"None — of — your — damn — business — what — I'm — drinking!"

"How many have you had?"

"Enough to know when somebody is shitting all over me."

Through her anger he heard her plea. Before you go to bed please talk to me and tell me what it's all about. What did you two talk about? He did not feel up to it. Not another long heart-to-heart talk now right on top of the other one. Christ, no. The light glinted on the glass again and then there was the flush of red at the end of her cigarette. He told her to go to bed.

"Don't tell me to go to bed, you bastard. You go move in with your new girlfriend — I don't need your lousy money. Maybe she's hard up and she'll give you free room and board in return for a good screw." He refused to rise to the bait and after she was sure he was going to remain silent she went on. "She's so high class muckity-muck maybe she won't let a dirty

slob like you move in and dirty up her bed. Her neighbors
might complain she's ruining the reputation of the whole
shitty-assed neighborhood. Tell her she can farm you out to all
the wives on the block and keep them all quiet. And you can
put in for a new job classification and ask your girlfriend to get
you a merit increase from the big boss. Male prostitute first
class and shit-heel specialist."

"Good-night," said Big Ben under tight control.

"You," said Queen Lila, following him into the kitchen, "you
take your things and get the hell out of my house."

He turned and stuck out his hand. "I'm paid up to the end of
the week, I'll take a refund."

"I'll refund you my ass."

He reached for her. "Let's have it, I'll take it with me."

She flicked his hand away. "To you all women are whores,
aren't they? Because you want to get paid for it you think all
women are like that too, don't you? — You *have* to think that
way, don't you?"

He went to the pantry and took out the bottle of whiskey
and showed it to her. Want a drink? She told him he had paid
for it — your bottle, you take it and get out. He filled his
shotglass and turned to her. Want a beer? Before she could
reply he told her she had paid for it, it's your beer. No answer
and he asked if he could borrow some. She told him to choke
down all the beer he wants but get sick outside, not in the
house. He went to the refrigerator and helped himself. I need a
taste of the hair of the dog that bit me. He tossed down the
whiskey and gulped the beer.

"Will she let you keep on working in the shop or is she
taking you into an office with her and a desk and a hot
couch?"

He looked at her and gulped his beer and his veiled eyes told
her to go on and spill her stupid fuck'n guts.

"Tell her to buy you a white shirt and a tie to wear to work.
And you want a new suit and a new car or no more nookie. No
car, honey, no nookie."

He kept his face insultingly blank.

"Does she let you drive her new station wagon?"

"I drive it," he said, flatly, and gulped the beer.

"And does she tell you to take out her little poodle dog for its
little walk?"

"I'm her little poodle dog. She takes me out for a walk."

"You mean lap dog. Lap-lap."

"Jealous?" he asked and poured from the bottle into the shotglass again.

"Why didn't she take you home with her?" When he ignored the question, replying only by tossing off the shot of whiskey, she stuck another barb into him. "What'd you do, say you wanted to get paid in advance? Hell, I wouldn't trust you either. You'd only go pass it over the bar to your redhead. Putting out to the ladies to pay it over to your redheaded pimp!"

Keeping his face stiff and his eyes narrowed to hide from her how much it hurt each time she slashed at him, Big Ben sipped the beer from the can with studied and steady moves. His stubborn silence only spurred Queen Lila on to become more and more abusive as she became more and more convinced by it that in his mind she had already been bypassed for a better prospect.

But Big Ben is not listening. He is off on an entirely different tack. At this moment he is trying to think of a way to escape from the whole mess, from everything, to get out of this trap which is ripping him apart inside. Right now the hell with it, the hell with everybody, he wants out.

How? How? How?

If the shop remains shut down he can look for a temporary job elsewhere and chip in to the Strike Welfare Fund to help those who put in full time manning picket lines and the strike kitchen. Many of the men will disappear anyway to do painting, papering, plastering, carpentering, and other repair work around the house. He knew Queen Lila would like him to push ahead on the projects in her place. The hell with her. Other men will disappear to fish and hunt in their camps back down in Pennsylvania. And a long strike, like this smells like it will be, is always a time when men and women try greener pastures they've been dreaming about, go out to California or Arizona or down to Florida, grabbing the opportunity to find out if they like it there better than working back here in the hoist and conveyor factory.

He had already volunteered for night picket duty with the vague thought that it can be a helluva lot of fun sometimes, especially if you can get one of the women pickets to keep you company all night parked in your car in front of the plant.

Tomorrow he would un-volunteer. A bright idea struck him and the gratifying picture it created in his mind's eye caused him to grin. *Maybe Mary Magdeline would take off with him.*

"What kind of funny shit are you stirring up now in that fat brain?" demanded Queen Lila, interrupting a derogatory remark she had already begun about his swollen idea of his superior intellect.

"Me?" he asked, looking straight into her eyes. "Nothing."

"You bastard," she said, and she took a deep breath and shook her head from side to side.

He gulped his beer without letting his eyes leave her face. The hell with you, babe. His mind went back on its previous track. Driving across country he can phone strike headquarters every few days and find out what's happening back here. Out in California he can get a job and let the Strike Committee know where he is, to notify him when they settle the strike, and then he can decide whether or not he wants to come back here. This way he can leave Big Ben the Shit behind here with Betty Lyons while Big Ben the True takes off free as a bird with luscious Mary Magdeline Kelly.

Queen Lila stood above him, studying him. "What are you thinking?" — Nothing. — "That's a crock of shit." — He poured another shot. — "Be careful, you might sober up and say something intelligent." — No danger of that. — "Who are you planning to shaft now, your new girlfriend?" — He went to the refrigerator and took another can of beer. — "I'll bet when she snaps the whip you lap-lap her shit and say it tastes like honey."

He came back to the kitchen table with the can of beer and he spoke quite pleasantly. "Y'know, you keep flapping that mouth of yours around loose like that you're liable to have a whole mouthful of teeth work loose all of a sudden and fly right across the room."

She reached for the bread knife and the same thought went through both their minds about that trained knife finding its own way between the ribs of the redhead's partner. Queen Lila steadied the shaky knife handle against her stomach.

With what he later admitted to himself was a phony shit-eating smile to hide that he was ready to crap in his pants, Big Ben turned his back to Queen Lila and carefully set the can of beer down on the edge of the kitchen table. He tossed off the shot of whiskey and picked up the can of beer and opened it and took a long drink of the cold bitter liquid and carefully replaced the can on its spot on the edge of the table. He took out a pack of cigarettes and slowly extracted one. He lit it and puffed it and then let it dangle from the corner of his mouth. He screwed the cap back on the whiskey bottle and put it away in the pantry. He stuck his hand into his pants pocket and took out a dollar bill and tossed it down on the table. ("For the beer.") He turned and walked to the door and opened it and went out into the night, carefully shutting the door behind him. From the moment Queen Lila had pointed the knife directly at him he had kept his back turned to her and he had never once looked at her and he had not heard her move or make any sound.

Chapter 19

His walk around the block decided nothing. By the time he came back to the house and saw the light on in the kitchen he was more anxious than ever to find some way to get the good life Betty Lyons told him was still possible, and at the same time to still be the great guy he liked to think he was to the people he worked with in the shop.

His car was parked in the gravel driveway beside the house. He opened the door on the driver's side and got in and then pulled the door shut. He saw Lila come to the kitchen window and peer out between the curtains and he started the motor and backed the car out onto the street. He saw the curtains on one of the front windows part as he drove away.

The strike tent was set up in a big lot along the bank of the creek directly opposite the factory administration building. From there you could yell over across the road to Mike's Bar. Big Ben parked the car at the curb as near to the strike tent as he could get. As he crossed from the car to the tent he saw that there were three cars parked on the other side of the creek directly in front of the main plant gate. Pickets were seated inside the cars. *On Strike* placards were tied to the door handles on the outer sides of the vehicles.

No one expected the company to try on the very first day to move out any dies or any completed work. But it was an indication of strength to be able to maintain round-the-clock picketing seven days a week. And it was a tradition in this union to show this kind of strength to the company from the very first day a strike started.

Big Ben's sweeper friend was in charge of the strike tent. Old Bill charged himself with the responsibility to keep the coffee always hot and ready on the kerosene stove for any hungry or chilly pickets or for any strikers who wandered in to find out what was going on. He also kept up the supply of doughnuts. Once the strike settled down for the long pull, the coffee and doughnuts and other provisions would be brought in by a scrounging committee who would get donations from friendly merchants and from workers employed at other factories in the area.

Old Bill was a widower. He lived alone in a furnished room on the second floor above Mike's Bar, next to the room Big Ben had occupied there. Strike tent duty gave him people to talk to and an important role to play. It also gave him the opportunity to pick up information he had to phone in to personnel man Dick Penfield each morning. In return for this and other similar favors he reluctantly performed for the company the old man was permitted to stay on the payroll past the age sixty-five compulsory retirement deadline specified in the contract between the company and the union.

When Big Ben walked into the strike tent Old Bill was washing dirty coffee mugs. He had an apron tied around his waist and he was dipping the mugs into a large sheetmetal washtub of soapy water and then rinsing them out in another washtub into which clean water was pouring from a garden hose hooked up to a faucet outside a small boathouse on the bank of the creek. When Old Bill looked up at Big Ben the light from a kerosene lamp carved dark hollows into his sunken cheeks.

"How's the coffee holding up?" Big Ben asked him.

"Always ready and waiting," boasted Old Bill, reaching for the pot. He poured the coffee into a mug and gave it to Big Ben. He brought over the box of doughnuts. A visitor now was most welcome. During these early morning hours it gets lonely being there by yourself in the strike tent.

It was easy for Big Ben to start the old man off on a talking jag. In his younger days Old Bill had toured the country with a song-and-dance act. He enjoyed boasting of his exploits with women when he had been in show business. But he was the first to say that this was because he had now reached the age where all he could do was talk about it. My sex life is all in my mind now, long on talk and short on performance.

"How," prompted Big Ben out of his own desperate need to ease his troubled mind by listening to the old sweeper, — "how the fuck could any man be so goddam stupid to leave the stage and settle down and go to work in this asshole factory in this asshole town?"

It was Old Bill's cue. He grinned and showed his even false teeth and hiked up his floppy pants and did a quick jig and then told the story. My married brother lived here with his wife and when vaudeville rolled over and gave up the ghost I moved in with him and used his place as a home base while I picked up odd jobs with the carnies — carnivals. When my brother died, his grieving widow kept my bed warm there and I was fool enough to offer to make it legal and she was fool enough to take me up on it. She had relatives working here in the plant and they put in the good word for me. That's how I got committed in this funny farm.

Big Ben asked him what happened to his wife and Old Bill said she died of cancer. By then all her children — my nephews and nieces — were grown and married and gone. Big Ben asked why he didn't get married again, and Old Bill said the next time he got that close he suppressed the urge to buy a wedding ring. Instead we made it legal in the eyes of the good Lord and the hell with the city clerk and we saved two bucks we would have wasted there. And she kept on drawing her widow's social security checks she would have lost if we signed a paper. She still had the farm and I moved in. That woman could cook. She cooked so well she ate her own cooking and she hit that scale way up over two hundred pounds. Now *there* was something to wrap your cold feet into on a cold winter night!

With only occasional prompting from Big Ben to keep him going, the veteran of vaudeville took advantage of this chance to relieve the tension that had overloaded his wiring system from living alone this past year since his two hundred pound roommate had passed on and left her farm to her children. His stream of chatter was exactly what Big Ben needed to heal the hurting wound inside him and by the time a thin line of gray began to show along the edge of the horizon a mantle of peace had gently settled down on him.

The old man said he had to prepare fresh coffee. He expected everybody on strike to be there this first morning for the mass picket line the strike committee had set for the starting time of the day shift.

Big Ben said to tell the guys he would be back, but he might be a little late. He wanted to go home and take a shower and pull himself together and he had to straighten out a problem.

He went over to his car. This visit with the old sweeper had smoothed out the jagged feelings which had driven him to the strike tent and now there was hope again and he was going to live the good, honest life so he could respect himself.

Driving back to the cottage he went over some of his

alternatives if the pressure here became too great and he had to
hit the road. He recognized — with a great deal of private
pleasure from being aware that he was recognizing it — that
he was reaching back into his memory to find a substitute for
Mary Magdeline Kelly if she would not take off with him. He
even thought about the possibility of going back to
Pennsylvania to see the wife of his neighbor friend he had
accidentally killed in the motorcycle accident. Even though he
had never tried to sleep with her she still kept the money he
sent her every week. But there was something unpleasant
about trying to find peace there where she would be a constant
reminder that he was responsible for the death of her young
husband. What about the girl he had picked up in Cleveland?
He had her phone number. She lived in Johnsonville in
southern Illinois. He wondered if she had already married her
boyfriend. And there was Donna Colangelo, his sister's
roommate. With her experience as a waitress it would be easy for
the two of them to work their way out to California. It was
comforting to think of these other women who had touched a
vulnerable spot inside him and to whom he might turn if
everything here collapsed out from under him. He still had
alternatives in reserve.

Queen Lila was getting breakfast ready for the kids when he
stepped into the kitchen. She spoke to him pleasantly.

"Where have you been?"

Without answering he went into the bedroom and closed the
door behind him. He could hear Lila telling the kids to hurry.
There was much calling back and forth. He stood there,
listening, and a deep regret filled him. He would miss this. He
might never get close to anything like this again. A home. But
it would be a relief to cut loose and go out into the unknown.
Adventure, with all these problems left behind.

He pulled his two old suitcases out from under the bed and
opened them and began to pack. He could hear Lila and the
kids talking in the kitchen. He would miss the kids and he
thought they would miss him too, at least until another uncle
moved in. He heard his name mentioned. The boy was asking
about him. He would miss the boy most of all. Maybe he could
come back and see the boy and take him to a ball game or to a
hockey match or out to go fishing.

The door unexpectedly opened and the thirteen year old boy

stuck his head in and disarmingly stared and waited for Big
Ben to say something to him.

"Come in or get out," said Ben.

"You come and eat your breakfast," said the boy.

Then the boy saw the opened suitcases lying on the bed. He
pointed but before he could ask anything Big Ben gently
pushed him out of the room and closed the door. Almost
immediately the door opened again and Queen Lila stepped in
and closed the door behind her. Big Ben went on with his
packing and Queen Lila silently watched. The doorknob turned
and Queen Lila stepped out of the way. The boy brushed past
his mother and went to Big Ben and took him by the hand.

"Ben, I want you to come and eat breakfast with me."

Big Ben allowed the boy to lead him into the kitchen and
Lila followed. His breakfast of orange juice, cooked cereal,
scrambled eggs and bacon, and toast and coffee were on the
table waiting for him. The two girls were already eating. A
loud good morning from Big Ben was echoed in subdued
fashion by the girls. The boy took Big Ben by the hand and led
him to his place. Sit down and eat. Big Ben tolerantly obeyed
the petulant command. The boy leaned against Big Ben's
shoulder and put an arm around Ben's neck. Ben disentwined
the boy's arms and gently shoved him away.

"Cut it out — sit and eat your breakfast."

The boy went to his seat. Big Ben silently ate. Lila busied
herself at the stove. Aren't you girls through yet? Hurry up,
you'll be late for school. Finish eating and get going. Where's
your books? Get them and get out of here. And don't talk back
to me today or I'll bat your heads off. The girls quietly hurried.
They kissed Lila and Big Ben and called goodbye as they went
out the door.

Big Ben chewed his toast. Didn't they know he was going?
Young kids, what the hell, another uncle will move in and take
my place. But the boy, he's smart, he knows what's cooking.
Stop looking at me and eat your egg, you little bastard.

The bright shaft of sunlight coming through the window
across the kitchen reached the point where it hit Big Ben in the
eyes. He ducked his head. Goddam miserable fuck'n sun. He
shifted his chair. There was the horn. The bus out in front of
the house. He motioned to the boy. Let's go. School. The boy
did not move. His lips were set and there was sadness in his

eyes. Smart little sonofabitch. The horn sounded. The boy's eyes did not leave Big Ben's face.

"Your bus, get going."

The boy did not move. His lips set tighter and his eyes would not let go of Big Ben.

The horn sounded.

Queen Lila took the boy by the arm. Come on. He pulled away. She reached for him. *School!* He shrank away and shook his head, his eyes filling with tears and still fixed on Big Ben. The horn. Queen Lila reached. *School!* — And the tears: *No!*

Big Ben went to the boy and held out his hand and the boy took it. They walked out to the school bus. It was parked in front of the house next door, its usual spot in front of Queen Lila's cottage occupied by a parked automobile in which sat two men who watched Big Ben as he pushed the boy up the steps into the bus.

The bus drove away and Big Ben started back toward the house. He was very much aware that the two men in business suits in the parked car were looking him over. He did not recognize them and he wondered what the hell they were doing there that early in the morning in this neighborhood. From the way they were dressed he thought they might be insurance salesmen up bright and early to start banging on doors with some fast pitch to sell some fuck'n shit insurance policies.

Queen Lila was clearing the kitchen table. He walked right by her into the bedroom and closed the door. The catch on one of his suitcases was broken. He had used a piece of cord to tie the suitcase together when he had moved in. He looked into the closet to see if the cord was somewhere in there. He thought of knotting a couple of old ties together to use them in place of cord. There was a knock on the door and he ignored it. Another knock and Queen Lila walked in. He continued to paw around among the odds and ends lying on the floor in the rear of the closet.

"What are you looking for?"

"Something to tie my suitcase."

There was the sound of her steps going away, into the kitchen, then returning. She handed him a ball of cord and a scissors.

"Here."

"Thanks."

He reopened the suitcase and rearranged some of the clothes so they would take up less space and then he lowered the lid again. The suitcase closed more easily now. He reached for the ball of heavy twine and unwound a good length of it and carefully wrapped it around the suitcase several times and then used the scissors to cut the twine. Lila shifted her feet. He bent further over the suitcase, pulling the cord tighter. Lila spoke.

"We're adult human beings, let's act like adult human beings."

To this he replied with a quick glance up into her eyes that said he was listening, and then went back to his work.

Her voice was under tight control, her diction extra good, her speech sounding somewhat formal. "I owe you an apology. I had no right to say what I said last night. We both went into this with our eyes wide open. I have no hold on you and you have the right to any relationship you want to have with anyone else — and vice versa."

Not looking up from the knot he was tying, he nodded curtly. Apology accepted, and I agree I have no more hold on you than you have on me. Both free as a bird.

Her breathing sounded. She was finding it hard to say it as easily as she had planned it. "The way it is, the best thing is for you to go and see how you like it, and I'll see how I like whatever I do then, and then later, whatever we both decide, that's the way it will be."

He swung the suitcase down to the floor beside the other suitcase and stuck out his hand to Queen Lila. She gripped it. — Friends? — Friends. — He nodded toward the closet. My guitar, give it to Frankie, a present. He indicated his suitcases. I'm going over to the picket line and I'll pick them up later. — No hurry. — Want a ride over there? — No, I'll clean up here first. Tell them I'll be over soon. — Another handshake. Friends? Friends.

The two men in business suits who were sitting in the automobile parked in front of Queen Lila's cottage got out of their car and motioned to Big Ben before he could get into his own car parked in the driveway. He waited for them as they approached him.

Special agent Rod Maybee showed Big Ben his identification. FBI, we'd like to talk to you. Big Ben, literally stunned by this totally unexpected confrontation, bewildered and frightened, his heart suddenly pounding, his face sweating, meekly went along with the agents on either side of him. He stepped into their car. All three sat on the front seat, with Big Ben in the middle. He realized he was cornered and he wished he had not been so quick to get into the car with them.

The younger agent started the motor. He drove several blocks and parked the car at the curb near one corner of the iron picket fence surrounding the sprawling rolling mill. The crashing sounds of the work being done on the steel ingots could be heard in the background.

Special agent Rod Maybee did the talking. He quickly and factually, with no element of approval or disapproval evident in his voice or manner, let Big Ben know that he knew a hell of a lot about what was going on between him and Queen Lila and Betty Lyons and Mary Magdeline Kelly. And then he asked how Big Ben liked Dave Newman's play. — "What play is that?" — Special agent Rod Maybee said he had seen a copy of the play and he had read it and thought it was pretty good for an amateur. A little too propagandistic maybe. But not too bad.

He asked Ben if he would be interested in taking over the job of administrator for an arts program sponsored by the central labor council. They could speak to the labor priest and give him a boost there.

"We know you're a registered Democrat, Ben. You're no commy. Maybe you have a few socialistic ideas. But every man's got a little socialism in him until he starts making a good buck. Then he becomes more concerned about getting some more salt on his own potatoes. — Ain't that right?"

Big Ben had to answer. "I guess so."

"You're doing this thing now with Dave Newman and his play. What we want to know, Ben, is what's that all about?"

A ton of lead dropped off Big Ben's back. They were not going to give him hell about his motion at the Labor Hall. They had not even mentioned the strike.

He told them about Dave Newman coming to him with the play and that he had already told Dick Penfield about that, and Dick Penfield had agreed that he should keep in touch with Dave Newman and see what more he could find out about what Dave wanted him to do with the play.

Big Ben's general idea at this moment, though he was too busy with other thoughts to define it specifically now, was to treat the two agents the same way he planned to treat Dick Penfield, to let them think he was going to play along with them the same way he had indicated to Dick Penfield he would play along with him, while at the same time in some way he would let Dave Newman and the college kids know that he had to appear to be playing this kind of game with those other people. Somehow — and he didn't yet know exactly how — he still had the idea that he could walk his own private tightrope down the middle between the contending forces in a way whereby he would not be cutting the throat of the people he worked with in the shop and at the same time in some way would advance the good cause on their behalf by getting something going in all this business about developing something on the side of the working people in the arts.

The special agents were very understanding. This play itself, Ben, it's not that it's radical, but it's a clever angle some people are trying to use to get a foothold in there. And there are other things Dave has written which *are* subversive, and this play will open the way for those other things to follow.

Big Ben, silent and listening to catch the full import of the words themselves and of the way they were spoken, began to shiver inside as the special agent coldly laid it out for him. Dave Newman is more dangerous now than when he was an out-and-out commy, because he's still friends with people who are commies and worse, and he opens the door for them. —Now you understand, Ben, that if you help Dave get his play done in the union hall, then you're working against your own country. We know you're not that kind, you don't want to do that —

Big Ben sweated blood. Bad enough to get caught between Jamison Langner and Dave Newman. Now this. *Christ, help!* He had to talk his way out of the tightening noose before it closed in all the way and pinned him where he now was certain they were trying to put him.

"I don't know what you fellas want, but there's a strike on over there at the shop now, and I think it might last a real long while. So I won't be around. I'm going out to look for another job."

"Why do you want to do that?"

"I'm fed up with that place."

"Stick around, Ben.'

"I think just for the hell of it I'll look for something."

"The strike won't last that long."

"I want to see what there is around — if I do decide to make a move.'

The special agent sharpened it up, though he still smiled. "We'd like you to stay right where you are over there, Ben."

"I don't know."

"*You — stay — there.*"

Big Ben looked at his wrist watch. Jesus Christ, look at the time, they're expecting me over there on the picket line, my turn on picket duty. There was no argument made about that. The special agent nodded to his younger partner who turned the ignition key and started the motor. The older agent patted Big Ben encouragingly on the back and told him they'd keep in touch. It'll be all right, Ben, it'll all come out clean in the wash — don't worry.

"Where do you want to be dropped off?" asked the younger agent.

They dropped him off where they'd picked him up and he saw Queen Lila's face appear at the kitchen window when he started the motor of his car in the driveway. He wondered why she was not over at the picket line. The fleeting thought presented him with a question. Did she see him drive off with those two in their car? As he backed his old Buick out of the driveway Lila opened the side door of the house. She called to him. But he kept the car moving. He had to get the hell away from her and everybody else, to be alone for a few minutes to pull his shivering shit together. — Oh, Christ!

He glanced at his side mirror and saw that Queen Lila was standing in front of the cottage and looking after him.

Chapter 20

He stopped at the strike kitchen, seeing a big crowd of strikers, more men than women, gathered in many small groups in the open field between the creek and the tent. He saw that only a few token pickets, carrying signs nailed to sticks, were on duty on the line. They were sauntering back and forth in front of the main gates of the plant on the other side of the creek.

"How's your head this morning?" said lift truck operator Wayne Henderson, grinning, as Big Ben elbowed his way into the kitchen tent. The confined space was jammed with men and women picking up their morning coffee and doughnuts.

"Fuck you," replied Big Ben, low enough not be overheard by some women nearby, tossing it off as his way of saying good morning, while not altering the glum expression on his face.

"Ben, you missed it this morning," Dusty Rhodes called out to him.

"Missed what?"

Men and women around him excitedly told what had happened, interrupting one another to fill out the story. You missed it. A mass picket line this morning. We kept out all the office people — all the foremen — all the bosses — all the big shots — no one got into that plant this morning — no one except the boilerhouse men — we sent them in to keep the place from blowing up. We kept them all out — and Dick Penfield led them all over to the Elks' hall — he's standing there himself at the door, the smart bastard, checking to make sure we don't send in no spies.

Big Ben touched the shirt sleeve of chief steward Don Mayer who just then hurried by. Hey, what happens now? But the chief steward continued on, as if he did not hear him. Other strikers answered Big Ben's question, each trying to squeeze in his bit of important information.

"Dick Penfield contacted the Chief of Police." — "The Chief is calling in all his men." — "He called the county sheriff for reinforcements." — "Jamison Langner says he's not going to let anybody keep out people who want to go in and work." —

"And our dear union president Baldy George, a sudden dying sister up in Watertown, last night, emergency, he took off."

Listening, grabbing all he could hear that was being said around him, while he ate a doughnut and drank the coffee that Old Bill the sweeper handed to him, Big Ben quickly tried to put it all together. He had to know where things stood in order to make an intelligent decision. Everybody around him was talking. A lot of nervous talking. A lot of arguing. Majority sentiment seemed to be against keeping the office force and the bosses out permanently, and even the worst agitators, he noted, were being careful. Keep them out the first few days to show the company we really mean business — make them fight their way in — make them use the police — make them go to court for an injunction — psychological warfare — keep a cloud threatening over the head of anybody who goes in — let them know they'd better not do any of our work in there.

Having quickly sensed that the majority disagreed with this, even though the few who did speak up against it were apologetic about their lack of militancy and were being beaten down by the louder voices, Big Ben gulped down the last of the doughnut and coffee and left the tent to seek out chief steward Don Mayer. On his way out of the tent and wading through the milling clusters of strikers in the field outside, he spoke out good and loud and clear.

"Whose stupid idea was it to keep the office and foremen out?" He asked it several times, saying it half humorously and half seriously, let others see that he was not afraid of the shouters. It worked. His loud, laughing, sneering challenge, immediately encouraged some of those who had been reluctant to risk the sharp counterattacks and they echoed his view, arguing with those who tried again to browbeat them into silence. What the hell are we keeping them out for? They can't do our work, the stupid bastards, they don't know how. How the hell can you settle anything if you keep giving the company the excuse not to meet and talk? Encouraged by this speedy reaction to his bold move, Big Ben found chief steward Don Mayer and this time angrily confronted him, swallowing the swear-words to keep women nearby from overhearing them.

"Goddamit, why don't we hold a special meeting right here and vote on this fuck'n thing right now? This is a democratic union, let's vote, goddamit — what the fuck are we waiting for?

"Vote on *what*?"

"The fuck'n office and the foremen — out or in? Decide by vote, and cut all the fuck'n bitching."

The chief steward welcomed the chance to transfer the heat to Big Ben. Someone brought him a chair from the tent and he mounted it and announced a special meeting in session right there and then in the field. The company has all the office people and foremen together over in the Elks' hall and we hear they're getting together a small army of cops and deputy sheriffs to take us on. What do we do? Do we fight it out and get a few heads busted and bust a few ourselves and see how it comes out? Or do we step aside and let them go in? Now you people decide.

Big Ben raised his hand. The chief steward pointed. Okay, Ben. He stepped down from the chair and Big Ben took his place and confidently attacked. He was certain he was expressing the overwhelmingly majority sentiment.

"What the hell are we, a bunch of stupid monkeys? The company needs a clash on the picket line and a couple heads busted, so they can go to some judge they got and pick up an injunction to cut us down to only three or four pickets at each gate. And we're giving them just what they want. We're setting it up for them. Why? We all know those people in the office can't do our work. And the foremen won't. So why keep them out? They can't hurt us. Let 'em go in."

At this point he was drowned out by a spontaneous, swelling noise of hooting and booing that caught him completely by surprise. He tried to shout above the yelling and catcalling, but he could not be heard. He saw young Purple Heart holding his cupped hands to his bearded face, booing. His heart began to race but he stood his ground. Grinning good-naturedly, he held up his hand, asking for a chance to go on. There were heckling shouts. Sit down! Who's paying you off? Big Ben kept the grin frozen into his face and waited until the heckling finally tapered off. He dropped his hand, but as he opened his mouth to speak the hooting and catcalling erupted again and drowned out his voice. He grinned and waited again for silence, but again when he tried to speak his voice was drowned out. He waited, internally sweating blood, but outwardly still smiling, and he tried again. Not a chance. Now the shouters yelled for him to step down from the chair.

"Motion to adjourn!"

The screaming voice of the Purple Heart out in the crowd began it, and the motion became a shouting chant.

"Motion to adjourn! — Motion to adjourn! — Motion to adjourn!"

The chief steward tugged at Big Ben's sleeve, and Big Ben bent forward, and the chief steward's mouth was close to Big Ben's ear. The chief steward took Big Ben's place on the chair. The shouting subsided except for a few isolated voices, with the bearded Purple Heart loudly insisting to the chairman that a motion to adjourn had been made and that it takes precedence over everything else and it requires a vote without any debate.

"Who's running this meeting, me or you?" The chief steward, face red, angrily shouted at his challenger.

"I made a motion to adjourn!" the Purple Heart yelled back from out in the crowd, not retreating an inch.

The chief steward shot back at his challenger. "You don't have the floor to make a motion. Because this brother here still has the floor. So shut up and let him finish. And then you can ask for the floor and make your motion after he's finished."

Now there was silence. Chief steward Don Mayer looked around, his eyes going from one face to another, daring anyone to challenge his ruling. There were no takers. He turned to Big Ben. You still have the floor. But Big Ben shook his head.

The chief steward squeezed in a careful stab in the direction that had been started by Big Ben. I'd like to hear from someone who wants to take the floor to support the suggestion of the previous speaker. Boos and shouts, and no volunteers. A hand was raised and the Purple Heart was recognized. He pushed through the crowd and stepped up to take the chief steward's place on the chair. Big Ben, standing only a few feet away, his face still a smiling mask, braced himself to receive the personal blast he expected. But the speaker went right to the main point. Let's keep that plant shut down so tight not even a mouse can go in and out! There were shouts from the men and women gathered in front of him. So move, Mr. Chairman! Second the motion! Call the question! Vote! Let's vote on the motion! The chief steward stepped up onto the chair as it was vacated. He looked to Big Ben to see if he could expect any help from there, but the frozen smile he saw told him to expect nothing now from that source. He looked out over

the heads of the large gathering of strikers. There was a
resigned weariness in his face and his voice when he quietly
spoke.

"Exactly what is the motion?"

"Nobody in, nobody out of that plant! Not without a private
police escort! Make them know it's not going to be an easy
picnic!"

"Is that the motion?" asked the chief steward.

"That's your goddam motion, *yes!*"

The reply was delivered in such an angry tone that even Big
Ben could not help laughing with others in the crowd, and he
thought about how funny it was to hear it said like that — like
hearing himself, the way he would have said it at the meeting
the day before if anyone had questioned *his* motion in that
skeptical tone of voice. He blamed himself for his predicament
and silently railed at himself for being so stupid with all that
fuck'n shit with Jamison Langner and Betty Lyons. It was his
own fault now that the part of himself he had always liked the
most, that part that had always made it possible for him to
respect himself, was down the drain. Jesus Christ, you sure
made a fuck'n mess of it.

There was a roar of support for the motion and then
absolute silence when the chief steward asked to hear from
those opposed. Several men called out to Big Ben, good-
naturedly kidding him for keeping his mouth shut. He called
back, in apparently good spirits, his voice matching their light
tone. Six months from now I'll be walking the picket line and
laughing while you brave bastards will be crying to the
company to let you crawl back in there on your hands and
knees.

With the meeting adjourned Big Ben grinned as he sparred
with the people around him. Open your big mouth and
somebody is bound to stick his foot into it. — Hey, Ben, what
was that you were gargling about up there before? — Me, I
never said a word. — Nobody seemed to harbor any ill feelings
toward him. Not even the Purple Heart. That was a relief. And
word might get back to Betty Lyons and to Jamison Langner
that he had made the effort.

When the report came a short while later that the entire
office and supervisory force was marching from the Elks' hall
to the plant, with a strong police and sheriff escort, Big Ben

raced with the others across the bridge over the creek to set up a mass picket line.

Chief steward Don Mayer directed them to the main gate where Big Ben saw Queen Lila already walking with a picket sign. This was where the confrontation would take place. The strikers knew that for psychological reasons the company had to take the office people and supervision in through the same main entrance where they usually entered to go to work. There would be no sneaking in through the back gate or the side gate, and certainly no climbing over the high fence.

Big Ben walked the picket line, carrying on a loud monologue aimed at the pickets near him. He played both straight man and comic, setting up the strained jokes and igniting them, and then, providing his own most receptive audience, laughed as if he was killing himself with his comedy act. Where's that stupid bastard who made that motion to let the office and foremen walk in on their own two feet? Him, he was promoted to a good job up in the front office! (Ha-ha-ha!) What do we do with the first cop who swings his club at anybody's head? Grab his club and shove it in through his belly button and build a tail for him in the rear. (Ha-ha-ha!) He heard himself, as if it was someone else performing, and he knew that what he was saying was not really funny, even though pickets near him, as nervous as he was, laughed loudly along with him. — Shut up, he yelled and he slapped himself on the cheek. (Ha-ha-ha!)— But he could not stop.

The main entrance to the factory grounds was only a little distance beyond the end of the short bridge over the muddy creek. An advance party of six uniformed policemen and deputy sheriffs on foot and carrying nightsticks moved into place and closed off both approaches to the bridge, directing motor traffic away from the chosen battleground.

Now the marching body of about one hundred men and women, two abreast, almost all of them dressed for office work, appeared. They were led in front and flanked on both sides by two-man teams of policemen and deputy sheriffs, carrying nightsticks. They marched across the bridge, and gathered in a group across from the pickets, both groups overflowing the sidewalks onto the paved street, but keeping a respectable distance in the middle between them. The moment of confrontation was yet to come.

There were about three hundred men and women massed on the picket line in front of the main gate, with an opposing group of about a third that number gathered across the street, standing, watching the moving pickets, waiting for the event to unfold itself. Two police cars, with red and white overhead lights flashing, appeared and slowly moved into position in the middle of the road, one on each side of the bridge. then a long string of cars, overhead lights whirling, sirens sadly wailing, appeared, stopping on the road connecting with the approach to the bridge across the creek from the factory, disgorging what must have seemed to the strikers to be a small army of uniformed policemen and deputy sheriffs, all carrying nightsticks. Big Ben looked across the creek and saw them and interrupted his comedy routine to marvel out loud: *Oh, shit!*

The fear became thick and oppressive, to those directly involved and to the crowd of onlookers who were gathering on the other side of the creek from the factory. To the strikers on the picket line it appeared that they were about to be attacked by a large and well-organized and well-trained unit of armed men, a force they could not defeat or repel but which they would resist somehow, even though it was to be expected that some of their own number would get hurt in the process. Within their fear was contained the vague hope that somehow in some way they would make those who attacked pay in kind for any hurt they delivered. The office people and foremen and executives thought they were endangered by a mob of angry men and women who seemed to have put aside individual friendship and were welded into an unfeeling force determined not to permit them to get into the plant without inflicting serious injury upon them. They expected that they would be punched and kicked as they pushed through the massed picket line, even if the uniformed police and deputy sheriffs could protect them from worse. As for the police and deputy sheriffs who had lined up between the two opposing groups, most of them were good friends, neighbors, even relatives, of men and women on both sides of the street, and they dreaded the dirty business lying ahead, their reluctance dramatized by their refusal to look at anyone in either group for fear their eyes might meet those of someone they knew. No one there wanted a battle that morning, but it was as if this was the script which had been written by the screenwriter, and the cameras were set to roll, and all expected they would be required to do their part when the director gave the signal to begin, and then they would play the scene as it was already written for them.

Several pickets, recovering from the initial shock at seeing the large force of police and deputy sheriffs, tried to pick up the spirits of the others with forced lightheartedness accompanied by a lot of nervous physical activity. Outstanding among these was Big Ben the True. He was in a strange state, marching cockily on the picket line, occasionally shouting out and jumping up and down in place, while consciously avoiding the eyes of Jamison Langner who, with Dick Penfield and Tom Watson on either side of him, stood across the street at the center of the opposing force.

When the Chief of Police went to Jamison Langner and conferred with him, Big Ben increased the tempo and volume of his one-man circus of laughs and shouts, whipping sharp quips at the pickets around him, prodding to make them shout their nervous shots back at him. And every so often he interrupted this to yell good-naturedly in the general direction of those gathered across the street.

"Go home, Sam — no work today."

It became a sort of battlecry he was encouraged to repeat, as each time it triggered a nervous flurry of supporting yells and cheers from pickets around him, along with his own loud, laughing punctuation to what he had just said. Go home, Sam, no work today! *Yeah!* — On the surface he was having a great time. But inside the brawling confidence of the outer shell his mind furiously worked at evaluating the situation in a search for the possibilities that would enable him to escape and start a new good life.

Then, hitting him like a slap in the face, he caught sight of the two government agents who had picked him up and then dropped him off again earlier that morning, and he abruptly broke off the jumping shenanigans and was silent. He wondered if they had already marked him and were watching him, and if over there they had been able to hear his stupid shouting. They were standing some distance away, on the sidewalk in front of Mike's Bar across the creek. Only one policeman was over there in that immediate vicinity, keeping curious onlookers up on the curb away from the bridge approach. Mike was behind the government men, with Mary

Magdeline Kelly, both standing on the wide concrete step directly in front of the entrance to the tavern. Seeing the redhead now reminded Big Ben of California, and he thought of some of the things he might have to do if he decided to go out there with her to escape the long reach of these government guys. He could change his name, grow a beard, maybe let his hair grow long, and he would have to pick a new social security number to go with a new name.

Now that he was again thinking about going away, he began to get an enjoyable excitement out of the possible adventure involved in creating an entirely new life and wiping out traces linking him to the old one. He wondered if he could construct a new personality for himself, to go with a different outer appearance and the new name and social security number. That would require real acting.

So preoccupied with this that he lapsed into silence, Big Ben kept moving back and forth in front of the main entrance to the factory grounds, moving along with the rest of the massed pickets in a tight, elongated elliptical path. He responded automatically with the others to orders from chief steward Don Mayer as they were echoed by the picket captains stationed along the streetside outer edge of the thickening ranks. — Close up, squeeze tight, no space, no air between — squeeze. Tight. Tighter. Climb inside your neighbor. A solid brick wall, nothing goes through. Not one single one gets through. No fights, no violence. If there's to be any violence, let it come from them, not from us. Don't be provoked. You hotheads, cool off, save it for later over at the bar. — And then, pleasing Big Ben and bringing him out of himself for the moment, he heard Don Mayer and the picket captains use what he had mentioned over in the field beside the strike tent: Don't get sucked in, don't give the company the violence they need to get an injunction.

Across the street from the massed picket line which was so tightly compressed now that it could barely keep moving, Jamison Langner and the Chief of Police terminated their tense consultation. Both turned to face the pickets who were intently watching them. The Chief of Police, beckoning, summoned his immediate subordinates. They huddled together, the capped heads of the three subordinates cocked forward to receive instructions from the head topped with the cap with the gold badge.

With the critical confrontation now imminent, Big Ben resumed his running fire of nervous quips to the men and women pressing tighter and tighter into him on all sides —(Get your hands out of my pockets!) — as the mass of several hundred bodies, responding to the cry of tighter, tighter, reduced itself in size to a solid thickness about four feet in width and about forty to fifty feet in length, the two elongated sides of the ellipse crushed together, still flowing very slowly in opposite directions, back and forth in front of the main plant gate — obeying the city ordinance requiring a citizen to keep moving to avoid arrest for loitering when asked to move by a police officer.

On the surface Big Ben was only another burly picket, a good candidate for the union's educational squad, getting mentally and emotionally set to resist the imminent attack. But Big Ben the True had already made several tentative decisions and — right there in the middle of the situation which seemed about to explode — he could not keep from quickly testing them, trying to spin them rapidly out to their logical conclusion. Assume he did go out to California and used a new name which he would adopt when he was sure he had cut off any possibility for anyone to follow his real name to the new name. Okay, long hair and a beard and maybe a mustache, and look for a job in a factory out there. But then they'll ask for your social security number. So better pick up a job some place on the way out there, maybe washing dishes in some one-arm joint. No, sir, I don't have any social security number. They'll know you're lying, but why the hell should they care? Apply for a new number, with the new name, and no questions asked. But what if they become suspicious and mention it to someone? A grown man without a social security number, how come? The hell with it, don't take the chance — use your own social security number, and change only one digit in the middle. Later, hell, you made a mistake in writing down the number, and if you want it you can still pick up the credit for retirement benefits. If they catch on now, the hell with them, move on and do the same thing all over again, until you get lost, and after a while they'll forget all about you. Benjamin Hood? Never heard of him.

It was sad to think of ending what he had only begun to

touch with Betty Lyons. But the hell with it, don't even say goodbye to her, she would never understand. Just walk away and don't look back. He tried to shut out the deep sense of regret flooding in on him as he thought of the good life she might have opened up for him: the theatre, the ballet, modern dance, long-hair music, art galleries, the life that included parties like the one given by Jamison Langner. It hurt to lose it all now when he was so close to getting it, to give up the once-in-a-lifetime chance he had accidently stumbled into. But if he was going to be a free man he had to pay the price. Yet, to turn away now and leave all that behind — it was such a damn hard thing to swallow and digest. It choked him up tight to even think about it.

Sharp, excited warnings from Don Mayer and the picket captains brought him out of himself. Here they come — hands down — don't be provoked — tighten up — squeeze together — nothing goes through!

The double line of police and deputy sheriffs, with office and supervision behind them, moved across the narrow no-man's land toward the massed picket line, and Big Ben physically and mentally braced himself for the collision.

Chapter 21

In the short huddle before the attack Jamison Langner had told the Chief of Police that he did not want anyone hurt. Tell your men to make a strong effort, but don't use their clubs. The Chief expressed doubt about breeching the massed picket line without force. Jamison Langner was disturbed by that. No. No broken heads. Not like you had there during the Rand strike. Don't. Not here. All we want is a strong effort, so you can honestly testify to that when we go to court.

(Your honor, we ask this court to issue an injunction limiting the number of pickets at each gate. Our city police, reinforced with deputy sheriffs from the county, tried unsuccessfully to break through a mob of several hundred pickets who were illegally blocking the main entrance to our property. As the police chief himself will testify, violence was certain and many people would have been hurt if we had insisted on use of legally justifiable force to gain our right of entry. Instead, choosing the intelligent and humane course, we are here to ask your Honor to remedy the situation by giving us injunctive relief.)

The ridiculous tussle lasted not more than a few minutes, but with the nervous arguing and shoving it seemed to last much longer. On both sides, the mouth was at a maximum and the shoving at a minimum. It was all being done for the record, to be blown up and batted about later by the lawyers. No violence, no club-swinging, no punching and no kicking; hit nobody, hurt nobody. Both sides obeyed instructions of their leaders, and the busiest man there was the photographer working under the direction of personnel man Dick Penfield. He snapped pictures as fast as he could, urged on to hurry and get it over with. Dick Penfield waved to Jamison Langner, and the Old Man nodded to the Chief of Police who called to his men and motioned for them to move back to the other side of the street. Police and deputy sheriffs herded the office and supervisory force away from the pickets. The funny little game was over.

The tension was gone and pickets laughed and called out friendly taunts to the men in uniform. Hey, where's that town constable who wanted to start a union? Here's somebody's badge I stole. Give that rolling pin you got there back to your wife, she's waiting to bake a cake for supper. Move along there, men — hup, two, three, four.

Police officers and deputy sheriffs huddled briefly around the Chief and then straggled across the bridge to the cars which had brought them there. A few of them, still careful not to show too much friendliness, nodded to strikers they knew. The marked cars, after loading up, moved out of sight, one by one, without sirens sounding and without lights flashing.

Picket captains called out instructions given by chief steward Don Mayer as the picket line disintegrated. Back to regular schedules. Those on duty stay here. The rest take off, and everybody report home first before you start playing around, so we don't get blamed.

Departing pickets joined friends from the office and supervisory force, walking together in the street, crossing the bridge to the other side of the creek. Come over to the strike tent and get some coffee. I'll buy you a beer. But all such invitations, though welcomed, were pleasantly refused. There was a line not be crossed, so long as the strike was still on.

Big Ben, joking with other strikers and calling out to office workers and foremen and to friends among the police and sheriff's deputies, wove in and out, hurrying across the bridge toward Mike's Bar. And then, almost over to the other side of the creek, he slipped between some strikers and some office workers and came face-to-face with Jamison Langner.

Surprise!

Jamison Langner involuntarily spoke. Hello, Ben. Then the Old Man flushed and turned to escape. But Big Ben had already instinctively said hello in reply, before he, equally embarrassed, turned his head away. They fled from each other and an elderly man who worked in the toolroom in the machine shop called out, mimicking what he had heard. Why, hello Ben. And Big Ben grinned back over his shoulder. Fuck you, sir.

Mike's Bar was filling up quickly with thirsty strikers. Men and women, released from the tension on the picket line, swapped stories about what had happened during the short skirmish. — "Did you see my next door neighbor? He took one look at me and shifted to the other end of the line. Crown me with his nightstick and I would never again let him use my power lawnmower." — "Big Gertie right there in front of me with her big ass, I owe her five bucks." — A squeal from the other end of the bar. "I'm worth more than that, you cheapskate." — "Excuse me, Gertie, I didn't see you down there." — "You see me now, and you better start running before I get hold of you and make you give me what I still got coming, because back there I didn't even know what you were doing behind my back, you dirty cheater."

Withdrawn into himself now, hearing but not taking part in the somewhat forced banter going back and forth all around him, Big Ben sat on a stool at the rear end of the bar and fingered the shot of whiskey which Mary Magdeline had put there with its beer chaser. He half-heartedly echoed each flurry of laughter that punctuated almost anything anyone said, while he thought he sensed the start of a coolness setting in around him. New arrivals were jovially invited to step up to the bar and have one, but no one had offered to buy one for him. People near him who were talking about what had happened earlier on the picket line seemed to be careful to address themselves to anyone else but him. He bent his head over his drink. Shit on all of you, you fuck'n bastards.

Mary Magdeline, passing by to get a drink order, rapped her knuckles on the bar to make him look up. Smile! He obediently showed his teeth and then he wondered how he could get her alone to sound her out on heading out with him to California.

It didn't take him long to figure it out. He borrowed a pencil from Mike and scribbled a note on the back of someone's business card he found in his wallet. (Important to talk to you, will phone). He folded the card twice into a small square and tapped his empty shotglass on the bar to get Mary Magdeline's attention. He was ready when she refilled his glass. He put some coins with the folded note into her hand. Her fingers closed into a fist and she walked away. He saw her shove her hand into her apron pocket and then he tossed down the drink and went into the backroom and slipped out through the family entrance.

Captain's Cabin was crowded with a lot of people he knew from the shop. Less than a block away from Mike's Bar, it was the chief rival for the drinking affections of the people working in the factory across the creek. Upon entering the place, through the family entrance and the backroom, Big Ben quickly checked to see if Queen Lila was there. Relieved at not seeing her, he guessed that she had gone home to be there when the girls came home for lunch.

A man at the bar taunted him about the motion he had made at the meeting that morning. The mood was friendly and Big Ben replied with a grin that there are two sides to every question. Another man at the bar got into the act. The right side and the wrong side. Big Ben, continuing on to the phone booth, called back his answer. Time will tell which is which. He stepped into the phone booth and closed the door. But he had to come back out to look up the number in the telephone book. The two men who had heckled him invited him to come over and have a drink. He saluted them. Thanks, I've got to make a phone call. Both accepted that in friendly fashion. Who is she, has she got a friend?

Inside the phone booth he dialed the number and someone answered after two rings, a man with a sense of humor who deepened his husky voice into a simulated toughness. Mike's Whiskey Bar, what the hell do you want? — "Can I speak to Mary Magdeline Kelly?" — Mary What Who? - "The redhead behind the bar." — A loud call: Mary Magdeline Kelly, your boyfriend! — Big Ben could hear the shouts mixing with ridiculing laughter, but he could not make out what was being said. Then hoarse voice was back, being tough again. She's busy now, call her later. — "Tell her I'm calling for her mother, an emergency." — A hoarse yell: Your boyfriend says he's calling for your mother, an emergency! — Big Ben heard the muted laughter this provoked. He waited.

Mary Magdeline Kelly said hello, and her impatient, angry tone burst the California bubble Big Ben had dreamed up for himself. The cold reality of their relationship caved in on him and dried up his mouth. He did not reply immediately and Mary Magdeline's annoyance apparently was aggravated by his silence.

"Who — is — this?" she demanded, hard as stone.

"Me — Ben — I just gave you the note over there."

"What's this about my mother?"

"Nothing — it's me, I got to talk to you. Can you meet me when you're through work?"

She was angry about being lied to. "I have to go home, I'm going away tomorrow."

"I'll drive you home."

"Listen, you — !" she began, but then she relented and her

voice softened. "I'm taking a plane back down to Miami first thing in the morning — so goodbye, sweetie, and thanks for everything."

"Wait — do you want company? I'll go down with you."

"I got company, thank you. Goodbye, sweetie, I got to work."

The click told him she had hung up. He walked back to Mike's Bar. Mary Magdeline did not give him any special sign of recognition when she placed a shot of whiskey and a glass of beer in front of him. She picked up the five dollar bill he put down and she brought him his change and hurried away.

He was still rooted in the same spot, deep into his own thoughts, when a head bent over to whisper into his ear. Ben, some dame in the car out in front wants to talk to you. Through the big window he saw and recognized the new station wagon. His first impulse was to duck into the backroom and out through the family entrance, but others in the crowded tavern, aware of the station wagon and the attractive woman sitting at the wheel, began tossing suggestive remarks at him. With that challenge to his manhood it was too late to duck out. The impulse to run was quickly replaced by the sense of satisfaction it gave him to see Mary Magdeline Kelly standing on tiptoe and straining to get a good look at the woman waiting out there for him. It made him feel good enough not to mind the slightly obscene curves being thrown at him, none of which were really malicious.

Grinning and growing taller, he slid off the stool and swaggered to the front door. Someone yelled to him not to keep the girlfriend waiting. She's sweet, can I come along? I'll bet that *tastes* real good. Big Ben turned his head toward where that came from. I'll let you know. He did not waste even a goodbye glance on the redhead.

The woman in the station wagon was frightened. But she hid it well. Her cheeks were warm, but otherwise she maintained her superior and self-assured air, looking straight ahead, ignoring the wisecracks she was attracting. The men gathered in front of the tavern were boldly gawking at her and there were whistles which she ignored. Nor did she let herself show any of the panic she felt when one of the men, with a beer belly and wearing a red leather hunting cap, sauntered over and opened the door of the car on the curb side.

He showed her a leering smile and big yellow teeth. Can I

help you, honey? She did not move. The man slid in and sat next to her. If you're looking for something, honey, maybe I can help you out. She pressed her lips thin. He reached over and pulled the door shut. Let's go for a ride, honey. The pounding rose in her ears. But her voice seemed cool and steady. She tried to sound as superior and aloof as she possibly could. "Will you please get out of my car?"

She saw Big Ben and she sounded the horn, and the man sitting beside her hurried to open the door and get out. Big Ben ran the gauntlet of good-natured kidding to get to the station wagon. The man who had vacated the seat to make room for him held the car door open. Keeping your seat warm. Big Ben passed him with a low growl. Get lost, you bastard. The self-appointed attendant slammed the station wagon door shut and Big Ben reached for the wheel and slapped the horn. Honk, honk to all you dirty sonsofbitches.

He knew that Betty Lyons was frightened and he felt sorry for her. Let's get the hell out of here. The car pulled away from the curb.

The two of them were silent. Betty Lyons concentrated on the driving, keeping her eyes fixed on the road ahead. Big Ben waited for her to speak first, while he wondered how bad a scene he was in for this time.

The car moved at a comparatively slow pace along the newly paved highway. The creek was off to their left. On their right were row after row of newly built homes thrown up by residential developers. Then they were beyond these. They were out into open country, with dairy farms off to their right, stretching away from the creek, green meadows turning brown and cows bunched together and chewing away.

There was very little traffic. Betty Lyons drove as if she were coping with a flood of automobiles, her driving requiring her undivided attention. Big Ben could not stand the prolonged silence.

"What's up?"

She glanced over at him and then looked ahead again. She drove a short distance further before applying the brake to slow down the vehicle. She guided the station wagon off the road, parking it on the wide, grassy shoulder, in a spot shaded by branches of some big trees. She sat still a while, not yet ready to talk. He waited for her to begin, bracing himself for the

miserable repeat of the night before, but determined this time
not to take it as quietly as he had accepted it then.

She turned to him.

"They're going to hold a special meeting of your union
tonight."

She said it with the pride of someone who knows she is
bringing important information not possessed by the person to
whom she is talking. Now she waited for the questions she was
sure this information would prompt from him. But he sat there,
not moving, with a faint smile fixing itself onto his face,
patiently waiting. She finally got the message and went on,
putting it together for him, piece by piece, reluctantly
volunteering another block of her secret material each time she
paused to hear from him and found his wall of silence had not
yet been breeched. Contradictorily, though his refusal to speak
was aggravating, her overall feeling was one of enjoyment,
because despite his silence she was aware of his intense interest
and his desire to know more — the mystery and suspense it
permitted her to build into the telling gave her a satisfying
sense of power.

She unconsciously slowed down and dramatized, her voice
changing in pitch and intensity as she highlighted the most
important aspects of her message. Jamison Langner and Dick
Penfield and the company's lawyers met with two officials from
the Washington office of the union. They threatened them with
a damage suit against the union, for interfering with
production. And the union officials asked the company to hold
off until they had a chance to speak to your local officers.
They're going to order them to send the people back to work.
(Big Ben's skin crinkled at the outer corners of his eyes,
discounting the possibility of the success of this effort.) If your
local officers don't go along, your charter will be lifted and an
administrator will be appointed, and he'll tell the people that
your union will not defend anyone who is fired for refusing to
go back to work. Dick Penfield is still arguing that anyone who
was in any way responsible for causing the strike should be
fired —because a strike is completely illegal, in violation of
your contract. But so far Jamison Langner still seems to have
some reservations about going all the way for that. His mind is
still open, I think, and he could be affected if something
constructive were done to affect him.

She stopped and earnestly stared into his eyes, trying to pierce the wall, straining to let him see how worried she was about what might happen to him. He refused to come out from behind the faint smile and since what she was trying to do for him was apparently not being sufficiently appreciated, a note of resentment was now evident as she went on, forced by his silence to be more specific.

"When you have your meeting tonight your officers will make their recommendations." Big Ben interrupted to tell her that union president Baldy George might go along. But he's out of town. — She was sure he would be back for the meeting. "They'll make their recommendation and then there should be a chance for someone to do the intelligent thing — to support them."

This broke his silence. "I tried something this morning and the people voted me down."

She asked him about it and she told him how glad she was to hear that he had tried and she would be sure to tell Jamison Langner and she knew it would be helpful. Her forehead was deeply wrinkled with the effort to let him know how much she was pulling for him and how much the right outcome meant to her. — "And tonight you won't be alone, there'll be others there to back you up."

Eyes still smiling, he sniffed, not convinced.

She reached out and touched him. "This is your chance, Ben. Please, don't throw it away. As it now stands, there's a good possibility that Dick Penfield may get you thrown out of there, and that will mean the end of everything we've been talking about, the things you want and that I can help you get — once we get by this bad time and it fades into the past."

He showed a flash of the bold bravado and anger.

"Fuck 'em! Fire me, I'll handle it myself and the hell with those bastards in the union, I'm not kissing their ass — I'll put in my own grievance and push it on up to arbitration!"

The schoolteacher rebuked her foolish pupil. "You're underestimating Dick Penfield. He expects grievances on this and he expects them to go to arbitration. A three-man board — and then what do you do when your union man on the board cooperates with the company man to make a majority against putting certain people back in?"

"He'd never get away with it, the people would raise holy

fuck'n hell!"

"I understand the union man and the company man pick the third man," she said, with patronizing tolerance for his utter lack of sophistication regarding something so blatantly self-evident. "They'll pick someone they know will vote on this with the company. Then, for the record and with a lot of noise, the union man votes the other way. Two to one, and you're out. The union walks away, smelling sweet."

He was quiet. She must have heard something. He had heard many times how it had happened this way to others, not at this shop, but it could easily happen here now. The only way to lick it would be to start a campaign to get rid of the officers or to get a different union in here. But the way the people felt about him after what happened this morning he would get nowhere with that. They had him cornered.

He asked about Riley and she said she believed Jamison Langner was ready to look the other way on Riley, to let him come back to work with only some mild penalty, maybe a week off without pay — *if* the people will call off the strike and go back to work. She could see that he seemed to think that had possibilities. Pleased, she touched his cheek. Relax, don't be so upset. Remember, I'm in your corner. She leaned forward and gently kissed the high cheekbone.

Inwardly torn, he pulled back and shook his head and said: oh shit.

She told him how much he meant to her, that he didn't know his own strength, that he had a quality she needed. You act rough, and tough, and deliberately uncouth and vulgar, and you don't know who you really are and what you really need —to develop the great potential you hardly even know you have there within yourself. But along with all your instability and your uncertainty you have something basic, something solid, something in you that you don't even know you have, something that comes from the kind of life you've lived, your down-to-earth background and experience in the world of work, all of which makes you what you are, a horrible adorable who has the possibility to give me what I need, so desperately need, for my own survival — if you don't destroy both of us in the process.

She held out a hand, showing the long, thin fingers, with well-manicured nails. Look, they're shaking, and you can't imagine how much I'm shaking inside; I'm getting high, manic, really sailing and ready for a nosedive into a deep depression if this blows up in my face. Because I know I'm leaving myself vulnerable, wide open, with a good chance to be hurt again. She wiped both hands down the sides of her face, a nervous, self-conscious gesture. My psychiatrist will approve of this, whichever way it goes, being able to leave myself open and to risk being hurt again.

Big Ben liked this kind of talk. It got to him, this fumbling effort to articulate feelings and thoughts which are so hard to define into something all cut-and-dried, her hesitant stuttering for the right word forcing him to listen intently and to strain to reach his own thoughts deep into his own self, trying to fit to his own indefinable yearnings what he could make out of what she was trying to get across to him.

She had touched exactly the right note, by making him reach this way into his own mind and emotions; he did not want to be cut off from this by some stupid, senseless, unappreciated sacrifice on his part; and unexpectedly a feeling possessed him which before he would not have permitted himself to recognize. But now he was not only aware of this feeling, even though he initially was embarrassed about it, but because Betty Lyons had made herself so vulnerable to him he did not shut it off from himself nor did he mask it from her. Instead he accepted it as evidence of a developing aesthetic sensitivity within himself, which he wished her to know about, and he leaned to her and pressed his forehead into the crook of her shoulder and clung to her — and wept.

This complete surrender shocked Betty Lyons and she reacted to his touch with a strong impulse to pull away from him. But because it was expected of her she forced herself to put her arms around him, his clinging arms combined with his crying acted on her like a file rasping a raw nerve. She had to fight off her need to shove his body away from hers and she franticly asked herself what it was. Did his surrender add up to a cloying weakness that repelled her? That seemed too obvious. She made herself keep her arms around him, while she underlined a reminder to herself to talk to her psychiatrist about this. Then she felt Big Ben rolling his body over on top of hers. She tried to push him away as he pulled up her dress and unzipped his pants. He had difficulty trying to insert. And then he couldn't, he had turned to rubber. He cried again. And apologized: sorry, sorry, sorry. She pushed him off her. It's all right. They sat there only a minute that seemed much longer. She did not want to talk and he did not know what to say except sorry, sorry, sorry. He wiped his eyes dry with the back of his hand and asked her to please drive him back and drop him off within walking distance of the strike tent.

She felt tremendous relief when she drove away, leaving him there. But even to think of the way he had been clinging to her and then what followed after made her shudder with distaste. *Did she want to see him again?* — But this thought deeply disturbed her, reminding her of her desperate times of emotional instability, and she fervently charged herself to treat it as a stupid, passing fancy that she would wipe out with a good night's sleep.

Chapter 22

Big Ben is seated on the end seat on the right, in the third row of folding chairs. He has been careful to find a seat far enough away from Queen Lila so she cannot question him. She is in the first row, far over on the left side of the Labor Hall. Several times he sees that she is looking back toward him. But he concentrates on the speaker and avoids meeting her eyes.

He envies the skill with which the fat man up there on the platform is handling the situation. Like a fine musician, he is playing the tune, hitting exactly the right notes in exactly the right way to move the crowd his way. Smart bastard, smart as shit, he is herding them in the direction Betty Lyons predicted. Knowing where the fat man intends to end up, it is fascinating to follow the criss-crossing turns and circles and sidetrips he is making on his way there. It's a real fucking education just to listen to this shitty bastard — the hatchet man.

It is a special meeting in the Labor Hall, as Betty Lyons had said it would be, and local union president Baldy George, returned from visiting his quickly recovered sister, has introduced the two men sent in by the national office. They've come in here to help us straighten out this company. The fat one has a barrel of a voice and he starts off in a conversational tone, briefly summarizing the history of their situation, saying this is how it has been told to him. He seems to be wandering aimlessly back and forth all over the place, but Big Ben recognizes that this is not so. The fat man is carefully making a thrust here and then there, feeling his way, gradually shaping the direction, now touching on the accumulated complaints of the people, now taking fiery potshots at the company, several times provoking spontaneous applause by the militancy of his words. Step by step, he works himself up to the level of ominous threats about what this company can expect if it does not deal fairly now with you people, and now he presents it as a victory that this company at last realizes that it cannot get away with pushing you people around. *You taught them that!* And now they know that this international union is standing one hundred percent behind you people on the legitimate complaints you have here. We made that clear to

297

them this afternoon. And I'm glad to be able to report to you now that this support from the international union and the great demonstration of strength you people put on here this morning on the picket line has finally produced a changed attitude on the part of this company. *You can be proud!* Every one of you can be proud of the wonderful job you are doing here. You can take great pride that you have compelled this company to recognize that you have the strength, the will, and the determination — to fight the long war and not give one single inch when this company, like any other backward-minded, arrogant, dictatorial employer, calls in the police and the sheriffs to push you around, when they try to shove their fist down your throat. *You can be proud!* Because it is you who deserve all the credit for having made it possible for me now to report to you that your great spirit that you have demonstrated here, especially here this morning in your fine demonstration on your picket line, has made it unnecessary for you to fight the bloody, long war.

This company now knows you've got what it takes to stick it out for that long war — and it is you who have made them anxious to settle quickly, to shorten this war and get it over with. Your readiness to *die* for your cause has made it possible for you to *live* for your cause!

Big Ben marvels — (What a fuck'n horseshit artist!) — as the fat man, working himself up gradually, begins to pound his points home, his powerful energy surging out into the hall, while he chops with his hand to drive each point into the skull of each man and woman out there. You have demonstrated unity; you have demonstrated strength; you have demonstrated intelligence; you have demonstrated great fortitude and great restraint in the face of great provocation; and now, having come this far so quickly — (Big Ben leans forward, sensing that the fat man is starting in for the big kill: getting out the hatchet) — you have forced this company to back away from you; you have compelled them to admit they have been in error; to admit that they were wrong from the very start; that on this crucial issue you are right, this crucial issue which you rightfully recognize as the most important issue facing you here, an important principle being involved, for which each and every one of you has demonstrated *that if it is necessary you are ready to sweat out the long and bloody war!* — Big Ben recognizes that it is all set up now. Okay, you fat, fuck'n sonofabitch, now trigger it! — bury the hatchet in their head.

"Brother — Riley!" — The entire hall swells with anticipation, and the hatchet man tops it with his powerful voice, triumphantly proclaiming the great victory. *"The company has dropped all charges against Brother Riley!"*

The cheers and applause swell again and the people in the hall rise to their feet, clapping their hands in appreciation of the good news brought by the speaker. It is only when the applause has subsided and the people are settling down again onto their seats that a lone voice from the rear, directly behind Big Ben, introduces a skeptical note.

"What about his job?"

"Full reinstatement," replies the fat man, easily, his face all one big, friendly smile — "full reinstatement to his job without any break in seniority."

The same voice in the rear, another shout: "What about back pay?"

The hatchet man fields that easily, with throaty warmth. No, there's no back pay for the time he didn't work. People can't walk around punching guards just for the hell of it and then get paid extra for clouting them. It would be nice if you could, but you can't. There has to be some kind of penalty, at least for the record, or we're going to have everyone using the guards for a punching bag. And if it's all right to punch the guards, then it's all right to lay a good, old-fashioned haymaker on the good brother or good sister working right next to you whose guts you hate after working with them for twenty years, and then we're all in for one helluva time in there — you'll need sawdust on the floor, like a butcher shop.

While the people are still chuckling with him on that, he off-handedly drops the other shoe. So Brother Riley will be returning to work with full seniority and all other rights restored — after something only for the record, some mild slap on the wrist your committee will work out with the company — maybe a few days off or maybe a week.

Big Ben is surprised by the sharp reaction this provokes. ("Back to work with no penalty!" — "No time off!" — "Sellout!" — "Full back pay for all time he's already lost!" — "Full back pay for all time already lost for everybody!") The hatchet man does not seem to be disturbed, as if he has expected this, as a usual reaction. He stands his ground, his fat face never letting go of that round smile, turning it to receive each new challenge from out there in the hall. His unperturbed aspect seems to further provoke the shouters, and Big Ben turns and cranes his neck, trying to see who it is back there who is stirring it up. ("Now we're out, let's stay out!" — "Full back pay for all time off for everybody!" — "Nobody back to work until we all get a wage increase!" — "C'mon, let's go fishing!") Big Ben wonders if the clever sonofabitch up there notices that not one person in the hall has raised a question about the grievance of the lathe operators. Smart bastard, he's letting the heckling roll on, in fact seems to be encouraging it; he's been in this shitty game so long he can breathe through his fuck'n pores that these loudmouths, given all the rope they'll take, are going too far, becoming so fuck'n ridiculous in what they're advocating that they're isolating themselves — even though it might not seem that way from all the noise they're still making. He must know that he has the overwhelming majority with him now or he couldn't be so confident up there. They'll thank him if he'll take on these supermilitant loudmouths and stop them cold, but he'll have to do most of the job himself — Big Ben knows the people will not openly express here how they feel, both for fear of retaliation later and because they are naturally reluctant to line up with an outsider against any of their own from the shop.

Tense, sitting on the edge of the folding chair, leaning forward, eagerly listening, searching for the key to where and how he himself might break in and hit the floor and carry the meeting with him, Big Ben watches, as if hypnotized, seeing the fat man produce a copy of the contract. He shows the little, red booklet, waving it high in the air over his head — and his reverberating voice cuts through. *Your contract, this is your contract!*

In anticipation of what the hatchet man is going to say about the contract, a voice in the rear — it sounds like the Purple Heart — yells for him to wipe his ass with it, and Big Ben can't help shaking his head from side to side with tremendous admiration — (Oh,. you fuck'n smart bastard!) — as the fat man grabs that wipe-your-ass and beautifully uses it as the launching platform for a blistering attack.

His barrel voice flattens the shouters. I don't think you people here want me to wipe my ass with your premium pay for overtime and for Saturday and Sunday and holiday work; you don't want me to wipe my ass with your paid vacations and your paid holidays; you don't want me to wipe my ass with your job classifications, with your wage increase, with your new minimum and maximum in your rate range; and you don't want me to wipe my ass with your pensions, with your seniority, your job posting, your grievance procedure, and every damn thing else you've got in there, you name it!

Absolute silence in the hall now. — It's this contract that is protecting all those things for you, and it's all one big ball of wax, the whole damn thing, and you damn well know it — all one whole contract negotiated by your committee, including some compromises here and there to arrive at a fair agreement. It's your contract, you people ratified it — this whole agreement — and you know that as an important part of this whole damn ball of wax you damn well agreed that there will be no strike, no stoppage of work in violation of this contract, and your officers are obligated — obligated by this contract here that you ratified! — *it says it right here in cold print and you voted to approve it, you know damn well you did, by secret ballot!* — your officers are obligated to publicly condemn this strike or stoppage of work as an illegal act in violation of this contract — and, further, to instruct you to live up to this contract and also to instruct you to report to work or be subject to drastic penalties which under the law they are powerless to prevent!

There is some subdued booing, and the fat hatchet man pauses briefly for breath and then his voice belligerently booms out again, compelling silence, while he threatens the detractors with the red booklet, stabbing it directly at them. You know damn well you are in violation of this contract! — (The lone voice of the Purple Heart again: Shove it up your ass!) — What you may not know and it is my duty to tell you, is that each and every man and woman here in this hall is laying yourself wide open to a suit for damages — this company can go to court tomorrow morning to seek an order from the judge, attaching your home, your car, your boat, your motorcycle, your bicycle, your summer cottage, your fishing camp — every damn thing you own, except maybe your wife or your husband and your kids and the clothes you got on your back.

He means to frighten them, and even Big Ben is frozen still, though he knows it is all a game. There is deadly silence and the fat man takes his time — he has the meeting all wrapped up in his pocket. He lets the silence drag out while he deliberately reaches inside his suitcoat and brings out a folded sheet of paper which he slowly and dramatically unfolds. Then he waits, letting them sweat, the silence out in the hall becoming even more loaded with apprehension. Big Ben is no longer on the outside looking at it, he is caught in it with the rest.

The speaker is studying the sheet of paper, reading it to himself as if seeing its message for the first time. Looking up, he speaks conversationally, a routine introduction to important material which will follow. This is a letter from the national secretary-treasurer of our union and I have been instructed to personally deliver this to the recording secretary of your local — *after* making its contents publicly known to you.

He twitches his round face and wets his fat lips and takes a firm stance with his thick legs and lifts the letter to read it aloud. Between phrases, as he reads, he looks up and his eyes have taken on the opaque, glassy look of the tough whore out working the street — he is the iceman laying it on the line.

"Please advise your membership that in the event of an illegal stoppage of work during the life of the existing labor-management agreement, the constitution and by-laws of this union, as adopted by the delegates in national convention, provide that they will not — I repeat: will not — be eligible to qualify for payment of weekly strike benefits."

The speaker cuts off the renewed booing at its start, lifting his powerful voice and increasing the intensity of his delivery to maintain control. His words ring clearly through the hall, delivering the dire sequel to the sharp warning in the letter.

"As the official representative of the national officers of your union, I have been instructed to inform you — that the original motion and the vote taken to engage in this illegal stoppage of work should have properly been ruled out of order by your chairman." — (Big Ben's thinking apparatus is in high gear: It is *his* motion the fat man is talking about.) — "Therefore in accordance with the interpretation and advice of the legal department of this union, I am now acting officially on behalf of the national officers to instruct you — every man and woman employed in that shop — that you are hereby officially notified to fulfill your legal obligations under the contract —

and starting with the day shift tomorrow morning you are hereby officially ordered to report to work at the regular starting time of your regular shift!"

Big Ben, instinctively shouting with the rest, rises from the seat of his folding chair along with almost everybody else in the hall. The fat man seems to be prepared for this explosive reaction, as if he has secretly enjoyed knowing what was going to happen, while he worked at setting it up to be ignited. The iceman is a warm human being again, and his big, fat face is divided by a broad grin. He lifts both arms overhead, as if he is blessing the noisy congregation, and his throaty voice tops all the uproar he has created.

"This — meeting — is — officially — adjourned!"

The meeting may be officially adjourned, but it is not over. This thought snaps across Big Ben's mind, as he sees a folding chair lazily sail up into the air toward the fat man. Men and women shouting, screaming and shaking fists, surge forward. The fat man reaches to catch the chair and lightly tosses it back up into the air again above the heads of those who are pressing toward him. Laughing with evident love of battle, he roars out his own inarticulate, but clearly defiant, battlecry. He seems to be enjoying tremendously what is happening, apparently already relishing the telling at the bars which will follow in the days and months and even years ahead. ("Some fuck'n bastard out there in the hall tosses a fuck'n chair at me, and I catch the goddam chair — and I toss it right back at the fuck'n sonofabitch!")

All eight members of the negotiating committee who have been sitting on the platform behind the fat man quickly move forward to shield him from the irate crowd. But he does not appear to be the least bit intimidated. He is laughing, retorting with genial defiance to the angry heckling, apparently not at all worried about the eventual outcome of the noisy, milling revolt he has caused down below on the floor.

This puzzles Big Ben who is pressing forward with others toward the speaker's platform, while feverishly trying to evaluate the situation. *(This is the moment to make your move! Now, now, it must be now! It's now or never!)* Every nerve alerted, he frantically checks out what might be the motivations of the fat man. Is it that he admires the guts the people are showing now? Does this uproar evoke for him memory of earlier days? Does he see a rank-and-filer, much thinner, still working in the shop, as wildly independent and unpredictable and untamed as are these people who are now yelling for him to be tossed out on his ear? Or is it that he has finished his job, having established the record, even if the people don't go back to work now? Is this all he's really been after, to establish a good legal defense for the international union to use in any damage suit filed by the company? The stoolpigeons will have to report that he really tried to do the job; and the company will have to concede, even in court, that no one can predict for certain what people will do in these situations — there are always surprises. And it *was* funny the way that folding chair, as if on cue and shot out of a circus cannon, had sailed up into the air toward the platform; it would have tickled anyone with a good sense of humor such as that possessed by the fat man.

At this point, without being aware precisely why he has pushed his way through the crush of people to get there — except that his head is swollen to bursting with the decision he has made: right now, quick as hell, to make the move! — Big Ben, his cheeks so hot they burn, stands halfway up the short flight of steps leading from the auditorium floor to the platform, facing the crowd, his hand stretching high to get attention, his voice straining to be heard above all the noise.

"I — am — the — man — who — made — that — original —motion — and — I — want — to — answer — this — man!"

He repeats this threat — again — and again — and again — until the noise in the hall subsides and it is only his voice which is heard.

"I made that original motion to shut that place down, and I'll answer this man!"

He sounds like he is so angry that it is difficult for him to speak, and those who had vociferously rejected him that same morning now call out encouragement.

The fat man appears behind Big Ben's head and his voice booms, ruling this man out of order. This immediately prompts more shouts, jeers and booing from the people in the hall. His face red with excitement, not even deigning to turn his head to see his opponent looming above him, Big Ben fires his hot reply.

"You just adjourned this damn meeting — so nobody's out of

order from nothing! And if you want to get the hell out of here
and go on home, goodbye, goddamit, and for chrissake don't
you come back here, nobody will goddam miss you!"

There is loud applause and some approving shouts, and the
fat man smiles, graciously conceding the quick thinking in that
angry reply.

Big Ben waits, until everyone in the hall sits down.
Chairman Baldy George, deciding to make the best of the
situation, announces that even though the meeting might or
might not be officially adjourned — we don't know for sure —
nobody is going to stop anyone from having his say if the
membership wants to listen — so go ahead, Ben. That brings
the chairman some muttered, derogatory heckling, and Big Ben
waits for absolute quiet. He gets it.

"Okay. Now for chrissakes let's get back to what the hell it
was that started all this. As I remember it, it was some goddam
thing about the men on the lathes having some kind of
grievance — !"

"Right!" The voice of the Purple Heart interrupted with a
loud yell from the rear.

That outburst prompts general laughter, both up on the
platform and throughout the hall, a nervous letting of pressure,
and Big Ben comicly points to the offender.

"Will that lathe operator with the funny beard back there
shut his big bazoo long enough for us to get back to where the
hell we're exactly supposed to be, which is back to his
grievance!"

The heckler, his voice now colored with friendly humor,
cannot resist repeating, "Right!"

"Sergeant-at-arms, throw that man out of the hall."

It is said with tongue in cheek, and Big Ben's outer
demeanor now seems to radiate an easy confidence, contrasting
with the feel of the tight knot cramping his stomach. A few
minutes earlier, still seated, every nerve on edge, his thoughts
fighting one another while he listened to the fat man, he had
suddenly tasted the vomit rising into his mouth against his will
and with a gulping swallow he had forced it back down again
into his stomach. Fortunately, he has too much else to think
about now, because even while he is running on, saying
whatever words instinctively come to mind, he is still trying at
the same time to decide what he can say to weave his way out

through this mess and come out on top in all directions. He knows there is no turning back now; there can be no further delay; he must say it now, whatever it will be, or the psychological moment will have passed.

"The lathe operators were given a bum time study and they couldn't get any satisfaction — " He rushes on, with so many words coming out so fast they trip over one another, reminding the people how they have come to where they are now, while at the same time he keeps on frantically ransacking his brain: *how the fuck to get out of this fuck'n box?* He scambles together fragments of thoughts about Betty Lyons and Jamison Langner and Dave Newman and the FBI pair, while he intensely reconstructs the familiar ground — "and it was after the lathe operators walked off the job the second time that Brother Riley left the shop with the rest of us to come over here to the Labor Hall, and then Brother Riley remembered his toolbox and he turned around to go back into the shop to get it, and the guard at the shack inside the gate tried to stop him, and then that was when Brother Riley dumped the guard into the creek, and after that was when the company filed charges with the police against Brother Riley, charging him with assault and with stealing his own toolbox out of the shop and whatever the hell else the company threw at him with the whole book there, and then that was when I made my motion and somebody seconded it and we all voted — and that's how we got to where the hell we are right now. *And right now where the hell are we?* The International tells us that they won't sanction the strike because they say it's illegal in violation of our contract with this company, so they're not going to pay us no strike benefits — and if you want my opinion, and whether you want it or not you're going to get it, *I think that's lousy —legal or illegal, that just plain stinks!"*

Applause.

The fat man, standing above Big Ben, wears his tolerant smile, telling those who are applauding that he is holding his fire until this loose-lipped screwball clarifies where the hell he is heading.

The applause does not stop the tumbling flow of words. Big Ben rides right over it, going on and on, and on and on, and on and on, going back to tell again how they came to where they are now, and then again asking: *"Now where the hell are we?"*

The fat man's smile is getting broader and a troubled silence begins to settle in on the people out in the hall as they begin to become aware of a lack of direction and a touch of incoherence creeping into all those goddam words spouting forth up front, while Big Ben ever more frantically rummages around in his brain for that one special dramatic thrust he can use to reconcile all the conflicting forces with his own undefined, obscure and inarticulate, but deeply ingrained, private principles and beliefs and desires, that single terrifically clever ploy which he can use to break him out of this iron band which is tightening in around him, making the cold sweat soak his armpits, making him breathe hard, increasingly desperate with the knowledge that having started this he can't stop, he has to come up with something brilliant to bring him out on top or sure as shit he will be in worse shape than he was before he opened his big stupid mouth, he'll fall flat on his face, make a ridiculous fuck'n asshole of himself — a ridiculous fool in everyone's eyes, falling between two stools in the shithouse, with people on both sides of the fence turning on him and laughing at him.

Desperately flailing around in his mind now, chagrined at the thought that everyone listening to him is recognizing that he is making a thorough ass of himself, drowning in his own words, he also starts to listen to himself, hearing all the words as if they come from the mouth of a stranger, and listening, he searches there for a clue, a life preserver, however fragile, to grab onto.

"Maybe later when the dust settles we can start shopping around and maybe we can find us ourselves some outfit that won't stab us in the back just when we need them most, but right now where are we? — we're out on the bricks and our union is condemning us for being there — so if the company goes to court against us they can quote the words from our own union to hang us by the neck until dead — and that's our lousy situation, whether we like it or not — so where the hell are we and what can we do about it? We know we got people here, some with families, some with homes and mortgages, and some with time payments on their cars, their furniture and their color TV sets and everything — and this official bigshot hatchet man we got here from the national office comes here and tells us that if we don't go back to work with our tails all stuck

between all our legs and if we don't kiss the company's big
brown asshole, then we're going to get ourselves sued, everyone
of us here, for everything we got, whatever the hell it is, and
they're going to leave us all with nothing else, goddamit, but
just our plain bare asses hanging out there in the cold!"

Unexpectedly, thank God, the shadow of a direction flicks
across his brain, and he desperately grabs it and pulls it in to
him.

"I made the original motion back then, and I know why I
made that original motion back then, and this character from
the national office breathing down my neck behind me, he
wasn't there, so he don't know — and nobody else knows what
went on in my head back when I made that original motion.
The important thing is the *intent* of my original motion, and
I'm the only one who can get inside my own brain and can get
to know what my original *intent* was back then when we
started this. And that is important — *because that is what we
voted for!* And I'm the only one who can interpret for myself
what was my *intent*, which you voted for, and now, goddamit,
I'll tell you my *intent* and interpret it for you — so everybody
shut up and listen and I'll interpret it."

There is some laughter, friendly but also containing
something Big Ben recognizes with some dismay. The people in
the hall are beginning to laugh *at* him. Disconcerted, he stops
and grins in a silly way and makes a funny face to ridicule his
own stupid way of saying things.

The pause is very brief, but as he starts talking again he
sees Queen Lila's face. There is a wondering expression there
that causes him to stutter and then stop again, and now he
hears the heavy voice of the fat man behind him, intended only
for his ears, telling him to sit down and shut up, and he
realizes he has a tough job on his hands to win back the
respectful attention of the people.

His hand touches his chest, pressing there, feeling the
heaving as he breathes. His palm is wet. The sweat has soaked
through his shirt. He begins again, and now the direction is
getting more clear, but as it takes shape, both for himself and
for the people out in the hall, he is aware of the growing
restlessness and loss of attention out there, with more and more
people talking to one another — and he hears the fat man,
quietly but insistently heckling him, over and over, from

behind his back.

(Sit down, you stupid bastard, sit down!)

But he is not yet aware of all this when he begins again, trying to recover from the effect of that look on Queen Lila's face. He is momentarily successful and he regains some inner confidence as he hears himself beginning to spell out, both for himself and for the rest of the strikers, a specific action for them at this time.

"In my original motion I said that we should stay out until the charges against Brother Riley are dropped, and now they tell us they're dropping the charges against Brother Riley — so the charges are dropped, and that was all my original motion was all about, so let's go back to see where we were on the day when we walked out of the shop and come over here to this same hall to decide what to do — and let's talk about the grievance of the lathe operators, and let's talk about the grievance we were going to talk about then, before that happened with Riley, the grievance of the lathe operators, and let's try to forget we been out here, walking the picket line for Brother Riley — because that's all behind us, and now let's all look ahead."

Chairman Baldy George has to step in to admonish the people to be quiet, and then he turns to Big Ben. Get to it, Ben.

Big Ben says okay, and he does his best to shut off from his ears that low, insistent voice behind him.

(Sit down, you stupid bastard!)

"Okay, here we are, back where we were when the lathe operators asked us to come over to the Labor Hall. Now what are we going to do about their grievance? It's been dragging on too long and they got a right to get it settled. All right, that's the reason we all came over here to the Labor Hall from the shop, to make our point that we're all one hundred percent behind them. The fact that we're all still out here now tells the company that they got to settle this grievance or we're ready to shut that place down the same way we shut it down tight for Brother Riley. That worked out all right there and there's no reason why, if we have to do the same thing here, it shouldn't work out the same way again for the lathe operators — "

The chairman has to admonish the people again to be quiet so the speaker can be heard. But before Big Ben resumes, the same voice that he earlier recognized as that of the Purple

Heart lathe operator is heard again, and this time it is an unfriendly challenge.

"What the hell is it? Jesus Christ, are you saying we should go back in there, or, goddamit, do we stay out until our grievance is settled?"

"I'm saying let's all do what's the most intelligent thing to do right now."

(Sit down, you stupid bastard.)

"Jesus Christ, stop dancing around up there and say it! In, or out? Get the hell off that fence!"

(Sit down, you stupid bastard.)

Big Ben is squirming, sweat pouring down his cheeks, but there is no turning back now, even though he realizes, as he replies, that what he is proposing can at this time only produce chaos out there in the hall.

(Sit down, you stupid bastard.)

"Let's do what we would have done if the company hadn't been so damn stupid and filed charges to get one of our union brothers arrested by the police. Now they dropped the charges, let's settle the grievance of you men working on the lathes — and I don't care for myself, but meanwhile all these good people here might as well not be losing any more money than they have to,.so while we go ahead and settle this grievance they might as well all be back at work!"

There it is, at last, out on the table, and there are the angry cries and shouts he expected to hear, people all over the hall up off their chairs, yelling for him to sit down, calling him names.

(Sit down, you stupid bastard.)

Big Ben thrusts his fist up into the air. (Fuck it, fuck 'em all!) And he screams with relief that it is all over —

"Mister Chairman, I so move!"

The legality of Big Ben's motion was immediately challenged by the shrieking voice of the Purple Heart, backed up by chief steward Don Mayer, on the grounds that the meeting had already been officially adjourned; and the battle raged, with fierce speeches, interruptions, charges, countercharges, threats, and invitations to step outside and settle it with fists, until finally it was agreed that a secret ballot vote would be taken to decide whether or not to return to work the next morning. There was no doubt about how the vote would go. There was so much dissension that even the Purple

Heart finally in disgust said the hell with it, there's no use staying out, not with the people all split up like this.

Big Ben did not stay to cast his ballot. While the torn slips of paper were being distributed to the people in the hall, he abruptly ran out, holding his hand to his mouth. He vomited into the street.

In the pay booth at Mike's place he phoned collect to his sister in New York City. She told him her roommate had met some new guy and moved out. Big Ben got a fistful of change from Old Frank who was behind the bar and he put in a person-to-person call to the girl he had put on the bus in Cleveland to go home to Johnsonville to marry her boyfriend. She told him the wedding was set for Saturday morning in church and he wished her good luck. After a couple shots of whiskey he went back into the phone booth and dialed Betty Lyons' number and hung up at the start of the first ring.

When Queen Lila awoke the next morning to get ready for work she found him asleep on the couch in the front room, smelling like someone had poured a bottle of booze over his head. She unpacked his suitcases and put away his things before she drove him to work. He was too shaky to handle the wheel of the car.

Neither Jamison Langner nor Betty Lyons got in touch with him again about the arts program. Big Ben blamed this on his own stupidity in handling the situation. He did not know that in addition to what had happened in the Labor Hall, which he thought had made him into somewhat of a stupid shit in both the eyes of the rest of the workers in the shop and in the eyes of Jamison Langner and Betty Lyons, something else very significant had been happening elsewhere, causing Jamison Langner to have second thoughts about his arts program for labor. With the nation's vice-president, Spiro Agnew, vigorously stumping the country, attacking the "intellectual slobs," accusing them of undermining the system with their elitist radicalism, Jamison Langner no longer felt the need to fill a cultural vacuum before radicals rushed in there. As one of the largest financial contributors in the area to help re-elect the vice-president's chief, Richard Nixon, Jamison Langner felt a new sense of security — the administration in Washington was

running a very tight ship now and those who had worried
about smart radicals making inroads through the arts could
now relax.

Big Ben read in the evening newspaper about Jamison
Langner withdrawing his financial support from The Dance
Center. There was one paragraph about Betty Lyons resigning
her position to go to Europe to study the relationship between
dance groups and their communities over there. He thought
about phoning to ask her when she would be leaving, but since
she did not call him he decided not to call her.

Shortly after that, Dick Penfield offered Big Ben the job of
foreman in the machine shop down at the plant in Virginia and
Queen Lila told him he had to make his own decision on that.
Big Ben shook hands with her and said it had been great. She
said she had no regrets. They said goodbye and wished each
other the best of luck.

About two years later — on the same springtime day when
police in the nation's capital carried out the largest lockup in
our country's history by arresting twelve thousand
demonstrators against the Vietnam War — Queen Lila heard
that Big Ben quit his foreman job in Virginia and was living in
a racially integrated religious commune in southern California,
along with his war veteran brother Tommy. This information
was passed along to her while she was walking on the picket
line. Mackenzie Machine Tool employees were striking to get
rid of the measured day work incentive system, to replace it
with substantially increased hourly wage rates, and to reinstate
automatic progression from minimum to maximum of the wage
rate range for each job classification. Heading the union's fight
were newly elected president Don Mayer and the new chief
steward, the still-bearded Purple Heart, now married and a
part-time student at the college. The union bought one hundred
copies of Dave Newman's play *Empty Hands* for its members
after their former union organizer, now a financially successful
life insurance broker, produced the play off-Broadway in New
York City and then published it himself. Queen Lila read the
play and liked it. — She received a card that year at Christmas-
time; a gold and red picture of Jesus Christ; postmarked
Houston, Texas; no return address: "My brother and me

working here in a machine shop now. Give my love to the kids. Tell them I miss them. Miss you too. Your friend — *Big Ben Hood.*"

OTHER BOOKS BY EMANUEL FRIED PROVIDE
FASCINATING AND ENJOYABLE READING . . .

THE DODO BIRD

"**The Dodo Bird** is a workingman, small, hapless, reliant on alcohol to keep him going. He is waiting to meet his daughter, determined not to have a drink. Two other foundry workers, one of them a noisy bully, make a bet on whether he can hold out. From this situation, and from the coarse, repetitious language of the workers, Emanuel Fried has created a drama that builds up quite a head of steam. That it does is a tribute most of all to an intensely concentrated plot."

— *Edwin Newman, NBC-TV*

"Compelling power and vibrant plausibility."

— *Associated Press*

"The most authentic portrayal of workingman in the history of the American theatre."

— *UE News (United Electrical,*
Radio & Machine Workers)

DROP HAMMER

"No important American playwright I can think of has ever dealt realistically with the lives and aspirations of blue-collar workers. Emanuel Fried's DROP HAMMER helps fill this void. Crudely eloquent and powerful, unfailingly honest in its observations, it is exactly the sort of play Odets might have written if, like Fried, he had actually worked in a factory. Unlike Odets, Fried knows his people too well to sentimentalize them. His workers are really dirty, they sweat real sweat; they also lie, cheat and betray each other just like the rest of us. The strength of the piece lies in its ferocious commitment to getting it right."

— *Wiliam Murray, New West Magazine*

"Odets 20 years later."

— *Dan Sullivan, Los Angeles Times*

"What would seem to be character studies within a union local proves instead to be a dynamic, often electric examination of people expressing basic responses; it's powerful stuff, a strong statement about survival."

— *Variety*

MESHUGAH AND OTHER STORIES

"Human down-to-earth atmosphere of real people. Packed with observation, tension, compassion, social conflict, presented with spare and tight writing — not a polysyllabic word nor a stray adjective. Bravo!

— *Jewish Currents*

"Fried's stories reveal more about being Jewish in the America of the Great Depression than do many epic works of fiction or sociology."

— *Humanistic Judaism*

ELEGY FOR STANLEY GORSKI
By Emanuel Fried

"No further proof that the American theatre mirrors fantasy and little else is needed than the fact that the vast and historically crucial working class is the forgotten subject. One can comb the literature for some hint that the dramatic possibilities have been explored and be disappointed. With the exception of Emanuel Fried's work. His plays singlehandedly redress the situation. An impressive achievement."

— Terry Doran, Theatre Critic
BUFFALO NEWS

"Some of us are old enough to remember the double shock of surprise and recognition when O'Neill's polyglot seamen first spoke on the American stage. Many of us experienced the same double shock on first hearing the unmistakable second generation immigrant voice from Odets' Jewish Americans. Now Fried gives us another first in the authentic accents of a foundry's hard hat blue collar workers."

— Annette T. Rubinstein
Editorial Board, SCIENCE
AND SOCIETY, Author of
THE GREAT TRADITION IN
ENGLISH LITERATURE FROM
SHAKESPEARE TO SHAW

"Manny Fried is one of the first in many years to explore the dramatic world of factory life."

— Leslie Orear, President
Illinois Labor History Society

"A writer in the NATION referred to me as 'the last of the proletarian writers.' All I can say is it ain't so as long as Emanuel Fried is alive and well and writing in Buffalo."

— Jack Conroy, Founding Editor,
ANVIL and THE NEW ANVIL,
Author of THE DISINHERITED